"**Extreme Prejudice** *is very compelling and true to Biblical prophecy. The Story naturally reveals these truths as the Johnson family experience unfolds. I found this book to be a great read and it helped me to see how things might possibly happen in our near future.*"
—**Mark Dekle, District Pastor, Pennsylvania Conference**

"*Like the book* **Faithful Fugitives**, **Extreme Prejudice** *brings to life one way the last days of earth's history might play out. This installment regularly includes biblical teachings relevant to the end of time in the characters' dialogue. It is a real blessing to read for anyone wanting to reawaken their interest in Bible prophecy.*
—**Eric J. C. Ellison, Doctoral Student in Theology at Trinity College, Chicago**

"*If end time events have always baffled you,* **Extreme Prejudice** *is the key to unlock its mysteries. Although written in fictional form, the reader will find answers to complex subjects with real life implications. With every twist and turn, you will find shocking revelations, pulse-pounding suspense and many parallels to current world events. The reader is sure to be left to ponder, 'Can extreme prejudice soon become a reality?'*"
—**Kay Stahl, Church Family Life Co-Director, etc. Williamsport SDA Church, PA**

"*If you are interested in eschatology—study of the climax of this world and humankind according to Bible prophecy, you must give this book a read. This novel leads you through the Biblical details using the experiences of a handful of people in a realistic 21st Century setting.*"
—**Buz Sterner, President, The Ministry Place, Inc.**

Extreme Prejudice

James A. Ellison

TEACH Services, Inc.
P U B L I S H I N G
www.TEACHServices.com • (800) 367-1844

Copyright © 2021 James Ellison
Copyright © 2021 TEACH Services, Inc.
ISBN-13: 978-1-4796-1276-5 (Paperback)
ISBN-13: 978-1-4796-1277-2 (ePub)
Library of Congress Control Number: 2020919154

Published by

TEACH Services, Inc.
P U B L I S H I N G
www.TEACHServices.com • (800) 367-1844

DEDICATION

I could never have written this book without the help of very good friends. They read my work, gave suggestions, and wrote reviews that I greatly appreciated. I want to mention Bob Maxwell, Buz Sterner, Kay Stahl, and Mark Dekle. And in particular, I appreciate my son Eric and his wife Tiffani. To these excellent friends, I dedicate this book.

TABLE OF CONTENTS

SIGNIFICANT CHARACTERS
(*In order of appearance*)

Chad Johnson: son to Daniel and Janine Johnson, home from an internship at a prestigious financial firm for the funeral of his parents. Had a sister named **Grace** who died when she was very young.

Daniel and Janine Johnson: Chad's deceased parents.

Detective Hardine: Investigating the murder of the Johnsons.

Diana Cross: Chad's childhood friend from his former church and youth class.

Vonnie Hixon (and later in the story, her parents): One of a foursome from the young adult class of the local SDA church.

Reverend Bill Tucker: New pastor of Chad's church of his formative years, who performs the funeral for Daniel and Janine.

Brian and Cynthia King: Two of a foursome from the young adult department of the local SDA church.

Raphael Wilson (and later in the story, his parents): A member of the four young people from SDA church.

Pastor Peter Lange: Pastor of the local SDA church where Vonnie, Raphael, Brian, and Cynthia attend.

Perkins Family, including their youngest, Emilee: Their home became a place of sanctuary for rescue.

Isa: Astonishing miracle worker on an international scale.

Naziya: Young peacemaker who works amazing miracles.

Leticia Greene: Vonnie Hixon's boss.

Richard: prisoner in the county jail.

AUTHOR'S MESSAGE

I magine if the Holy Spirit would be suddenly withdrawn from the world; there would be chaos, neighbor would rise up against neighbor, animals would no longer fear humans, and the forces of nature would be unchecked. Governments would seek control, and when they fail, they would unite to achieve equilibrium. This is not totally imaginary; it is a realistic scenario for the future, not hypothetical, but biblically sound. It will be a herculean task for governments to control humanity because normally "good" people will no longer retain virtue or ethic. Nominal Christians, nominal Jews, nominal Muslims, and other faiths will not maintain their false friendly façade. All bets will be off, so to speak. Survival of the fittest or allegiances with power brokers will compel humankind to act on behalf of self. Prejudicial behavior will excel to the extreme.

In talking about the Spirit of God's relationship with humans, we read in Genesis 6:3, "Then the LORD said, 'My Spirit will not contend with humans forever ...'" (NIV). Here the Lord is specifically talking about length of life, yet the reason He is limiting life is because of sinfulness. God mercifully allows life to be limited to curtail the spread of evil to the point of overcoming true believers. Even so, Satan's nature spreads and increases, and God's intervention to save His people is in jeopardy. As time passes, the evil that was before the flood returns.

The days in which we live are solemn and important. The Spirit of God is gradually but surely being withdrawn from the earth. Plagues and judgments are already falling upon the despisers of

11

the grace of God. The calamities by land and sea, the unsettled state of society, the alarms of war, are portentous. They forecast approaching events of the greatest magnitude. The agencies of evil are combining their forces and consolidating. They are strengthening for the last great crisis. Great changes are soon to take place in our world, and the final movements will be rapid ones. (*Testimonies to the Church*, Vol. 9, p. 11)

It is the author's conviction that once-revered individuals will turn into self-serving, malicious tyrants. In the name of decorum, force and punishment will be used to bring into line outlying elements to a single all-encompassing directive for humanity. Even religious leaders will be at the forefront advocating compliance with the requirements of the new world order.

Reader, please don't blindly follow the majority. It may look noble. It will look logical. It will appear to be the solution to world chaos. It will be the only avenue to acquire sustenance. But, evaluating the big picture will reveal that the principles of God will be subverted. Satan has his counterfeits for every true doctrine, and you can count on the fact that his counterfeits will be more convenient, more comfortable, or more trouble-free.

Satan is almost here. He will not be able to exactly mimic Christ's return, "This Jesus, who was taken up from you into heaven, will come in the same way that you saw Him go into heaven"[1] Satan will not come in the clouds and return to heaven with the redeemed like our Savior (see 1 Thess. 4:16–17). The devil needs to stay on earth and fabricate his artful deception of acting like Jesus. He will be here on earth in all incredibly believable reality. His ability to persuade is beyond human capacity to equal. Without the Holy Spirit's help and without knowing the Bible's description of Jesus' return, humankind will be duped, lost in his evil sophistries. Fortunately for true believers, the Holy Spirit will attend to their requests for help, and the Bible is easily accessible for study.

The following work of fiction is presented to the reader as a possibility of what could happen. It also presents how characters might react to the dynamics of a world gone mad at the hand of an evil angel who wants to be worshipped as a god. This work is written to stimulate thought and emotion, an attempt to encourage Bible study and to nudge the reader to get spiritually ready. Live the story. Feel the pressures of compromise. Decide not to be scammed by Satan. And most of all, put Jesus into the center of your life!

---

[1] Acts 1:11, CEB

CHAPTER 1

The house was quiet. All the police tape had been removed. News vans were no longer parked in the street, and the forensics truck had vacated the driveway. The detectives and lab techs were gone. Chad had his parents' house all to himself. The dining room table had all the extra extension leaves put into the center; all the chairs were pushed against the walls, except one. Chad sat in the lone chair with boxes stacked and arranged to one side. He was ready to sift, study, scan, and sort the contents. This was not a task he was looking forward to accomplishing. He never expected or wanted to do this. This was something older people or lawyers did.

The only noise was the familiar tick-tock of the old clock on the mantel in the living room, an heirloom from great-great-grandparents. The clock reminded him of home when he had returned from college for holidays or special occasions. The singular sound had been comforting in the past when he was a child, pretending to go to sleep in his bedroom around the corner and down the hall. Now it signaled an end to the past and a beginning to a new reality without his parents. The clock was almost irritating in that he would prefer to hear his dad's bass voice or his mother's diminutive soprano. Grief was feasting on the life sound of the clock, plunging him deeper into the feelings of loss with regret. There was also a foreign feeling of revenge that rose up within and surprised him.

First to be sorted were the important documents found safely hidden in the security lock-box under the bed next to the nightstand. He emptied the box onto the table and planned to put back into the box those papers he felt he needed to keep safe. The box had been unlocked with a key attached to the handle by a rubber band. *Some security*, he said to himself. The deeds to the house and titles to the two cars were first to go back into the box. Then he discovered his original birth certificate. He had official copies, of course, but reading his mother and father's names in full gave him pause. It compelled him to realize that he was an orphan, a grown-up orphan. His roots were now memories rather than realities.

He had to stop. He didn't want to be set free from his moorings like this. He would have wanted to fix things up a little better. Not that they were bad, it was that he and his folks were not seeing, and now, never able to see, eye to eye on church attendance. It wouldn't have hurt him to show up at church once in a while. It would have meant so much to them, especially his mom. Then he went away to college, fifteen hundred miles away. Casually showing up at church was a distinct impossibility. For four years of college, he maintained his independence from church. It was not his thing. The discussions with his folks ground down to respectful silence on the subject. Then, an internship meant his comings home were even rarer. He regretted not doing the right thing to please his folks. Guilt bothered him, and anger returned. He hated the individual or individuals who took away his chance to reconcile.

The will came to his hand next. He was an only child, so the assumption was that he would inherit everything. He couldn't even show his gratitude to his folks. More bile rose in his throat. Again, he had to stop what he was doing. It was too much for him. He had to get up and take a break to clear his head of the thoughts that occupied his brain. He had only just begun. He was halfway to the kitchen when the front doorbell rang. He went to the entrance, even though it was futile to attempt to open the door. A large piece of plywood had been nailed over the damaged beautiful heavy oak entryway.

"Yes?" he spoke tentatively through the barrier.

"Mr. Johnson? I'm Detective Hardine. Can I come around to the side door and talk with you?"

"Yes. I'll meet you there." Chad walked back through to the garage and met the detective at the service entrance door, which led into one side of the garage and next to the auxiliary door leading into the mudroom where coats and boots were neatly hung and lined up along one wall.

He invited the detective through to the kitchen, a strange act for Chad because guests and friends always came through the main entrance.

He knew Detective Hardine from a couple of previous conversations, initially on the phone, and when they had spoken face to face at the police station. It was the detective who had broken the news over the phone about his parents' murder. They settled at the kitchen counter on stools.

"I came to let you know that the investigation is still ongoing. However, we have not gotten any firm leads as yet. I have been assigned as the lead investigator and will keep you informed of any developments. Perhaps, you can help with some general information."

"I don't know if there's anything more I can say that will help."

"I know this must seem tedious to you, but it is surprising how one little tidbit can get us going on the right track."

"I'll help in any way I can."

"Thank you. I wish I could make this easier. This has to be a terrible shock for you. I can recommend some grief counselors if you think it would help. They're all here in town, so I don't know if they would help you when you return to your work back east. When are you planning to go back?"

"I've been granted a leave of absence for four weeks, with assurances that I could extend that if need be."

Detective Hardine continued to ask several seemingly unimportant questions. What had happened was that he had been assigned solely to work on this case. An overload of homicides at the precinct station, plus the nature of this case, had dictated that only one detective could be spared to work on a murder without clear leads or possible suspects. It was his first time working solo on a case. They rambled through some general questions about the folks: occupations, friends, hobbies, favorite restaurants, church attendance, clubs, fraternal organizations, etc. The detective made a few notes on his notepad even though the entire conversation, just like all previous conversations, was being recorded. Then he pulled a plastic evidence bag out of his jacket pocket.

"This piece of literature was found lying on your father. It's an advertisement for some religious meetings. It probably means nothing. Could've blown in the open door when it was kicked in, you know how they tuck these advertisements into every crevice imaginable, but in this business, anything can be a clue. Does this make any sense to you at all? Did your folks attend these meetings?"

Chad took the plastic-encased leaflet in hand. Examining the brochure, he saw a red multi-headed dragon with sharp teeth and a gaudily dressed woman with a crown on her head riding the winged beast looking like it was ready to breathe fire. The title line read, "Unveiling the Secrets of the Book Revelation," and the rest of the front page indicated meetings to be held to explain the prophetic symbols. On the back there was more information as to time and place. There was a blank place to write an address and a return address. No information was written in the blank spaces. Obviously, this was hand-delivered. An incongruous thought crossed his mind. *It's a leaflet; it must have blown in the door with the other leaves.*

"No, this doesn't seem like anything my folks would do or be interested in doing. They attend, I mean, attended a church regularly, the one I grew up in, but this isn't something my church does."

"I didn't think so, but in this business … one never knows. So far, this looks like a random act of violence. If it had been a robbery, I think more things would have been taken. Electronic devices were left behind, as were the sterling silver items, including gold and jewelry. Maybe the perps were interrupted for some reason and left suddenly. I'm still trying to figure that out. I know I asked you this before, but it bears repeating. Did your folks have enemies? Maybe you thought of someone since the last time I asked you?"

"No, my folks were pretty straightforward people, Pete and Polly pew-sitters. I don't think they would have had a single enemy to speak of."

"That's all I've got for now. Do you have any questions for me?"

"Do you know when we will be able to schedule the funeral?"

"I'm sorry, not until forensics releases the bodies. They are pretty thorough, you know. As soon as I know, you'll know. The lab will call the funeral home, the one you gave them, and then they'll call me. I'll call you immediately when they do."

"Thank you." Chad didn't hold eye contact with the detective. His head was down, studying the countertop and thinking about the phrase, "Pete and Polly pew sitters." He had used it on his folks during one of their arguments. He walked Hardine to the service door and watched as the detective went to the neighbors instead of his sedan. Again, he was alone in a house with a distinctive "tick-tock" sound in the background. He decided to turn on some music to drown out the irritating sound that reminded him of years past.

Being in the house where murders had occurred and where bodies had been lying on the floor didn't bother him. He didn't believe in ghosts.

The blood on the floor didn't scare him. He was not the squeamish type. He found himself standing in the entryway between the front door and the living room, staring down at the remnants of his parents. Their blood stained the carpet in two rugged pools a meter apart. He tried to construct a video image of what had happened. His father must have stood in front of his mother, protecting her. Furniture remained where it had always been. No struggle was apparent. The only wreckage was the front door. He turned to look at it. Plywood encased the outside. The door jamb was shattered inward. A chunk of the door jamb dangled from a security chain attached to the door. The door had to have been kicked in violently. The simplicity of the two pieces of evidence told Chad that someone or some persons had come through the door for the purpose of killing his folks. Nothing of great value was taken. No other part of the house had been rampaged or pillaged. He questioned this as a random act of violence. It seemed so purposeful. He tried to think of any instance where his folks could have created an enemy. Nothing came to mind. All their social activities were with the church. His father's work was with the bank in a corporate position where he worked on establishing new branches in new neighborhoods. He shook his head in negative wonder.

He returned to the dining room table to sort through more of the documents. He finished the important legal material. He closed the lockbox and put the key on his own keychain. Next, he opened a box of files containing all the warranties for every appliance and electronic device in the house. He closed it almost as soon as he opened it, setting it next to the lockbox. His next task was to plow through a number of papers taken from his father's office. That took an hour.

Walking into his father's office, he took a break. He sat in his dad's leather desk chair and took in the world that used to be his father's domain. Next to the work area was a small table where a Bible sat on top of a paperback book. He took the Bible into his hands and

He sat in his dad's leather desk chair and took in the world that used to be his father's domain. He took the Bible into his hands and felt its worn, pliable cover.

felt its worn, pliable cover. It obviously had been opened repeatedly and used often enough to have a lived-in comfort to its pages. Then his attention was attracted to the paperback book which had been underneath the Bible. His father never put another book on top of his Bible out of respect for divine inspiration. The paperback was also worn and in worse condition than the Bible, owing to the fact that a paper cover was its only protection. The spine was broken, the pages folded over, dog-eared. It was a tattered copy of *The Great Controversy*, a book he had never seen before. The book practically fell open in his hands. Most of the rough wear was in the last quarter of the tome. His father had marked passages, written stars, exclamation points, and question marks in the margins. Many a passage was underlined with notes in the margin. His eyes read one of those highlighted passages:

> One reason why many theologians have no clearer understanding of God's word is, they close their eyes to truths which they do not wish to practice. An understanding of Bible truths depends not so much on the power of intellect brought to the search as on the singleness of purpose, the earnest longing after righteousness. The Bible should never be studied without prayer. (*The Great Controversy*, p. 599)

Next to this underlined passage, Chad's father had written "Amen." He could see his father reading this book with a desire to be a better Christian. He, too, had to agree that personal character needed to be open to the direction of the Holy Spirit. He almost said, "Amen," as well. It caused him to look at his father's Bible with reverence. Looking at the Sacred Book, his eyes moved to the gold edges of the pages, which were almost bereft of their original golden luster due to usage. No corners were turned down or dog-eared. The treatment of the Bible was different than the other book. Then he saw an insert, a bookmark. He opened the Bible to the book of Revelation to find a leaflet invitation to some meetings. It was the same brochure as the one Detective Hardine had shown him with a multi-headed red dragon with a woman riding upon its back. It marked a place where Revelation chapter 17, verse 3, was located. "…a woman sitting on a scarlet beast which was full of blasphemous names, and it had seven heads and ten horns" (RSV).

The slick, glossy leaflet with the symbolic image on its front had been something his parents, or at least his father, was interested in studying. He, out of ignorance, had given the detective the wrong answer. He glanced out of the study window to see that the detective's car was gone. He scrutinized the paper with more intensity. The dates were from five months ago. The meetings were finished. *Did Mom and Dad attend?* he asked himself, adding, *Was it important?* He put the book back where it had been. He didn't know why, but he felt a compunction to place the Bible on top of it in the same alignment as before. It was like a shrine to his father's behavior. The new thought added some mystery to what his folks had been doing before their sudden deaths. He thought about it for a few moments and then rose to return to the dining room. He was startled by the doorbell immediately overhead in the hallway. "Yes?"

"Chad, is that you? This is Diana, Diana Cross from church. Do you remember me?"

"Yes, I do. Ah, can you meet me by the door next to the garage? It's just around the corner to your right."

Chad went to the service door for the second time, thinking about Diana. She was from the youth group at church. They had come up through Sunday School classes together. She was the fun girl of the group, all ears, neck, and goofy rimmed glasses, always with messy, dirty lenses. All the boys enjoyed her wit but never thought of her in romantic terms. She was just one of the crowd.

He opened the door to see a dramatic change. The glasses were gone, obviously replaced by contacts. Her eyes were an entrancing emerald blue-green. Her medium-long hair framed a delicate face with a radiant yet subdued smile. The hair curled just above her shoulders, enhancing the snowy white pedestal for her head. She was a latent beauty fully out of her chrysalis.

"Chad. I'm so sorry. This is awful. I don't know what to say. Words fail me. You must be in a lot of pain." She blurted out her words as she wrapped her arms around his chest. He could smell her perfume and feel the light fabric of her dress. Her outburst thrust him into a moment, solidly on the side of emotional grief. He felt like letting it go. Instead of holding it in, he wanted to loosen the tight mesh of strings binding his heart. In a rush the body started to shake. His eyes were clamped shut to prevent tears from pouring out. They came anyway. Then he had a moment of machismo. He had to quell the outburst in the face of a comely woman. He broke away from her grasp and turned away, hiding his eyes. He wiped the moisture away as if a dust particle had flown in his eye. Diana kept one hand on his shoulder while he composed himself. She understood more than he did about his desire to keep a manly exterior. She waited.

"Ah, come on in. We can go into the kitchen," he said, trying to keep a normal tone to his voice.

"I have some food in the car. I need help carrying it."

"Sure, let me help."

They went to her car. All of the food was in a box sitting on the front seat, which he could manage. It would have been cumbersome for her to bring it to the door by herself. "What do you have in here? It's heavy. This isn't Thanksgiving."

"I wanted to bring you a meal when no one else was bringing you one. After the funeral, there will be a bunch of food brought to your house, but I thought you would need some now." She held the door for him to go through.

"But this is a lot. I'm only one person. A sandwich would have been enough." Then thinking that he might not seem grateful, he added, "This is very thoughtful of you, more than thoughtful really, very kind, thank you. I was getting ready to eat lunch. Have you eaten?"

"No. I was planning to drop this off and go."

"Do you have someplace you need to be?"

"No, not really."

"Then, you must help me eat this food." Chad slid the box onto the counter and went to the cabinet for two plates. She was debating whether to stay, but when he placed the dishes on the kitchen table, she gave in. She helped him retrieve the items out of the box. She was proud of what she had made.

"It's still warm, but we can warm it up some more if you'd like."

"What is it?"

"Salisbury steak casserole, mashed potatoes, and I thought you needed a vegetable too, so I made a green bean casserole. The Salisbury steak is a recipe from my mother," she added with a dash of humility.

"You went to a lot of trouble just for me. Thank you. This is almost like a Thanksgiving feast."

"For that, you would need dinner rolls and, at least, pumpkin pie. I actually thought of doing that too, but then you are single, ah, you know, one person. I didn't want to overwhelm you with food." Her tone lowered at the end. She immediately knew she had said too much, using the word single was a give-away. Chad felt the attraction come through as well. She was trying to make a connection with him. It moved him to realize that this formerly frumpy female had graduated to the point where she wanted to be attractive to him and be beneficent to his needs.

"This is perfect timing; I am hungry."

"Good."

XXXXX

"This is wrong! Stop it! Please!"

"Lady, if you don't pay your bills, you get evicted. It's as simple as that," the policeman stated.

"But, I do pay my bills; I've always paid my bills! You can check. My bank records will prove it!" Vonnie Hixon pulled out her smartphone to access her bank account. "Here, I'll show you," her fingers danced across the face of the phone, trying to bring up her banking data and online statement.

"It won't do you any good. I have to see to it that you vacate the property immediately. The owner needs to clean out the apartment and re-let it to someone who pays their rent." To add emphasis to his words, he held up an official eviction notice. Then a worker entered the apartment with a carpet cleaner and carrying cleaning materials and a roll of garbage bags. This packed another layer of frustration on top of what she was already experiencing.

"But, this is not fair! I should have had a warning notice. But, I do pay my rent. I've never missed a single payment! Here, look, my bank statement will prove …" Vonnie paused as she puzzled over the data on her screen. It showed her account overdrawn. "I don't understand? Why? What happened? I should have at least a thousand dollars in my account after paying all of this month's bills," Her voice trailing off in a whisper, then suddenly, "I've been e-robbed!"

"Look, lady, I've heard all this before. Everyone is a perfect citizen. I'll give you ten minutes to get important papers, and then you have to go," he emphasized.

"Ten minutes! I can't move everything out in ten minutes. I have clothes and books, and, and …"

"Get going, Miss, I don't have all day!"

"Okay, okay, but don't let him touch any of my things." Vonnie rushed to her closet and yanked out her suitcases. She dragged them into her bedroom and started to fling clothes from her dresser and nightstand into them. She wanted to scream. She wanted to stomp her feet and demand that the intruders leave immediately. Her Christian demeanor was being taxed to the limit. Her possessions were being taken from her without due process of the law. Her mind raced over her rights, and what she could do to stop the loss she was sustaining. The law would take time to rectify this injustice. In the meantime, her stuff would be taken to who knows where. She may never get all of it back. Perhaps she would get some kind of compensation for her unreturned property. She had learned that when a person is being evacuated from a home due to some forthcoming natural disaster such as a wildfire, the five "P's" should be observed: People, pets, papers, pictures, property, in that order. She stopped to follow that rule of thumb. She didn't have a pet, so she went to her important papers; passport, diplomas, certificates, cramming them into a smaller suitcase from a drawer, then she went after her computer laptop, which had more important data on it along with a myriad of folders with digital pictures. Next, she resumed stuffing her clothes into what space was left. Plastic garbage bags were brought out and filled with whatever could be hastily obtained.

The officer, more accurately a rental cop, an individual under contract in certain circumstances, followed her everywhere. It annoyed her that he watched as she emptied her top dresser drawer of dainties. She used her body to shield his view, but he moved around to get a better line of sight. She was getting angrier by the second. It was a violation of her privacy. It was a violation of everything sensible. No warning allowed her to get help before this happened. There was no way she could stop the process and make a proper appeal. She was helplessly trapped. Her dander rose to a point where she was shooting angry eyes at her oppressor. The storm was about to explode inside. She wanted to beat her fists against the officer's chest. She was feeling decidedly unchristian, a feeling she didn't want. That's when she noticed that he wasn't wearing a name tag. *Who was he?* She asked herself. He was big, overweight, and not as diplomatic as policemen were supposed to be. Her worries about her situation started spinning in a slightly different direction. *Is this person authentic? Is this invasion of her world a contrived perpetration based on an elaborate e-crime scheme?* Her eyes darted toward the other man who was supposedly there to clean the apartment. He was more imposing than the officer, lean and muscular. He lolled around, waiting for her to leave. She now felt she was in the presence of thieves. Her life might be in danger. Tentatively, she asked, "May I have your names so I will have someone I can refer to when I make a proper appeal?"

"Just get your stuff and leave. You've got two more minutes, and then I kick you out, with or without your things. Got it?"

She had no choice; she had to get what she could and get away from these men. The apartment was rented fully furnished; however, she had a few items of her own, a bookcase and some lamps, odds and ends. She was overwhelmed with the task. She piled suitcases and bags outside the front door and returned for a last quick grab and go. There, on her nightstand, was her Bible open to her morning reading for the day, "Lay up your treasure in heaven where moth and rust does not consume."[2] She didn't know why she had opened her Bible to that particular text; usually, she did systematic reading through a book alternating between the Old and New Testaments. She always marveled at how no matter what passage she read for that day, it always had something for the problems and issues she would face. Today, she thought she was being lazy by simply reading the page it opened to. In the brief moment she had to look at her Bible on the nightstand, her heart was calmed by the memory of the moment of reflection the passage gave her. The words were God's preprogrammed advice for the trouble she was in at the present. Comforting, she clutched the Bible to her breast, turning to leave her apartment, chagrined that the most valuable possession was the last one she took out of her former home.

She looked at her oppressors as she moved from the bedroom through to the living room and the front door. The fire of anger was no longer in her eyes. The internal storm was becalmed. God would take care of her. The two men saw her look at them. The officer had his prepared statement.

"Maybe that church group of yours, that sect you belong to, will take you in."

Vonnie was shocked. His words were spat out with a sneer rather than offered as a suggestion of help. This man had seen something in the apartment that identified her as a member of a church he considered heretical. He was ridiculing in a simple way the members of her church. She tried to think of objects in her home that would communicate her membership.

XXXXX

"Chad, look at you. You're so grown up!"

"I don't know what you mean?"

"The last time I saw you, you were still a kid with messy hair all combed up to look like it wasn't combed. And you wore your pants below your butt. Now you look like a serious businessman in casual dress."

---

[2]Matt. 6:20, RSV

"Has it been that long?" Chad had a fork full of mashed potatoes half-way to his mouth. "You've changed too. I thought you wore glasses, well, I guess you're wearing contacts, but it makes you look entirely different than before—nice."

"Thank you. I've been wearing them since twelfth grade. I hated those klutzy old Harry Potter rims always sliding down my nose."

"This Salisbury steak is delicious. You're a good cook. Thank you for bringing it over."

> *He was fit, a chiseled definition to his chest and arms. His brown hair was neatly trimmed with just enough to sweep back to one side.*

Diana smiled while she looked at her plate. So far, her efforts were received in the exact manner she had anticipated. What she had not anticipated was how Chad had matured. He was fit, a chiseled definition to his chest and arms. His brown hair was neatly trimmed with just enough to sweep back to one side. Not a single hair was out of place. His sharp eyes were alive with intelligence, and his jaw communicated quiet strength. She wanted to change the conversation to his loss without pushing at his emotion; she knew it was just under the surface.

"Do you know when the funeral is going to be?"

"Not yet. Forensics has to release the bodies, um, my folks, to the mortuary."

"Do you have any ideas of what you want for a funeral service?"

"No, not really. I thought I'd leave it up to the minister. They know these things; they perform them all the time."

"The funeral director can help, too. Did your folks ever say what they wanted?"

"Not to me," Chad answered.

"You know, I've heard that funerals are for the living. I guess it's for the survi— I mean the ones who are grieving. This service should be for you and the ones who knew your folks," she explained.

"I think Reverend Wells will do a good job. He knew my folks pretty well."

"So you are going to ask Reverend Wells to come here? Do you know where he went? It's been a while since he went to California. Then I heard that church didn't work out, and he was retiring. Do you know where he is?"

"Ah, I guess I need to catch up. I thought Reverend Wells was still here." Chad felt even more out of sync with his church. It was odd to feel uninformed, believing that life would just remain the same. He needed to get some more information. "Who's the pastor now?"

"Reverend Bill Tucker," she answered.

"My folks never talked of him."

"Maybe they didn't like his style. A number of people left the church after he came. Your folks did too, sort of. It's only been the last couple of months or so that they stopped coming."

Chad had to mentally blink with that information. He was counting on Reverend Wells to do the funeral. Now he was in a bind. He would have to make arrangements with a minister he didn't know and who didn't know his folks. It was an awkward feeling, but no more awkward than having a funeral for his folks after they were murdered by a person or persons unknown. The news of his folks not attending added another dimension of mystery. Why did his folks stop attending the church they wanted so desperately for him to attend when he was home? As he pushed green beans around his plate, the phone twittered. It was Detective Hardine who called, as promised, to tell him that the morgue had released his parents to the mortuary. He thanked him and hung up. He stared at the casserole for a moment, collecting his thoughts. Diana knew what was happening based on the half conversation she overheard.

"Would you like it if I went along with you to the funeral home to give you support? You shouldn't have to do this all by yourself. I was involved when my grandfather died. I helped Grandma and my mom while they made preparations," she asked quietly.

Chad could tell she was trying to be the rescue woman. Her cooking, planning, and guessing at his needs were becoming more and more apparent as a desire to get connected with him on a deeper level. Women had attempted to catch his attention through the intervening years. He had had several dates, and some lasted past the initial first three. But, he found it difficult to get serious. Marriage was a big deal for him. It meant providing for a wife and a family. The thought of having children and raising them also meant he had to settle in his mind what the family would do with regard to faith. Church and worship didn't speak to him in its present mode. The style that he was accustomed to was the style of the church his parents raised him within. He had to settle that issue and many other issues in life in his mind before getting down to dating with a mission to find a life partner. If he didn't know what he was, then he didn't know what he wanted in a companion. He couldn't look for a woman of faith if he didn't know what shape his faith was in. Given all that, he was drawn to this caring friend from the past. Her transformation into a beautiful woman was an extra plus.

"Yes, I would appreciate it if you would help me make arrangements. It is very kind of you to offer.

CHAPTER 2

The walls of the room were lined with sofas. End tables and lamps added a relatively cozy feel to the room. Stackable chairs were lined up side-by-side in the middle of the room, available for people to sit down when or if a service would begin. The funeral director had planned for any possibility, owing to the fact that the Reverend Tucker hadn't coordinated with him ahead of time. Up front there was a smallish viewing area. Chad stood to one side of the caskets. The mortician had performed excellent work repairing the damage to his parents' heads. He was alone before the scheduled time for the viewing. It was difficult to approach them as they lay in separate caskets side-by-side jutting out into the room. It was as if they were sleeping in a divided double bed. By chance the funeral home had put them on their customary sides; Mom on the left, Dad on the right. It was difficult for him to approach them because he knew what he had to say. He wiped a tear out of his eye and walked to his mother's side.

"Mom, Dad, I'm sorry. I know you wanted me to attend church, but I just couldn't. It wasn't for me. It was like church was out there somewhere and couldn't find me. I wish I had at least attended for you when I came home from college. At best, I wouldn't have to be apologizing to you now. I'm sorry.

"I also want to know what happened. Why would anyone want to kill you? I don't get it. I'm angry, no, I am livid! Why? If I can, I will find those,

27

those … I'll find them and bring them to justice. I will see to it that the police arrest them and make them pay for what they did to you.

"I wanted you to be proud of me. I know you said you were proud of me and meant it, but it's different from my side of the equation. I wanted to show you my success. I never got a chance to show you. I was just getting started." Chad stopped talking to think about his parents' expectations of him. A memory flitted across his mind. It brought a smile. His mother's humor drove the memory.

"Mom, I know you wanted me to get married and have a lot of grand-kids for you to spoil. Remember that time you assisted one of the women at church with a wedding? You promised to take care of her bridal gown while they were on their honeymoon. Then, when I was home, you brought the dress out of the closet and handed it to me. You said, 'Here, take this. Fill it up, and bring it back to me.'" Chad thought about that for another moment. "I think I got my sense of humor from you, Mom. Thanks."

A quiet knock came on the door. He moved to open the door and came face to face with the director. "People are starting to arrive. I can keep them out if you need more time."

"No, they can come in now." He looked over the director's shoulder to see Diana waiting for him. She was the first to greet him with a warm embrace. She held it longer than he expected. She started the evening by performing all the rituals of a wake—signing the guest book and standing before the casket to pray, and then hovering near Chad as he greeted friends and acquaintances, many of whom he could not remember properly. Strangers from his dad's work had to introduce themselves and tell stories. All of the visitors were horrified by the murder and wanted to express their outrage at what had happened. Every time they spoke of it, it was like a jab to the ribs. The multiplicity of encounters and the discussions were taking their toll on his fortitude. He was young and healthy, but he felt weak as the night progressed. He revived when Diana showed up with a cold Coke. The caffeine kept him going.

Some of the people he knew from church wanted to know why his parents had stopped attending. This added to what he already knew from Diana, but no one had an answer for why.

A small group of young people his age approached. They introduced themselves as Brian, Raphael, Vonnie, and Cynthia. They started by saying that Chad's folks had talked a lot about him when they met in church. Chad immediately looked to Diana for help. She shrugged her shoulders, indicating she had never met them before.

"Pardon me for asking, but you're not from the church my folks attended."

"Oh, ah, well, your folks have been attending our church for the last several months. Four, maybe five months, I think," Brian King answered.

"What church would that be?"

"We belong to the Forest Glen SDA church. It's located on the corner of Seventh and Crestline Boulevard. Have you ever been there?"

"No, I haven't. I didn't know my folks were attending a different church. This is the first I have heard of it. Is it Mormon?" Chad asked.

"Sometimes, people confuse us with the LDS church because of the initials. It happens all the time. Our church is called the Seventh-day Adventist church, hence the SDA initials."

"You say that my folks have been attending your church?"

"Yes, they started after the Revelation studies we had. They came to the meetings and started to join us as a church family. Everyone loves your parents; they're so nice. And another thing, they always talked about you. I feel like I already know you," Vonnie Hixon answered.

At this point Chad reeled with conflicting feelings competing for his full attention. He wanted to explore in detail the folks' strange behavior of uniting with this new church; he wanted to know why they departed from the old church family; then, his understanding that his folks were proud of him and talked of him to these strangers opened wounds of grief and guilt. Not knowing what his parents were doing in their final days caused him guilt for being so out of touch. It must have registered on his face because Vonnie made a quick covering statement, "We are so sorry for your loss. We want you to know we grieve with you and also for our friends, Daniel and Janine." She gently touched his lower arm in compassion.

Diana could see the consternation on his face. She moved in like a defending mother bear. Without looking at the foursome, she spoke to Chad, "Reverend Tucker wanted a moment with you about tomorrow's service. I think now would be a good time. I see him standing alone over there." She pointed with her full arm and hand and then took his arm with her other hand, leading him away.

XXXXX

"Any luck?"

Detective Hardine stood when his captain appeared suddenly at his desk. His presence and question took him by surprise. "No, I'm afraid not, not yet anyway. I'm of the opinion that the usual scenarios like domestic issues, suicide, robbery, jealousy, and competition in business, or a drug deal gone bad, are not probable causes for this. At least, not now, with the evidence we've found. I can't find a motive or a suspect, but I'm still digging around." He wanted to defend his work to his boss, so he continued to explain more. "I've interviewed everyone I can think of and just came back from the viewing service at the funeral home. I tried to see if there might be some hint of a lead I could get there. Nothing. I'll keep trying. These days with the world going crazy, it could be anything; a hate crime is a possibility, or a gang-related initiation rite, or maybe a mistaken address or identity for a drug assassination. I'm checking my sources for those last ones to see if there was a contract that went down, and they missed their real target. I know I'll find the answers. I can feel it."

"Keep up the good work. Don't worry if nothing shows up right away. I've seen cases similar to this where the truth comes out later when defenses are down, and people start to blab. It's late. Go home to your family and start tomorrow with a clear head." The captain turned on his heel and left Hardine's desk. The captain was unaware he didn't have a family. His cell phone rang.

"Hello, this is Detective Hardine."

"Detective, I just wanted to call and say that I found out that that leaflet you had about those meetings … Well, my folks attended those meetings, and I think that they were attending another church because of that, a Seventh-day Adventist church."

"Interesting."

"Yes, well, could it mean anything? I mean, you showed that to me and asked, and I wanted to let you know what I found out about it. My dad could have been holding it when they came in the door. Or, it could be a coincidence, maybe."

"Yes, it could be a simple coincidence. It's hard to tell. I want to thank you for telling me what you found out. I'll keep you posted, okay?"

"Thank you, sir."

The detective turned off his phone and started to ponder the leaflet. *It was not a simple coincidence that Mr. Johnson was holding the advertisement at the moment of his death?* He didn't believe in coincidence. Then his mind pulled up some data. *Mr. or Mrs. Johnson's fingerprints were not on the brochure. No fingerprints were found on the paper! Maybe I have my first lead. The Johnsons were lured into a strange church.*

XXXXX

When Chad concluded his call with the detective, he looked at his friend.

"I didn't know your parents were attending another church. That was a surprise to me," Diana said. She had taken Chad to a sports bar for a bite to eat after the viewing at the funeral home. They talked as they waited for burgers to arrive.

"They didn't stop attending church altogether; they evidently started attending another one, maybe at the same time. That's a surprise to me, too. They have always been members of our church. Dad was always fond of saying, 'don't fix what isn't broken.' They were happy where they were," he answered.

"So these Adventists stole them away from us."

"Looks like it. I wonder what attracted them," he said more as a statement rather than a question.

"Did you see the news about one of those SDAers? It's been on the internet. It's a big legal blowout, and people are taking sides. Opinions are going back and forth in social media, for and against this one guy who got fired for no reason it seems."

"No, I have been off-line ever since the news about my folks."

"It seems as if this one person is taking on an international health provider, kind of a David and Goliath story. He has some backing from some lawyers and special interest organizations. The ACLU is in this big time. Possibly because of their making a noise about it, that's why the story is bigger than it is."

"This might make it easier for me."

"How so?"

"I was thinking that I should try to figure out what the attraction was for my folks. The best way to do that is to attend their church, but I didn't want to go trooping in there. They'd get the idea I was interested in it too. I'll just gather as much information about this SD, ah, Adventist fellow. There must be a lot of info and blogs about him and his beliefs."

> *"I was thinking that I should try to figure out what the attraction was for my folks. The best way to do that is to attend their church, but I didn't want to go trooping in there. They'd get the idea I was interested in it too.*

"I get what you mean. Can I study with you? I would like to know why they left our church for this church I've never heard before."

"Okay, let's start now. Tell me what you've heard so far."

XXXXX

Brian and Cynthia dropped Vonnie off at her parents' home. It was awkward for her because it was like she was back in high school. They had given her a ride. She had a car, but with her bank account gone and her debit card non-functional, she couldn't afford to drive it very far on one tank of gas. They talked first of Chad and the funeral home viewing.

"I think it was good for us to go to the viewing. We had a better chance to show our support than if we just went to the funeral," Cynthia stated.

"I agree," Vonnie answered.

"It will be more meaningful for him to see us tomorrow. He'll know we really liked his folks," Brian said. "Changing the subject, Vonnie, have you gotten any encouragement from the bank or police about what happened?" he added.

"The bank is horrified that their security systems got hacked. They're alerting their customers. They're tracking down the source with the police. Hopefully, they'll find who did this. There are things that don't add up."

"Like what?"

"Like, if they wanted to steal my money, why did they erase my banking history as well? Then, why is it that my only unpaid bill is this bogus claim that I haven't paid my rent for three months? Other businesses, such as my car loan, haven't contacted me for nonpayment. It doesn't make sense," Vonnie explained.

"My guess is that the landlord is in this, but I don't know why. Why would he want to get rid of a dependable renter, especially one who doesn't make a lot of noise and throw wild parties?" Brian commented.

"Exactly!" Cynthia agreed. "Vonnie, what are you going to do?"

"Right now, I'm going to reestablish my credit and open a different bank account; get back on my feet."

"You know we're here for you. Brian and I agree that if you need to stay at our place or if you need some money, no matter how much, just ask us, okay?" Cynthia put her hand out to touch Vonnie's shoulder.

"Before you go, let's pray together."

"Yes, thank you. And let's not forget to pray for Chad Johnson."

Before Brian could finish his prayer, there was a sudden rap on his window. It caused them to jump in surprise. Brian rolled down the window as the officer demanded.

"What's going on here? Keep your hands where I can see them. You, too." The policeman shifted his flashlight from Brian to Cynthia. His voice was gruff and strident. He did not immediately see Vonnie in the back seat.

"Yes, sir. We were just dropping off our—"

"Shut up! Nigger! Step out of the car, slowly. Keep your hands in front of you so I can see them at all times. You first." He pointed the bright light into Brian's eyes, blinding him. "Make no attempt to hide your drugs; we'll find them anyway." Brian complied slowly and carefully. The officer had his service revolver pointed at Brian's chest. "Now, face the car and keep your hands up." The officer patted Brian from his armpits to his legs. "Okay, sit on the curb, and don't move. You're next. Get out slowly and keep your hands where I can see them." The beam of light illuminated Cynthia's worried face.

"Please don't shoot us. We'll comply," Cynthia answered nervously. She exited the car on the passenger side, and the officer kept his revolver on her. "Sir, can I ask why you are doing this?"

"Shut up!"

"I would also like to have you answer that question," Vonnie's father stated firmly while standing on the front lawn. Officer Kimmel swung around suddenly in response to the voice behind him. The gun aimed at his chest.

"Get back in your house! This does not concern you. You are hindering a police investigation."

"On the contrary, this does concern me. That is my daughter in the back seat, and I want to know what's going on."

Vonnie had rolled down the window and answered, "That is my father, and this is where I live. I, too, want to know what you are doing. These people are my friends and have done nothing wrong."

"Shut up, all of you! Get out of the car and sit on the grass. I'll get to the bottom of this. If there are drugs in this vehicle, I will find them."

"Sir, don't you need to have probable cause to search this car? What is your probable cause?" stated Mr. Hixon.

"What are you, some kind of lawyer?"

"I'm a paralegal. I know enough that this is an illegal search unless you have probable cause. I repeat, what is your probable cause for mistreating these citizens?"

"They were hiding. I saw their heads go down. They're acting guilty. They're hiding something."

"Oh, for Pete's sake, we were praying," Vonnie exclaimed.

"You were praying? That's a new one! I've never heard that excuse before."

"Nevertheless, it's true; we were praying." Vonnie looked to Brian and Cynthia, who, in turn, nodded their heads in the affirmative.

"I think you owe these young adults an apology," Mr. Hixon stated.

"I don't owe them anything. Get in your car and get out of here." Officer Kimmel re-holstered his service revolver and went for his cruiser, demanding that they leave. He was obviously upset and outmaneuvered.

"Sir, with your permission, I'm going to invite them into my house."

"Whatever." Frustrated, he slammed the police car door closed and roared down the street.

Quiet disbelief dominated the atmosphere around them until Mr. Hixon suggested they go into the house.

XXXXX

Around the kitchen table, they discussed what had happened, "I can't believe what he said, and his use of *that* word," Vonnie spoke her frustration. "It was demeaning, and I resented it!" she added.

"Thank you for your words. It is not the first time we have been stopped because we're black. This is not the first time I have heard that word, either. It has happened more often when it is just me, but Cynthia has also gone through this before."

"Really? The police treat you like that often?"

"I wouldn't say often, but it does happen from time to time."

"Oh, how awful! I'm so sorry."

"My sentiments, too. I never realized. My heart aches for you guys," Mr. Hixon added.

"It was nice that you were there this evening. It stopped him from continuing. We are always concerned if we make a wrong move or something, we might get hauled into the police station."

"Or worse," Cynthia added.

"I want you to know you are always welcome here, and if there is anything that I can do to help, I will come running," Mr. Hixon stated with feeling.

"It was God's will that you were here this evening. I know He protects us. This time, He used you," Brian pronounced.

"Amen," Cynthia seconded.

"You know, things like this are going to get worse and worse now that we are near to the second coming. It won't be just us; it will be all of us struggling to get through to the end," Brian explained.

XXXXX

"Look what I found." Diana was accessing the Internet on her smartphone. They had pushed their plates to the center of the table and were occasionally munching on steak fries and dipping them in ranch sauce as they started their research. Chad changed sides of the booth to sit next to her and look at her phone.

She explained, "Well, we know that Jeremy Richards' lawyer is suing CentraHealing for wrongful termination, but what I found is that CentraHealing did not inform Jeremy that CentraHealing supposedly had a standard of strict compliance about in-service meetings, whether or not they conflict with individual belief. CentraHealing is a huge organization that spans the world operating hospitals everywhere. Many of these hospitals are owned by church organizations, like the Catholics, Presbyterians, even the SDA church. Something doesn't add up. Jeremy Richards has had a perfect record of efficiency reports. His lawyer has copies of all of them. Then, suddenly, for no reason, CentraHealing fires him because he was unwilling to work on his Sabbath."

"That can't be all of it. There has to be something else that is going on behind the scenes."

"Then why doesn't CenturaHealing explain whatever that is?"

"Because if they did release their real reasons to the press, then they could be sued for slander. They'll save that information for the courtroom. I found some different stuff. I went to the chat rooms and Twitter to see what they were saying. I'm not so interested in what this Jeremy is doing to fight for his job or his retirement. I'm interested in learning who and what he believes."

"Did you find anything?"

"Yes. I found different things. This Sabbath thing is one issue. They keep it like the Jews do, from sundown Friday to sundown Saturday. Jeremy never had a conflict because he worked Monday to Friday, eight to four-thirty. Supposedly, he wasn't going to have a conflict in the future, but they scheduled this one-day conference he had to attend. It was nothing more than a board meeting switched from a Tuesday morning to a Saturday afternoon. Other workers who attended said it was a sham, and are sympathetic with him. He tried to take vacation time for the weekend, but they wouldn't let him."

"That sounds like a set-up and not his fault. Do you still think that Jeremy did something wrong, and they needed to precipitate an issue?"

"I don't know. The chats from individuals inside the organization are mostly positive for their friend. Chats from admin officials or people close to the leadership are absent like there's a gag order that went out. There are a lot of comments from sympathizers who are or look like they are SDAs. They say lots of things about him being a good family man, loves Jesus, is humble, quiet, holds offices in the church, gives Bible studies, and is a great soul-winner."

"So he goes house to house like JWs?"

"No, he invites people to his home and gives them Bible studies."

"Humm, sounds like a dedicated Christian, maybe a little over the top, almost too good to be true," Diana summarized. She went back to scrolling through her phone screen. She was still looking at the subject of wrongful termination. Then she hit something.

"Wait a minute. Here's something." She kept speed reading the material. Chad leaned over to look. "Look at this comment. A receptionist for one of the offices said that she is afraid of losing her job, too. She has worked for the organization for almost as long as Mr. Richards and has watched over the years as other Adventists have been removed for little things they did. She says a mistake that would normally get a counseling moment with the boss, was different for SDAs; they got the boot while others went back to work. Very few SDAs work for the organization and the hospital that is, or started out as, an SDA hospital."

"If true, that sounds like prejudice. Is there anything about the doctrines of this church that would generate prejudice?"

"Here, this sounds like something." Diana touched her screen to access the whole story. "Someone is blaming Jeremy for disrupting the workplace. He's a department head who says that several of his best workers started asking for the Sabbath off so they could attend church. They were shift workers in the hospital, and it started to destroy his scheduling, causing a lot of angry feelings. The organization had to hire more people to fill the vacancies. The workers had been receiving studies from Jeremy. Then, here is another person who said that the request for Sabbaths off in their department was a real godsend because that meant people who wanted Sunday off would have the Sabbathkeepers take their shift. This report shows pro and con. But, Jeremy is on the hot seat because of persuading people to keep the Saturday Sabbath."

"Maybe you found the reason for why CentraHealing wanted Jeremy Richards gone. It doesn't make it right, but it might have been a motivation on their part."

XXXXX

Chad stopped the clock on the mantel and went to his old bedroom to sleep. Everything was the same as when he was in high school. He had moved his small suitcase out of the hotel room and brought it home. A cleaning company that specializes in cleaning crime scenes had come in, disinfected everything about the living room, and had removed the carpet. A handyman fixed the front door. The plywood was gone. The only thing yet to be accomplished was new carpeting. The house almost looked like nothing had happened. His bedroom was no exception.

Looking around the bedroom, he saw evidence of his childhood. On the shelf in the closet was a box, partially exposed by the open sliding door. He knew the contents of the box—some Power Ranger toys, a Lego set, some storybooks that were his favorite when he was young. On shelves near his desk were more mature objects. A baseball he acquired from a professional game where a foul ball had landed almost exactly in his mitt; a cluster of books next to an e-reader that had a multitude of books stored in its memory chip. On the top shelf, several electronic helicopters and a drone lay gathering dust. The drone was his pride and joy in high school. He had used it to get a bird's eye view of sporting events and some sunbathing girls at a neighborhood swimming pool. It seemed silly now to hang on to those trinkets from his past. He stretched out on top of his bed. Another stray memory crossed his mind. He remembered how he would sleep on top of his bed with only a blanket thrown over him. In the morning, he would toss the small blanket in the closet, tug on the bedspread, and his bed was made. It was his way of meeting his mother's demand of making his bed every morning. The sheets never got used. He lay there thinking about the past and how much he wished his folks were still here. Tomorrow would be their funeral. It was supposed to put a cap on their passing, to bring about a resolution to their deaths. There wasn't a resolution. It was too soon to be thinking about putting this all behind him. Too many questions fought to dominate his thoughts. He decided that tomorrow afternoon's funeral would not end anything. He would find out why and then maybe …

He couldn't sleep. Grief, anger, curiosity, revenge, and a dozen more reactions to his condition rattled through his consciousness. Finally, they settled on curiosity. He got up and went to the study to get the paperback book under his dad's Bible. He started to read.

The first part of the book talked of the progress of the Christian church in history. Chad could see the author setting the stage for something big later on. He flipped back to the back from time to time to read the chapter headings. This writer was moving through history from Jesus' ascension to His return. Clearly, she laid out the battle that was going on unseen between Satan and God, more specifically, between Satan and Jesus. This was not something he had visualized in his understanding of what Jesus was doing now and how Satan figured into the picture. The book demonstrated that the Word of God was being obliterated, unseen, unknown, unread by the general populace. Recorded history during this time spoke of the dark ages. This book exposed the reason why it was so dark—it was dark spiritually. He had had world history classes, but this was a revelation to him about the powers of darkness prevailing within the dominant church of the time, the medieval Christian church. No wonder his history professor was so negative about church in general. His professor's favorite phrase was, 'Absolute power corrupts absolutely." In contrast the writer was telling the truth about God's work to save His people. This writer had a strong belief in the literal second coming of Jesus and the saving work of Jesus on the cross. The why of His second coming was centered on the need to rescue His believers from Satan's continued attempt to pry them away from a salvation already accomplished. Chapter after chapter illuminated the work of uncovering biblical truth before the end. Satan was trying to cloud the issues, and he was also corrupting church leaders with the feeling of power over potentates.

Chad's eyes hurt. He rubbed them and then looked at the clock. It was after four in the morning. He was physically tired and somewhat settled in his mind. The Scripture passages quoted in the book had a soothing effect on him. God was in control. God had a plan. Jesus was going to finish that plan. Instead of being adrift about his folks, and what they were doing in another church, he was now attacking the mystery and learning why they were attracted to this new church. He still didn't know why, but he was on a mission to find out. Half the battle is having a plan.

CHAPTER 3

The funeral was in his home church. The familiar neighborhood, the familiar entrance to the parking lot, his folks' customary slot close, but not too close to the entrance; these were his roots. Some of the members noticed Johnsons' car in its regular place. Chad was filling a spot on the pavement between painted lines. He was also reminding grieving friends of the empty spot they had in their hearts. Once he climbed the steps to the narthex, the ritual of the funeral began. Diana was waiting. She would be his only family. He greeted everyone standing by the guest book. Hugs and kisses on the cheeks came from ladies; hearty, lingering handshakes from the men. The comments were almost predictable; "We're so sorry," "This is a tragedy," "We missed you at church," "How are you doing?" "Where are you living?" "It's so good to see you again, wish it were under different circumstances." Chad was prepared to hear those remarks; he was experienced now after the viewing at the funeral home the night before.

When the time came, he and Diana were ushered to the front row of the almost-full church. Murmurs could be heard, unintelligible to the ear, but understandable by intent. The members were remarking about the presence of Diana at his right side. He took note of where Brian, Cynthia, Vonnie, and Raphael sat. They had greeted him at the front door but yielded their time to some members who suddenly broke into the conversation. He nodded toward them. As the soloist sang the opening song, he thought of the foursome who was from his folks' new church. Had they read the same book that occupied his mind and had kept him awake until late? Because of that initial reading, he wanted to talk with them more, but now was not the time. His eyes drifted toward the caskets. They were not open; his parents were tucked in for the last time.

Reverend Bill Tucker performed the expected rites. The eulogy was omitted in favor of a sermon preached, using their service to the church as an example to everyone on how church members should serve their congregations. Some of the facts were slightly inaccurate as to how many years and which positions they held. The minister kept saying Jane instead of Janine, causing some of the longtime members to wince every time he made the mistake. The form and order of the service were familiar, and the prayers had been heard many a time before, as they were written in a book of prayers. This kind of church behavior, familiar to the members and to Chad's folks, was meaningful by its pattern and words. It reminded Chad how he had difficulty trying to apply the traditional ways of the church to his desire for a church that had relevance, that met him where he was intellectually. The funeral didn't speak to his heart or to his grief. He knew that God would save his parents with their deep faith in Jesus and what He did for them on the cross. He did not fear for their losing out on eternity. He feared that *he* might lose out on eternity if he didn't find the Jesus of the here and now. As he mulled this over in his thoughts, the service concluded, the music played, and he was invited to follow the caskets out of the church as they were guided by the pallbearers out to the narthex led by the pastor. Two hearses were waiting to take his folks to the cemetery.

The well-wishers were out in force at the graveside. The small awning provided only enough cover for Chad, Diana, and a few of the more elderly mourners with shade and seating. The graveside consisted of a read prayer, a committal, and another read prayer. The reverend was done in less than three, four minutes tops. Chad wanted more. The moment he was in now required something—something that could speak to him. It all seemed so formal and dry. He wanted people to know what he felt. He wanted people to understand how good his folks were to their community and to their friends. He wanted someone to understand the loss of their personalities, their humor, their wisdom, their understanding of him, and their patience with his divergent opinions. His loss was too great to wrap up in a thirty-minute funeral and a couple-minute graveside farewell.

This was a perfect example of how his church couldn't reach him, and he didn't know where he was or how he could be found.

Condolences were made all around. Some were coming to the reception at the church afterward; others had to get to work, and so gave Chad their remarks before leaving. Chad still invited everyone to come and take some of the food, as the caterers had prepared plenty. He found himself wrapped up in the needs of others with no time for himself. The four young people from the strange church, with whom he wanted to talk, were unable to get any good time with him. Brian and Cynthia quickly explained that they planned on coming over the next day with a dish his mother had always brought to potluck. He asked if they needed directions, and they replied that they had been there many times before. He was unable to react to the knowledge that they had been in his home because some of his father's bank associates were leaving and needed to say goodbye. He didn't have a chance to get back to the foursome before they left.

He didn't eat a single bite. He spent the entire time talking with mourners. It felt strange to be responsible to them somehow. It was like he had to console them from an empty reservoir of compassion. When he finally got a plate, he wasn't hungry. He sat there, staring at the table two inches in front of his plate.

"It was a nice service." Diana's voice came through the fog.

"Huh?"

"I said, 'It was a nice service,'"

"I suppose so."

"It wasn't nice for you?" she asked. "The people said they liked it."

"To be honest, I had a feeling that it was missing something."

Diana sat down next to Chad. "Maybe it was because the pastor didn't know your folks as you do. He got your mother's name mixed up. Everyone can forgive him for that—he barely knew them. But he did the best he could under the circumstances. He did a lovely tribute on their service to the church. Don't you agree?"

"Yes, he did that. It's just that ..."

Diana hesitated, wondering if he would continue. When the silence lasted too long, she asked, "What is it? Maybe I can help."

"The service today reminded me of something. It's something about me, not the service. Other people get something out of what was done, but I didn't. The service reminded me of my difficulty with the church in general. It's hard to explain all the different feelings I have about it. One thing comes to mind immediately is the fact that I feel like I'm an observer and not a participant. I watch. I don't do anything. My mind drifts."

"You could have read something, maybe your own tribute. That would've been nice," Diana added.

"That's not exactly what I'm talking about. Sure, I could've participated, but what I'm saying applies to the worship we do on Sundays. This funeral is not exactly the problem with me; it reminds me of …, well, it's the feeling that if God is real, I should see or feel something, understand Him on a deeper level. It should make sense to my life today. I should do something that is meaningful to Him and to me. I shouldn't just watch. I don't want to look forward or back for some token of God's love. I want *now* to be meaningful. Do you see what I mean? My folks' murder was meaningless, senseless. In many ways church for me is the same, without meaning, empty."

"Is this why you stopped attending?" she asked.

"Yes."

"Chad, you can't find God if you turn your back on Him," she stated tentatively.

"I didn't turn my back on Him. I just stopped attending our church because it wasn't working for me. I studied. I tried to find some other way. I even tried some other churches."

"What is it you are looking for, some emotional pizzazz, maybe?"

"I don't think it's emotion that I'm looking for. If I knew exactly what it is that I'm missing, I'd go looking for it. If I find it, it should make me happy. Let me ask you, are you happy with your present state as a Christian?" He looked at her for the first time in the conversation.

"Yesss … I guess so. I've never analyzed it like you have. Faith is what one has or doesn't have. I guess I was predestined to have it."

"But, haven't you wondered about why it is that you believe? Isn't there supposed to be a living link with you and God, and also with you and the people who believe in God?"

"I have faith in God, in Jesus Christ, and I come to church with others who do too. Isn't that what it's all about?" she questioned.

"Yes, but I think there should be more. I love what Jesus did for me. I have asked God to forgive me for my sins, whatever they may be. Once that is complete, then there is worship. We're supposed to worship God. And, that's where I get messed up. It all seems one-dimensional."

"What do you mean, one-dimensional?"

"When we worship, at least the way I've been taught, worship is a single vertical line between me and God. We listen to the pastor as he directs us to look at God, hopefully. Sometimes, I hear sermons about current events and humanitarian issues and not God or Jesus. If we come together to worship individually, why do we need to come together? If each one has a different experience, then we are separate cubicles of understanding, not needing each other or this big building to perform worship. There has to be more is all I'm saying. Shouldn't religion be interconnected? Not just a single vertical line, but a web, maybe." Chad was trying to explain his need for a fellowship of believers, something he didn't fully understand. He also felt that this wasn't all that bothered him about church. There were the intellectual element and the emotional aspect, which he didn't feel comfortable exploring.

"You're making this too difficult for yourself. Just go to church, and let it go at that," she instructed. Diana was at sea with the discussion and wanted this discussion to move on to something else.

"I can't," he responded.

"Well, whatever it is that you're looking for, I hope you find it. Not to change the subject, but to totally change the subject, there were a lot of different people here today. People I've never seen before."

'Maybe some came from my folks' new church. I know Brian, Cynthia, Vonnie, and Raphael did."

"I saw them too, but there was one strange little guy in a tweed jacket that took pictures of the guest register. I thought that was too much."

"Ah, I think that was Detective Hardine. He's desperate because he doesn't have any leads. Did anyone else see him take the pictures besides you?"

"I don't think so. He was trying to be secretive about it. I saw it because I watched the guest book to make sure everyone signed in. I was trying to make sure you had a good record of those who came. I have in my purse all the cards that people left. You'll want to go through them later. I'll do that with you if it will make it easier."

Chad had a sudden thought about how Diana was so extremely helpful and felt a little embarrassed at not thanking her for all her help. He knew she was trying to make herself more than a helpful friend. She was making a play for his heart. Nonetheless, he needed to thank her. "Diana, you have been very helpful. I can't begin to thank you for all you have done for me and for my folks. I'm feeling embarrassed about the amount of time you have spent helping me. You must have been taking time off of work. I, I, ah, don't even know what you do. I've been wrapped up in my own problems, and I haven't thought about what it may have cost you."

"Chad, please don't worry on account of me. I wanted to be here for you. To answer your almost question, I'm a student. I'm working on my PhD, and I've finished my classwork. The only thing I have left is my dissertation. I'm in the research phase, and I can work at my own pace as long as I get it done by the deadline."

"Whoa, that's impressive, but still, I've taken you away from your research. I don't feel comfortable using you so much."

Diana reached out and brushed a tiny strand of Chad's hair off of his forehead and then put her hand on his cheek. "I want to help you. There is a lot more that you have to go through with settling your parents' estate. I want to be there for all of those difficult times because … I'm attracted to you. I always have been since we were kids in Sunday School class." She didn't drop her hand, and her eyes never left his. She was measuring his response. Chad was in a spot, and their relationship was at the jumping-off point. She watched for a glimmer of hope only to be interrupted by the chief caterer asking if Chad wanted them to box up the leftovers for him to take home. It was too much food for him to eat.

Diana came to the rescue. "I know a shelter that could use the food. We could give it to them?" she asked Chad. The conversation ended with the distribution of the food and telling the funeral director to deliver the flowers to a senior living center. Diana had wished for much more to transpire from that moment but had to settle for holding his hand as they walked out of the church. As they walked, Chad asked, "So what is your study discipline? What are you getting your PhD in?"

"Sociology. My dissertation is on the long-term behavioral effects of drug-use passed down through family dynamics."

"That sounds like a lot of work."

"It is, but probably not any more than getting a partnership in a prestigious financial firm like you."

"You know?"

"Yep. Like I said, I'm attracted to you. I've been following you by asking your folks a lot of questions. Your mother was on to me."

Chad's mind went to the scene where his mother was holding up an empty wedding dress. *Now I know another reason why she wanted me to attend church when I came home!*

XXXXX

Detective Hardine was in Reverend Tucker's study. He was asking him to review the attendance record and pointing out which individuals he recognized from his church. The task unnerved him to have a detective asking him questions about individuals, murderers. The detective could see the reverend's reticence, assuming it was due to the possibility of the killers in his service. He reassured him that he was only looking for connections and the possibility that someone, maybe a stranger, would attend out of curiosity and know something that would break the case open. In his thoughts he knew that many times killers liked to attend funerals for whatever maudlin motivations that compelled them. He did not share that thought with the reverend, instead reassured the minister that he would not be unnecessarily interviewing his tried and true members. Detective Hardine was grasping at whims and whistles; the only thing coming to the surface was this mystery church and the leaflet.

XXXXX

The news conference was broadcast on national as well as some international television networks. The BBC carried the conference only because another controversy on the subject of religious free exercise was happening in Europe, and this story added to what the network thought was a bigger story. Jeremy Richards sat next to his wife and lawyer and read a prepared statement.

ZZZZZ

I didn't ask for this conflict, and I certainly did not want to be the center of a public spectacle. I was loyal to CentraHealing and gave them my service for most of my adult life. I think they should give me my retirement, which I have earned after twenty-six years.

His lawyer made his comments next.

Mr. Richards has earned more than his rightfully-deserved retirement. He has been shamed by this termination. The emotional damages need to be acknowledged. He is a respected man in the community and a leader in his church. The damages to his social standing as a person in his community have to be acknowledged in a financial manner.

ZZZZZ

The BBC anchor segued from this US issue dealing with a minority religion to the struggle of unsponsored minority denominations being taxed by the state in five different countries. State-sanctioned churches were not taxed for their property and holdings. But when the economic crunch affected budgets, the governments were looking into tax-free entities that were getting a free ride when it came to emergency services such as fire, police, and ambulance protection. In the countries where national medicine underwrote the bill for all medical needs, unsponsored churches again were singled out for special attention. In some cases the cost would close smaller churches unable to carry the extra financial burden of property tax and income/sales tax off of offerings received. Larger churches felt an additional squeeze on their handling of offerings. Many of the churches that were world church entities and had their offices in other countries would normally send a portion of their tithe and offerings forward to their central headquarters. Countries saw this outflow of money as a drain on their strapped economies and made it illegal to send away those amounts. Liberal opinions, which predominated, tended to side with governments in their positions.

Chad wondered about the cost of state-sanctioned churches, common in Europe. Missing from the BBC dialogue was the drain on the budgets that the state-sanctioned churches posed. Ministers' salaries were subsidized along with building maintenance of structures, some of which were quite old and expensive to maintain. Chad turned off the television and went to bed. The day's events played on his mind. Finances were his forte. He saw the investment of capital in local economies crucial. Money needed to have velocity. The turnover of legal tender from one person to another was velocity. When people slowed their spending, velocity diminished, and the GNP suffered, recessions could occur. States needed to jump-start the economy with new capital. They could print more, or they could find resources that would generate revenue. Printing more added to the national debt. His mind mulled over the issues pro and con, and it kept him awake. In one sense he favored raising revenue, but only if it was plowed back into the economy. On the other side was the issue of separation of church and state. The church already generated velocity by spending their offerings on the needy and in services to support church operations. Taxing the churches might not produce the desired result, especially if the revenue was lost in the debt-ridden treasury. He inclined toward leaving the churches alone when it came to taxation. Somewhat settled in his mind, he drifted off to sleep.

XXXXX

Emotional fatigue weighed on him more than physical fatigue. He awoke tired after sleeping almost nine hours. He lay in bed, looking at the opposite wall. The living room clock did not tick away the moments of this new phase of his life. He was now alone, silently alone. Not like when he was at school or working in his internship. He was really alone. As he contemplated his new status, he had to shake himself out of a doldrums mood that settled into his psyche like water into a depression. He could feel it cling to him like gooey paste. He panicked. He had to move, physically move to sprint away from the sorrowful swamp. He cast off the light throw, straightened the wrinkles to his bedspread, and tossed the mini blanket in his closet. A smile came to his serious face remembering his mother. He dressed for exercise: a t-shirt, jogging shorts, tube socks, and an old pair of sneakers.

He went out the back door through the garden fence to the street and then down to the open area that led to a park a quarter-mile away. It was a route he had taken when he trained for high school football. He virtually sprinted to the park to freshen his mind with a blast of oxygen. He fought off the effects of depression by pumping oxygenated blood around his body. As he ran, his brain focused on his course of action. He would grieve, but not from the morass of "Woe is me."

He performed interval training, varying his speed around the park to challenge both his cardio and muscular fitness. It was exhilarating and brought him home with a better positive attitude. Maybe he could shower and dress for church. Make a stab at finding God. A car pulling in front of his house changed his mind. It wasn't Diana's or Detective Hardine's, which caused his mind to wonder as to who it might be. When Vonnie stepped out of the car, he found his mind leaping forward, thinking that it was a perfect opportunity to get some more information about his folks and their unexpected change of churches. He surprised Vonnie by coming up behind her on the walkway.

"Hello. Nice morning for a run. What brings you to my home?"

"Oh! You surprised me. I didn't hear you behind me."

"It must be my sneakers. I guess that's what they're supposed to do, sneak up on people."

"Yes, I guess so. Ah, I brought you breakfast."

"Your friends said they were coming over today, and here, you have come with breakfast. I can't begin to express my gratitude for what everyone is doing for me. Thank you. You didn't have to do this. I appreciate your kindness. Won't you please help me eat it? Stay a little. I would like to ask you some questions about your church."

Vonnie could not resist the last request. Her plan was to leave the food as a gesture of thoughtfulness, but when he said he wanted to ask about her church, she immediately changed her mind. "Okay, I would be happy to answer any of your questions if I can."

Vonnie carried the food while Chad opened the door. He had to run around to the back door and let her in the front. He led her to the kitchen and excused himself for a moment to go to his room to slip on sweats over his running gear. Back in the kitchen, he began his investigation.

"What is different about your church as opposed to say, my church? I want to know what it was that attracted my folks to leave my church."

"The most obvious difference is, of course, the day of worship, but then, less obvious is our theology on various subjects, such as last-day events, what happens when you die, what Jesus is doing now in heaven, things like that."

"I know about the Saturday worship. I don't think that would attract them. I think it might be the last days' events that you mentioned because my father had this brochure with symbols from the book of Revelation on it."

"That might be it because they did attend our seminar on Revelation. They came every night. How many do you want?" she asked while holding a plate ready to serve him. It was the first he noticed what the food was that she had brought. He had been looking at her in a different way. He watched her face as she talked. She didn't wear make-up, no lipstick or gloss, no mascara or eye shadow. He concluded that she was not trying to attract him in any romantic way. She was there to be nice. She was good-looking with a pleasant smile coming from a petite mouth, hazel eyes under playful bangs and short hair.

"Oh, yeah, food. I almost forgot. Is that what I think it is, little chili rellenos soufflés?"

"Yes, it is. Your mother brought these to a ladies' prayer breakfast we had. Everyone wanted the recipe. I figured I would bring them today."

"Did she tell you that they were my favorite?"

"No."

"Well, they are. I'll take a bunch." Chad momentarily forgot his desire for information.

"I brought salsa just in case you didn't have any on hand, and some hash browns."

"Thanks. This is going to be a feast! It's just like when I always come—home …" Chad had to stop talking because the memory of his mother overwhelmed him. She was gone, ripped from his life by murderers unknown. His eyes filled up with tears, and he couldn't look at the woman from the strange church. His head went down, and his eyes tried to focus on his plate. The little tokens of memory didn't help him control his equilibrium. He closed his eyes. Vonnie placed her hand gently on his shoulder. Silence ruled the moment. Unseen by Chad, Vonnie was also grieving. Tears were in her eyes. She remembered the nice couple who were so enthusiastic about the Bible and the mysteries of Revelation. For her, it was an incredible loss, a loss generated by a crazy mad world of sin. Chad went for a box of tissues, and Vonnie helped herself too. They looked at each other with understanding.

"You liked my folks," he said with conviction.

"Very much so. Both your mom and dad were great people. Your mom had a great sense of humor, and it was like she was on a mission to—"

"Get me married off." Chad tried to finish her sentence.

Vonnie smiled. "Probably so. I was going to say she was on a mission to convince everyone you were a perfect son. Now that I think of it, she did a lot of talking to the unmarried girls our age, so you're probably right on."

"Mom was definitely on a mission. She loved children and wanted hordes of grandchildren. She always worked in the Sunday School department."

"She volunteered in our Sabbath School divisions, too."

Chad took a deep breath. "I know why. It's because we lost my baby sister at one year, and for some reason, I don't know why, my folks didn't or couldn't have any more. They didn't talk about it much."

"What was your sister's name?"

"Grace."

"Would you mind terribly if I had prayer with you?" she requested.

"Not at all."

"Dear Father in heaven, this family has been broken by Satan, attacked on so many levels. And yet they have stayed true to You. I pray for Chad. He is now all that is left of this wonderful family. He needs to be comforted by You, Lord. Only You can comfort him. We were never designed to grieve. You designed us at Creation to live forever, never grieve, never to lose anyone that we love. So, I appeal to You, Lord, our Creator, the one who knows how we are made, to comfort him in this time of need. Comfort me, too, Lord, because I grieve as well. Help us to look forward to the time when all this will be resolved. That soon, very soon, we will be reunited with those we have lost, and Janine will be able to hold Grace in her arms again. We pray, and for this food as well, we pray in the name of Jesus, amen."

"Amen," Chad repeated.

XXXXX

Detective Hardine met Pastor Peter Lange in his front lawn. He stopped the lawnmower and invited the detective into his home.

"How can I help you?"

"I am investigating the murder of the Johnsons."

"That was awful; very hard to believe that that could happen to such good people," the pastor replied.

"I noticed you attended their funeral. Were you close?"

"I wouldn't say close, close. We got to be friends, and I baptized them. I liked them very much. I really only knew them for a few months. They were becoming a part of our church family. I visited them in their home several times."

"You baptized them?"

"That is correct."

"Baptism is an initiation rite for your church membership, I assume. Are there any other initiation rites that they had to perform, any special ceremonies or secret rituals?"

"No, not at all."

"Did the Johnsons have any trouble with the other members of your sect?"

Pastor Lange could see that the detective was uninformed of the SDA church and its practices. "Daniel and Janine were first-class people. The members of my church liked them and welcomed them as family. We are as mystified as you as to why anyone would want to hurt them. No one had trouble with them or disliked them in any way. Our church is a church that loves Jesus, and we try to be like Him."

"I found this brochure near Mr. Johnson's body at the scene of the murder. Are you familiar with it?" Detective Hardine produced the brochure in its plastic envelope.

"Yes, I am. This is our invitation for our seminar on Revelation. The Johnsons came to our meetings because they received one of these in our distribution in their neighborhood. Do you think this had anything to do with their murder?"

> *I found this brochure near Mr. Johnson's body at the scene of the murder. Are you familiar with it?*

"I don't know, but I am running down every possible lead. I am wondering why it was by his body."

"Do you think Daniel was holding it when he was murdered?" Pastor Lange asked. "I can't see how murderers would be interested in something like this. This is about the Bible, about understanding the Bible," he added.

"If you can think of anything or anyone that could help me solve this crime, please, don't hesitate to call me. Here's my card."

XXXXX

They started to eat. "Something in your prayer bothered me," Chad spoke quietly.

"Oh, no, I didn't mean to hurt you in any way. Please accept my apology."

"I know you didn't mean to hurt me. What bothered me was you don't think my mother is with Grace yet, like it's still in the future before she will get to hold her."

"Oh, I see. That is another one of our beliefs that is different from other Christians. We believe that when we are dead, we remain in the grave until Jesus calls us at His second coming."

"That's different. I haven't heard that before. Where does your church get that from?"

"From the Bible."

"Where?"

"In the book of Thessalonians for one place. It says that when Jesus returns, the dead will rise first, and then we who are still alive will join them and meet the Lord in the air. The dead have to be in the grave before they can be resurrected."

"I'm not ready to swallow that," Chad blurted out loud before he thought of how it could offend Vonnie.

"The idea, at first thought, is very comforting to picture your loved ones happy in heaven, but with a little more examination, one can see that it might be a torment for them to be up there, watching what is happening down here to their family or friends. Their loved ones might be in pain or in trouble or, worse yet, turning their backs on Jesus' free gift of salvation."

Chad didn't want to argue the point with her because he thought he had been a bit too abrupt about not swallowing her belief. The idea of his folks seeing and hearing his resistance to church affected him in a way he didn't expect. However, he still wanted to find out what the attraction was to her church. Vonnie continued, "Besides, the time when Jesus comes is very near."

"My dad was interested in the last days. He was reading this book. It's in his study. I'll go get it." He went to the study, slipped the book out from under the Bible, and brought it back to the kitchen. It was worn, tattered, and because of that, it looked old. "Here it is. There are so many parts underlined and starred. He has folded down corners to mark pages. In some places whole pages were underlined. I guess that indicates he was really interested in the subject." Chad handed the book to Vonnie.

"I see. He really was interested in the subject. This book was new when we gave it out at the seminar. Your dad has poured through this pretty thoroughly. Look at this." She pointed to one page. In the margin there were multiple numbers written with countries or states noted.

"Those are dates," he reacted. "The author is listing all these things that are going to happen, and my dad is putting dates and places next to them. It's a month and a year, but the year is either this year or late last year." He put his finger on the text. "Here, where it says, 'calamities by sea and land,' my dad wrote last month, and last December when there were plane crashes in Europe and Canada and then a ferry that capsized in Hong Kong. Here, where it says, 'cyclones,' he has April, Kansas. Now where it says, 'tidal waves and earthquakes,' he has January, which is when the huge earthquake happened in Chile in November of last year with the tidal wave that hurt other countries. My dad was confirming the words in this book."

"And the Bible," she added. "Jesus predicted many of these same things, earthquakes and famines, at the end of time. We are coming so close to the end of time that we don't have much time to be ready."

"Why do you say that?"

"Because it is soon; His coming is near."

"It has always been near. Since my parents and grandparents were children, it was near. The rapture could happen at any moment. After a while, you get tired of hearing that Jesus could come at any moment. It's like overkill. It's one of those things that makes me feel that religion doesn't seem relevant. If He's always coming soon, when does the word 'soon' get worn out?" Chad vented a personal frustration.

"I'm not a theologian, and I don't know all the answers, but I'll try to help you if I can. We have a study group at church that tries to bring all this information together. We study the Bible and compare notes on world events. Even our pastor attends and adds what he knows from his personal study. You could join us, see what we're learning, and see what we see in the world around us that gives us the conviction that Jesus' second coming is very near." Vonnie suggested.

"Give me an example. Ah, I mean specifically, give me an example of why you think His coming is near."

"Okay, I'll do my best. In the book of Revelation—"

"Good, I'm glad you are referring to that book because my dad was very interested in that book," Chad interrupted.

"In the middle of Revelation, in chapter thirteen, I'm pretty sure, it describes a political-religious organization that makes people worship incorrectly. It coerces them to worship a system of false principles, and if people won't, they will be killed. Before that, it also prevents those who disagree from buying and selling. That looks very much like prejudice against the true people of God. It is a system of false worship. Jesus said in His own words that when we see the desolating sacrilege standing in the holy place, we're supposed to flee. He was talking about the same thing mentioned in Revelation thirteen. Before all this can happen, there has to be an environment of prejudice against people who live by the standards of the Bible. We are seeing that prejudice building right now. It's in the news, and it is all around the world. Ministers are being put in prison and killed in countries where Christianity is a minority faith. We can see that in the news right now."

"I need to see that in the Bible myself." Chad left for his dad's study once again and returned with the Bible. "Now, where is that exactly?" he asked.

They paged to the book of Revelation, and then Vonnie found chapter 13. They read it together. First, there was the description of the beast that comes out of the sea. Chad looked at Vonnie questioningly after reading that section.

"Chad, keep in mind that Revelation uses symbols and metaphors to describe things and events of the future. The beast simply means some kind of organization or power. It's obvious from the writing that it has religious worship in its nature."

"Okay."

Then, they read about the second beast that comes from the land.

Because of the signs he was given power to do on behalf of the first beast, he deceived the inhabitants of the earth. He ordered them to set up an image of the beast … He was given power to give breath to the image of the beast, so that it could speak and cause all who refused to worship the image to be killed. He also forced everyone, small and great, rich and poor, free and slave, to receive a mark on his right hand or in his forehead, so that no one could buy or sell unless he had the mark, which is the name of the beast and the number of his name. (Rev. 13:14–18, NIV 1984)

Chad thought about that for a moment. Then he spoke, "I don't see that happening now."

"The way I figure it, before that can come to complete fulfillment, there has to be an environment of religious prejudice that the general public accepts. Laws are made based on the majority opinion of the people. What we just read has to have the right environment for the majority of people to agree. I see religious prejudice rising big time," she responded.

"I have heard of religious people, Christians, being beheaded and imprisoned in Islamic countries, but America has laws against that happening."

"I'm an example."

"How?"

"I got thrown out of my apartment. They said I didn't pay my rent, but I did. I found out later that my bank account was hacked, my funds were stolen, and my record-of-payment for rent was erased. I used electronic withdrawal. It was funny that my record-of-payment for my other bills was not erased. It looked like the hack was purposeful in getting me out of that apartment complex. The day I was thrown out, they made reference to my 'sect' taking care of me. As I look back at it, it only makes sense that it was all contrived. The manager had made several remarks to me before-hand about me having religious meetings in my apartment that were not allowed because this was not a business but a residence. All I ever did was to have my friends over for Bible studies and refreshments."

"You think that was because of your faith?"

"I can't think of anything else that makes sense."

"Did you tell the police?"

"Yes, and they're investigating."

"I think they should follow the money. Wherever it went, might lead to the culprits. You could get it back. Some Black Hat somewhere is responsible for this."

"You're right. Thanks for the advice. I'll tell the police the next time I talk to them. There are other instances of prejudice happening to my people and my church. In Alaska the Bible camps they have are on public forest lands. They had agreements with the U.S. Forest Service for one-hundred-year leases. Now, suddenly, they are terminating all those lease agreements and confiscating the lodges, cabins, and facilities that were built. Other church camps are not being treated in the same way. In two states the governments are taxing church lands and offerings. They are not doing that for the mainstream Protestant, Catholic, and other churches in those locations. SDA's are losing their jobs in some businesses. For the most part, these things are not being reported in the media."

"I know about that. There's that case of Jeremy Richards losing his job because he wouldn't attend a staff meeting on Saturday. I'm wondering how that's going to work out. The trial starts tomorrow."

"Either way, for or against, it is an indication of growing religious prejudice against God's people."

"You believe that SDAs are God's people? Don't you think that might be a little arrogant?"

"Yes, I agree with you. Seventh-day Adventists don't believe they are the only ones going to heaven or are the people described in Revelation. Although, I would say that there are some, very few members of my church that hold that false idea. What we are trying to do as a church is align ourselves with Scripture as much as possible, to be what God wants us to be and to follow the teachings of the Bible."

"Every denomination says that and believes it, too."

"In our Bible study last week, we were studying these chapters in Revelation, so it is fresh in my mind. I don't want to look like some know-it-all. I think the Holy Spirit wanted me to learn this so I could answer your questions. Here, look in the last verses of chapter twelve. It describes God's people as *those who obey God's commandments and hold to the testimony of Jesus*. We as Adventists are doing our best to keep all of His commandments with the power of the indwelling Spirit of God, and we are teaching others about salvation in Jesus using His testimony of instruction for these last days."

"Okay, so you think God's people, SDAs too, are being singled out for abuse, and that is an indication that Jesus' coming is near?"

"Exactly. It's a fulfilling prophecy, which indicates the end is near. This passage is also telling us some other things that tell me the end is near. For instance, this paragraph we read indicated a grouping or coming together of world faith groups." Vonnie pointed with her finger to the line in verses 14 and 15, where it indicated that the beast deceived the inhabitants of the earth to set up an image and caused everyone to worship it. "I believe that as these groups come together, God's true people will be among them, but then, when true faith and true worship are sacrificed in the name of togetherness, God's people will refuse to worship incorrectly. They will not participate. My point is that a world religion has to form for this prediction to be fulfilled. I see that happening in the world today. There's a conference going on right now in Brazil. Maybe you've heard about it. The National Association of Spiritualist Churches (NASC) has organized a conference bringing together the heads, or representatives, of all the Protestant, Catholic, Jewish, Islamic, Buddhist, you name it, faith groups of the world. They are trying to hammer out points of common agreement and create an organization to represent them all."

"I have not heard about this but, I have been a little pre-occupied. Is the SDA church participating in this conference?"

"No way! Like Daniel in the Old Testament, we can see and understand the handwriting on the wall. It's the first step in making this prophecy come true."

"I see."

"Chad, there's another thing this prophecy is talking about that could be in the stages of being fulfilled. It talks about being unable to buy or sell. Are you aware of the plan for America and other countries to go to a cashless society next month?"

"Yes, I am. My work is in the world of finance. Having a cashless society, or the digital dollar as some call it, a good thing. It saves the government from the cost of minting and printing money, managing it, and safeguarding it in banks and armored cars. But, best of all, it thwarts the criminal element, which uses cash instead of credit cards. Credit card usage can be traced, and cash is harder to trace. That's why thieves steal it, and murderers use it to buy motel rooms and food on the run. Taking away cash hamstrings the bad elements of society."

"I see your point that that can be a good thing. However, if everyone is required to use plastic either in the form of a bank card or credit card and have their personal identity tied to it, then it would be a very easy thing to turn off one's card or cards and red-flag their usage as individuals. People can be coerced into compliance with a national law that violates conscience by using that tool. The power of the pocketbook."

"It could be used that way, I suppose."

"From this one description of the end of time, three things are happening today to make the elements of this prophecy possible: a move toward extreme prejudice to the point of beheading Christians, formation of a dominating religious coalition, and the matrix for restrictions on buying and selling."

> *"From this one description of the end of time, three things are happening today to make the elements of this prophecy possible: a move toward extreme prejudice to the point of beheading Christians, formation of a dominating religious coalition, and the matrix for restrictions on buying and selling."*

"Interesting. And this book, *Great Controversy*, is interesting, too. This author has an amazing grasp of the Bible and Revelation. I've been reading it because my dad read it, but now I want to finish the last couple of chapters because I am genuinely interested in it myself," Chad explained.

"In our Wednesday night study group, we are studying a chapter at a time and comparing it to Bible prophecy. You're welcome to join us if you would like."

"I just might do that."

CHAPTER 4

"M r. Johnson didn't come to church today," Reverend Tucker commented. It was more of a question than a statement. He was greeting congregants by the front door after the service was over. Diana was the point of his inquiry.

"No, he didn't. I looked for him, but I didn't see him," she answered.

"Is he going to attend that cult church his folks joined?"

"No, I don't think so. Chad hasn't been attending any church for the last couple of years. He has a thing about churches. He doesn't think they speak to him."

"It seems that is true for a lot of our young people today. However, the world is changing, and soon faith in God will become globally important again. I expect many young people will see the light and come back on their own terms. God hasn't changed His message to accommodate the post-modernists. The post-modernists will need to adapt to a world that is coming back to God."

"I hope that is true for Chad. I would like to see him come back to church, and I'm doing my best to get him re-interested."

"I'll pray that you are successful. He comes from an affluent family." Reverend Tucker turned to greet the next couple standing in line. Diana started to walk down the front steps while fishing her cell phone out of her purse. She was going to call Chad but decided against it. She didn't want to be the one to put him on a guilt trip. Instead, she decided to give him some space after spending almost every day with him for the past week.

XXXXX

Vonnie called Brian and Cynthia after she left Chad's place. She knew they were planning to drop off a meal that afternoon and wanted to let them know how eager Chad was to learn about Revelation and last-day events. Their plan was to refresh their memories on some of the things they had studied in case he would ask them some questions. They also planned to extend an invite to the Wednesday night study group. They were in their living room, rereading their notes when the doorbell chimed. It was Detective Hardine. After explanations, they invited him in to answer questions. They were a little nervous, given the recent experience with officers of the law.

"You attended the Johnsons' funeral, why?" he asked.

The two looked at each other, a little surprised. "Because they're our friends," Cynthia answered. "And, they are fellow church members and have been guests in our home," Brian added. "We know them. Why do you ask?"

"The Johnsons' murder is a mystery to me. None of the regular motives for murder seem to be relevant. This leaflet from your church was found by Mr. Johnson's body. Can you think of any reason why someone would kill them? And, why was this leaflet nearby?" Hardine showed the plastic-covered brochure. He was sitting in a chair opposite the couple sitting on their couch. They recognized it immediately without having to rise up to get it.

"That's one of our invitations," Cynthia said to her husband.

"Yes, sir. That's an advertisement for our Revelation seminar. The Johnsons attended," Brian explained. Detective Hardine expected that response, yet he still needed to press forward, but this time with a more specific question.

"Is there anyone who could be angry with your church or with the Johnsons for attending these meetings?"

Again the couple looked at each other, this time with a look of consternation. "I haven't heard of anything. Have you, Sweetheart?" Brian shook his head no. "No. We have not heard of anything like that."

"So far, everyone has said the same thing. The Johnsons were nice people, and everyone liked them. Did they, either one of them, mention any groups, maybe a person or persons they were having trouble with?"

"Nothing comes to mind. We're sorry. We wish we could help you and give you an answer that would help you solve this crime. This is a great injustice to our friends. We'll pray for your success."

They were thanked for their time and given a card before the detective left.

XXXXX

That afternoon, Brian and Cynthia were able to drop off a dish at Chad's place but were unable to have any lengthy conversation with him. Several ladies from Chad's church were also there serving up a first-rate late Sunday dinner. At the door they extended an invitation for him to come to the Wednesday study and then left when he was suddenly called back by the ladies in the dining room. After he came back, he detected an altered attitude in the room. It was quieter. The ladies were setting everything up but not talking.

"What's wrong? Did something happen?"

"Chad, you're not thinking of going to that study of theirs, are you?"

"Why?"

"Because it's one of those cults."

"A cult?" he asked, eyebrows raised.

"Yes. They're listed in the book, *Kingdom of the Cults*."

"That old book?" another asked.

"Yes, that old book. It's still true today. Things haven't changed."

"They call themselves Latter-day Saints, and they have their own Bible, the Book of Mormon."

"No, I don't think they're Mormon. They're SDAs," Chad tried to correct. At this point it was like Chad wasn't even in the room. The women started their own conversation. He could have swung like a monkey from the chandelier, and they wouldn't have noticed.

"SDA, LDS, it doesn't matter. None of them believe in the Bible or Jesus."

"Don't forget the Jehovah Witnesses. They're part of them somehow."

"No, Ethel. They're all separate groups with their own beliefs if you call them beliefs. It's really fanaticism."

"Whoever they are, they're not Christian in the right sense. They're offshoots who steal members from legitimate congregations like ours. They do some type of fancy brainwashing once they get you to attend their meetings. I know, because the pastor told me so."

"It's because of their diet. They don't eat meat, and that makes them susceptible to suggestion. That's how they brainwash them. They're protein-deficient."

Chad listened because he had to. The rapid-fire comments kept coming in one after another. He felt some of them were unfair, some were confused with other denominations, and some might have a grain of truth to them. He didn't know much about this new church his folks adopted, but because his folks were careful and intelligent, wary of tricks and scams, he didn't think they were taken-in without careful thought. As the ladies continued their babble, there grew within him a desire to ask more. Vonnie that morning seemed genuine enough, and his folks were no dimwits. The prejudice he was hearing felt like it was driven by some inner frustration on the part of the present company. Regardless of their prejudicial behavior, he still had to thank them for their wonderful Sunday dinner. His thoughts were jostled back to the conversation with the newest wrinkle in the conversation.

"What did that black couple bring? I'll bet it didn't have any meat. Where did you put it, Karen?"

"I put it in the kitchen next to the trash. It should be thrown out anyway," she answered.

Like a school of fish, the women, of one accord, moved to the kitchen. Chad followed. The foil cover was ripped off, and one took a wooden spoon and dug into the casserole. She scooped up a healthy amount and let it dribble back into the Pyrex dish. "You're right, no meat. How do they live without proper protein? Their children can't develop proper brain function."

"It doesn't look very appetizing."

"Kinda yucky."

"It's supposed to be baked first," Chad cut in. "They said I should bake it for an hour at 350 degrees." Chad went to the counter and tried to put the foil back on, but it was ripped. He did the best he could and then found a place for it in the refrigerator. He didn't feel it would be wise to tell the ladies that the recipe was one that his mother used. "I think it was nice of them to think of me like that. Just like you ladies are doing for me today. What you brought smells delicious. I'm starving."

XXXXX

He woke earlier than normal. His mind was wrestling with the imaginary tick of the clock and the unmistakable feeling that time was running out. He finished the tattered book before he went to bed the previous evening. The last two chapters were wonderful in the resolution of the earth's great violence. Heaven and the gift of eternal life were a welcome relief to the descriptions of the chapters before. He thought of the scenes where the redeemed were reunited. He thought of his parents being there, with Grace, and his meeting them in the air, as the Bible indicated. The underside of his emotions was that he didn't feel completely ready. It was not in the front of his thinking, it was a dread, without form, lurking behind curtains he had drawn himself, curtains of frustration about church, worship, and meaningless rites. If he were to be ready, he would have to tear down the curtain from top to bottom and launch himself on an honest appraisal of God.

Another competing focus was the need to make here and now decisions about the house and cars and furniture. The funeral was complete. His folks laid to rest. He had to wrap up the personal effects and get back to his life. He was in the kitchen eating leftovers and making a list of the things he needed to do. The phone rang. He looked at the clock first before he looked at the phone. The last time he had been called at an early hour, it was to be informed of his parents' death. This time, what he thought was early was 8:05. His musings had burnt the time.

"Hello?"

"Chad, this is Bill Bennington, your father's associate. Do you remember me?"

"Of course, I do. We've been in your home many times."

"I'm afraid I've got some bad news."

"Now what?"

"Your folks' bank account has been emptied, checking but not savings."

"Oh, no. Was it hacked?"

"Well, I don't think so. Let me start at the beginning. I wanted to do something for your folks and for you. I got our corporate lawyer, who is also your parents' lawyer for the estate, to draw up a power of attorney for you so you can access all your parents' assets. Then I checked the accounts. The savings hasn't been touched but, the checking had a lot of card activity the day after your folks were murdered. You have a card for their account, but you haven't used it for several years. If I remember right, they wanted you to have the card in case of emergency. Neither you nor your folks have switched over to the fingerprint reader cards as yet. What I wanted to do is have you simply come in, sign the POA, and your work would be done. Now, I see the sinister side of this horrible crime.

They were after their money and stole their debit cards. I've blocked the cards, and the card company is not paying on the charges, so you'll get at least some of the money back."

"Mr. Bennington, I think you've given Detective Hardine his first break. I'm going to call him as soon as we're done."

"Chad, when you get a chance, come into the office and sign the POA, get a new fingerprint debit card, and I can answer any questions you might have. Also, bring in any cash you have around the house so that we can exchange it for digital dollars. The government has moved up the deadline to the end of this month."

"Thanks, I'll be in today, say about eleven." Chad had two competing thoughts as he dialed the detective's number—a lead to the murder and the fulfillment of Vonnie's comments less than twenty-four hours ago made concentration difficult.

"Detective Hardine speaking."

"Sir, this is Chad Johnson, I just acquired some information that might help you."

"What did you hear?"

"My folks were robbed."

"This represents a motive. Tell me about it."

XXXXX

It was five minutes past eleven when Chad and Detective Hardine walked into the bank office. They had arranged to meet and then talk with Bill Bennington. Greetings were exchanged, and then Chad was handed off to the lawyer, who would square away his legal rights to his folks' various accounts and investments. Detective Hardine huddled with Bennington and started the tracing of activity on the cards. The deductions were fast and furious for the day after their time of death, and then, when the account was emptied, the cards would no longer work. Hardine copied down addresses of businesses where withdrawals were made. He hoped store videos would provide faces and clues. When armed with a plethora of information, he hurriedly left. His steps were eager because of the upturn of events in his favor. He thought about the leaflet in his coat pocket; it was a dead end. Chad didn't see him go. He was getting the numbers for a fortune in stocks, money market certificates, and precious metals. The safety deposit box contained over $45,000 in gold American Eagles, which amounted to about thirty coins at their present market value. His head was spinning with the knowledge that his folks, as frugal as they were, had amassed a sizable retirement. He couldn't resist slipping one coin into his pocket before leaving with a sheaf of documents in a leather briefcase provided as a gift from Bill Bennington.

Chad went to a restaurant across from the bank and contemplated his future and fortune. He studied the papers as he drank a soda. His training as an intern was preparing him to manage portfolios just like this one. He would collect a fee for doing so. If he managed his folks' account, he wouldn't collect a fee; he would reap the benefits directly. He could live comfortably off of this alone. With the house and cars paid for, he would never have to work another day in a brokerage. He was comfortably set for life.

Given his training, he was curious as to how his father managed his own money against the common norm for a diversified folio. He had to praise his father for his investment acumen. The only departure from the accepted was the larger weight he had given to precious metals. The suggested amount was 10 percent of a total portfolio to precious metals when the market was plunging or volatile. With his father's emphasis on gold and silver stocks, not counting the smaller amount of physical coin in the bank security box, made his father's emphasis on metals nearly 25 percent; a bit heavy in that category. He wondered if his father was accounting for the scary issues in the financial world. If that was true, then his father was ahead of the game and sitting pretty for what may come. He again had two competing thoughts contend for his attention at the same moment. This was no longer his parents' portfolio; it was his. And the other thought was that his father might have been reading the signs of the times from the same perspective as Vonnie had from the previous morning. He was musing over those two strains of thought when his food arrived. It caused him to be distracted enough to hear the news on the overhead TV screen. A reporter was commenting on the proceedings of the Jeremy Richards case while standing on the front steps of the county courthouse.

ZZZZZ

"Mr. Richards had to defend his church when he was grilled on the position of the church on various topics. When asked how his church stood on the ordination of gays, Mr. Richards wisely answered that he couldn't answer for the world church. The lawyer switched his question to a more personal application

and asked if he himself supported the ordination of gays. Mr. Richards had to answer that he did not support the practice. Then the lawyer for the defense asked him if his personally-held beliefs were different from those of his church; if he was a maverick, not believing the same as his church's position on gay ordination. When challenged by the prosecution, the defense responded by indicating that they were trying to establish whether Mr. Richards was a true Seventh-day Adventist. The line of questioning was allowed, and Mr. Richards' position on gay ordination was exposed along with his church. Gay rights action groups are reacting to this news. Some are planning demonstrations for tomorrow at the courthouse and on Saturday at area SDA churches. Then the defense switched slightly to the subject of the ordination of women. Richards was submitted to the same line of questioning, and another issue that the defense brought up was the practice on the part of some Seventh-day Adventists to work on their Sabbath. This was important because Mr. Richards didn't work on his Sabbath, but many Adventists do work on Sabbath. The cross-examination put Jeremy Richards in a difficult position, trying to explain his position as opposed to other SDAs in the same organization/hospital who do work on the day. All in all, Mr. Richards did not present himself in a favorable light.

> *Gay rights action groups are reacting to this news. Some are planning demonstrations for tomorrow at the courthouse and on Saturday at area SDA churches.*

We'll see if tomorrow is a better day for Mr. Richards' case. This is Justine Rudd reporting from the county courthouse."

ZZZZZ

Chad listened to the report and wondered about how much of this church he didn't know anything about. To his thinking, it seemed as if all churches had accepted the alternate lifestyle as a norm. It was an old issue that hadn't been reported on as of late. Most people and organizations wanted to be politically correct and not call down trouble from political action groups. He had heard that the ACLU was helping Jeremy Richards, and now, maybe they would distance themselves from his conservative views.

The news report jumped to another subject.

ZZZZZ

"The elderly and some businesses are having difficulty making the big change to a cashless society. Barry Whitmore has a report for us. Barry?"

"I am standing here at Toni's Pizzeria where Toni has been in business for thirty-eight years. This establishment is a favorite place for many retirees. They have strong opinions about this cashless move by our government. All these years, Toni has always been a cash-only establishment, never accepting credit cards or checks. Now, because of the change, he has to rent a card-reader at a monthly fee. On top of that, he must pay the card company a two-percent charge for every transaction. He doesn't like it, and he is thinking of throwing in the towel and retiring.

"While I was in the restaurant talking with Toni, Esther, a longtime customer, sympathized with Toni and then encouraged me to taste the product. As you can see, I am taking her advice ... hmmmm, delicious. She said it is a 'crying shame' that Toni can't stay in business.

"Floyd, another regular customer, added that this move to cashless status ruins his coin-collecting hobby. Serena, yet another senior, said she doesn't trust the banks to be fair with the debit cards. She said, 'They charge me a monthly fee and another fee for using my card. It's my money. Why do they take it away from me for using my money? It's mine!'

"As you can see, not everyone is in agreement with this modern move to electronic money. This is Barry Whitmore from Toni's pizzeria on the east side.

ZZZZZ

Chad looked at the gold coin in his hand. It was so insignificant, just one ounce, but it was worth close to fifteen hundred dollars. Gold was still the basis of worth for printed currency. Theoretically, it was also the basis for electronic money. He knew the Federal Reserve controlled the money supply, so he wondered if maybe governments could manipulate digital currency to control people. It was a compelling thought. People would have to knuckle under to access their money. Given that possibility, *Could the world end up with an elite cabal where one was either in or out of the accepted group?* he thought. He had heard of the New World Order concept where individuals were categorized according to their contributions to society. *Would the world descend into a morass of haves and have-nots?* he mused even further. He shook off the disturbing possibilities about the newscast and turned to the briefcase to review his father's transactions.

He pulled up the hard copy statements going back three years. He studied the withdrawals and deposits.

At first, he examined the withdrawals immediately after the murder of his folks. It was his primary concern. He, however, did not find any new information. It seemed that the individual or individuals had used the cards primarily to purchase gift cards for restaurants and large chain-stores. The purchases occurred all in the same zip code within twenty-four hours after the death of his folks. He paused for a few moments of reflection on the thought of how horrible it was for someone to die for something that they would gladly exchange for their lives—money. It made their loss cheap and unnecessary.

Then, he studied the withdrawals and deposits to see what expenses they had. Tax and insurance payments were noted at regular intervals. Peppered everywhere were charges for restaurants, gas stations, and grocery stores. Recently, he noticed monthly payments by e-check to the new church they attended. The amounts were almost always the same. He went back further and found payments to his former church. These were mostly less in amount with the occasional very large payment that also had an accompanying deposit from his parents' investment account. The large contributions made his head spin, one of which was huge. His parents seemed to underwrite major projects of the church. Chad was impressed by their commitment and chagrined when he compared it to his own connection to God's work. He felt guilty for not sharing their love for the church.

His analysis of his parents' accounts gave him a sobering perspective of how they had used their success to better their world. The repeating mantra of politics and special-interest groups calling for people to make a difference was fulfilled in his folks' local financial ministry.

"Sir, wouldja like a refill on your soda?" the waitress interrupted his thoughts.

"No, thank you. I've had enough caffeine. Can I have a glass of water?"

"Ah, well, we don't put out water glasses anymore. But I can getcha bottled water and a glass wit' ice." He looked at her with a quizzical look. She felt she had to explain. "It's now a restaurant chain policy wit' ta drought. We needs ta preserve water for crops and all. Ya know what I mean?"

"I thought the drought was on the West Coast, not here."

"The news people say that it's spreading east. Our parent organization is just being proactive. It's sad really, the animals are a-sufferin', and the crops are a-dyin'. I was watchin' last night, and they was a-sayin' that ranchers are sellin' their stock ta get some payback before their cattle die off."

"I see. I don't need the water, thanks anyway."

It was at that moment that the local news broadcast ended with a cute human interest story.

ZZZZZ

It seems as though a puppy and a raccoon have become friends. The owners of the beagle pup say that the raccoon is not a pet but comes regularly in the morning to take a nap with the three-month-old puppy. Here are some pictures. [Instead of pictures a red screen with blocked white letters filled the screen with the words, 'BREAKING NEWS.' Attention-getting sound effects filled the restaurant. A female reporter was holding her clip-on microphone in her hand, sitting at the anchor desk. It was apparent that she had barely arrived at her desk when the station had begun the broadcast. A tech was trying to attach the mini-receiver to her belt.]

"We apologize for breaking into your regularly scheduled programs. This just in from Jacksonville, Florida. A sizable earthquake has caused major damage to the city, toppling some buildings and shaking residents—wait a moment, [the reporter held her hand to her earphone.] *Another report has Miami reporting damage to buil ..., and Virginia Beach is also experiencing a major quake. The reports of damages and shaking and moving streets are flooding into affiliate news stations. We are attempting to get a report from seismologists, who can give us more information. Miami is reporting that their harbor is empty; that boats are sitting on muddy ground. This indicates a tidal wave is about to approach. Reverse 911 calls are going out to warn people to climb or drive to higher ground. Charleston, South Carolina, is also expecting floods, issuing flood warnings along coastal regions. They also are reporting damage to structures.* [The reporter was disjointed in her presentation as news collided with concurrent messages inundating the newsroom and her earpiece.]

"Ladies and gentlemen, this appears to be a major earthquake event with the epicenter of the quake being near the Georgia/Florida state line on the East Coast. We will endeavor to bring you more information as it comes to us. We will return you to your ... Just a moment ... Oh, my goodness! More destruction is being reported at this moment. New York City is shaking with tremors, no, it's shock waves as of this moment. It seems as if this earthquake is larger than expected. Oh! Oh! I can feel the tremors under my feet! It isn't

very noticeable, but I can feel it. I hope it doesn't get bigger. [The reporter paused for a moment showing some anxiety over whether she should run for cover. Then the tremors subsided, and she focused back on the camera while listening to reports on her earphone.] *I think we can continue our report now as it seems the studio is not shaking. I understand we have videos of some of the areas affected by this quake. We have a static view of Miami from a tall building downtown. There is no audio, so we will be talking over the scene as you see it.* [Looking down at the seafront, the viewer's perspective was of a muddy field dotted with slimy stones. Buoys were resting on the seafloor. The normally scenic oceanfront appeared to be a salt flat at low tide. Faraway in the background, the water seemed to be placid.] *What you are seeing as a viewer is a large oceanfront avenue, which normally would have gentle waves rolling into the beach. The absence of water means a tidal wave is coming. Anyone seeing this who lives within visual distance of the ocean should—*

"We are taking you to our affiliate in Miami. Dillon Kramer is standing by."

"The ground is still rumbling, and it is very much a dangerous situation here. As you can see, I am standing in a solid doorway here in case, well ... My cameraman caught some of the destruction from just minutes ago. [The video showed clouds of dust rising from a street where a wall had collapsed. People were running for their lives. Cars were stopping, and other cars were running into the vehicles that had stopped. Some were fully aware of the earthquake, some were in shock, and others were just coming to the realization that a catastrophe was in the making. The video abruptly changed to a close-up of a gas station carport that was crashing down on some cars lined up for gas. The field reporter came back on briefly.] *We have been told to get to high ground. We are not safe here. Dillon Kramer, WVWA channel 8."*

"Very disturbing. We are receiving a report from Jacksonville ... Ah, we apologize for the disjointed nature of the report; instead, we have on the phone a representative from the National Geological and Seismic Activity Institute. Sir, can you tell us what's going on?

"Yes, the event we are experiencing is a 9.7 earthquake located in the new subduction zone in the Caribbean. It has been suspected for years that the tectonic plates are moving together, bringing North American closer to Europe. This earthquake is proof that this theory is correct."

"Are you saying that the United States is going to join Europe, physically?" The reporter asked.

"Yes, but not for billions of years from now. It will take a number of serious earthquakes over millennia before that will happen."

"Okay, but what about today's quake, where is it? Is it in the Caribbean ocean?"

"From our calculations the epicenter is east of the Caribbean close to the Atlantic ridge. We are thinking that this seismic event is between the North American, Caribbean, and maybe South American plates moving against each other. This is not a common event. We didn't expect it because this is not a real active area. Now—"

"Instead of a geological lesson, let's move to another more important topic. What's happening now, and who's in danger? Where should people take cover? Where are people going to be safe?"

"Well, ah, coastal regions should expect tidal waves. If it were me, I would go to high ground. But …"

"Thank you for your information. We are jumping to a live shot in Miami. [The anchor cut off the expert who was not on the moment of tragedy, which was the real story of safety and information, not a geography lesson. What was visible was an additional anchor reporter sitting next to her. The new anchor introduced the next on-the-scene report. However, this time there was no reporter doing a lead-in. The scene was of beachfront property next to marinas empty of water. In the background was a building tidal wave. Flotsam cluttered the wave with small watercraft tipping upward on the looming danger. At first, it looked like a great surfing wave, but as it grew, it became more ominous by the second. Palm trees in the foreground began to look tiny in comparison. As the wave ascended upward, the camera began to shake. It was obvious that the photographer was beginning to see the developing disaster and his risky position. The view changed violently as the photographer began to run, affording those watching a stomach-churning journey through doorjambs, stairways, and juddering, moving snapshots between floor and ceiling. The station broke back to the anchors at their desk.] *Oh my, that's scary! I hope and pray the cameraman will be okay—. A warning has been issued for all coastal regions south of Virginia. Any individuals living within two miles of the ocean are strongly advised to seek high ground immediately. The best we can say is the tidal wave is very dangerous, and our viewers who live in those areas should move quickly to avoid this catastrophe. We are safe here in our nation's capital, but we have to underline how dangerous this is to those areas near the oceanfront. We're bringing you the news as it happens; we apologize for our disjointed story. We are returning to the live shot we had earlier from the top of*

the Marriot Hotel. You are looking north along the beachfront with the ocean to your right. The wave is coming in from that direction. Oh! That's really bigger than I have ever seen. [The anchors went silent as the catastrophe played in front of the cameras.]

ZZZZZ

Chad could not take his eyes off of the images as one scene after another flashed by the screen. Activity in the restaurant was nil. No one ate; no one ordered food. Cooks stood next to waitresses watching. The tidal waves slammed against buildings and rolled cars over and over. Palm trees were uprooted and washed down streets and against buildings. There wasn't any need to repeat the same images because all up and down the East Coast, videos were available to choose from. Houses and boats were crushed against land structures. In one, the water was white and foamy. In another, the water was muddy and filled with trash. In a couple of scenes, bodies could be seen struggling to find something to grasp. In one short video, a comatose body was caught next to a light pole, contorted around it until the pole broke under the stress of thousands of gallons of water pushing it over. When the body was seen sliding under the waves, a gasp came from a waitress standing directly behind Chad. She commented,

> *Activity in the restaurant was nil. No one ate; no one ordered food. Cooks stood next to waitresses watching.*

"Oh, how awful. That poor soul. We're getting so close to the end of the world. People and even animals are dying everywhere." Chad turned to look at her when one of the cooks asked her what she meant. Chad listened to their exchange.

"Whaddya mean?"

"The things Jesus said will happen are happening: earthquakes, famines, pestilence, wars, and more wars. My pastor was talking about it last Sunday. There's the drought on the West Coast and the failure of crops; Ebola and AIDS, plus the swarms of locusts eating all the crops in Africa. This morning, I was hearing about the big hurricane headed for Florida and the East Coast, maybe, and then this earthquake happens just before the hurricane is supposed to arrive. It's too much to dismiss as bad luck. I think it's the end of the world."

"Like an act of God? I mean acts of God?"

"No, no, I don't believe God is doing this. God saw ahead of time this would happen."

"So, we're all going to die in one of these disasters. Is that it? Is that how the world ends?"

"Not necessarily. It's kinda like Noah's ark. We all have the choice ta get in if we want, but if we don't, well …"

"I'll keep my eye out for animals walking two by two," the cook said with a chuckle. He moved back into the kitchen to avoid more religious dialogue. Chad felt sorry for the waitress.

"I agree. I, too, think the world is coming to an end. Too many things are happening at the same time in fulfillment of prophecy," he said to the waitress with a wan smile. Inside, he was surprised at himself. He had never spoken about Bible prophecy with conviction as he did with this stranger. It marked a transition in his life toward a stronger certainty that God was relevant, at least in the area of understanding of end-time events. There was an urge on his part to be closer to God as these final events unfolded. His recent reading had plucked on responsive chords deep inside and had manifested in this short statement. He could now admit he was drawing closer to what he thought before as ambiguous.

"Yes, yes, thank you for agreein' with me. I needed ta hear you say that. I'm getting' more worried every time something like this happens," she spoke, pointing at the television set on the wall. "Except for the people at my church, I feel kinda like the Lone Ranger about my beliefs," she added, looking over her shoulder at the kitchen.

"I'm with you on this. I recently read a book that brings together a lot of the predictions from the Bible. It helped me to understand these things better," he answered.

"Whadja learn?" She sat down opposite Chad at his table.

"Well, I learned that there are political and financial issues that will happen in the end."

"How so?"

"The book of Revelation says that no one will be able to 'buy or sell' unless they have the mark of the beast. If you can't buy groceries, for instance, that is coercive and would need to be enforced by some power like a government or a police force."

"I don't see that happnin' yet. Do you?"

"Yes. Financially, there is the move to digital dollars, which means that the government could, at some future date, require banks to turn off unsubscribing individuals accessing their bank accounts. We can already see people competing for essentials because there is a crisis of resources that seems to be getting severe as plagues, droughts, and natural disasters are ruining crops and infrastructures. Like that," Chad pointed to the TV as another scene showed houses being swept away and slamming into brick buildings and splintering into kindling.

"Oh, no. Those poor people!" The conversation could not go on as the scene depicted was too horrific to ignore. It seemed callous to talk as people were dying before their eyes. They alternated between watching and hanging their heads down in dismay. Then the anchor reporters switched their focus to a BBC video from Bermuda. The anchors cautioned the viewers that the scenes could be very disturbing, which meant that everyone riveted their eyes on the television screen.

The video started with a view of streets and structures, focusing downhill from the white and brown two-towered municipal building with a flag in the foreground. Birds were rising from everywhere in a mass flock. The camera began to shake violently as the ground started to roll in waves like a turbulent sea. The flag pole toppled. Then the camera seemed to lie on its side as the distant sea approached from three different directions. Before anyone could fathom the fact that the island nation was sinking, the view of the catastrophe abruptly stopped when electricity no longer fed the camera.

Everyone in the restaurant was stunned into silence and barely heard the announcers say that all communications with Bermuda have been cut off. An approaching cruise ship had radioed a distress signal to all ships at sea to converge on the island for rescue operations. The communication from the captain indicated they were launching all tenders and rafts to pick up survivors. The island could not be seen, only floating wreckage.

The death and the destruction on the east shore of the United States paled in comparison to the loss of an entire community, let alone a sovereign nation. The world came to a halt as it watched/heard helplessly the loss of life. No one knew how many were lost. They could only guess. Bermuda was gone, never to exist again.

CHAPTER 5

The week of unremitting news stories about the earthquake and its sequelia stormed the media assets of every city, in every state, day in and day out. Disaster sufferers struggled with basic essentials of water, food, medicine, and housing. Growing in the background was the looming danger of diminished resources of federal, state, and local governments. No one wanted Hurricane George to reach landfall, but all indicators were projecting that it would hit the Carolinas. Congress would have to appropriate more monies and deepen the national debt. Calls were going out for donations to help the needy. That is why a local story made national headlines.

Brian and Cynthia had made major donations to ADRA and the Red Cross. Tens of thousands of dollars might make local headlines, but when several million went to ADRA, and a million went to the Red Cross, people take notice. Local reporters were clamoring to interview the couple. What they found was an African American couple living in a middle-income apartment complex near a local college. It made the story even more sensational.

Chad hadn't turned on the TV, choosing to access news on the internet where he could control and select the stories he preferred, avoiding the dismal earthquake reports. The cataclysmic loss of human life had added to his sorrow, and he was battling a strong grief-generated depression.

Diana's phone call jolted him out of a negative mood while on the couch, contemplating his future.

"Chad, quick! Turn on your TV. There's a couple that I think we've met. They're interviewing them."

"Okay, which channel?"

"Channel one hundred six."

ZZZZZZ

[The news channel banner across the bottom of the screen noted the couple's last name and a brief statement, "Couple donates $1 million to Red Cross."]

"*... you agree?*"

"*Yes, I guess I can see your point. We are a couple that doesn't fit the mold.*" [Brian answered.]

"*But don't you want to, umm ... buy your own home? You have more than enough money to do so. You have limited space. Your car is out in the weather. Why wouldn't you want to change to a residence that is a little more, ah, maybe, comfortable? I'm not saying your place here is bad, it isn't, but it is not what one would expect of multi, multi-millionaires.*"

"*Normally, that would be the expected, but we are not in a normal situation. The world, as we know it, is coming to an end. We believe there is not much time left here on earth. Why buy a home we do not need? It would be better if we helped to relieve suffering with the wonderful gift we have received. God trusts us with this money.*" [Cynthia explained.]

"*I'm impressed by your generosity. What you did for the earthquake victims was wonderful. But, I have to ask, you have hundreds of millions of dollars. Aren't you going to put some of it into safe investments so you can maintain your philanthropy?*" [The reporter asked.]

"*We've talked about this, haven't we, honey? We fully expect this world to spiral downward politically and religiously. We can already see the events described in the Bible happening. Our concern is to get the word out to everyone that everyone needs to turn to God and accept the free gift of salvation provided by Jesus. Cynthia and I are paying for media advertising to warn everyone of the coming danger of falling into Satan's trap. He will unite the world in false faith against true believers. We have to avoid—*"

"*Excuse me, who or what do you think is this false faith, as you say? Islam? Do you think Islam is the false faith that Satan will lead?*

No. What the Bible teaches is an international coalition of people under the guise of religion; a movement of world opinion that is controlled by satanic forces to exclude God's true people from scarce resources like food and water; basic sustenance. The book of Revelation tells of a time when these people will not be able to 'buy or sell,'" [Brian explained.]

"Who are these people of God, 'God's true people,' as you say?"

"They are those who 'keep the commandments of God and hold to the testimony of Jesus.'" [Cynthia quoted Rev. 14:12.]

"So, you believe it is all Christians, and not Atheists, Buddhists, and Islamics, for example? A holy war?" [the reporter asked.]

"I do not mean a war between Christians and other faiths. I believe it is a war between Christ and Satan, a struggle that involves God's people who are loyal to God's principles. Not all Christians keep God's commandments. This is the time for all people to decide if they are going to be true to God in every way, which is manifested in their commitment to live by the standard God has clearly stated in the Ten Commandments."

"What faith are you?"

"Right now, it doesn't matter what denomination you are; it matters if you are true to Him in what He asks you to do."

"What church do you attend?" [She asked, intending to expose them.]

"The Seventh-day Adventist Church." [he answered reluctantly because he knew that the reporter was trying to identify who and what they were.]

"So the only true believers are the Seventh-dayers"?

"I didn't say that. God's true people are from all backgrounds and beliefs, but

> ***God's true people are from all backgrounds and beliefs, but the one thing they have in common is that they are followers of Jesus and keep God the Father's precepts as their mark of loyalty to Him.***

the one thing they have in common is that they are followers of Jesus and keep God the Father's precepts as their mark of loyalty to Him." [Brian finished his statement, which was followed by a pause. The interviewing reporter wanted to conclude by getting back to the initial subject and away from religious sentiment.]

"This is so important to you that you are going to spend your vast inheritance on warning the people?"

"And, we want to relieve suffering if we can." [Cynthia added.]

"Thank you, Mr. and Mrs. King, Brian and Cynthia, this has been ... interesting to say the least. Now back to you, Sherry and Tim."

ZZZZZ

Chad and Diana reacted over the phone. "Are they the ones who came to your folks' funeral?"

"Yes, they came to my home with a casserole as well. Nice people. The casserole wasn't bad either; I remember my mom making something like it. I'm guessing they have recently come into a lot of money?"

"Yes, and it seems they are throwing it away."

"Did a rich relative die and give them a big inheritance?"

"As the story goes, it was not a relative. I guess Cynthia was taking care of some terminally-ill lady that gave everything to them because she was pleased with her compassion and tender nursing. The couple planned on keeping everything quiet and then started giving it all away," Diana answered.

"A large donation of a million dollars begs for notice," Chad remarked.

"Right. Maybe they need some guidance on how to manage their fortune. Interested?"

"Not really. They seem to be determined to give it away because of the felt belief that the end is near," he said.

"Maybe we could talk them into helping our church. We really need to repair the foundation, which is sinking in multiple places and cracking the walls. It's going to take a lot of money. And then there's the parking lot that needs to be redone. There's discussion about selling the building and moving out to the suburbs."

"I doubt they would help out the church—"

"Because they're SDAs, and we are not, right?"

"No, I was going to say that they really believe the second coming is soon, so why would they help build a building when Christians aren't going to be here to use it?"

Diana felt like getting their conversation turned to a more personal slant. Twice now, he had defended the couple's belief on last-day events. She sought a way to spend more time with him. "So, what have you been doing?"

"Thinking."

"About what?"

"Oh, things. I've been thinking of not returning to my internship, and I've been trying to find out who killed my folks, and, you know, why they ..."

"Joined another church?"

"Yes, that, and then there's the reason they were murdered; for a couple thousand dollars?! Why kill them? Detective Hardine has been tracking where the money went. It turns out that it was a robbery; no other motive has surfaced. I would kinda like to be here when or if he apprehends the killers. I know it's a slim possibility, but I want to be nearby anyway, maybe ask them why they had to murder them. After that, I can go back to my internship."

"Have you been talking to anyone about this? I can tell by the tone of your voice that you are discouraged. Can I help? I'm a good listener."

Chad was tired of being alone, eating leftover food, and fighting off negative thoughts of death and destruction. Every time he dwelt on the loss of life in the earthquake and subsequent tsunami, he would think of his parents. When he thought of his parents, he would identify with the grieving families. He was in a cybernetic loop. He fought off morose musings by exercising to excess. "I would like to have someone to talk to, but I think I would prefer talking about anything else but the loss of life."

"Okay, it's a deal. Is it alright if I come over now?"

"I suppose ..."

"I'll see you in a little bit."

"Right n—" Diana clicked off before Chad could ask her to come a little later, maybe after lunch.

XXXXX

Detective Hardine hit another dead end. One out of nine convenience stores had a clear video showing the individual purchasing ten money cards with the Johnsons' credit card and never turned to reveal himself to the camera. An interview with the clerk got a description of the perp that would fit 200,000 males in the city. The other stores either had broken cameras, or they were pointed in the wrong direction because they had been turned by a mysterious hand just before the transaction. Interviews with all clerks got basically the same descriptions only with different clothes. He knew the numbers on all of the money cards, but not one had been used. He was wondering why they were waiting. He rounded up five of the clerks and had artist sketches made. It was clear from that exercise that two individuals were making the exchanges, and thus hiding the money tracks. His newest clue was withering on the vine. Frustrated, he went to play a round of golf. He had not taken time for himself in weeks.

XXXXX

Chad went to the mailbox and was sorting through the mail. The bulk of the mail was advertisements, the others were addressed to his parents, and one for him. It was from the bank and had his new debit card. What surprised him was the technology employed. The card was a fingerprint reader device. The entire card was made of miniature computer chips. It came in a plastic sleeve to protect it from activating. A warning label explained that step one was to call the 800 number to activate the bank system to validate; step two was to open the sleeve and place all four fingers and the thumb anywhere on the card front and back. The fingers activated the card with an imprinting of the owner's prints. No other person could touch the card. If one did touch the card, it would not work, not until the owner handled the card once again. He marveled at the wonder of modern technology.

Chad was reading the specs on how the card worked when the doorbell rang. It was Diana. He was amazed at how fast she had gotten to his home. She must have broken speed limits to get there so soon. He had to smile at the thought.

"Good morning. Come on in," Chad said as he opened the door for Diana.

"Thank you." She wrapped her arms around him and kissed him on the cheek. "You shouldn't be here alone. You need to talk about this and get your grief out in the open. Don't hide it inside, okay?"

"I'm okay." He shrugged.

"Have you been sleeping enough? Your eyes look a little tired. Eating, have you been eating properly?" She began to mother him whether or not he needed it.

He was thinking that he would prefer to talk with her about the different things he had discovered, rather than his health and welfare. She was safe in that respect. She was not an Adventist and not one to defend their position. Maybe she could offer a different slant on what he had read.

"Yeah, I've been eating … maybe too much. There's plenty of food, too much for me to finish by myself. I've been doing a lot of reading, and I would like to bounce some stuff off of you if you don't mind. Let's go into the living room."

They sat side by side on the couch. It was Diana's choice to wait until he sat, and then she took to his left side, which meant she would have less space and end up closer.

"So, what do you want to tell me?"

"This disaster on the East Coast really bothers me."

"I know, isn't it awful? You're grieving both for them and your folks. I'm so sorry."

"I suppose I'm grieving for both, but I'm also thinking about something I read. Look." Chad reached for the worn-out copy of *The Great Controversy* sitting next to the Bible on the coffee table. He opened to where one paperclip of several marked a specific passage. "Here it's talking about Satan in the last days. 'He will bring disease and disaster, until populous cities are reduced to ruin and desolation. Even now he is at work. In accidents and calamities by sea and by land, in great conflagrations, in fierce tornados and terrific hailstorms, in tempests, floods, cyclones, tidal waves, and earthquakes, in every place and in a thousand forms, Satan is exercising his power.'[3] It goes on and on. That's what just happened. A whole island nation was destroyed!"

"I know it's terrible! But things like that are always happening, right?"

"Yes, but this mentions specifically that Satan is the cause, and he is blaming God's people for not worshiping properly."

"So? That's true, isn't it? No, wait, Satan blaming God's people for not worshipping? That doesn't make sense. Why would Satan want anybody to worship at all?"

"Yes, but here it says, 'It will be declared that men are offending God by the violation of the Sunday sabbath; that this sin has brought calamities which will not cease until Sunday observance shall be strictly enforced; and those who present the claims of the fourth commandment, thus destroying reverence for Sunday, are troublers of the people, preventing their restoration to divine favor and temporal prosperity.'[4] This Saturday versus Sunday thing seems to be a big issue in this book. And Satan is promoting Sunday over Saturday."

"Come on. Why would one day be more important than another? We should worship God every day, right?"

---

[3]White, *The Great Controversy* (Mountain View, CA, 1911). p. 589
[4]White, *The Great Controversy* (Mountain View, CA, 1911). p. 590

"Yes and no. We should be dedicated every day if we are to be true Christians, but God asks that we worship Him one specific day every week. And this little book says it must be Saturday because it is in the Ten Commandments."

"I don't see that happening now. There's no big discussion on the Saturday worship issue apart from this Jeremy Richards. We've had a huge disaster, but no one's blaming anybody except God, maybe. I don't see how the day we worship is relevant."

"That would have been my take on the subject last week, but this week things are different. I haven't watched the news on TV because it is nothing but the earthquake. I have been reading the news on the internet. There's a Reverend So-and-so, I forget his name, at an ecumenical conference in Rio, who is blaming the world for not honoring the Sunday worship hour. He said that we need to get back to basics, and God will protect us. That's what this book predicts."

"One crackpot doesn't make this book true," she replied.

"Well, he did say that standing in front of a number of clergy that was attending the conference. They didn't disagree with him," he answered.

"If you ask me, the Ten Commandments are no longer relevant; therefore, the day is not relevant. Sunday is like everyone's day off. Going to church on Sunday is the common thing to do. The majority of Christians worship on Sunday. If they're making Sunday observance a requirement, it's a move to get us all on the same sheet music. I think it's time we all get along."

"You're in agreement then?" he asked.

"I guess so. Look at you! You're getting more serious about religion." Diana looked pleased.

"Instead of serious, I would use the word 'curious.' I'm still trying to find out why my folks switched churches. To change meant that they had to adopt some unpopular practices. The day of worship is one of them. I'm planning on attending their church tomorrow to see what the attraction might be. Want to come along?"

"Ah, okay. It would be nice to do something together. We could make a day of it and go out to lunch somewhere special after their service is done. That is if they have a service like we do." Her angling to be a couple was not lost on him.

"I was planning on taking a run in the park. I can change it to a walk if you want to come along. We could talk as we walked."

"Okay."

XXXXX

Vonnie was surprised when she heard of Brian and Cynthia's fortune. They had not mentioned a word to anyone as it turned out. The church treasurer knew because of the incredible amount in tithe and offerings that had come in the church's offering the previous weekend. She was not supposed to gossip about members' giving, but she had to tell the pastor pronto. Vonnie got her news like Chad, through human channels. Several texts hit her phone in rapid succession, each one telling her to turn on the news. She had to slip down to the breakroom to watch the broadcast. She rejoiced at her friends' serendipity.

"Don't you wish that was you?" Vonnie was surprised again, this time by a voice behind her. She turned to see her boss standing behind her. "Mrs. Greene, you surprised me."

"I didn't mean to. But what would you do if that happened to you?" She pointed to the screen.

"I haven't thought of it, but I guess I would do the same thing that Brian and Cynthia are doing."

"Wait, do you know them?"

"Yes, they're very good friends. We go to the same church."

"You're an SDA, then?"

"That's right."

"Why do SDAs want to give away their money? Is it a requirement of the church?" she asked somewhat in jest. But Vonnie came back serious.

"Under normal circumstances my friends and I would give some to our church and to charities, and we would also invest it so we would be able to help more in the future."

"I admire you and your friends, but why would you not want to save or invest now? What's the 'abnormal circumstances'?" Mrs. Greene used her fingers to make quotation marks in the air.

Life as we experience it now is ending. Jesus is coming soon, and money will mean nothing when that happens. Why not use the money for good when it can be effective?

"The difference is that life as we experience it now is ending. Jesus is coming soon, and money will mean nothing when that happens. Why not use the money for good when it can be effective?"

"To be strictly honest, I would be selfish and squirrel the money away for a great retirement, which would begin immediately. I would feather my nest for the future. I think you and I are the proverbial Ant and the Grasshopper. I'm the ant. I hope that doesn't bother you when I say that."

"No, that doesn't bother me, because I am an ant, too."

"How so?"

"Because the Bible says, 'Lay up for yourselves treasure in heaven, where neither moth nor rust destroys and where thieves do not break in and steal.'[5] What one focuses on down here has an effect on your commitment to live up there."

"You're right. And I can't help but see the parallel with that verse and what you experienced recently. Incidentally, I wanted to ask you if the police are any closer to finding who hacked your bank account?"

"No. They haven't found anything yet."

"When I heard about it, I immediately checked my account because I have the same bank as you. Are you the only one that was hacked?"

"It seems so. The bank manager told me that someone must have gotten my number and guessed my passcode. I'm guessing that the apartment manager has something to do with it because only my rent payments were affected. Proving it is going to be difficult. It has been given to the cybercrime people, and they are supposedly overloaded. I'll probably never know, but I'm happy that God has got my back. He'll take care of me."

"I admire your faith, both you and your friends."

"Thank you."

XXXXX

"Are we late? Look, the parking lot is full, and there are no people walking toward the front door. We're ten minutes early," Diana observed.

"Their worship hour starts at eleven, but they have Sunday School before that. The sign says that starts at nine-thirty. I guess they all came for the study first," Chad answered.

"Correction, how can they call it Sunday School if it's on Saturday?"

"My mistake, I guess they call it Sabbath School." Chad glanced at the sign on the front lawn. "Maybe we should've come for that too."

"I think for now, one hour is all I can take."

---

[5]Matt. 6:20, NKJV

Diana hung onto Chad's arm as they entered the foyer. A greeter welcomed them and asked them to sign their guestbook. The lobby was full of conversational clusters that were slowly migrating toward the sanctuary doors. Children were seeking out parents and skipping toward the same doors. Several of the clusters broke up and approached Chad and Diana. At first, they thought they were a young married couple, but when Vonnie saw them, she welcomed both by name, which cleared the misconception.

"I'm so glad you came today. Would you like to sit with me?"

"Sure, why not," Chad replied. They slipped into the sanctuary and took a pew near the back. It wasn't two seconds before Cynthia and Brian joined them. Brian sat next to Chad, and on the other side, Vonnie was next to Diana.

"Good morning." Brian extended his hand to first Chad and then Diana. Cynthia leaned forward and greeted warmly, but without the handshake.

"When I came this morning, I didn't expect to be sitting with celebrities," Chad said to Brian.

"We didn't expect to be in the spotlight. Things got a little out of hand. Have you been to an SDA church before?" Brian deftly changed the subject.

"No, this is our first time. Should we expect any surprises?"

"I don't think so. I'm guessing our service will be a little less formal than what you might be used to."

"I guess we will see."

Meditative music played as the platform filled with worship leaders who knelt for a few moments before taking seats. The choir was already in place. A dignified gentleman spoke about announcements in the bulletin, which gave the couple a chance to open theirs and scan the order of service. They were attracted by the title of the sermon, *Symptoms of The Last Days of Earth*. Diana pointed to it for Chad to see. He nodded his head. Her interest perked up because she knew this was a topic Chad was mulling over. Prior to reading the title, the only reason she was here was because she wanted to be relevant to Chad. Their minds were brought back to the gentleman because he said all visitors were invited to dinner in the fellowship room. On cue Brian, Cynthia, and Vonnie extended their own encouragements to come. They felt a little awkward about accepting.

The first hymn was announced, and they stood to sing. After all four stanzas were sung, Diana whispered to Chad, "They sing the same songs as us."

Chad thought about her remark. He knew that most denominations sang similar songs coming from all mainline traditions. He remembered his father's singing. It was louder than necessary and not altogether on key, but always enthusiastic. The lines of the hymn they had just finished were some of his father's favorites.

The offertory came next, and Chad felt compelled to give something. When he reached for his wallet, Diana followed suit in case someone was watching. He used the portable card-readers to put in a respectable ten but knew he could manage more. They sang the Doxology for dedicating the offering, and that was familiar to the couple as well. A children's story followed. The storyteller read from a book entitled, *The Little Lightning Bug Who Couldn't Play Hide-n-Seek*. The lady had their attention by the way she inflected her voice. She ended by saying that each child had their own light and should not try to hide it. They sang "This Little Light of Mine," as they returned to their parents. The pastoral prayer followed, and the congregation knelt. That was not new to them, but the fact that there weren't any kneelers was. Scripture followed, and then a soloist sang, "O Soul, Are You Weary and Troubled." It set the mood for the sermon. Chad and Diana took note of the fact that it was 11:25, more than enough time for a typical ten-minute sermon. It also surprised them a little to see the pastor leave the pulpit and walk down into the audience.

Pastor Peter Lange spoke extemporaneously. "Do we have enough time?" He paused for effect. "In past Sabbaths, my sermons have been on the fulfillment of Bible prophecies and the nearness of the second coming of Jesus. It is indeed near, very near. Every week we see more indications of just how near it must be. This past week is no exception with the earthquake and tidal wave, and now the hurricane assaulting the Carolinas. Affected people need our prayers and support. Today, I want to put a different perspective on the nearness of His coming. Do we have enough time? Do we have enough time to accomplish what we need to accomplish?

"You have heard my sermons on the prophecies. As I have said, you have heard my sermons about the signs of the times. Today I want to talk to you about symptoms of the earth and the end of time. Symptoms are a step away from the signs and the prophecies. Precursors, if you will, conditions that preclude a fulfillment of a sign or a prophecy. There are five areas in which I see these symptoms; the natural world, the financial world, the world of media, the political world, and the religious world. I can't finish all of these today, so this will be a two-part sermon.

"First, let's look quickly at the natural world. Our population is burgeoning. As of today, we are way beyond the seven-and-a-half billion mark. Soon, we will have nine billion. At seven-and-a-half this mass of people requires one-and-three quarters worlds to eat and live. That means that a high percentage of individuals are suffering from malnutrition. 16,000-plus children are dying of starvation every day. When we reach nine billion, we can't sustain our present life. Food production must rise to meet the demand. Agricultural science is telling us that we have to double plant productivity or double land productivity, or both. That requires fertilizer, and fertilizer requires phosphate. We are in a crisis of phosphate availability. North Africa had the largest source of that ingredient, and it is now depleted. Science must come up with a different resource. Land is at a premium. Forty percent of this earth's land is no longer arable. We must plant vertically or use a different substance than soil. Is it any wonder that our government and world governments have put in place 'Build Up, Not Out' requirements to save land for food. Also, all golf courses are being taxed unless they can produce food in non-playing surfaces to match the loss of arable ground to recreation. Public parks are being considered for the same restriction. Scientists are racing to find alternate food sources such as insect powder for protein and/or fish protein. More on that in a moment.

"Citrus crops are affected adversely. Florida produces more citrus than any other country except Brazil. Florida is suffering from 'greening,' wiping out grove after grove. A Chinese insect carries a parasite that kills the trees. Science has a solution; they have bred a parasite-resistant tree. However, a grove has to be cut down and replanted with seedlings, which take twelve years to produce small amounts of fruit.

"Freshwater resources are dwindling. Seventy percent of our freshwater is used for food production. Now, more than 25 percent of the world's population does not have access to feces-free water for drinking. Forty percent of the world lives in severe water scarcity. They need clean water. We all need clean water. Aquifers are very important sources of water to produce crops. There are thirty-seven large aquifers in the world. Every one of them is being taxed to the limit, and some are disappearing altogether. Twenty-one are past the replenishment point. The Ogallala aquifer in the United States once was the source of 20 percent of the country's wheat, corn, and beef. This underground source of water is critical for food for America. If we were to stop using water from that source, it would take a thousand years to replenish it. When we need to produce, as the National Geographic says, 60 percent more food to sustain humanity, we are in a back-stepping posture. The quest to find more water seems to point in one direction. Desalinization is an option. But that cost lots of money to produce. That will add to our financial crisis. I will mention more about that later. Scientists are finding ways to grow plants in saltwater. I wonder if that will be enough to solve the problem in time because plants also need oxygen.

"We are running out of fresh air. More and more CO_2 is unable to be converted back to oxygen. On land our primary resource for the conversion of CO_2 is trees. Trees once covered 12 percent of the earth's surface. Now it is less than 2 percent and getting steadily lower. Every year 15.3 billion trees are being cut. Then forest fires, pine beetles, ash borers, and host of other parasites kill more. One place where you would expect trees to help us is Alaska and Canada, where there are lots of trees. They have the same problem with tree loss and an added problem of melting permafrost where CO_2 is trapped and now being released due to the warming of sub-polar regions.

"Ocean plankton was once responsible for 50 to 85 percent of O_2 production. But, that is no longer happening at the same levels. Almost half of the phytoplankton population has been decimated. Why? Because global warming of our seas is affecting plankton where they can no longer perform the photosynthesis required. That is affecting oceanic animal populations, thus decreasing marine-related food production.

"Ozone is an increasing issue. Governments have excelled at banning chlorofluorocarbons and neglecting to restrict other substances, like dichloromethanes. The loss of our protective ozone layer increases skin cancers, cortical cataracts, and now, through increased UV radiation, rice crop production is greatly affected. Rice is a number-one staple for a majority of the world. Again, all these facts put together show a merging of issues that attack mankind's survivability. Science is attacking these problems, but can they get to all of them and solve all of them in time?

"At this point you are probably wondering, 'Is this a sermon or an ecology report?' To answer that, let me quote Isaiah 51:6, 'The heavens will vanish like smoke, the earth will wear out like a garment, and they who dwell in it will die like gnats; and my salvation will be for ever.'[6] I have to ask you, Will Jesus let us starve, die of thirst, or run out of air? No, of course not. He loves us. He died for us. The conditions of a worn-out

---

[6]RSV

earth are symptoms of the end. God mentions, 'My salvation is for ever' in the same breath as an earth in an almost uninhabitable state, worn out like a garment. The earth's suitability for life is coming to an end. Jesus' rescue is near as our world is almost finished. How much longer can it last?

"Animal life is not lasting. Zoologists are saying we are on the cusp of a mass extinction of wildlife. Already various species are disappearing. The World Wildlife Federation, in its Living Planet Report, tells of all the species already extinct; 83 percent of vertebrates in Latin America. In the world we have lost 52 percent of the earth's bird, mammal, fish, reptile, and amphibian populations. Just a few years ago, one type of antelope died out, all 120,000 of them, half in just four days! We have lost three-quarters of our freshwater populations. Ocean populations are following suit. They're losing necessary O_2 and food sources. The plans for fish farms to feed the world are in jeopardy. The coral reefs are in peril, as well. The Great Barrier Reef is two-thirds dead. This concerns Australia greatly because so much of their economy in Northeast Australia depends on it. They fear if they lose the last third, that alone will be a mass extinction event for marine life. Bees are dying. In the *New York Times*, August of 2016, an article said if we lose all our bees at once, then the world would last only four more years. One-third of all our crops are possible because of bees. Colony Collapse Disorder is destroying bee populations everywhere, some places more than others, 30-50 percent worldwide. Wisconsin has lost 60 percent of its hives. Pesticides are blamed for CCD, and so are pests. But they are not sure. Spraying for Zika wipes out any bee colony it touches. Spray or not to spray—that is the question. When we need to increase resources, we are losing resources.

"This next topic will serve for me to transition to my next major point, coffee. Coffee crops are dying. Coffee is not necessary for survival (some will disagree with me, especially in the morning.), but the communities who rely on coffee crops are on the edge of ruin, financial ruin. Financial collapse is my second point this morning. Continuing, coffee is a cash crop that they use to buy food. A financial crisis in the middle of a commodity crisis means chaos. Without trusting God, people fall back on their own limited resources. Less money to buy less food and less water has to lead to anarchy. Desperate times lead to desperate behaviors, which are symptoms of the end. People will be fearful, hungry, selfishly grabbing for what they need, and claiming scarce resources in a false name of justice. Eventually, it will be a battle of the haves and the have-nots. Vigilante groups such as the Neo-KKK (also known as Circle of Christian

Cleansing, KKK) will step into the melee and carve out their own share that they think they own, deciding who should have and who should go without. And at that point, we see Revelation 13 coming into clear focus, marking the citizenry as to who can buy and who can sell. With the condi-

> *We see Revelation 13 coming into clear focus, marking the citizenry as to who can buy and who can sell.*

tions I have detailed to this point, I see this issue coming to a head now. Look at the way people are behaving.

"In James chapter 5, the first verses, we see these words, 'Come now, you rich, weep and howl for your miseries that are coming upon you ...' (NKJV). Leaders of countries, including our own federal and state governments, have been borrowing prosperity for today from tomorrow. They have been enacting legislation for wonderful benefits their budgets can't afford, like raised salaries for politicians and state and federal employees, comfortable retirements, subsidies for every popular program that can get a mayor, governor, or president reelected. These are nice things to do, but we must be able to afford them. The national debt is over twenty trillion dollars. This is growing, but what is even more concerning is the amount of accounts receivable. Those are things that must be paid, such as Social Security, federal and military retirements, FHA, Medicare, Medicaid, student loans, and so on. Local and state governments are in the same boat. Accounts receivable are ten times greater than the national debt.

"Our society has a crime crisis. When we put criminals behind bars, we have to guard, feed, and house them. Our governments can't afford to do that. Thousands of dollars are siphoned from state and federal accounts that have zero balances if all account receivables are factored in. It is yet another drain on depleted public funds. For example, it costs $900,000 a year to house a detainee in Guantanamo.

"How do governments do it? Maybe I should say, why do the governments do it? They sell treasury bills and municipal bonds. Many decades ago, they discovered that going into debt stimulated the economy. In 1960 a dollar of debt created $2.41 in economic stimulation. In 1970 a dollar would artificially grow the economy by $.41. Then in 2014, a dollar of debt could help the economy by $.03. Nowadays, debt doesn't help at all, and the bills need to be paid.

"A financial collapse by itself might be surmounted after a significant debilitating struggle. But if a financial calamity comes at the same time as a crisis of commodities, we could have competition for basic necessities. If we had the same economy as Israel once had, a year of Jubilee could solve these financial crises in one fell swoop. But, without that, the world's financial woes continue. We can see in Scripture that the end times will be difficult, very difficult. Jesus said it would be so bad that the elect might not make it. Matthew 24:21–22 says, 'For then there will be great tribulation, such as has not been from the beginning of the world until now, no, and never will be. And if those days had not been cut short, no human being would be saved. But for the sake of the elect those days will be cut short' (ESV). Jesus was concerned for us then and even more so now.

"Personally, I am looking forward to that time when I will eat food like the five thousand did. I want to break bread with Jesus. I want to sit down at the marriage supper of the Lamb. I plan to drink from springs of living water. And I will breathe in the perfect air of God's righteous glory. It may be difficult between now and then, yet, Jesus and His Holy Spirit will guide me through. This is my hope and assurance; it is yours as well."

This was an interesting perspective for Chad and Diana. They were squeezing each other's hands in confirmation of what they were learning. Occasionally, they showed each other's smartphones with articles that they Googled that confirmed some of the subjects that the pastor had mentioned. They both agreed that the time spent was worth it to see and hear what the Adventists believed and get a feeling for why his folks were attracted to this religion.

CHAPTER 6

C had and Diana hadn't planned on going to the visitor's potluck after the worship service. They wanted to slip out and compare notes at a local restaurant. But their peers asked them with a genuine desire to get to know them. Brian, Cynthia, and Vonnie made them feel welcome and special, and even Diana felt the warmth despite her reticence to mix with individuals of the sect. After shaking the pastor's hand, they walked down to the fellowship hall and stood with their new friends in the back. After prayer, the guests were asked to go first if they wanted to. They really didn't want to go to the front of the line and be made the center of attention. They hung back and went through with their three new friends. Cynthia helped Diana to decipher the different dishes that she saw. The experience was raising more questions. These people were different in many ways, from dogma to diet. She couldn't fathom how people could change to a lifestyle like what she was seeing. It was foreign to what she knew. She took a small forkful and found it to be savory. Because she had been dubious, she had not taken a large portion. Finishing that, she wanted more but didn't want to go back a second time and look like an overeater.

"I know it might be a little strange to eat at a vegetarian potluck, but did you find anything you liked?" Vonnie asked.

"As a matter of fact, yes, yes, I did," she replied.

"So it wasn't a complete loss."

"No, it wasn't. This pasta dish was very tasty." She pointed to the one she liked on Chad's dish.

"I liked that one, too. I'm going back up to get some more. Can I get you some more?"

"I'll go with you."

Diana felt better about going with another and felt better about Vonnie. She didn't see her as a competitor for Chad's attention. When they got to the table, the dish in question was gone. So they took a few samples of other dishes and then went to the dessert table. They chatted about the food, and Diana didn't feel like Vonnie was trying to convince her to be a vegetarian. Instead, the conversation progressed like two friends enjoying a day together. There was a companionship quality to her that pulled her into friendship. They came back to the table to find Pastor Lange personally welcoming Chad for the second time. They were talking about the funeral and the fact that the pastor had attended. Chad thanked him for coming to the funeral.

"Brian, Cynthia, I was wondering if you've made a decision about what form of evangelism you were going to support?"

"Our first reaction was to go with printing literature for distribution. But, then we thought of the fact that the Internet is more popular. Social media, emails, phones, computers are the norm now. Our idea is to establish an Internet media center. They call it a 'Beowulf Cluster,' a bunch of computers linked together to create a supercomputer. We would search with it and then use separate stations to dialogue. We could flood social media, connect with interested people, dialogue on Instagram, Twitter, chat rooms, blogs, and so on. We could even use translators from our Adventist universities and reach the world. We still will purchase some literature for follow-up."

"Great idea! We need to get specific truths out so that everyone can make an intelligent decision. *The Great Controversy* mentions that. If you need help, let me know. I would like to help."

"Yes, we do need you. Tomorrow morning or even tonight if you can spare the time."

"Okay, I will love to help. Tomorrow morning will work for me."

"Thanks, Pastor, I'll text you the address and when we'll be there."

Pastor Lange moved to visit at another table. Chad didn't want to let him go. "Ah, Pastor Lange, I have a question."

"Sure thing, what do you want to know? I'll do my best to help."

"You mentioned in your sermon about the Neo-KKK's involvement in last-day events. I have only heard of the KKK way back during the Civil War. Something about purifying Christianity, I think. Are they active today?"

"Chad, that's a good question. Great minds think of the same things. Your father asked me that same basic question. I got that information through church channels. It came up in a minister's meeting about two months ago. Several SDA students have been kidnapped out of our schools, both academies and colleges, and subjected to deprogramming. Involved in some of those cases, the Neo-KKK turned out to be the culprits. A couple of those incidents ended in court with kidnapping charges. The perpetrators are out on bail, and litigation seems to be delayed. In the past, the KKK was basically a secret cabal supporting Christian slave ownership. It seems their racism animated their Christianity. I guess they made a step from racial dominance to maintaining the purity of their supposed doctrines of Christianity."

"Interesting. I thought they were has-beens. I didn't think they were very prevalent."

"As far as my limited knowledge goes, I think they're more prevalent in the South. That's where those kidnappings occurred. No incidents up here that I know of."

"Reverend Lange?" Diana joined the conversation.

"Yes?"

"Why were they deprogrammed?"

"Because some people think Adventists are wrong in worshipping on Saturday. They call us a cult. This is behavior we saw back in the seventies and has been resurrected recently for reasons I cannot fathom. There's a lot of anger in the world, as seen by all the demonstrations taking place for various reasons. It seems that if one holds an opinion different than the norm, then you are un-American or non-Christian. As Adventists, we have expected this as a sign of end times."

"You expected this? How so? Is the world against you as Adventists?" Diana thought this a martyr complex. She wondered if they were playing the sympathy card.

"Not just Adventists, anyone who keeps the commandments of God. You see, in the book of Revelation, it identifies two groups—those 'who worship the image of the beast' and those 'who keep the commandments of God and the testimony of Jesus.' This is a call for the true believers, 'those who keep the commandments of God and have the faith of Jesus.' SDAs, along with any other Christians who have the characteristics of keeping the faith of Jesus and are keeping all of the commandments."

"You believe that people don't like you because of the difference in the day of worship?"

"Yes and no. There are many people who know why we worship on Saturday and are sympathetic, and then there are others that think we are wrong and need to be coerced to worship on Sunday. We have seen that behavior in some of the dialogue in the media. There are people who think that this country is losing out on God's blessing and need to make America prosperous again. It is their desire to legislate conscience. For some, they think having everyone act like a Christian and worship on Sunday will make America great, and thus, merit the favor of His blessing."

"But, the day of worship has changed, right? I think I remember somewhere that the Ten Commandments were nullified by Jesus' death on the cross. The cross ended a dispensation of the law, and now we're in the dispensation of grace."

"I understand a lot of people sincerely believe that. I don't want you to think I am putting you down if I answer from my point of view."

"No, I would like to know why SDAs believe the way they do. Jeremy Richards is raising the question in the media."

"Okay, Jesus said, 'Do not think that I have come to abolish the Law or the Prophets; I have not come to abolish them but to fulfill them.'[7] Twice He said He didn't come to abolish. Many look at the 'fulfill' and not at the two times He said He wouldn't abolish. To me and many Adventists, we believe that fulfilling the law means validating the law. Then there is another way to look at it. Throughout the Bible God's Spirit inspired Scripture through human writers, but when it came to the Ten Commandments, He wrote them with His own finger. Do you think He would abolish something He felt was so important that He would write it with His own finger?"

"I guess not. But, all this is new to me. I have to study it myself."

"Yes, that's the best way. Bible study is very important, and taking my words or anybody else's words is not the best. Let the Holy Spirit speak to you through Scripture after you pray first and ask Him to guide you. There are two ways to interpret Scripture. The best way is to let the Bible speak for itself. Study a passage in its greater context. Let the passage

---

[7](Matt. 5:17, NIV)

talk to you without pre-conceived bias. A pre-conceived bias can be called confirmation theology, using the Bible to confirm what you want it to say. A technical term for that is called eisegesis. The right way to interpret the Bible is called exegesis, which is a serious analysis without foregone conclusions. I guess I might be getting too technical."

"Not to change the subject, but to change the subject; why do you think my parents changed from a church they attended for years to your church? What do you think made them switch?"

"Everyone has their own reasons; your father was very interested in last-day events. Your mother was quieter but demonstrated interest in the answers to your father's questions. When I interviewed them for baptism, your mother had very informed responses. I think the subject of last-day events attracted them, but what really impressed them was the role of the Sabbath in the final conflict."

"Really?" Diana reacted. "That seems a bit farfetched to believe that everything boils down to a day of worship."

> *At this time, which is so close to the end, we will see forces attempting to coerce us to worship on Satan's false Sabbath. To most, it will look like a good thing. In reality it will be an attack on the kingdom of God established at the very beginning.*

"It does seem to be too simple to be true, but it is more significant than it seems. In the Garden of Eden, not eating of one tree when there were thousands to eat from seemed simple and arbitrary. The result of taking from that one designated tree was a world of sin and evil. The evil didn't come from Adam and Eve. It came from the architect of evil, Satan. This is his rebellion, his kingdom, and it is against the kingdom of heaven. The Saturday Sabbath is one day out of seven. The Sabbath was before the fall of Adam and Eve, the seventh day of creation. So it was a part of God's kingdom. Sunday observance came after the Garden of Eden. It is pagan in origin. It is linked to sun worship and stands in opposition to the Saturday Sabbath observance. Satan will require worship of all people at the end. It will be the culmination of his kingdom. He will not want worship on God's day, but a day of his own choosing. At this time, which is so close to the end, we will see forces attempting to coerce us to worship on Satan's false Sabbath. To most, it will look like a good thing. In reality it will be an attack on the kingdom of God established at the very beginning."

Diana was interested in the logic presented. She was about to ask another question when the table was distracted by a newcomer.

"Hi, everyone," Raphael Wilson greeted.

"How did it go?" the pastor asked.

"Well, I think God blessed."

"He always does," answered Brian.

"Chad, Diana, you remember Raphael, don't you?" Vonnie introduced.

"Yes, I do. How are you, Raphael? Did you just do special music or something at another church?" Chad asked.

"No, I had a sermon at the Atterberry Church. They needed someone for pulpit fill while their minister was temporarily doing evangelism in Eastern Europe."

"Laymen preach in your churches?" Diana queried. She and Chad looked at Pastor Lange.

"Once in a while, it happens. As a matter of fact, your dad gave a sermon here over a month ago," the pastor answered.

"He did!?" Chad exclaimed more than questioned. His words matched Diana's thoughts exactly.

"Yes, he did. And he was good, especially as it was his first sermon," Vonnie added.

"Yeah. I was surprised because his title was so obscure. It was 'FLL.' That didn't tell us anything, and then when he told us what it meant, we expected a straightforward sermon on faith, loyalty, and love, which it wasn't, which it was, but it wasn't really—" Brian was cut off by Vonnie.

"Don't tell him. He'll want to listen to it himself on the church's website."

"You're right. I think Chad would appreciate that," Brian responded.

"It was a very interesting sermon. As a pastor, I know that if anyone in the congregation can remember one of my sermons after a couple of weeks, it was worth preaching. Your father's sermon is still being talked about. I was asked by some of the members if I had heard it, so I listened to it. Very compelling," Pastor Lange explained.

"What's the church's website?" Chad asked.

"Oh, easy. It's on the back of the bulletin," Raphael directed. "I had been asked to preach at the Atterberry Church several months ago, but when I heard your dad's sermon, I felt he should preach instead of me. Then … well, I preached. I hope you don't mind, but I preached his sermon because I was under the conviction that others needed to hear it."

Chad and Diana were curious and intrigued by the fact that there was a recording that they could listen to. Chad immediately thought of how emotional he might become when he heard his dad's voice. Inwardly, they both wanted to get back to Chad's home and listen to it. However, the friendship of the church was so pure and comfortable. They all liked them as much as they loved Chad's parents. It was another half hour before they left, filing out of the fellowship hall surrounded by Brian and Cynthia, Vonnie and Raphael.

XXXXX

They drove into the garage and parked. It was like a couple coming home. The similarity did not escape either of them, but neither said anything to the other. They had talked every moment of the trip away from the church. They compared observations and related their expectations to what they observed. The overall opinion was favorable. The church people were friendly and not pushy. The four friends, their age, created an impression that compelled them to want to associate on a social basis. Diana's aversion was breaking down. Chad's curiosity was jumping beyond a ten if that were possible. They both wanted to jump on the computer and listen to Mr. Johnson's sermon. They stopped in the kitchen and pulled a couple of Cokes out of the refrigerator.

"Did you notice that they only had water for a drink option?" Diana commented.

"Yes, I guess it's healthier that way," he responded. "It seems like they have a reason for everything they do."

"Purposeful or obsessive, what do you think?" she asked.

"Maybe both. Some might have good reasons, others it could be obsessive. Are they all super health-conscious? There wasn't a single meat entrée, and some of the items were labeled vegan. Perhaps, they are making sure that vegetarians are catered to. I'm guessing a majority are at least vegetarians. Maybe we should have asked them about that," Chad commented as he got up and moved away from the kitchen. "I want to change into some more comfortable clothes."

"Me too. Do you have an old pair of pants I might be able to use?"

"I do."

"Continuing on the conversation about their health practices, we had enough to question them about as it was. I will say that it seems a total commitment on many levels. I have to compliment them about that," she finished.

Chad opened his chest-of-drawers and pulled out some new polo slacks. He had a shirt out of his closet on a hanger that he presented. Diana nodded at the combination. She would wear the shirttails out to cover the empty belt loops. She looked around for a place to change, and he said, "Here, use my bathroom." He finished before she did, and he moved out to the living room, threading a belt into his pants.

The doorbell rang, and he went to see who it was. It was Reverend Bill Tucker. "Reverend Tucker, thank you for coming over." Chad opened the door wide and let him in. Diana was laying her dress over one end of the sofa arm. Chad finished buckling his belt.

"Hello, friends, I wanted to visit you and see how you are doing. I came earlier and saw Diana's car, but no one answered the door. I figured you needed some alone time. So I went and had lunch and came back. Diana, I want to thank you for your personal attention to Chad at this terrible time of grief."

Diana was seething at the reference the pastor made about them spending alone time. She knew what he meant and wanted to set him straight. Before she opened her mouth, Chad spoke, "You didn't need to get lunch; I have plenty of food here. Only you didn't know when we would get back home, I suppose. We just got home about twenty minutes ago."

The pastor's eyes went immediately to the dress on the sofa; looked at Diana and exhaled, "So, how are you doing?" Diana, still steaming, said nothing. Chad came to the rescue, "Diana has been a great spiritual support, supporting me as I questioned spiritual things. She's a great spiritual, I mean Christian friend. Won't you take a seat?"

"Thanks, ah, I can't think of a more horrible cross to bear than to grieve over parents who were murdered. As I understand, there are still no answers and always a bunch of questions in these cases. I'll pray for you."

"Thank you," Chad spoke to the floor.

"I thought of you this morning. There was more bad news today. An earthquake in Oklahoma caused extensive damage, and the ruptured oil lines caught fire and started a massive fire that is burning refineries and area buildings and homes. The death count is rising."

"Why are you telling me this?" he asked.

"Yeah, why are you telling him this? It's not appropriate," Diana interrupted her silence.

"I didn't mean to be inappropriate. I just felt concern for you. I know that when one experiences loss, additional loss can launch an increase in the burden even if that trauma is far away but brought near on TV."

"Still—"

"I came because I wanted to help you with your grief response."

"What happens when you get overburdened with grief?" Chad then looked to Diana and continued, "I really want to know. I couldn't watch the news about the East Coast earthquake and tidal wave. It made me sick, ah, sad sick. That sounds stupid. What I mean is, I identified with every survivor, and I felt a strong sadness settling in, a depression. So I exercised to get out of it."

"See! He's handling it just fine." She stopped short of saying, *he doesn't need your help*. She could see there might be some help for the man she loved.

"He might be. Exercise may be a good way to avoid depression. Another way to deal with grief is to come to church. God heals all our wounds. If you worship God in the right way and on the Lord's Day, He will heal you."

"What are you preaching on tomorrow? Chad asked.

"Oh, I haven't completely decided yet. I was thinking that I might show what the governments of this world are doing to get God to bless us again. Very promising. Normally, I would probably preach out of the lectionary, but this news is so sudden. All Christians need to know about this. The more I think and talk about it, I guess I will preach on it."

"Tell us what you are going to say," Diana spoke.

"Oh, I think I'll hold out until tomorrow. You'll have to come and hear what I have to say," he said with a wink. "Chad, I do have a personal request I wanted to make with this visit."

"What request would that be?"

"Your father was a great help to me and to the church with his knowledge of finances. He spoke of your training and internship. So, I was wondering if you would be able to give us some advice. I don't know how long you plan on staying in the area, but we could use you this Tuesday evening."

"Oh, well, I'll do what I can. I'm not sure if I will be able to help."

"Thank you, Chad, I knew I could count on you. Well, I must get going. See you guys tomorrow."

They bid Reverend Tucker farewell at the door and watched him go to his car. Then they closed the door. Diana slumped against the door jamb and gave off an exasperated look. "Thank you for defending my honor."

"He couldn't've come at a more awkward moment. He saw me putting on my belt and you laying your dress over there. He definitely saw stuff that made it look like we, ah. You know what I mean."

"I suppose, but he didn't have to say what he did. He assumed. Anyway, you stuck up for me whether he believed it or not, which for me earned you beaucoup points, thanks. And, to change the subject, as the Rev asked, have you decided when you're going back?"

"I guess I have to make a decision. I don't need to go back to support myself. If I went back, it would be to learn more and build my résumé. It all boils down to what I want to achieve in my life. I have to decide what's most important in my life."

"Whatever you decide, I guess I will understand. But, I would prefer you stayed here where I can do this." Diana wrapped her arms around his neck and planted a kiss square on his mouth. Chad didn't resist.

XXXXX

The glossy photos were a little blurry owing to the fact that they were reproductions off the video camera at the gas station. The lens hadn't been cleaned in years. Finally, one of the cards had been used, and the camera caught the individual standing near the pump, looking at his cell phone. Unfortunately, a bike on a bike rack obscured the license plate. There was one moment where the young man looked up, and the face was clear for one second. That was all that was needed to capture a likeness. Hardine compared the picture with the driver's license database and checked against registered sedans of the same make and model as in the video. He had a match, and the photos were sitting on the front seat as he drove to the residence to interview the lead.

"I knew there was something fishy! A two-hundred-dollar card for one hundred and eighty dollars. The guy said he needed cash, and I needed to get rid of my cash because of the transition to digital money. It was all so surreal!"

"You bought just the one card?" the detective asked.

"Yes, I would have bought more, but I didn't have enough cash for the second one."

"I'm going to have to confiscate that card as evidence."

"Why? I haven't spent the whole two hundred. Will I get the card back?" the young man retorted.

"I'm afraid not. It's stolen property."

"I paid good money for that."

"As you said, you knew something was fishy. It certainly was, and it is connected with a double murder. I expect you will tell me everything you know to avoid becoming a suspect."

"Ah, yes. What do you want to know?"

"Can you give a sketch artist a description of the fellow who sold you the card?"

"Yeah, sure."

"Tell me where you encountered this person."

"In the mall."

"Would you be willing to go to the mall with me and point him out?"

"I guess so. Would I be able to get my money back?"

"Probably not."

XXXXX

The laptop sat on the coffee table with the screen tilted upward for good viewing for the couple who sat on the couch. They were as close as they could be without occupying the same space. Diana held Chad's right hand with both of her hands. She knew this would be emotional for him because she felt her own heartstrings plucked with a master's touch. The sight and sound of Chad's father crashed down upon both viewers. The opening words were lost in favor of a rush of nostalgia. There he was, talking to his son like nothing had taken him away. The same bass intonation, the same turn of a phrase, Mr. Johnson's sermon sounded like a man of authority with his characteristic booming voice. He spoke to the congregation and also to the camera.

When the video went in for a close-up, Chad could hold it no longer. He broke with a rush of anguish. Diana had to hit pause.

Later, when control was mastered, they went back to the video. Chad watched through moist eyes as his father introduced himself and told of his profession. Then he talked about making financial plans for retirement where treasures are laid up for later. Then he transitioned to a spiritual application. He quoted a passage from a devotional book titled, *That I May Know Him* (page 257), "The riches of the grace of Christ must be kept before the mind. Treasure up the lessons that His love provides… The trial of your faith is more precious than gold."[8] Then, he applied the quote to the main points to his sermon, faith, loyalty, and love (FLL, the answer to his obscure sermon title). He made the point that real financial planning starts with the soul. The treasures of the soul are faith, loyalty, and love. Your trial of *Faith* is more precious than gold. Your *Loyalty* is to Jesus, who has all the riches of grace, and your *Love* is for the Father who created you, who provides for you, and who gave you life. And, because He gave you life, He can give it back to you when you go and are in your grave. That is because you are loyal to Him."

Chad nodded his head in agreement. "He's right, of course. It's a blessing to know I will see them again when he and mom will be resurrected." The gripping of hands intensified. As they listened, the words flowed into their hearts. It probably was the dearest and best sermon they had ever heard. Any resistance to God's message was gone. They wanted to believe every spoken word.

Daniel Johnson made his points about faith, loyalty, and love. "We need to trust, have faith in God in the coming perilous time. Our faith will be rewarded by His almighty hand. Our trust in Him is like pure gold. Our spiritual financial stock in heaven doubles and triples as we demonstrate our faith." Chad had to smile at his father's application of banking and investing to high finance. He had to smile at his own thought reference to 'high' finance. It was, indeed, very *high* finance. Chad listened as his father merged his talking point about the results of our faith, loyalty, and love.

"Faith can be a real trial; for example, I have to trust Jesus to lead my son back to God in time. My wife and I pray that he will be convicted of the nearness of God's kingdom and the principles that will be at stake at the end. We have to trust God that He will bring issues before him that

---

[8]White, *That I May Know Him* (Washington, D.C., 1964) p. 257.

will lead him back. I think many of you can relate with me on how difficult it is to trust Him and His will when it comes to our children."

"Because of the Scripture text, 'Lay up treasure in heaven,' we tend to think that we have to put something up there ahead of time. We don't. All the treasure is already there. By *faith,* we grasp it ahead of time. Our *loyalty* acknowledges His Creator-Lordship, which means we exist in His universe in all its perfection. That is a treasure to come. Our *love* is what we have for Him because He loves us and prepares the gifts He promises us. So, laying up treasure in heaven really means laying hold of the promise of His benevolence. It is so simple. You can remember it with this mnemonic, **FLL**.

"Are there any catches to this wonderful promise? No. Everything is plainly laid out in Scripture. If there is a catch, Satan put it there. He obscured some detail, which then looks like a catch to people just beginning to understand. Like me. I thought Adventists were putting in a catch by saying we had to keep the Saturday Sabbath. To be honest, I thought this was a satanic device. Then, as I read Scripture, I found many New Testament references to God's commandments. In the book of Revelation, the people of God are described as 'those who keep the commandments of God and have the testimony of Jesus.' And then I found the commandments of God are referenced throughout the New Testament, such as Second Peter chapter three, and Matthew 5:17, 1 Corinthians 7:19, John 14:15. All of these are just examples of the many passages in the New Testament mentioning the commandments of God, and these that I have cited are all from different biblical authors. The Sabbath is a loyalty issue, yet if you think of it, it requires faith to keep it and love to enjoy it. God wants to meet us every Sabbath to give us a blessing, as indicated in Genesis 2:3, and He wants to meet with us throughout eternity. Salvation is nothing more than a restoration of a Creator/Created love relationship. Because of sin, we have little in the way of experience as to how wonderful that relationship is. We need to trust God, i.e., have faith in God. His plan for our happiness is far beyond our comprehension. I can't wait."

Chad thought of how different his father's sermon was from so many others that he had heard over the years. Usually, a preacher will progress through his points, one after another. But, his father was blending them together into an essay of the Christian life. It was simple and profound. He prayed as he listened to the remainder of the sermon, praying for help from the Holy Spirit to guide him into the truth and unite him to the

Savior. This was different from many Christians; approaches to theology. They tend to follow 'confirmation bias,' the practice of looking for texts, or portions of texts that support their preconceived opinion. Chad was open to what the Scripture said, letting it speak within its context. He remembered part of the quote his father had underlined in the book under his Bible, "One reason why many theologians have no clearer understanding of God's word is, they close their eyes to truths which they do not wish to practice."[9] His folks had changed because of what they discovered. He now wanted to study to know for himself. Before he knew it, the sermon concluded. He would listen to it again and again.

He turned to Diana, who still had moisture in her eyes. "That was good. It was simple and good. Not some flashy oratory, but from the heart. I liked it," Diana pronounced.

"I did too. In all the years growing up, I never heard him preach a sermon. Then, here it is, a sermon for me to hear after he is gone. This is not a coincidence."

"No, it wasn't. I think it was just for me. God was speaking to me," she answered.

"To us."

A quiet pause occupied the room as they sat together, thinking. "So, what are you going to do?" she asked.

"I am going to follow God with all my heart and mind. And mind means study," he responded simply.

"Me too."

The couple bowed in silent prayer. Each knew what the other was doing. They were committing their lives to God anew. They held hands, gently squeezing for mutual confirmation of the felt presence of the Holy Spirit. Daniel Johnson would receive a precious moment of gratitude later in heaven.

Time collapsed as they reveled in joy at their newfound revival to a real Savior. Spiritual appetites could not be sated. They studied with relish and were surprised when they had to turn on lights as night had fallen. Finally, they had to recognize they needed to go to their respective residences.

"Monday, I need to do some work on my research. I have to interview some volunteers coming into the office where I am allowed to do my study. I'll have to do some preparation tomorrow after church rather than us getting together. Is that okay?" Diana explained.

[9]White, *The Great Controversy* (Mountain View, CA, 1911) p. 599

"Oh, please don't feel you have to explain. I think you have been more than helpful to me, and I have probably taken up too much of your time. Although what just happened was timeless."

"Indeed," she smiled in reply.

They kissed by her car before she slipped into the driver seat. It was another long passionate kiss; their second with meaning.

XXXXX

Reverend Tucker sat on the dais as the liturgies were completed. Diana sat on the right side, about halfway down from the foyer. She was alone. Reverend Tucker was in the middle of composing his after-service remark to her about Chad's absence when Chad showed up in the back of the sanctuary. It was a relief. If Chad started attending, then the former status quo could return. If they married, an affluent couple could once again be relied upon to help carry the church forward. Some of his pastoral concerns were relieved. He could concentrate on his sermon.

It turned out to be a short treatise on the plans announced at the Rio conference with no Scripture and no references to the last-day events mentioned in the Bible. The reverend's homily was a list of the resolutions. *First*, the conference of churches said that all agreed that the world's natural disasters can be curtailed by God's almighty hand. *Second*, all agreed that God can stop the madness of terrorism and rampant violence in the streets through a united world government. *Third*, the world's moral and social ills can be diminished by God's people coming together to worship God on common ground and on a common day. And *last*, God would reward this practice with protection from natural calamities. The conclusion of the conference was that everyone has a baseline of mutual interdependence that boils down to surviving this planet's disasters and its uncontrolled hoards. God is the only source that can control both.

Reverend Tucker spent time with each of these resolutions, explaining their simple beauty and the ability to bring this world back to its Christian values. He put in plain words that because most everyone recognizes that Sunday is the Lord's Day, it, therefore, must be the correct day of worship. And this majority is confirmed in their practice of observance by Christ's resurrection on Sunday. He predicted that Sunday observance would bring about a new, stronger moral united society, and God would reward His believers with the blessing of fewer and maybe no more natural disasters. His excitement bubbled over when he spoke of the conference's support from world leadership to support and enact legislation to keep the Sunday Sabbath. He said, "The world is finally turning its face toward God." He then became even more excited about the news that peace-loving Muslims were joining the world church on the commonality they hold together with the Roman Catholic church on Mary, the mother of God. They are also willing to go along with the Sunday ordinance to create peace in the world. "These peace-loving Muslims stand in stark contrast with radical Muslims that are creating so much trouble and violence, sometimes, violence for violence's sake alone. They usually follow a Friday day of worship, but for the sake of a better world, they plan on keeping both days for worship, Friday and Sunday. It symbolizes their desire to cooperate with this international endeavor to clean up this world so prosperity can come back."

As an afterthought, the reverend added some more good news. "In addressing the crisis of world hunger, the Conference announced that the Catholic organization, the Knights of Malta, will be in charge of equitable distribution of provisions for the world population. The Knights of Malta are a large operation that has been standing ready for this day. Resources of ships, planes, trains, and trucks are promised from practically every industrial nation to carry the foodstuffs to the people in need. This is the beginning of turning our world around for good."

Chad was alarmed by the treatise. He could see the fulfillment of prophecy and the closing scenes of earth's history. He whispered in Diana's ear, "This confirms what I have been studying." She nodded in return. "I'm going to study more of this when I get home. I read something about this, and I'm going to find the quotes," he added.

"I have to prepare for tomorrow's interviews. Do you mind if we wait and compare notes on your study?" she whispered in return.

"Does this mean our lunch together is out?"

"No, I just need a couple of good hours to get ready."

"Okay, so where do you want to eat?"

XXXXX

Over hors d'oeuvres Chad broke the news he knew Diana would appreciate. "I'm staying."

"What? Really? Oh, Chad!" Diana wrapped her arms around her beau. "This is great news. I love you! When did you decide?"

"I guess I decided last night after I watched my father's sermon for the third time. Here is where I can learn more about these truths and continue my parents' legacy."

"You didn't decide because of me?"

"That was the extra bonus. I want to get to know you better. Maybe I should have told you that first."

"Yes, you should have. It would have been more romantic."

"You're right; I should have. Maybe I'm a little out of practice. That reminds me, can you do me a quick favor after we eat?"

"Sure, what is it?"

"I would like you to come with me to my parents' grave. It would be easier if you were there. It won't be more than a couple of minutes."

"I'd be happy to do that with you."

XXXXX

Chad had a small bouquet of flowers he had acquired before coming to church that morning. He carried them as the couple walked to the grave. He bent and set the flowers crossways over his mother's grave and spoke, "These are for you, Mom. I know Dad didn't go for flowers too much, but he would appreciate the fact that I gave them to you." Diana cooed at his words. He continued.

"Dad, Mom, if the Adventists are correct, then you won't be able to hear this until the resurrection, but I'm going to say it anyway. Your prayers are being answered. I am coming back to God. Maybe you didn't understand how I thought the church wasn't relevant to me. Now, I am beginning to see its relevance. The church is supposed to get us ready for the end of time. Your deaths, I mean your murders, made me want to find out why you would change churches. That is why I started studying, but now I am studying for myself. I have found a purpose in knowing, and in knowing well enough to tell others like you did in your sermon. I only wish you could see me now, and for me to join with you in telling others. Thanks to you, the both of you, and your sermon, Dad; I think I'm on the right track.

Mom, you will be happy to know that Diana and I are dating. I just might need that dress. Who knows?

"And, Mom, you will be happy to know that Diana and I are dating. I just might need that dress. Who knows?"

Diana laid her head on his chest for the quiet pause that came afterward. She was smiling at the sentiments he expressed as they walked to the cars. Chad had a larger bouquet of roses for her. Her hopes from way back in years past were on the cusp of becoming true.

"What did you mean about that dress?"

"It's a story I'll tell you later when we have more time."

XXXXX

Chad contemplated Romans 7:7–12 and spoke aloud to himself, "God is holy, just, and good, but here it says the law is holy, just, and good. Paul speaks of how the law makes him die, so how can the law be good? Unless ... hmmm. Of course, 'the wages of sin is death,'[10] so the law teaches us what sin is. As the teacher of what sin is ... we are led to the solution, which is Jesus' death for us. The law is based on God's character. God wrote the law with His own finger ... I get it! The law and God are synonymous. No wonder the law is holy, just, and good. Huh!"

Chad felt relieved as he sorted out this conundrum. Again, he was reminded of the quote where people 'have no clearer understanding of God's word ...' because ... 'they close their eyes to truths which they do not wish to practice.' He was also reminded of the practice of Confirmation Bias, people searching for texts to try and confirm their bias, or, more accurately, their prejudice against keeping the law of God, God's ten-commandment law.

With that settled, he moved on to find the text he remembered reading before. The one provoked by Rev. Tucker's homily. He Googled, "commerce in Bible," to see what that would yield. He found one site that had sixty-six verses listed. He was pretty sure he had read it in the book of Revelation. So he went to that verse immediately when he spotted it among the sixty-six. Revelation 18 spoke of the merchants weeping and mourning because no one purchased their cargo anymore when Babylon, the harlot, had fallen. He knew from Revelation 13 that the symbol of the beast was a religious organization formed to control people in their worship. And that they would also control redistribution of wealth, making it

---

[10]Rom. 6:23, NIV

easy to control buying and selling. No wonder the merchants were connected with the harlot that sat on the beast. What he couldn't discern was why no one bought their cargo anymore. He asked himself the question, *What does this picture represent? Is it symbolic? And, if so, what?*

This text could go both ways, he reasoned. Revelation 13 talks of religious coercion, so the cargo would have to be religious cargo or doctrines. Then in Revelation 18, the cargo is listed specifically in commodities. *Could it be both?* he asked. *It could.* Either way, at the culmination of history, when Jesus comes, Babylon falls, and all commerce ends. Then he compared what he was reading with what he had heard that morning. The Knights of Malta would take over world commerce in an effort to provide even distribution of commodities, food primarily.

He had to assume that what he was hearing was fulfillment of biblical prophecy. Near the first of Chapter 18, was a call to come out of that coalition of religious organizations. He saw that heaven was sending out a warning. In the homily of the morning, there was definite purpose in forming a group for religious leadership with the desire to keep a day of worship other than the one established at Creation. His conclusions drove him to prayer.

"Father, God, hallowed is Your name. I can see Your kingdom is coming soon, and Satan is exercising his power to corner the market in his false rule of faith. Please forgive me for not seeing this earlier and for not studying this earlier. Help me to be a part of Your true people, the ones who keep Your commandments and have the testimony of Jesus. I am Yours. I will seek to do your will in all things. In Jesus' name, amen."

CHAPTER 7

Diana was struck by the number of stories she was hearing. In social work one always heard tales of abuse and unruly children. However, this was a wake-up call. What fellow workers were saying around the proverbial water fountain amounted to catastrophic in the domestic realm. Social work services were overloaded with first occurrence incidents. Workers were complaining before the start of a busy day. It was as if they were trying to top each other with a greater horrendous story.

"Children are turning on their parents for silly stuff, really. Yesterday, this kid wanted ice cream. His mom said they didn't have any, that they had to go to the store. This six-year-old kid attacked his mother with a kitchen knife. She received some cuts on her hands and arms before she could corral him, and then she beat on him excessively; liked to kill him if the husband hadn't knocked her out with a breadboard. They all lost it. It was as if they were at war," a middle-aged man related.

Another related, "There were these two boys I had a consult with that had no concept of harm or death. They are seven and nine, and for fun, they shoot each other with BB guns. The older one told me about talking to evil spirits in his bedroom, who have glowing red eyes, and his pet dog can see them and greets them like friends. Then, there was this incident where the boys got into their father's gun cabinet and started shooting at cars and pedestrians in front of their house."

"I heard about that on the news," an associate cut in.

"That's right; it was on the news. Well, when I talked to the older one, he acted as if there wasn't a problem because all people come back to life. The spirits told him so."

"I heard kinda the same thing," a young first-year interjected hesitantly. "Twin girls were stabbing pet cats with pointed combs. One of the cats was killed, and they waited for it to come back to life so they could continue stabbing it. When it didn't come back, they attacked each other. When I asked them why they did that, they said the visitors told them—'visitors with red eyes.'"

"I've heard some paranormal stuff—"

"Hey, turn on the TV. We've got another disaster on our hands, some earthquakes, and maybe volcanoes." The conversational group suddenly became quiet as they focused on the plasma screen hanging on the break-room wall. The picture that came into focus was in the middle of a report showing snow, which was really ash, falling obliquely across the screen. A reporter was explaining that a 6,000-year-dormant volcano suddenly rumbled to life and then blew a small cap, sending ash into the sky. The report was interrupted by another news flash. A verbal report spoke over the visual display of snowy ash saying,

ZZZZZ

"Our affiliate in Klamath Falls is telling us that Crater Lake is smoking and Wizard Island in the middle of the old crater has disappeared. Videos are coming in, and we are switching to Angela Nash at the scene. Angela?"

"This is a surprise to everyone here at the National Park Headquarters. An earthquake caused Wizard Island to submerge. Crater Lake has heated up. Temperature readings are off the chart ... excuse me."

ZZZZZ

A park ranger came into the picture his arms spread wide as if he was herding people away. With urgency, he told the reporter to announce quickly to everyone in the vicinity to evacuate the park immediately. His words weren't totally clear over the microphone. The reporter rebutted by saying,

ZZZZZ

"We just got here!"

"You and everyone in the park are in danger. We must evacuate now!"
[He turned and spoke into her microphone.]

"You heard it here, folks, we are evacuating. This is a very dangerous situation. Everyone hearing this broadcast, if you are in this park, get out, the situation is unstable. Evacuate now!"

ZZZZZ

The cameraman remained on scene as the reporter started to move away from the front of the Sinnott Memorial Observation Station. The pre-dawn sky, slightly luminous, lent no help in showing the roily water of Crater Lake and the absence of the iconic Wizard Island. A close-up of a green uniform with patches blocked the camera as a ranger tried to move the cameraman. The picture juddered about and ended pointing into the dark void of the crater as it moved away. Suddenly there was an orange glow beneath the waters in the form of cracks like lightning bolts. The illumination below accented the boiling, bubbly surface of the lake. Steam jets shot geysers skyward. Three seconds later, an explosion erupted in searing hot light and expanded outward in all directions, including directly toward the camera. Hot globular shards of lava emanated like pyrotechnics away from an epicenter assaulting every square foot of the landscape. Screams were the last thing heard as the picture winked off.

Anchor personnel were visibly in a state of shock. Out of character they sat speechless in various postures, four humans in body shock, distress written on stooped shoulders, hands to temples, and eyes staring at imaginary scenes. The senior national anchor for CNN news cleared his throat.

ZZZZZ

"Our hearts and prayers go out to the people at Crater Lake. Ah, we are now receiving multiple reports of breaking news from the international and national desks. We are trying to sort out what we must cover first. Our producer says we should direct the viewers to our international correspondent, Roland Conkel. Roland, what do you have for us?"

"*The Ring of Fire is lighting up all along the Pacific Rim. We don't have videos, but we do have phone contacts with Japan, Mexico, and the Philippines. Just a minute … I am told we just have received confirmation from the Aleutian Islands. But, wait, now … an earthquake, ah, Mt Fuji has erupted. Will take you there first by phone. Jack?*"

"*Yes, I hear you. I hope you can hear me. Mt Fuji started spewing ash and smoke about an hour ago. Now it has lit up with blobs of magma being thrown out in all directions. There is no large lava flow as yet, but some are suggesting that that is only a matter of time. The size of the magma release is indicative of much more to come. I am hearing that the western half of the U.S. is also coming to life with smoke and some ash. Roland, assumptions are that the tectonic plates are shifting, allowing for the release of gases and super-hot magma to move up old volcanic tubes. We felt earth tremors off and on for hours before reports came in on Mt. Fuji.*"

"*Jack, pardon me for cutting in, but wouldn't that mean that earthquakes are causing the volcanic activity?*"

"*Yes, of course. Some of the rumbling we have heard and felt might have been Mt Fuji coming to life. I asked Sachi Herakowa, an expert volcanologist, to be on this interview, but she is too busy estimating the magnitude of this eruption and its risk to the local population. I wish you could see this eruption; it seems to be growing every minute. Just this moment, the east face started flowing with magma. From this distance it appears to be moving at a fast pace, which means it is probably faster close up.*"

"*Jack, thank you for your report. We have another story coming out of Mexico. It seems Paricutin has blown a portion of its cone away. An eyewitness is on the phone. Hello, you're on the air.*"

"*Hola, am I on?*"

"*Yes, you are on the air. Could we have your name?*"

"*Man, we are seeing a volcano going up in the sky. The sky is cloudy with black dust, man. See, we saw a whole half of the mountain shoot off thataway. Big explosion, like a boom craaash! And then—*"

"*It seems we have lost the connection with the eyewitness who phoned our affiliate. We don't seem to have a reporter on the scene. Paricutin was a recently active volcano in the middle of Mexico. It sure seems to us here in CNN headquarters that the Pacific Rim is becoming active with earthquakes and eruptions all along the fault line around the Pacific. Our science specialist, Merlyn Shorr, has a map to show us what's happening. Merlyn?*"

"*Roland, here is a map of the Pacific. We have a purple line showing the Ring of Fire that stretches up the west coast of the Americas, South, Central,*

*and North. And, after reaching the Aleutians, it curves down along the east-
ern shores of Asia down into the South Pacific. So far, we are aware of these
volcanoes that are erupting right now. They are marked in red on our map.
Mt. Saint Helens, Mt. Rainer, and Crater Lake that was formed when Mt.
Mazama erupted millenia ago here in the mainland of the United States.
And, then up in the Aleutians, there is Pavlof. Then, down in Japan is Fuji,
and then in the Philippines is Mt. Pinatubo. Now, with the news of Paricutin,
we can see a crescent up and down the edges of the Pacific Ocean. This is very
significant. It means that the north Pacific Tectonic plate is shifting."*

*"Thank you, Merlyn. We now have some more to add to this catastrophe.
Mount Baker at the northern border of Washington State is shooting ejecta
into forests that are catching fire. We have reports of forest fires in the Mount
Baker-Snoqualmie National Forest, and it is feared that fires are spreading
northeast into British Columbia."*

ZZZZZ

Diana could not remove her attention from the plasma monitor. That was
true despite the fact that she was being paged from the front desk. Some
of her research subjects were waiting for her at the entrance. The totality of events in the natural world, coupled with the pastor's words last
Saturday about the 'earth wearing out like a garment,' convinced her that
prophecies were being fulfilled. Deep in thought she had to be aroused by
another, saying, "They're calling you at the front desk."

"Oh, they are? Thank you." Diana went to the front desk to greet her
study subjects. She wondered if this interview would also include strange
and violent behaviors like the others had related.

XXXXX

Reverse 911 calls came through on all phones at the same moment. A
cacophony of ring tones, buzzers, and musical scores came from every
cubicle and office door. A perfectly inflected computer-generated voice
called for everyone to turn on TVs or listen to the president of the United
States on their phones.

Vonnie jumped at the initial noise of all the devices. She turned to her
cell phone and then decided in favor of watching the video of President
Crenshaw on the wall TV in the break room. Her inner voice asked, *What
next?* This was the second time that day she had gone to the break room to

watch unfolding news stories. This time she stood behind her boss, Mrs. Greene. It was difficult to see the screen from where she stood because the room was crowded.

ZZZZZ

"Ladies and gentlemen, the President of the United States of America."

"Americans, one and all, my brothers and sisters, we are in the midst of unbelievable circumstances, circumstances that seem to be beyond our control. If you have been watching the newscasts, you will know of what is happening on the West Coast. Before that, not too long ago, the East Coast was hit with a disaster. Food productivity is declining. Our natural resources are disappearing. Crime is rampant. And, domestic unrest is ruining our homes and schools. This cannot continue. Many feel there is no remedy. However, there is hope.

"The world is suffering from many disasters of natural and human origins, for example, calamities by sea and land, huge forest fires (like the one raging from Washington State into neighboring British Columbia at the present), hurricanes spawning hailstorms, floods and tornadoes, earthquakes with massive tidal waves or volcanoes or both. The world community suffers as much or more than we do. Yet, there is a spark of optimism upon the horizon.

> **The World Coalition of Faith, the WCF, has come up with a proposal to bring an end to all this chaos. God can and has demonstrated He can fix this broken world. We must get back to basics.**

"I come to you today with a solution. Not a pie-in-the-sky dream idea, but a real solution, tried and proven. The World Coalition of Faith, the WCF, has come up with a proposal to bring an end to all this chaos. God can and has demonstrated He can fix this broken world. We must get back to basics.

"As I speak to you now, other world leaders are communicating with their people about this answer. I am pleased to tell you I have been able to persuade them to follow the WCF's recommendation. We are resolved to work together. The WCF has proposed that as the world starts worshipping God on His day of holy worship, our problems of crime and natural disasters will come to an end. Italy has tried this. One year ago, Italy required Sunday worship; 95 percent of the country's

population agreed by keeping Sunday holy. Records of attendance were kept, and non-compliants were urged to help the nation with incentives. The results were phenomenal. Italy has had in the recent past more than 300 earthquakes per year with painful destruction of property and dreadful cost of human life. That stopped. Crop failures ceased. Crime dropped to very low levels and is still dropping. Their economy revived. Tourism returned.

"This was not on the news. Why? Because when there are no earthquakes, no disasters, no droughts, there is nothing to report. Quietly, Italy has had a resurgence of its fortunes, and they owe it to their commitment to God. It is time we apply their success on a global level. If an entire country can turn the tide, we should take note. The WCF has called for unity in the faith. I am calling for a unity of faith. We all can benefit from compliance with these rulings.

"I call for solidarity with brothers and sisters around the world. We can title this the 'Great Endeavor.' Think of the simple beauty of this concept, all of us coming together on Sunday in fellowship, learning from the Word, and demonstrating to God above our unity with Him. He would be more than pleased with us and would honor our prayers. His Almighty Hand would be on our side. Also, by worshipping together, the social morals of our society will improve.

"All last night, I huddled with Congress, both sides of the aisle. We are agreed; this is no time for partisan politics. With our disastrous circumstances, we have to be, must be, one voice, one body, one nation, one world to affect global change. And, I must add, one faith!"

ZZZZZ

Vonnie put her head down in prayer. This was it. As she prayed silently to herself to be prepared for the trials of the end, she heard the room erupt in applause. It interrupted her concentration. Without hearing what President Crenshaw had said, she could see there was agreement with the elements of the proclamation. She turned to exit the break room and return to her desk. Two steps out of the room, her elbow was touched. She turned to see who had touched her.

"Miss Hixon, I thought of you when the president was talking just now."

"Mrs. Greene, ah, hello. Why did you think of me?" she asked out of curiosity.

"Because you don't go to church on Sunday."

"No, I don't."

"What are you going to do?"

"I will follow my conscience, which is guided by my belief in the Bible."

"But don't you want to help our country? I mean the world?"

"I must do what God asks of me to do."

"I hear you," she said as she walked back toward her office. Vonnie watched her go, wondering at the meaning behind her words.

XXXXX

A light shone through the window of one of the basement windows where the teens held Sunday School. It was obvious to Chad that the finance meeting was being held down there. He locked the car with a chirp of the key remote and went to the side door. This would be an interesting evening. His knowledge of finance could be used, and he wondered if the committee would listen to any suggestions he might have. He resigned himself to the possibility that they might not understand what he had to say.

"Oh, good, Mr. Johnson is here. We can start early," the treasurer said. Committee members shifted in their seats and faced the pastor. Not one said hello or shook his hand. He found a seat near the end opposite from the pastor. An agenda was written on an ancient blackboard. The reverend started with a prayer, and they jumped to the minutes from the last meeting. A few clarifications were made, and then the treasurer's report was handed out. The dismal story of a church hanging on by its fingernails assaulted Chad's sensibilities. No regular business could stay above the drain in this condition. He had a few suggestions, like using the church's tax exemption number on common purchases and budgeting utilities rather than getting hit with big bills in the winter. He couldn't believe that the church hadn't moved to the use of card readers in the church services. Money in the form of cash was all but obsolete. He tried as gently as he could to persuade them to move with the times. Their response, "But we can't afford them. We need to pay our bills first."

The end of the treasurer's report came to the conclusion that if they paid just the essential bills that month, they would be short by over $600. When that point was made, everyone on the committee made eye contact with Chad. It made him uncomfortable.

The next agenda item dealt with the insurance premium. They had to hope that the offerings would revive in time to cover the six-month premium when it came due next month. Pastor Tucker said he would make an appeal in next Sunday's sermon. "I'll ask if anyone would like to pay the premium as their gift to the Lord," he promised. Again, every eye around the table went to Chad. The history of his parents' relationship with the church and the expectation they had about his role in their membership became abundantly clear.

"I think I can help," Chad said. As one, they smiled. He reached into his pocket and drew out the gold piece. "I inherited this coin from my folks. It's pure gold worth about $1,400 or $1,500. If you cash it in the right place, you should get full value. It will make up for the shortfall, pay the insurance premium, and have some left over for some portable card readers. My folks have bailed you out." He wanted to add the word "again," but chose not to. Instead, he rose and tossed the coin on the table. Everyone's eyes went straight to the coin. Three hands reached for it simultaneously. Chad left the church.

XXXXX

Chad's habit of keeping the TV news off to avoid dismal accounts about multitudes of people dying changed. He now had the news on continually because almost every news event was a fulfillment of prophecy. The president's speech confirmed a number of predictions. Today, he listened only casually while he worked on paying bills and transferring accounts into his own name. Outside, the landscaping crew worked on grass-mowing, tree-trimming, and weed-spraying. They had asked him what he wanted. This was new; a change in his status as head of household. On a lunch break, he washed dishes as another duty of the head of household.

A dripping plate hovered halfway to the dishwasher. The shocking news this time was criminal. Automatic weapon noise filled the air as amateur videographers tried to capture the scene while ducking for safety. Screaming dominated the audio. Chad couldn't tell what or where the video was coming from. He stood, dreading the next catastrophe.

An amateur video shook up and down as the person holding it ran for protection. Underneath the picture an information band appeared, indicating the network and the planned report about Jeremy Richards' court decision. As quickly as it appeared, it changed to "Breaking news." Richards and his lawyer were about to give a statement, but before they could set up the news conference, shots were fired. Everything went chaotic, and only this video was available. Then the picture changed to a reporter talking from behind a panel truck.

ZZZZZ

This was an assassination. Automatic weapons opened fire before a news conference could begin. Everything here is a mess. I think the Richards were killed. People and police are everywhere. Ambulances and medical teams are racing up the steps. The shots were fired from over there, I think. It is difficult to know for sure; the echoes were coming off of the buildings there and over there. O, this is awful. Who would want to hurt these people? They're gentle, just … why? They are not crimin … Oh, my! I can see blood running down the steps.

ZZZZZ

Chad couldn't move. This was different from other newscasts he had witnessed before. This hurt. Why? Before, he sympathized with victims of disasters and terrorist acts. Sometimes, he even prayed for them, but this was in small measure like what he experienced with his folks. He could recognize grief easier. This wasn't as massive as what he endured. It was similar. Why? Diana might understand, so he called her.

She was working at her desk, compiling interview material. She answered her cell phone on the first ring. "Chad, honey, I'm glad you called me. I need a break."

"I'm not sure this will be a nice break."

"Why do you say that?"

"Because I think I'm grieving for someone I've never met."

"Ahm, Chad, you've had a traumatic event most people don't experience in a lifetime. You are very sensitive to loss. Do you know what I mean?"

"Yes, you know I have had trouble watching tragedies because of the loss of life, but this is different. It hurts."

"What happened to bring this up now?"

"The Richards have most probably been assassinated. It's on the news now."

"What? The Richards, Jeremy Richards, the Adventist who is suing for his retirement?"

"Yes, them."

"Both of them? Even his wife?"

"Yes. I think so."

Diana went silent for a while and then started to talk quietly. "I see what you mean. It's affecting me in the same way." There was a small pause. "Chad, grief has a lot to do with proximity and identity with the deceased. Proximity has to do with nearness, and identity is about who you are, how you see yourself. A neighbor who dies is nearby. A death of a parent is both. The death of a policeman, for example, is about identity. Other policemen can identify with that individual. Chad, I am grieving for this couple because I have been drawn into their story and because of getting to know their church identity. I think you might be grieving for them for the same reason."

"Yes, you're right; that is why I am struck by this loss. Why would anyone want to kill these people? They are not a threat to anyone."

"It doesn't make sense. It's like maybe a hate crime against who they are if that is possible," she guessed.

"I don't know. I guess it could be prejudice. This shouldn't happen to people who live by a principle. They're better than 99 percent of the rest of the world, like my folks. Very sad."

"Chad, stay there. I'm coming over."

XXXXX

Brian and Cynthia were listening, with their paid volunteers, to Pastor Lange talk about priorities for their ministry in the E-Center. "We are in a unique situation. There may not be enough time to do traditional evangelism. Because of that fact, I take the counsel from the predictions for the end of time. We have to streamline our dialogues to dealing with the primary issues of the very end of time. First is the knowledge of the saving grace of Jesus. This is primary above all else. In Matthew 24 it says, "And this gospel of the kingdom shall be preached throughout the whole world ... and then the end will come."[11] Everyone needs to know there is nothing better than Jesus. Second, is living the life of Jesus Christ, perfect in Him. This leads to the issue of keeping the fundamentals of God's character, His love and holiness. That means keeping the commandments, which is our third issue, which includes the most contradicted of the ten, the Saturday Sabbath. Then lastly, we have to spell out the predictions of the end. We have to warn people of what's happening and tell them to avoid the trap Satan is setting for the world. We are told the world needs to know the issues before the end can come. As I understand it, in our blogs and chats we have to be concise; use Bible

---

[11](vs. 14)

texts and short statements of truth. I suggest that when you use a Bible verse, instead of citing chapter and verse, give them book and chapter. It will make them search, and therefore, read the context. Before you hit send, check your theol—"

"Oh, no! Everybody, something terrible has happened! Look! The Richards have been murdered!" a student exclaimed, pointing to her computer screen. The group clustered around the monitor. This time, the report of the assassination had a more coherent progression. The settlement became a feature and was proffered as a possible motive. Millions of dollars were to be awarded to the Richards. Protestors were flooding the scene with handmade signs made before the murder. They were swung about. "No $ for Sluggards," "Get a Job Not a Lawyer," and "Keep the Lord's Day." The small group could only shake their heads in response. Pastor Lange called for prayer. One teen led out immediately; others followed. They prayed for the Richards' family and for themselves as they neared the great conflict between good and evil that lay before them. Silently standing together, they found they were holding hands and sensing the presence of the Holy Spirit. This was their moment of understanding. They were going to finish the work. The Holy Spirit would attend their efforts. They sang, "Sweet Spirit" and prayed some more. Kneeling came naturally. They were being rewarded from heaven with God's presence; knighted for their commitment to the King. It was a while before they felt the need to move to their work stations. Being anointed for a purpose drove them to cleanse their hearts of any possible lingering sin.

XXXXX

Conflicted, Brian and Cynthia returned to their apartment to lead in the Bible study. They wanted to be in two places at the same time. For them, Bible study, like food, couldn't be missed, especially when it came to soul winning. However, the activity at the E-Center was hopping with possibilities. There were so many chats and conversations going on that it tore at their nature to leave for a meaningful time with friends in study. They had less than a half-hour to get ready for their guests.

Vonnie arrived first, asking if they had seen the news. That conversation increased when several more came in the door. Pastor Lange arrived, and the assembly went again over the horror and asked the pastor what it meant. Diana came in with a tentative knock, and Chad followed. Nobody sat down. Faces demonstrated concern and compassion for the victims and their families. When "their families," was mentioned, Vonnie said, "That includes us. We're part of their church family." A sobering thought which led to an introspective moment. Both Chad and Diana felt the identification with the Richards and with this alarmed company. In their afternoon together, they had gone over the pangs of the identity grief they were experiencing. Chad could see his emotional coupling with his folks and other loss of human life. The silenced friends were ready for prayer.

Pastor led off first. His prayer echoed the sentiments at the E-Center that afternoon. He called upon God to sustain His people in perilous times. He even prayed that those who carried out this violence would reverse their opinions and find salvation with Jesus. While he prayed, Chad and Diana were surprised by this concern for the salvation of hateful murderers. It was difficult to swallow for Chad, as he did not want the perpetrators of his parents' murder to gain entrance into the kingdom of heaven. The thought

It was difficult to swallow for Chad, as he did not want the perpetrators of his parents' murder to gain entrance into the kingdom of heaven.

wrestled with his conscience. He had reached a testing point. God pulled upon his newly acquired commitment. Diana peeked at Chad to see how he handled the thought. She could see his furrowed brow, wondering how he would process this. After a battle, he relented and yielded to the providence of God. He rested in his changed opinion, albeit with a slight regret. He asked God to help him and forgive him for his reticence. He sought Diana's hand.

Group prayer followed naturally, several joining in at various times. Raphael's humble prayer reflected sentiments at the E-Center. Again, the Spirit moved. A permeating feeling of warmth animated the words, tones, and inflections of their voices. The presence of God made a bond between the individuals better than the hands that were finding each other just like they did at the Center. Moments later, they knelt in reverent supplication. For some, this moment carried over from the rich aura that animated them earlier that day. For the new initiates, like Chad and Diana, this overwhelmed their senses. They reveled in the feeling of a rich nearness to the Holy Spirit. They couldn't explain it; they could only feel it. No one wanted to stop praying. They enjoyed communicating with a very real Deity. Without discomfort they knelt for almost a half an hour. A Bible study was being replaced by a Spirit study, a lesson taught by senses other than the normal five. Tears of happiness trickled down cheeks.

Enthusiasm for the Lord's work bubbled over into the discussion after the prayers ended. They compared notes on what had happened and what had happened at the center. Pastor Lange told them that the Spirit attends those who are performing God's will and will attend them in a larger measure at the end of time. Chad asked how the Center was developing because of the outpouring of the Holy Spirit. In answering, Brian explained that they were deluged with opportunities for dialogue. Entering into chat rooms afforded chances to talk directly with people who normally would shy away from personal face-to-face debatable topics. The anonymity of the net encourages people to be more open. Brian hastened to tell them that the reaction to the murder of the Richards had opinions all over the spectrum. "The bigotry exhibited is extraordinary! Some are saying they deserved to be killed. Another said that the Richards are throwbacks to the Old Testament. Several called them prejudiced because of their views on gays."

"And then, when we answer them with Scripture, others join the discussion," Cynthia added.

"That's what we're looking for, dialogue on the issues," Brian averred.

"In my conversations I noticed that many of the hardliners didn't want to continue the discussion after several more moderates entered the chat room," Pastor Lange explained.

"The more, the merrier, I guess," Brian added.

"The 'more' means a wider net. I'm sure some of the participants in my group were overseas. That's what we want, right? Get our message out to the world," Cynthia said.

"There's an additional way to get the message out," Chad put in. Everyone looked at him. "Look, what you are doing is raising awareness, and that's good. But, if you really want to reach the world, you have to use the 'seven degrees of separation' principle."

"What's that?"

"It's the principle that there are only seven people between you and everyone else in the world. You have friends who have friends who have friends. Statistical studies have confirmed this several times. My suggestion is this; if you can get people talking and sharing with everyone they know, it can theoretically get to everyone. And, with the Holy Spirit helping us, we just might reach the world." Diana heard the 'us' loud and clear. She agreed. The total experience of studying Scripture, seeing fulfillments, and feeling an attending Holy Spirit carried with it conviction, very strong conviction. Her quiet demeanor yielded a broad smile and a subtle nod of affirmation.

"Chad, that is fantastic!" Vonnie exclaimed. "We coax them to share what they have heard with their friends and relatives, following the multiplication principle of relationships."

"I agree," The quiet Raphael spoke up.

"I'm really encouraged by what's happening here," the pastor remarked. "We need to pray for God's help every step of the way. When we do something great for God, Satan always attacks. We need to keep a strong connection with the Lord."

On the way out of the apartment, Chad talked with his best friend, "That was wonderful."

"It was, I agree. I've never experienced that before. It wasn't a whooping and hollering type of meeting. It was fellowship with God, I mean with the Holy Spirit."

"Yeah, like I said, wonderful. I think I'm going down to the E-Center tomorrow afternoon. Want to come?"

"I will, but I've got to catch up on my data collection. When I get more done, I'll come with you."

"Okay." Chad kissed her before she slipped into her car and watched as she drove away.

CHAPTER 8

S itting in his father's study still felt like he was entering an inner sanctum where he should be invited. He read the Scriptures focusing on New Testament prophecies from Paul's and Peter's letters. The Bible study last evening confirmed his understanding of the closeness of the second coming. He wanted to nail down more of what was predicted. He read again the words in 2 Peter, "You should remember the predictions of the holy prophets and the commandment of the Lord and Savior through your apostles."[12] Then later, he read, "But the day of the Lord will come like a thief, and then the heavens will pass away with a roar …" (vs. 10). Already the heavens were on fire out west. Then he kept going back and forth from the two pages. It was intriguing to him how many times in the New Testament the word commandment (or its plural form commandments) were a part of the discussion. It was important to note what his father had said about many Christians wanting a Savior but not a Lord, especially when the earth seems to be falling apart. Having a Lord means loyalty and obedience. The president's speech rang in his ears as the prediction that the false Sabbath became an issue because of the recent natural calamities. Another sound rang in his ears.

---

[12](2 Peter 3:2, ESV)

The phone rang next to his elbow, startling him back to this time and place where the heavens were quiet. *A phone call at this early hour?* he questioned himself. Then he noticed the time, seven a.m.

"Hello?"

"Chad? This is Diana's mother. I don't mean to be rude, but is Diana there?"

"No, Mrs. Cross, is she on her way here?"

"Ah, well, this is awkward. Diana didn't come home last night, and I, well, I assumed. I shouldn't have, but Diana adores you, she always has. I assumed she might have stayed with you last n ... I apologize I shouldn't have made the assumption. But now, I don't know where she is."

Mrs. Cross, the last time I saw her was last night after the Bible study. We drove away in separate cars. I'd say about nine, maybe?"

"Where could she be?"

"Did you try to call her?"

"Yes, many times. The phone goes immediately to voice mail. I'm really worried now. It's not like her to stay out all night."

"Don't be worried. I'm sure there is some logical explanation. I'll check it out. I'll retrace her route from the Kings' apartment to your house. Maybe she had an accident or something. I'll call as soon as I find something."

"Thank you. If she shows up here, I'll call you."

Chad was worried. This was out of place. Diana would always answer her phone. He tried to reach her but got the same response. She must have had an accident and was in a hospital, or something. He jumped into the car and went to Brian and Cynthia King's apartment. He ran to the door. Out of breath, he waited for an answer to his ring.

Without a greeting, he asked, "Do you know where Diana might be? Did she say anything to you? Did she come back here to ask more questions?"

"Chad, what's the matter? Come in. Tell us what's happening." Brian invited Chad in by taking him by the arm and gently leading him to the couch. "What's going on?"

"Diana didn't get home last night. Her mother is worried. Did she come back here to ask more questions?"

Brian and Cynthia asked the same questions Chad asked Mrs. Cross with the same results. They both instantly leaped into action. Brian said, "What can we do?"

"I don't know. I was going to retrace her route to home. Oh, I know, can you check the hospitals?"

"Okay, we'll do it. We'll let you know what we find."

Chad wasted no time rushing out the door and hurtling down the steps three at a time. From the parking lot, he drove the route she would most probably take to her home. Every street, he cased with eyes isolated on the color blue. He then remonstrated himself and opened his search to include broken glass. He looked for glass on the street and in intersections, the telltale indication of an accident. Any blue car or reflective sparkles were his signposts for Diana. As he drove, intellect and emotion spoke to each other. He knew he was attracted to her, but now he could feel the desperation of love. Potential loss pushed his mind to a conclusion. He recognized his protectorship, an atavistic urge. If she were lying in a hospital bed somewhere, comatose, or worse, she needed to know that he reciprocated her love. He had to tell her.

The closer he got to her apartment, the more concerned he became, if that were possible. He cruised through a green light and then screeched to a stop. Was his mind playing tricks on him? He had to go back. Turning a volte-face, he went back to find her car down a side street. Pulling in behind, he saw minor damage to the rear, which spoke of a fender bender. There appeared to be no serious damage that could result in hospitalization. He was relieved and mystified simultaneously. He found something, but what?

There underneath his hand was a brochure exactly the same as the one found atop his father's body. He froze, his mind toggling between despair and horror.

Approaching the car carefully, he peered first in the left side back window. Nothing was on the back seat. He wondered why he bothered to look there first. Looking in the driver's window, he saw her Bible sitting on the passenger's seat. Her phone was in the cupholder. Without hesitation he opened the door to reach for the phone. There underneath his hand was a brochure exactly the same as the one found atop his father's body. He froze, his mind toggling between despair and horror.

"No! Not my Diana!" He didn't want to believe his eyes. He didn't want to be awake. He wanted it to be a nightmare. He reached for the leaflet and stopped. This was a crime scene. He called Detective Hardine immediately.

XXXXX

"Are these cards all that you have left from your purchase through cash-cards.com?" asked Hardine.

"Yes, sir."

"All of these will be analyzed by the lab boys. We may get lucky. After this is all done, you'll get back the cards that are not involved in crimes."

"How long will that take?"

"I don't know, forever? This will teach you to not get involved in stolen goods." He had zero tolerance for those who helped criminals knowingly or unknowingly.

"How am I supposed to know what's stolen or–"

Hardine's phone rang. "Excuse me. Hello? This is Detective Hardine."

"Detective Hardine, this is Chad Johnson. I need you to see something quick."

"I'm in the middle of somethin'—"

"My girlfriend, Diana, has disappeared, and I found her car. Her phone is here, but she's not here. Get this—one of those leaflets, like you said was on my father, is lying on the front seat. I thought—"

"Don't touch anything. I'll be right there. Gimme your location."

XXXXX

Chad pushed the red phone icon to close the communication after giving the detective the cross streets where he was standing. He stood there as if the air was as heavy as solid lead. He was a man of action with nothing to do. He backed up toward his car and looked at her car with the dents on the back. He looked at it and got yet another ghastly thought: *is Diana in the trunk*? He hesitated to look. But because it was something he could do, he went to the front to pop the trunk. It loosened and then caught. He had to pull on the edge to spring it away from the bent rim. It indicated that it hadn't been opened, a moment of deliverance from his misery. Looking in, he found nothing of note. He closed the lid almost to the latching point. He stood there, staring at the back of her car. A vile taste of anger entered his mouth. A similar emotion to the one he endured with his folks swept into his thinking. Awful sentiments were taking charge of his mind; idleness breeds alarming applications. He had to control this rush downward by getting practical. He had to focus on finding her. He gazed at her car, trying to visualize the incident in the same way he stared at his parents' front door. A minor accident that tapped her rear end, her red turn signal light broken, these were his first observations. He knew that the broken glass had to be near where the collision occurred. He went back around the corner and scanned every inch. There it was; a ruby sparkle in the grassy verge. He bent over to pick it up and again remembered not to touch anything. He left it.

Slowly walking back, he gazed at the car, saw it, and wondered why he didn't see it before—a pattern to the dents, double H's. What had hit Diana was a vehicle with a brush grill used in off-road peregrinations. He knew the whole scenario. Diana had been taken alive for some reason. There was a chance to save her if he could find her … in time.

He heard the tires screech as they came around a corner several blocks away. Detective Hardine was not wasting any time. He rolled up and jumped out, leaving the door open. "Mr. Johnson, show me what you found."

"Well, this is Diana's car. It was rear-ended up there." He pointed to the spot around the corner. "Then Diana and whoever hit her car pulled around to here. And then she was abducted."

"What makes you think she was abducted?"

"She's nowhere to be found. Her mother doesn't know where she could be. Friends are checking out hospitals. Here, look inside. Her phone and Bible are here. And the brochure. See?"

Detective Hardine took in the scene, looking closely at the brochure and the keys still in the ignition. Pointing at them, he mumbled, "Why would she leave those in the ignition?" He whipped out his phone to call in forensics and another unit to secure the scene. Chad's phone rang while he watched. It was Brian.

"Chad, we've been checking, and we found one hospital with a Jane Doe admitted. I'm driving there now to see if it's Diana. Cynthia is checking some other hospitals and some urgent care centers. Have you found anything?"

"I found her car. It has been in a minor accident."

"A minor accident? That doesn't sound like something that would send someone to a hospital. What do you think?"

"No, it doesn't. I'm worried. Ah, please know that I'm thankful for what you're doing, but I don't know if she went to a hospital, I'm thinking it was an abduction."

"An abduction! No way, man! Can't be!"

"I know. I'm hoping it isn't, but what else could it be? Her phone is here, and the detective found her keys in the ignition."

"Should I still go to the hospital?"

"It might be good to rule that out for sure. Again, thanks for doing that."

"No need to thank me. I'm as concerned as you. I want to know, too."

When Chad ended the call, he looked at Hardine, who was gazing back at him. "Mr. Johnson, you did good calling me. This is very suspicious. How do you know the accident occurred around the corner?"

"There's a piece of her taillight in the grass up there." Without answering, the detective started walking in that direction. "Also, sir, she was hit with a vehicle with a special grill. The kind of grill that off-roaders use when bushwhacking." That stopped Hardine in his tracks, looking back at her car.

"What?"

"If you look at the back, you can see a pattern to the dents. It looks like a brush grill."

"You're right. Have you ever thought of being a detective?"

"No, not at all." Chad thought of how this had come about. None of this should be happening. The world shouldn't be unraveling like a broken strand on a knitted sweater. Being a detective never entered his mind because he had always thought of carving a niche in society. Now, all he wanted was to find Diana, and then find a way to get through the problems facing believers in this chaotic period of history.

A forensics truck pulled up to the scene at the same time as a police cruiser. They went to work, cordoning off the area and setting up police tape. The area included the entire corner back to and beyond where the flake of taillight lay on the ground. Little numbered cones were placed, and cameras recorded every nuance of the crime. Evidence bags were in abundance, but very few were used. A tow truck arrived to take her car to the forensics lot but had to wait as fingerprints were taken. Chad explained that his prints would be on the outside door handle and on the trunk. They took his prints to rule him out of anything they would find. Then the tow truck started to back into place, but Hardine had a thought and stopped everything. He instructed the police cruiser to pull in behind Diana's car. He directed it to the point of touching the back bumper. Chad watched and then reacted to the truth before him. The traffic grill on the front of the cruiser matched. "Detective, does that mean a policeman abducted Diana?"

"No, not necessarily. It means we can't rule it out."

"Are police grills the same as civilian brush guards?"

"Could be, and then again, maybe not. It all depends on the contract in effect when new cruisers come in. Brush grills are used on cruisers to remove vehicles from traffic or for interrupting a chase." Hardine instructed the cruiser to back up and signaled the tow truck to move in. He turned to Chad, "I'm going to track down brush grills on traffic cameras in the area. I've got hours of work, and I've got to get started. I'll call you when I find anything. About what time would she have been here at this intersection?"

"I think about nine-twenty, give or take a few."

"Thanks." He left, leaving Chad standing on the curb. It seemed highly contradictory to have been at such a spiritual high at nine o'clock and have evil stalk twenty minutes later. He knew who he needed to call—Mrs. Cross.

XXXXX

A dull ache dominated her thoughts as she tried to clear her vision. Distinct details refused to form, only light and lumps. She wanted to rub her eyes to make them comply with her wishes. It was then the memory of her wearing contacts entered her mind. The contacts were coated with film from being in her eyes far too long. They needed to be cleaned. Her first inclination was to chastise herself for going to bed with them in. Then, reality dawned. *Where was she?* The question forced itself upon her aching brain. Diana groaned. The sound stabbed with sharp pain. A foul odor affixed itself to the discomfort. Her consternation grew with each added sense. Her hands were on the floor, and the stickiness of the floor gave her tactile revulsion. Movement in front of her told her that her encumbered vision came from some other source. Her mind clouded with an unknown drug gave her double lines to each hazy form. Two eyes, in a pattern of four, were not more than a foot away. Somebody looked at her.

"Shhhhh. Don't move. If they see you moving, they'll give you another injection. You need to be awake." A finger moved ever-so-slowly to the person's lips to emphasize her point. The whisper Diana heard had to be feminine in origin. She needed to see, to understand, to put it all together. Her mind couldn't help her; neither could her eyes.

Taking stock, her body spoke to her. An ache in her shoulder told her of a bump with an object. As she concentrated, it felt more like it had collided with something hard. Colliding reminded her of a collision or an accident, and then she remembered her fender bender with ... what? She couldn't fully remember.

XXXXX

Chad couldn't be more discouraged. Mrs. Cross was understandably distraught. He tried to reassure her that the police were looking into every possibility. He told her that he had been praying and that she should too. Nothing seemed to comfort her. The thought crossed his mind that he should go over to her apartment but thought better of it. Instead, he suggested she call a friend to come and sit with her. She agreed. He said a short prayer with her before they closed the conversation. He paced the living room, wishing he could do something.

Pastor Lange came directly to Chad's home. Instead of a greeting, Chad found himself enveloped in a compassionate hug. "We have to pray!" he spoke softly into his ear. They went straight to the couch and bowed in prayer. Pastor Lange prayed first for Diana's safety and then about Chad's worry, asking that he be given the confidence that Diana was safe in God's plans. He then used a rather confident tone that called for God's intervention. There wasn't a caveat, "if it be Your will." He prayed with the assurance of God rescuing Diana soon. The pastor's cell vibrated while he prayed, and he shut it off to continue. He thanked God for the outpouring of the Holy Spirit and its help putting the message out to the world. He put finding Diana in the same category as performing His will with the Spirit and the Holy Spirit rescuing Diana. After Pastor's prayer, Chad prayed and then needed to know why he was so sure that God could find Diana.

"Chad, I can't explain it. I always pray, understanding that God has a better plan than I can ever think of. Just now, the words came out differently than I normally pray. Sensing the Spirit everywhere and feeling Him close has changed my attitude. I'm willing to trust the Spirit as I talk and write. My impression is this: Diana has recently encountered some new important truths. In that sense she is just getting started in the truth God wants her to learn. I think He is more than willing (if that be possible) to have her continue, study, and search the Scriptures; therefore, I am confident He still has a purpose for her to perform. Like I say, I can't explain it. It happens wonderfully."

"Why do you think she has a purpose to perform?"

"Sometimes, you can tell what God wants you to do by seeing the gifts the Holy Spirit has given to you. Both you and Diana have spiritual gifts. Diana has a gift for reading people's spirit, their moods. It is her purpose. I have seen it in her as she relates to you and helps you in your grief."

Chad wanted to explain that it was because she was in love with him, but felt it might be in poor form to disagree. Having a God-given purpose raised his curiosity for Diana and himself. It struck at the very foundation of his concern about relevance. "What's my gift, providing money for church projects?" his cynicism showing in the middle of his worry.

"I saw your gifts last night."

"You did?"

"The gifts I see in you are listed in I Corinthians 12—wisdom and knowledge. You took some facts from the statistical world and applied them to our desire to reach the world. Your knowledge applied in a completely different subject is wisdom, two of the spiritual gifts listed. It makes you important to God and the need to reach the world. Everyone has the gift of giving money to the church. Spiritual gifts like yours and Diana's are for equipping the people of the church to perform ministry."

"So, you're confident that Diana can be found because she has a gift God needs."

"Absolutely. I'm trying to explain a feeling for why I prayed in a way I didn't expect. I'm confident He will protect her."

"I hope you're right. I don't want to lose her."

"Keep praying and be positive. God is on our side. I will pray, and so will all your friends."

XXXXX

Concentrating on videos rolling at high speed can give one a severe headache, especially if you have been at it for hours. Detective Hardine rubbed his temples in minute circles watching for brush grills on vehicles in intersections.

"Detective! What's going on?"

"Captain, you surprised me!" He stood out of respect.

"What's going on? Are you taking cases without permission?"

"No, sir. I'm working on another wrinkle of the same case."

"Explain."

"In the Johnson murder, the unsubs left a religious brochure. Last night, there was an abduction, and the same brochure was left in the victim's car. One is linked to the other."

"Okay, you have a legit excuse. But! Keep me informed. I don't want any surprises. Oh, and tell me why you were checking every squad car in the motor pool?"

"Because whoever hit the victim's car had a front grill that matches our police cruiser grills."

"Did you find anything?"

"No, all our cruisers were washed per usual."

"Per usual, that's good. I mean, the motor pool is following procedure, that's good. But, for solving the case, that's not good. Keep me up to date. Got it?"

"Yes, sir."

XXXXX

"Chad Johnson, I just heard. Terrible, just terrible. I don't know what to say. Mrs. Cross called me after she talked with you."

"Hello, Reverend Tucker, thank you for calling."

"I activated the prayer chain of the church. That should help, I think. You know, I hate to say this but, the first forty-eight hours are crucial. They ship their victims away as soon as they can to get away from the scene of the crime. They don't want to get caught red-handed."

"That's not very comforting."

"Oh, I'm sorry. I guess I was saying how important it is to get as many praying as soon as possible. God moves when the many call. I'll start calling the ones on my section of the prayer chain right now. Please call me if you hear anything. Gotta go."

XXXXX

"If they come in, they'll check to see if you're awake. They'll kick you, don't react. I've seen it. They'll push you around, and if you do anything, they'll give you another hypo. Don't fight back 'cause they'll beat you up, then give an injection."

"Wha'?" Diana asked at the same time as she lifted her hand from the gummy floor, wondering what made it sticky.

"Can't talk much. They might hear."

"But ..."

"I know, I know, it's all too much to take in."

"How, how much, I mean, long have you been ... here?" She rubbed her fingers together to ascertain the consistency. It felt like honey and smelled like desiccated mice.

"I think two days, maybe more. I got several injections 'afore I wised up."

Diana pieced the information together, realizing she had been abducted and now lay on a dirty floor in some isolated hovel. Panic started to overtake her questioning fog. *Where could she be? Why was she taken? What was the purpose for why she was hidden and abused?* She wrestled to sit up. Blinking to clear her vision helped. A murky window became her focus. It looked like someone had thrown vomit against the glass. Despite her revulsion, she planned to break the glass and get out. Stumbling to her feet, it became clear that the window was larger and much further away and at least twenty feet higher than her head. Her shoulder ached. Her hair was mired in muck from the floor. Her slacks and jacket were slick on one side from the effluvia she had slept upon. One shoe was missing,

If they come in, they'll check to see if you're awake. They'll kick you, don't react. I've seen it. They'll push you around, and if you do anything, they'll give you another hypo. Don't fight back 'cause they'll beat you up, then give an injection.

which caused her to stand on a slant. She threw her head from side to side, seeking an exit. Desperation assaulted her thoughts, causing her to gather air to scream. She stifled the reaction in time when she looked at the person that had spoken to her before. There were six other bodies lying on the floor. The one nearest had her finger to her lips while weeping quietly, pleading silently. At this moment, it became clear that the individual asking her to "play dead," as it were, asked out of desperation to protect herself from more suffering. One other body rolled over enough for the individual in a dress to make eye contact. Diana saw misery. Her fellow prisoner had ugly red and purple swollen lumps on her legs. If she had seen this person in a photo or in an emergency room, her empathy would flow out in swells of compassion. In this circumstance she saw a fellow victim.

"Please, lay down. Don't let them know you're up. Please."

Her instructor sounded miserable, not the least confident. The miasma started to become stark reality. She had to get out. Even though the room had a high ceiling and perhaps enough room for a typical church, the walls were closing inward. She wasn't claustrophobic; she was bereft of control. She couldn't predict where or when or even how she could exist in the next second or minute. There wasn't a place to go, no place to sit, and she certainly would not go back on the nasty, gummy, creepy floor. She neither couldn't nor wouldn't.

Six bodies shuddered in fear as footsteps fell near a sliding metal door. Diana tottered and almost fell in her attempt to turn to the misunderstood threat. Three huge figures burst through the widening aperture. A fist slammed her to the unwanted floor, and pain shot from her jaw to her brain. The absurd blessing of being knocked out kept her from feeling agony, both physical and emotional.

XXXXX

Chad wandered from room to room, praying and chastising himself for not driving or following Diana home. He tried to rationalize with himself that he couldn't have known, but that didn't change his conviction that he could have done more to keep her safe. A stray thought bothered him. He didn't have a photograph of Diana. Beating himself with grief and survivor guilt, he now added the fact that he didn't have so much as a selfie to remind him of his new-found love. Absurd, irrational thoughts and emotions kept him from relaxing and trusting in the Lord. His prayers for Diana seemed circular. He went from calling for God's intervention, to asking Him to bring the criminals to justice, to begging for Diana's safety, to asking again for God to do something, anything.

When the phone rang, a feeling of hope entered. *Could this be good news?* he wondered.

"Chad, this is Pastor Lange. Are you okay?"

"Well, not really. I thought this call would be from the detective."

"I'm sorry. I don't have any good news, but I thought you might want to be kept in the loop about what's happening.

"What's happening?"

"This is not good news. A young woman from our church in Beaver Crossing has gone missing. Then, at our academy, a teacher's aide and a student were on their way home after an evening concert. They never got home. It seems like there is a coordinated effort to kidnap young SDA females. It's a hate crime on our young women."

"Oh, no. This is terrible. Did anyone see the abductions?"

"I don't think so. The way we got the news was the girls never made it home. The pastor from Beaver Crossing called me because of members calling for prayer. We pieced together the picture of this dreadful behavior. I can't imagine what these girls are going through. Our church leadership is in anguish over this. All we can do is pray."

Chad wanted to act. He could see that solving one of these crimes would unravel all of them. One clue from one instance could lead to the solution for Diana's rescue. He jumped into action. "Pastor, where is your academy located?" He went on to gather information on the car color and the addresses of the student and the aide. He grabbed his jacket in a rush out of the door to the garage, knocking two other coats to the floor. He pushed the speed limit to get to the school. His plan was to repeat what he had done to find Diana's car with one addition; he called Detective Hardine on his way. His prayers included the phrase, "Help me to find something that will find Diana!"

Hardine, savvy enough to see the connection, responded immediately and met Chad at the school grounds. They plotted out possible routes to the younger girl's home and began their search. Less than a mile away, they found the young teacher's car. It was the only plausible route to begin traveling home, and Chad had followed the unmarked police car. Two couples, obviously parents, were standing next to it, making phone calls, 911 calls to the police. The detective showed his badge and started to secure the scene. The same brochure was in the hands of one of the parents. Detective Hardine produced an evidence bag and had it safeguarded, even though he knew that it had been touched at least once and maybe several times by the parents. After backing the family members away, he made good on his promise to keep his boss informed.

Chad introduced himself and explained his reason for calling the detective into this crime. Learning of his relationship to this similar crime horrified the parents. The two women were at the point of hysteria. A conspiracy contrived upon their daughters dumped more concern on them than they could bear. Husbands comforted them while unsuccessfully stifling their own emotions. One woman had to sit down, rather fall upon the grassy verge. Their grief renewed his. What exacerbated his grief was the absence of any new evidence. Everything seemed to be identical; the dents on the rear of the car, the keys in the ignition, personal phones left behind, and no purses.

Detective Hardine's expression changed as he listened to his captain. It was as if he had really stepped in it and now received a remonstration. He looked at his phone as if it was an infectious disease. His involvement in collecting information from the scene changed to the general behavior of securing the area and waiting for support. What observers didn't know was that his captain was en route.

XXXXX

Vonnie could not work, so she prayed. Having received the news about Diana and the other abductions, her heart throbbed with agony to the point that other considerations of everyday life evaporated. This escalation worked on her sensibilities. A cascade of thoughts competed to be recognized. In anticipation of the final conflict, she didn't recon on people she knew to be hurt or tortured. She couldn't know how she would act if she had been snatched away, but she would rather it was her than them. Another thought asked if she was ready for what lay ahead. Yet another pressed on her responsibility to witness. Was there enough time was a question that competed for attention as well. Then she thought of the text, "The prayer of a righteous man has great power in its effects."[13] She hoped she was righteous enough to pray with effect. Then she remembered a quote from Oswald Chambers, "Prayer does not equip you for greater works. Prayer is the greater work." She knelt next to her work desk, performing the greater work.

A sound at her work station caused her to look up. She saw Mrs. Greene standing there, wondering if she should come back, having intruded on a sacred moment. "Please excuse my interrupting you. I didn't know you were praying."

"That's okay. I can always call upon the Lord. He understands. How can I help you?" she stood, wiping a tear from her eye.

"Is everything okay? You're crying."

"No, I just got word that several girls I know have been kidnapped."

"Kidnapped! That's terrible! How old are they? Are they young? How did you know them?"

"They're from my church, my age. Actually, they are from three different SDA churches."

"What!? How can that be? All from your denomination? Maybe ..."

"The only thing I can think of is a hate crime. You know, like what happened with Mr. and Mrs. Richards."

"I hate to bring you bad news, but the reason I came to you is because of what I heard on the news about the Richards' murder. Ah, and it has

---

[13]James 5:16, RSV

something to do with their church, I mean, your church. It sounded serious, and I thought I'd talk to you. I can come back at another time. I think you might need some time alone."

"No, that's okay, let me help if I can." Vonnie really didn't want to hear any more bad news. She desperately needed to spend time with her Savior to restore her confidence that God is in control and will protect her. Mrs. Greene was her boss, so she felt obligated.

"The news is talking about polls that the network made about the Richards. They're saying that Seventh-day Adventists are intolerant of gays and female ministers. Is that true?"

"I have been an SDA all my life, and I haven't seen intolerance for anyone. I think where the misunderstanding comes from is our stand on Bible truth. For example, the Ten Commandments say it is wrong to murder, yet we have active ministries in prisons, bringing murderers into a loving relationship with Jesus. The Commandments tell us not to steal, and we follow Jesus' example on the cross who told the thief next to Him that He would see him in heaven. It is the principle of 'hate the sin and love the sinner.'"

"However, the news reports say that SDAs don't ordain women or gays. Is that not a fact?"

"That is true, but what the press doesn't understand is that doesn't mean intolerance. We still love our gay friends, but we can't endorse gays as ministers because the Bible identifies the gay lifestyle as sinful. We love prostitutes but not their occupation. Same concept."

"Okay, but what about women ministers? The Bible isn't against women."

"No, it isn't. Ordaining women has been our desire for decades. We are a world church with thirteen divisions of the church organization covering every country. We follow a democratic process of voting changes. At every world conference, the subject is on the agenda. There is only one division, the North American Division, which is calling for women to be ordained. The rest of the world divisions have majorities with a more patriarchal stance. So, we have adopted a compromise of commissioning women, which is just a different word for exactly the same thing. Commissioning means they have all the privileges as an ordained man. The rest of the world accepts that compromise. One interesting fact about SDAs is that one of our founders was a woman. She was a minister in every way."

"The media is saying there is a sizable slice of the public that believes that SDAs are bigots, and that is why some are taking the law into their own hands. Judging by what you told me, the kidnappings are coming from those prejudicial attitudes. Maybe it's time for you to avoid the spotlight."

XXXXX

Chad didn't expect the hug he got from Diana's mother. It was more like clinging. It lasted a few uncomfortable moments before she stepped back, and he could see the tears running down her face. He had come over personally to tell her what he had learned. He didn't want to repeat the same feeling of helplessness of being at an impersonal distance over a phone call. After a minute of composure, Mrs. Cross introduced him to her good friend Rose, who had a box of Kleenex in her lap.

"Chad, have you heard anything?"

"Not much. Detective Hardine is on the case, as I told you before. He has been checking video records of the intersections near where her car was found."

"Rose, Chad found Diana's car and called Detective Hardine because he knew him because of his folks' … hmm … death. This detective is supposed to be good at his job," she explained to her friend, adding some information that hope had been constructing in her mind. Chad didn't know if Hardine was good or bad at his job and recognized Mrs. Cross's grasping at straws. "Go ahead, Chad, you have anything to add?"

"The case has expanded to include two more kidnappings." He saw the look of fright on both of their faces. He plunged onward. "Three more young women have been taken in the same manner, a teacher's aide and a student in one car and another girl up near Beaver Crossings."

"How awful! What's the connection?"

"The connection is that all of them have connections with the Seventh-day Adventist Church. The teacher and student were driving home from an Adventist academy. The one in Beaver Crossings had just left a prayer meeting at the SDA church there, and Diana and I had finished an Adventist Bible study. I should have driven Diana home or at least followed her car. Then she would be here now." He spoke a little of his irrational guilt.

"Why the Adventist church? Is there something wrong with it, are they doing, you know, bad things? Are the kidnappers SDAs?"

"No, I doubt that. These, I believe, are hate crimes. They're linked to my parents' murder."

Still trying to suppress her shock, Mrs. Cross asked, "How so?"

"There was a brochure at every one of the scenes."

"What kind of a brochure?"

"A leaflet that describes some meetings they were having at the SDA church. I talked with Pastor Lange about it, and he said that they had a mass mailing and distribution to several zip codes, and the only people who came were from personally handed-out invitations. Upon checking, they found several of the zip codes never got the mailing. The brochures must have been dumped."

"Who's this Pastor Lange?" Rose asked.

"He's the pastor of the church where my folks were attending."

"His story is an unlikely story. The post office is required by law to deliver every piece of mail they receive. What is he trying to do, blame the postal service for these kidnappings?" Rose exclaimed. Chad didn't think her misplaced accusations were helping Mrs. Cross until he heard her comment.

"Chad, promise me. Please don't take Diana to that church again. It's much too dangerous. Reverend Tucker told me as much. He said they're against all Christian principles. Keep her safe when she comes home ... if she ..." she ended in a sob.

> *They don't seem to be worth the effort. I know we're supposed to solve the murder, it's our job, but some things have priority over religious turf wars. They are on the outs with trends anyway.*

He wanted to satisfy her concern and her sorrow, yet, he had a different view on these Adventists. Nothing indicated that SDAs were dangerous; everything pointed to prejudicial behavior aimed at them. He totaled up the different individuals who had denigrated these people. He thought of the comments spoken moments before. He remembered the bits of the conversation he heard from Hardine's superior at the last scene, "They don't seem to be worth the effort. I know we're supposed to solve the murder, it's our job, but some things have priority over religious turf wars. They are on the outs with trends anyway." He wondered if Hardine would remain on the case.

CHAPTER 9

S oft whimpering crept slowly into her consciousness. Then screaming pain assaulted the left side of her face. A groan emanated from
her throat. She couldn't help it. Her hand went to her face to find a
bulky swelling extending from her chin to her hairline by her ear. It ached,
throbbed, and stabbed at her face simultaneously. Another fog clouded
her vision but not from administered drugs. This time, her awareness
snapped back faster than before because of the pain. No drug prevented
her awareness from returning. It was a haze from being knocked out. She
gritted her teeth against the pain and felt the grinding of bone ends in her
jaw. She had a fractured mandible.

Having learned from the last time she was awake, she didn't stand and
didn't speak. She edged around to see the others. One young girl cradled
her lower leg and whimpered. Another held her against her chest, gently
massaging her back. They were either unaware or unconcerned about the
thugs who could be observing or ready to enter the room at any moment.
This ongoing trauma of imprisonment destroyed a sense of order and
self-determination. All signs of control over one's life disappeared, even
the simple act of taking an aspirin for the pain. She could do nothing, and
the fellow humans in the room could not help. Then the feeling of helplessness doubled in perspective with the injury. She knew of nothing that
she could do for herself, absolutely nothing. Her wish was to go back in

time to Chad and the comfort of his presence. The night before, or was it two, maybe three days before, they had knelt together in prayer, holding hands. A rush of memory reconstructed an experience of spiritual joy. It commanded her to flee in prayer as the sanctuary for her tortured status. Her emotional core reached out to Jesus in a petition, a cry of her tortured heart. He hears every request. He heard her appeal. The Holy Spirit performed the sacrament Jesus said He would carry out. He comforted Diana with His presence. Through the pain and lingering fog of the drug, her communion with God brought her to a safe place. Her pain diminished to a manageable level, which shocked her. It was a miracle. She wanted to share the experience with her fellow sufferers. She didn't know if they were Christians, but almost anyone would accept a sincere offer to pray for them.

She shuffled over to the weeping girl and her companion. "May I pray with you?" she whispered.

"Yes, please. He's our only hope."

"Yes, He is." Diana realized they were believers like her, another comforting factor. "Loving Father in heaven, we are Your children and the apple of Your eye. We know You want our best. We can call on Your power, and You will respond." Diana couldn't believe that she spoke such confident words. All her life, she had asked, "according to Your will." "Our need calls out, and we know You will answer. Because of Your loving care, we know for sure that we will walk out of here—" the reaction next to her interrupted her prayer. She opened her eyes to see and hear the loud sobs from the younger girl had increased, and her friend shook her head in the negative. An eye signal directed Diana's gaze down to the leg that she cradled. Her reaction matched the ugly mess. Two compound fractures bent the leg in unnatural directions. Empathy went out from her core to the girl who wept in total defeat. Involuntarily, her hand reached out to touch the mangled limb. The reaction to withdraw the leg came reflexively. Diana paused and then proceeded. As soon as she touched the leg, it started to stretch. In a couple of seconds, the leg returned to normal. Another second, the swelling went down, and then the next second, bruises of red, blue, and purple vanished.

Diana was surprised in a magnitude commensurate with witnessing a resurrection from a coffin. Instantly, she felt the triangulation of a miracle, the power of the Holy Spirit, the recipient of grace, and the ecstatic exuberance of being God's conduit of love. Finishing the prayer became forgotten in the moment. The teen and teacher concentrated alternatively on two points of focus, the leg and Diana's face. Absentmindedly, in her wonder of the moment, Diana put her hands to both sides of her face in a typical gesture of unbelief. Warmth emanated from her hands to her cheek, and the painful stabbing and throbbing ceased. Gratitude overwhelmed her; His power was for her too. Now the observers fixed their eyes on Diana alone. The oversized jaw became a beautiful delicate attribute to beauty once again.

Amazingly, the inert bodies in the room began to turn toward the miracles as if Diana had said, "May I have your attention?" The Holy Spirit in the sleazy room transformed it into a tabernacle of glory. None cared if they were overheard. This took precedence. God's protection thrilled them all and gave hope where none existed before.

"You have the gift of healing, that's wonderful!" the teacher exclaimed.

"It's more than wonderful; it's fantastic! God will take care of us," another remarked, then asked, "How long have you had this gift?" They all looked at Diana.

"I didn't know I had this gift. It just … just happened. I'm as surprised as you are."

"But, you prayed so confidently, saying we will walk out of here."

"It was an impression I had. Last night, or whenever, I don't know when, we prayed at the Bible study, and we experienced the Holy Spirit. I guess it gave me confidence when I prayed just now. The words just came out. I don't know your names. My name is Diana."

"Diana, my name is Karen, and I know why you prayed so confidently. In John 15:7 it says, 'If you abide in me, and my words abide in you, ask whatever you will, and it shall be done for you' (RSV). When you prayed in the Bible study, your will and His will were blended. You must have continued praying in your heart."

"I was thrilled by the experience and prayed on my way home. I couldn't stop until … when I was knocked out." That comment brought them all back to reality, a reality they still didn't control.

"What are we going to do?" Diana asked. The others grew quiet, and sadness began to creep back into their lives.

"We are going to trust in the Lord. We just saw evidence He is with us," Karen answered.

XXXXX

A notification order landed at the administration building at Andrews University by courier. The president's secretary had to sign for the envelope and brought it directly to President Hertzog for opening. It looked ominous with its law firm return address. He looked at his secretary and instantly read her facial expression to open it immediately. He did. After a quick scan, he asked,

"Do you know what this is?"

"No, but I can guess it has something to do with all these indications of the final conflict."

"You're right. It does. We are being told to open our married housing to gay couples, or we will be sued for violation of equal rights."

"So, now they're making us comply with their agenda. How much time do we—" The phone rang. "I should get that." She went to the outer office to answer the incoming call. A minute later, she came back through the door. "It's President Mackey from Oakwood."

"Hello, Jocelyn?"

"Yes, it just arrived by messenger. My thoughts exactly. Wait, no. We haven't received one of those. You got two registered letters? From different sources? Tell me what the second one is about." President Hertzog stood for about thirty seconds and then sat down. He looked like he had been fired. "What am *I* going to do? I haven't had time to think about what I'm going to do. I guess I'm going to talk to the faculty first and then the student body. Thanks, Jocelyn, and I'll be praying for you and your people there. God bless." He hung up the phone and looked at his secretary of eight years. They were friends and had compared notes on the transpiring events in the world. They knew time was ending."

"I can see that Jocelyn Mackey had some bad news."

"She did. They received a directive that because they are a Christian college, they are asked to take attendance, by name and social security number, of those who are attending church on Sunday. It seems that the IRS will give a tax credit for those who attend. Any church or church-related organization, like us, who doesn't will lose their tax-exempt status. It seems to be an extension of the old Johnson amendment of 1954."

"And now it starts. It's only a matter of time before they shut us down."

"I hear you. It's interesting. You work all your life providing quality Christian education as a calling, and then, when the Lord's coming is so near, you have to drop all your career goals and aspirations. You know what's on my desk. It's all plans and budgets for next year and the year after that. My appointment calendar is meaningless. I feel empty and elated at the same time."

"I know what you mean. The last couple of weeks, I have been wondering when I should just go home and not come back. When will my paycheck mean nothing? My husband and I are paying for the kids' tuition here at Andrews. The time is fast approaching when educating the kids is not important. All of our former priorities are gone."

"In the time we have, what are we going to do?"

"That is the question I'm going to ask the faculty, and later, I'll ask the students."

XXXXX

Seven in the morning outside his precinct, Hardine sat in his unmarked cruiser meditating on his predicament. He never gave up on a case. He always kept them on his desk until something broke, and the case was solved. This case had grown in scope from an isolated murder to mass kidnapping with the added prejudicial hate crime. This was huge, and his captain was telling him to let up and stay on the murder if anything developed that warranted his attention. Otherwise, he was to let the kidnappings go and let special crimes take over what was becoming an international sexual slavery investigation. He was told the girls were probably out of the country by now. His professionalism rebelled. The females were in jeopardy and may still be in the area. He couldn't dismiss the disturbing information that a police officer, or officers, might be involved. Why would any policeman want to violate his or her oath to serve and protect? The only answer had to be money. This presented another dilemma. In a cashless society, following the money had to be in bank and card transactions. Looking back at his train of thought, it told him he wasn't going to let it go. But, he would have to work below the captain's radar.

He got out of his vehicle and went to his desk on the second floor. He went immediately to viewing video tape on the road crossings near to all the abductions. He had a legal-sized tablet where he jotted down license plate numbers of vehicles with matching grills. He recorded on separate pages the intersections related to the kidnapping, comparing them with plates from intersections near Miss Cross's car. A folder stood at the ready to cover up his data if the captain came near his door.

His phone rang. The front desk told him he had a visitor. Chad was at the entrance, asking to meet with him. He asked the front desk to bring him up. Chad wanted to know if there had been any breaks in the case. What he really wanted to know is would Hardine continue looking. Detective Hardine could not disappoint him, even though he was under direction to leave off the kidnappings. He invited Chad into his office and told him quietly his strategy, which included trying to follow the money if nothing yielded itself in town relative to the vehicle used. The money might not show itself until much later when a person or persons unknown received a payoff. Chad didn't like hearing of plan B. It might be too late at that point. He offered to help. He offered to search from the crime scene outward to find any further evidence. Hardine saw it as futile as trying to follow tiny bread crumbs on a sandy beach. However, he set him loose, knowing it was better than sitting around the house, worrying.

Chad immediately drove to the corner and began checking every inch of ground on both sides of every road leading away from the scene.

XXXXX

"Yes, you're right, why whimper in the corner? We should stand together in dignity," a captive named Monica added.

"Like Paul and Silas in prison. We can pray and sing," Karen added.

"But, they'll just come in and kick us around like they did before. Look!" Cheryl lifted her dress above her knee to show the bruises. Dark purple blotches encompassed her legs. It was a moment before every-one looked to Diana. She felt awkward, not knowing if this was a call to heal. There was an inkling that God had prompted her to reach out and touch, but she was not sure if that inclination came from the Holy Spirit. The other two miraculous events were unplanned and totally involun-tary. Their captivity provided extenuating circumstances where the Holy Spirit could demonstrate His intervention. Diana silently asked God if this was the appropriate time. In her heart prayer, she felt compelled to pray aloud. "No matter what we decide to do, we should try to stay connected to God. Let's pray." All their heads went down in unison, yet some peeked at Cheryl's legs, "Dear Lord, we feel your Spirit among us. It gives us great comfort to know You are going to help us. You are going to help the right people to find us. We are worried about being abused and beaten. Bless us and also help these men who have hurt us to feel guilty for what they have done or at least feel reticent to continue their abuse. Protect us—" Her prayer was interrupted by the sigh that went out from the group. She peeked and saw healthy, unmarked legs. Cheryl immediately massaged her legs, not for comfort but for confirmation of what her eyes could see. "Once again, Lord, You have proved Your love and of our safekeeping. Thank You. Thank You. In Jesus' name, amen." Diana's God was creating a leader for this dispirited group. Diana would be a hero of His making.

The wonder of the moment did not escape anyone of them. Karen felt compelled to sing, "Thank You, Lord, for saving my soul. Thank You, Lord, for making me whole. Thank You, Lord, for giving to me Thy great salvation so rich and free."

"Thank you for singing that song. My sentiments exactly," Cheryl said. "Out of curiosity, I'm wondering, are you Seventh-day Adventist?"

"Why, yes. As a matter of fact, I am. Are you?"

"I am."

"Me too."

"And me."

"And me." The rest nodded in agreement. Diana didn't accede with the rest of them, but they didn't notice because it was dawning on all of them the enormity of the crime.

"This is a hate crime against Adventists, commandment-keepers!" Diana said what they all knew.

"It's more than that," the high school student began. They all turned their gaze at her. "I heard them talking after they knocked out Diana. One said that he wanted, like, to sample the merchandise. Then the other one said that we will bring a higher price if we're virgins. They are going to sell us as sex slaves." Amazingly enough, that horror did not surprise them. They were already at the peak of terror, being at the mercy of evil minions of Satan. At this point nothing could surprise them from the extremes of God's miracle-working power to the opposite of thugs selling them as slaves. The former fortified their resolve. They would not whimper when they could demonstrate trust. Their chins were held higher, and their hands were on their hips. No matter what, they expected to be God's instruments in victory. The Gray man syndrome of personal survival by blending in and not confronting the perpetrators gave way to solidarity of the women to face danger in unity.

> *They would not whimper when they could demonstrate trust. Their chins were held higher, and their hands were on their hips. No matter what, they expected to be God's instruments in victory.*

XXXXX

President Hertzog stood before the student body, informing them of current events. He explained the one registered letter that they had received and of the other letters that sister universities had received. After spelling out the details of their predicament, he was about to turn it over for questions when his secretary brought in the expected second letter. He read it aloud. The students were quiet, as was the faculty that stood around the gymnasium walls listening. Most of the listeners understood the omens behind the orders. One female freshman stood up, waving her arms. Because they were ready for questions, an usher handed her a live microphone.

"This is absolutely unfair! I'm a local attendee and not an Adventist. I only attend Andrews because it is so close, but I understand why you worship on Saturday. I worship on Sunday. Religious freedom is the hallmark of America's Bill of Rights. This is not fair! It's wrong. I'm going to ask my pastor to help out. I'm inviting you all down to my church to get registered for Sunday. Then you won't get into trouble. I'm not going to let them do this to you."

The president, moved by her sincerity, graciously thanked her for her kind invitation. Others were affected too. And some were giggling over her lack of knowledge. Thankfully, she didn't notice them. She was proud of herself for helping her friends.

The discussion abruptly turned to the future of how long the university would keep normal operations. The consensus boiled down to one month of watching. The plan was to make a coordinated legal appeal to the violation of constitutional rights, formed by the lawyers on hire with the General Conference. If the appeal failed, then the faculty and student body would plan from there.

To say the least, uneasy feelings permeated the totality of the institutions involved. Most could understand the developing dangers. Some were hoping things would resolve and go back to the status quo. A few worried about losing tuition money for future semesters because of the talk of closing schools.

XXXXX

National news did not include local vandalism as a rule, unless it came up as a trend over-reaching state lines. Several fire bombings of

Adventist churches got the attention of the local media in Des Moines. One exception was a non-SDA church. The Eastbro Baptist church building got hit with several gasoline bombs, ostensibly for their anti-gay demonstrations. It was an unlikely pairing with Adventists at best. Prejudice does not decipher the finer points of belief, such as loving the person and not the sin. When Molotov cocktails destroyed Adventist churches in Arkansas, Missouri, and Indiana, media attention spread to the national stage. When this happened, the media had to recognize the perpetrators had to be a much bigger organism with a longer malevolent reach.

XXXXX

Chad found Diana's purse. He used plastic gloves to put it into an evidence bag, both of which were furnished by Detective Hardine. The chain of custody was violated, but the hope of Chad finding anything was remote. Chad felt some confidence return. This find would tell the detective which direction the abductors took. It narrowed the search for vehicles considerably. However, two days of trying to find a direction to search didn't yield a lot of confidence, but anything was better than nothing. He screwed up his flagging spirit by reminding himself that Hardine was still on the case. There must be something in the history between Hardine and his captain that was interfering.

Checking the purse yielded nothing of value, except the direction of exit from the scene of abduction. Her credit cards were gone, and he didn't know what other valuables she might have had. Hardine thanked Chad, and then there was nothing to do but pray. He had no one to go to. Mrs. Cross was not an option because of her severe grief. She would not be able to help him. People at church were too far back in history. The new friends were an option, but he didn't want to distract them from their evangelism. Then he thought of the Bible study prayer. Maybe the Spirit could instill in him the hope he so desperately desired. He called Brian to ask where the E-Center was located.

Upon arrival, Pastor Lange gave him a short update on the activity in the center and then said, "You are here because of Diana. We had a prayer for her earlier and then went to work. You and I are going to pray together." They moved into a prayer room set up with carpeting and comfortable seating, couches, loungers, and end tables. They had no sooner settled in than Brian and Cynthia came through the door.

"We couldn't work while you were praying for Diana. Can we join you?" Then two others joined in without comment. Their concern comforted Chad. This is what he needed. His grief worked overtime. Loss compounded upon loss. He couldn't bear it alone. A perceived future assumed that his parents would be there in his childhood home. That vision disappeared in one short phone call. A future starting to develop in his head was a friendship developing into a serious relationship. He could envision dinners together in a restaurant. That beginning shattered with a blue car stopped on the side of the road. Grief makes the future painful.

They prayed, kneeling with arms linked around shoulders. The glow from before returned. The Spirit animated the words and emotions. Tears flowed, and spirits rose. Chad was convinced that Diana would be okay. His faith doubled and tripled. He felt good enough to go home and sleep; however, he instead went to Diana's mother to bolster her faith.

XXXXX

The young ladies were standing together when the latches on the sliding metal door rattled, indicating that they were coming. They turned in unison, and Karen led out, "Our God is an awesome God. He reigns in heaven above. With wisdom, power, and love, our God is an awesome God." The men stopped in their tracks as they were met with a different scenario than they expected. The women were not afraid. The men looked around for any altered circumstance that could lend sense to the changed behavior. Once the initial shock passed, they moved forward to cuff them with zip-ties. They had expected to carry them out two at a time, but now they walked them out four at a time without incident, without a struggle. They were locked in a large truck box without any light or air from the outside. They did know it was daytime from the dirty window in their prison room. They kept singing. When the truck began to move, they had to sit down to avoid falling down.

Time ticked by without them knowing the length. The turns and hills swayed them around unnaturally because they couldn't anticipate what was next. It lulled them into a stupor. Then suddenly, the vehicle's brakes screeched in an emergency halt, jolting them to attention. The back door rolled up, and a man in jeans and a blue and green plaid shirt beckoned them to get out in a soothing, quiet voice. They stood and walked to the back door, using the side to steady their steps. The moment of understanding that the zip-ties were gone came at different times for each of the ladies. The minor miracle, along with the gentle voice, communicated to them that they were now in the hands of an angel. Once on the ground, they were directed to walk directly back up the road to a house on the hill, the Perkins, by name. The angel rolled the back door of the truck closed and disappeared around the side of the vehicle. When they looked around the edge of the truck, he was nowhere to be seen. They were free, just as simple as that.

They looked back, and the truck stood alone; no traffic, no obstructions, no reason to stop. Black rubber marks ran up the pavement leading to the rear tires. No human anywhere, not even an angel to thank. "Thank You, Lord, for saving my soul …" they sang as they walked up the hill to the house with lights on the first floor. They had no inkling of what time it was. They did what they were told. Coming to the front door, the lady of the house opened the door before they rang the bell.

"We were expecting you. How can we help?"

At this point nothing could surprise them. They entered the home as if it were a palace inside a fortress. Knees went weak, and stress went out the window. They were safe. The occupants saw their need immediately. The messy, stained clothes and the clumped hair spoke of the ordeal. The news stories and what stood in front them gelled. These young women were the ones who had been abducted. The woman of the house and her two daughters went into action, asking if they needed food, or clean clothes, or a place to clean up. Diana asked for a phone. The man of the house quickly gave her his cell. She was about to be reconnected with the man she loved.

XXXXX

Chad knocked quietly on the door. He worried that if Mrs. Cross had managed to get some sleep, he didn't want to wake her up. After all, it was late Friday night. He saw a shadow on the front room curtain. Then the door swung wide with little regard for what might be standing on the other side.

"Chad! Oh, thank you for coming. I couldn't sleep, and I felt awful. Poor Diana, what must she be suffering! It's been two days." Chad could tell she'd been counting the hours and minutes. "Come in, come in. Have you heard anything? Is the news good, or is it bad?"

Chad held her hands in his. "I don't have any news. I found Diana's purse, which told us very little. But other than that, I have heard of nothing."

"Oh. When I heard the knock, I knew it had to be news of something. I don't know if I can make it through this. I need to know something. Reverend Tucker said the first forty-eight hours are the most important. Otherwise, the news is usually bad. Oh, oh, why is this happening to my little Diana?"

"Mrs. Cross, I just came from a prayer session."

"With Reverend Tucker? Why wasn't I invited?"

"No, it wasn't. It was with Pastor Lange and with Diana's and my new friends."

"Oh, them," her tone went flat.

"When we prayed, I felt the Holy Spirit in a very special way. This is the second time I have experienced this. The first time was with Diana at the Bible study we attended. This time, I felt sure that she is going to be okay. I can't explain it, but I was completely sure. No one spoke to me. God didn't speak to me. It was just a positive notion that I didn't have to worry. I came here in hopes I could help you feel better. Feel like I am feeling now."

"Well, those Holy Ghost groups don't seem to help me. I'm more rooted in reality." She sat down on the sofa, defeated.

"Here, let's pray together."

"You can pray. I don't feel like it."

"Okay, I'll start, but if you feel like it, you can jump in and simply say, 'Protect my Diana.'"

"All right. If I feel like it."

"Dear Father in heaven, we come to You knowing that You have the whole universe in Your hands. We also know that You are concerned with every one of Your children. You heard me say to Mrs. Cross—"

"Silvia, please."

"—to Silvia that I was convinced that Diana is safe. You gave me that impression. You encouraged me and gave me hope. I am trusting You to do the same for Silvia. I know You will answer my request. No matter how much time it takes, we will trust—"

"Protect my Diana!" Silvia's desire reached out to claim the hope that Chad possessed. Their eyes opened to look directly at each other. Silvia smiled, and Chad returned the smile. He closed his eyes to continue when his phone rang.

"Hello? Diana?! Oh, my! Praise the Lord! Where are you?"

"I'm okay, and we have an amazing story to tell you. Can you come?"

"Yes, of course, I can come. I'll bring your mother; she's right here."

Silvia snatched the phone from Chad in an instant. "Sweetie, are you okay?"

"Yes, I'm okay. We have a fantastic story. God protected us. Can you come with Chad?"

"Yes, of course, I can."

"I have to share this phone with some of the other girls. Give the phone back to Chad, and I'll give him the address, okay?"

She did, and Chad jotted down the number on his hand. When he clicked off, they both rejoiced, bouncing up from the couch and holding arms in the air. Then Chad suggested, "We left God on hold. We need to finish this prayer. Thank You, Lord, for confirming our confidence in You."

"And, thank You for protecting my Diana!"

"Amen! Let's run. It's a little bit of a ride."

Diana's mom turned herself inside out trying to think of what she needed to do to get ready. She jumped up and went around in circles. "She needs some clothes! Oh, she needs food! No, she needs her make-up kit. She'd want to look nice when she sees you. Shoes, she needs some nice shoes. What kind of shoes? I need to pack a bag."

Chad stood up and held her by her elbows, "All she wants is to see us. She'll look beautiful to both of us."

"I suppose you're right."

"Grab a coat, and we'll go." Diana's mom did grab a coat out of the closet, and then took some extra shoes and ran up to her room to get Diana's glasses from off her dresser. Then, going out the door, she took another coat out of the closet. Chad, in the meantime, called Detective Hardine. The detective had already gone to bed in a rare occurrence of going to bed early on a Friday night. He felt defeated, and then now, elated with Chad's call. He had to call his captain but held off before calling so he could get to the scene first and gather information.

Chad had quality time to talk with Silvia about his quest to understand his folks' change to another theology.

XXXXX

A soft, overstuffed couch with multiple pillows soothed Diana in luxury, a luxury beyond description. She was offered sandwiches and tea or coffee.

She took a sandwich and surprised herself with her internal hunger. Being subjected to the worrisome trauma of captivity swept away a normal function of wanting to eat. The host family wanted to know why this had happened. No adequate answer could explain evil behavior. They wanted to know if their faith sustained them. The answer was an emphatic, "yes." The story of the healing focused attention on Diana. After a while, it became apparent that this family had been under conviction that the world was going crazy, and prejudice seemed to be swinging against a certain type of Christian. They didn't know why, and here sitting before them were nine young women who had tasted that prejudice. They quizzed them about their faith.

Diana found herself on the spot with a question that asked how she felt to have God pick her out for the gift of healing. She revealed that she had been studying with her boyfriend because of the murder of his folks because they had made the switch to the SDA church. Her point of view matched the family's search. The many anti-Adventist hate crimes spurred them to ask why. And that why led them to search online about what SDAs believed. Diana explained that her search almost went in the same direction. Asking questions helped her to find the reasons behind Adventist faith. She said one Bible text stuck in her mind. Mark 7:8, "For laying aside the commandment of God, ye hold the tradition of men" (KJV).

> *The Adventist Church showed me the principle of letting Scripture talk. When I studied, I found the commandments of God important. God wrote them with His own hand.*

"I never thought of this before. For me, denomination and faith were synonymous. It mattered that I was attending and keeping the traditions. The Adventist Church showed me the principle of letting Scripture talk. When I studied, I found the commandments of God important. God wrote them with His own hand. Once I learned that, I experienced one revelation after another."

"And you were given the gift of the Spirit, healing," Karen added. All nodded ascent around the living room. Diana didn't feel comfortable being singled out in this way.

Converging on the house of sanctuary were many cars with happy occupants. All of the girls had called home. Hardine was on his way, and he had called an ambulance and critical stress debriefing teams. When he figured he was halfway there, he called his captain with the good news. The captain didn't seem happy. Maybe because it meant coming out late on a Friday night. He promised to show up. Several other vehicles were on their way, news vans. Soon there would be a large kerfuffle.

The youngest daughter of the house sat close to Diana and held her hand. "You are so lucky you have the gift of healing. I wish I could heal people."

"I guess it's a matter of focus. I could say how horrible it was to be kidnapped, or, like you, I can focus on what God has given. I'd rather forget the past. By the way, He has a gift reserved just for you."

"What is it? Do you know what my gift is?"

"No, I don't. God will let you know at the right time."

"How did you know?"

"Well, it just happened to me. I didn't know it until it happened. I am still very surprised by it all."

"We would like to learn more about your journey to the Adventist belief," the father asked.

"I can study with you. My boyfriend and I would be happy to come to your home."

The surreal moment with the family and the nine talking in the living room, sitting on soft seating and dining room chairs, gave the impression no horror had preceded. The only giveaway that indicated their ordeal was the condition of their clothing and hair. Comfort reigned supreme as they settled into the cushions and the pillows. Sirens in the distance almost drowned out the quiet comment by the little one, "I wish I could be like you."

Detective Hardine drove up with lights blinking and left them on as he dashed to the door. He came through as the father opened the door and abruptly halted when he saw everyone sitting calmly. He had to take in the scene and then start his questioning. He also eased his hand off of his holstered pistol. "Is everyone all right?" Nods indicated they were. "Ah, how'd you get away?"

"An angel." The look on his face appeared almost comical if it wasn't for the seriousness of the crime that had gone before. "Okay, let's start at the beginning and work up to how you got away. Did any of you see the perps that kidnapped you?"

"Yes," some of them said in unison. The others nodded in the affirmative. "Would you be willing to go to the station and look through some photos?" He got the same response. "Good, I have a quick question before others arrive. All of you, it seems, had a slight rear-end accident that caused you to get abducted. What kind of vehicles did they use?"

"A pickup truck."

"Yes, me, too."

"Mine was a car."

"So was mine."

"Okay, okay, that means they used different vehicles. What color were they?" Hardine was working toward a statement that a cop car was used. The answers came back with mostly dark hues, no black and white cruisers. He had to ask directly. "Were any of them police vehicles?" He felt time running out to get a disclosure. Sirens were wailing in the distance. Diana answered,

"Come to think of it, I thought something was weird. The car that hit me had some short aerials and had an emergency spotlight in front of the side view mirror.

"What color was it?"

"Grayish, I think." Hardine's mind went directly to trying to remember how many dark gray unmarked squad cars were in the precinct that had brush grills. He had hoped to rule out any police involvement in the crime. This discovery made him drop in his emotions.

Then the kerfuffle began. First, Chad and Silvia came in a step ahead of two EMTs. Diana was off the couch and into Chad's arms immediately. Silvia got pulled in with Chad and Diana's arms. Diana almost melted on the spot when Chad confidently told her, "I love you." Silvia kept repeating, "God protected you. God protected you." Then tears of relief and happiness began to flow. Diana lost it as well. Hands were stroking her lower back, which didn't add up with all their arms up high. Diana looked down to see her young disciple comforting her because of her tears.

Other family members entered the crowded living room, along with police officers trying to control the scene. More EMTs entered and tried to assess if there were injuries to treat. They asked permission to take individuals out to ambulances for health checks. Reporters with cameras elbowed their way to the front door. Something had to be done. Detective Hardine corralled a couple of officers to get a police line set up. One team of a reporter plus a cameraman tried to come through the back door after the older daughter of the house answered their knock. They ignored her in their dash to get the story. A scuffle broke out between a cameraman and a police officer who firmly pushed the grip across the yellow tape. More officers arrived, and the media had to stand in the street and do their reports from there. One reporter could be heard saying, "The poor girls abducted at gunpoint were found at this address. We are not allowed inside to interview them, which gives us the impression that their injuries are severe. No one knows why this quiet neighborhood could be home to such an awful crime against young girls."

Hardine found Karen sitting on a gurney behind an ambulance with a blood pressure cuff on her right arm. He asked her to tell her story interrupted by a medico. The detective asked, "Who got hurt?" She looked to be in relatively good condition. "All of us got roughed up and kicked. Diana got her jaw broken, and they stomped on Jane's leg, and it broke in two places. It was awful to look at."

"Where is this Jane? It sounds like she's in greater need of attention than the others."

"Oh, she doesn't need help. Her leg was healed."

"Healed? Did you say healed?" the medic asked. Detective Hardine also lost his train of thought. This case and the case starting this chain of events held religious overtones he had not expected. His job never allowed much time for quality church life. He wouldn't classify himself an unbeliever. He would rather say, "Religion comes later when I have more time." He disbelieved this healing. All his life, people claiming a miracle were those who were possibly healed by conventional medicine.

"Yes," she answered. "Also, I got kicked around a lot, and Diana prayed for me, and the aches and bruises disappeared." She showed the EMT and the detective her legs with no signs of abuse. It was her words against their thoughts. Ambulances were loading up and taking their cargo to hospitals for observation. CIS (Critical Incident Stress) teams went with them to continue their debriefing to stave off PTSD.

Hardine wanted to see Diana's jaw. He moved in her direction when the captain cut him off.

"How did you get this tip?'

"Mr. Johnson called me and told me all the kidnapped women were here."

"How did they end up here? Isn't it a bit too remarkable?"

"Yes, it is. They say an angel helped them to get away."

"Yeah, right, and my uncle is Batman. Did you get any good intel on the perps?"

"No, not yet. I have to get the ladies down to the precinct to look at mugshots."

"They saw their faces?"

"Indeed."

XXXXX

In the hospital room, Diana, her mother, and Chad had an opportunity to talk. They were amazed by the story of God's intervention. They had to pray their gratitude for His awesome providence, a natural response in light of the method of deliverance. They spent a great deal of time talking about the healings. All wondered at God's purpose for giving Diana this special gift of the Holy Spirit. Would He have more instances in the future that required her gift? This discussion of the future worried Diana.

A nurse came into the room with a tranquilizer. "No, no way. I don't want any more drugs!" Diana reacted quickly.

"It'll calm you down and help you to sleep. You've been through a lot."

"But ... well ... all right," she gave in. "Every time I close my eyes ..." She shuddered.

"Mom, Chad, I'm worried about the future. I don't want to go through what I've already gone through."

"I understand," Chad agreed.

"I don't think I can stay in our apartment. I just don't feel safe in our place with just us two females. You know the neighborhood and what it's like, right, Mom? Chad, I'd like to stay with you, but, Mom, I want you to be there too. People would get the wrong idea if it were just the two of us."

"Sweetheart, Chad can stay with us at our place," Silvia suggested as a matter of fact.

"No, that wouldn't work. We only have two bedrooms."

"Oh, well, let's talk about this tomorrow. You've been through a lot, and you need to sleep in a real bed for a night. We'll talk tomorrow when we get home. Night-night, my little sweetheart." She kissed her on the head and strode to the door. Chad wanted to stay all night in the chair next to her bed, but he had to give Silvia a ride home. He kissed Diana and left, promising to come back.

After taking Silvia home, he went straight back to the hospital. Upon entering her room, he found her deep in sleep. The doctors had prescribed a strong sedative. He settled into the uncomfortable molded plastic chair, thinking this could not be worse than what she had endured.

CHAPTER 10

Diana awoke rested and hungry. Snatching her glasses off of the tray table, she saw the clock which read eleven-forty. A breakfast tray sat on the table, and then, behind the rolling table, slept a handsome young man in what looked like the most uncomfortable position possible. She jumped out of bed and kissed her beau awake.

"Why didn't you wake me when you came in?"

"'Cause I came back last night."

"You slept here all night?"

"More like early this morning, two-thirty. I knew you were scared. So I came back."

"O, Chad, I love you so much!"

"I would have stayed here if it wasn't for getting Chad home in time for his bedtime," Silvia said, from the doorway.

"Mom, I just woke up. What a joy to have both of you here."

"I come bearing gifts. Well, used gifts. I brought you some clean clothes and a few extras for me and you if Chad will be so kind as to let us stay with him for a while."

"Yes, absolutely. I don't want you out of my sight during these times. I can't bear to lose you again," he answered enthusiastically.

XXXXX

At Chad's home they were just getting comfortable when the doorbell rang. Pastor Lange had come to rejoice in Diana's safe return.

"I'm so happy you're safe," he said without introductions. A celebratory hug followed immediately.

With a guarded smile, Mrs. Cross stood with her arms folded in front of her. She guessed correctly that this visitor had to be from the new, strange church. Her concern of the moment would be to communicate that her daughter was a chaste woman, and she was here as a chaperone. Before this duty came upon her, her priority focused on Diana feeling safe. Any discomfort to her ranked low in comparison to restoring Diana's sense of safety. Right below that primary purpose followed her daughter's marriage to her teenage heartthrob. Changing her mind the night before centered upon the opportunity to promote this blossoming romance. She would be the matchmaker from in-house. She approached this new person with her priorities in crisp order. To her, Pastor Lange presented a disruption to Diana's feeling of security.

"Pastor Peter Lange, let me introduce Diana's mother, Mrs. Cross."

"Silvia, please call me Silvia. So, you're the pastor of the Seventh Advent Church."

"Yes, I am. It is nice to meet you, Silvia." He did not correct her missing the full name of the church. "Diana has been very much in the middle of our prayers these last several days. I'm glad God sent His angel to rescue her and them. A real answer to our prayers."

"Silvia, Pastor Lange was leading the prayer session I attended before coming to you last night when Diana was rescued. Let's all have a seat." Chad led the way to the living room, where they sat down. Diana and Chad sat close on the settee holding hands.

"I can't stop thanking God for His answer to our many prayers. There have been so many I can't think of all of them at the same time. I end up praying off and on all day. Would you like to pray now?"

"I would like that," Diana answered immediately. They bowed and rejoiced with the Lord. They acknowledged His omnipotence and the wonderful way He saved all of the girls. Chad added a prayer of thanksgiving, and Diana tearfully spoke of her gratitude. Silvia also thanked God, "For protecting my Diana." She felt somewhat intimidated by this unknown reverend. They finished praying, smiling at each other, thinking about how great God is to them. Quiet ambiance lingered, then Silvia asked the question nagging her thoughts.

"Why are people so angry at Seventh Advents? They are stealing their women, killing their members on TV. What can they be doing that we don't know of?"

"We expected this would happen."

"That sounds ridiculous like you have a martyr complex. Who would want to be a part of that expectation?" She looked at Diana for a brief moment after saying that.

"What I am talking about is found in Scripture. Jesus said, 'I did not come to bring peace but a sword.'[14] We can expect Satan to take out his anger on God's people. When we study Revelation chapter 12, we find a description of what the devil is up to today."

> *Why are people so angry at Seventh Advents? They are stealing their women, killing their members on TV. What can they be doing that we don't know of?*

"The book of Revelation is full of symbols that can't be understood unless you are a minister. We have to leave that book alone."

"Believe me, a lot of people feel the same way. But they miss some of the most beautiful metaphors and descriptions in the Bible."

"Like what? May I ask."

"'Behold, I stand at the door and knock. If anyone hears My voice and opens the door, I will come in to him and dine with him, and he with Me.'[15] I have always wanted to dine with Jesus. Then there's this that I long for with all my heart, 'Behold, the dwelling place of God is with man. He will dwell with them, and they will be his people, and God himself will be with them as their God. He will wipe away every tear from their eyes, and death shall be no more, neither shall there be mourning, nor crying, nor pain anymore, for the former things have passed away.'"[16]

"I see what you mean. I, too, want to have my tears wiped away. I must've cried a bucketful these last several days." Then Silvia told her story of grief at her husband's death.

"To answer your question about why people are angry with Seventh-day Adventists. Chapter 12 opens with a picture of a pregnant woman clothed with the sun, with the moon under her feet, and on her head a crown of twelve stars. What would you guess this picture to mean?"

[14](Matt. 10:34, NKJV)
[15](Rev. 3:20, NKJV)
[16](Rev. 21:3–4, ESV)

"I don't know. Someone who is fragile or something. Ah, if she is clothed with the sun, she might be special, maybe one who is in favor with God."

"That's good. I like that. The story continues with her in agony of childbirth ready to deliver. Then a great red dragon stood before the woman wanting to devour her child. She gave birth to a male child who was to rule the nations. And the child was caught up to God in heaven. I'm summarizing and leaving out some symbolic details. People tend to get hung up on some of the symbols and miss the simple story. Who do you think this male child is?"

"It sounds like Jesus."

"I agree. The story continues with the woman fleeing into the wilderness, and the dragon pursues the woman. God protects the woman, and finally, at the end, the dragon is angry with the woman and makes war with the rest of her offspring, those 'who keep the commandments of God and have the testimony of Jesus' (vs. 17). That last statement validates what you guessed that the male child is Jesus. If the rest of her children are people who bear witness to Jesus, that must mean the Christian church. With that conclusion, one can go back and look at some of the symbols and see what they mean. For instance, at the beginning, the twelve stars are a clue. The number twelve in the Bible is interesting. We know Jesus' church was founded upon twelve disciples. When Judas betrayed Jesus, we see in the book of Acts where they felt compelled to replace him among the disciples, making the number twelve again. In the Old Testament, we see twelve tribes, which make up the nation of Israel. Another way of looking at Israel is to see them as God's Old Testament church. That brings us back to Revelation, chapter twelve and the pregnant woman. That was the Old Testament church giving birth to the Messiah, which then generated the New Testament church, which is being persecuted by the dragon. It is not too far off to say that the dragon is Satan, who is angry with the people who keep God's Commandments and testify of Jesus. The Seventh-day Adventist church tries to follow that description; we keep all of the commandments, and we teach the world about Jesus and His wonderful salvation."

"That is the clearest explanation I have ever heard from that book."

"I urge you to read Revelation carefully and thoughtfully. I find it able to teach me again and again, every time I read it."

"I will definitely read it for myself. The persecution of God's people disturbs me. But, there has to be a reason why they get singled out for discrimination. Reverend Tucker says a lot of people are angry with SDAs for stealing their members. Is that true?"

"Like every evangelical denomination, we are trying our best to win souls for the kingdom. We advertise for meetings with mailings, print media, and door-to-door invitations. Sometimes we end up with Christians from other churches wanting to learn more about prophecy. Like Daniel and Janine. If they join our church, we are accused of 'sheep-stealing.' We want everyone to grow and develop in God's truth, and we also want to call people to live in accordance with the description of His faithful people at the end of time, specifically, keeping the commandments and witnessing for Jesus."

"Who do you think is doing this persecution?"

"I can only guess. When we mailed out our advertisement leaflets, many did not make it to the homes. We paid for a mass mailing to several zip codes. Some boys playing around some Dumpsters discovered boxes of our literature dumped. They never got to the intended. Then these leaflets showed up at the scenes of the abductions and with the Johnsons. I can speculate that someone in or near to the post office, or knows someone in the post office, got a hold of those un-mailed brochures. That's locally; now in other states, the leaflets are now showing up at hate crimes and church firebombings. A large scale effort is developing, which means individuals acting alone and groups are working against Adventists. I have one friend who said he believes it is the Neo-KKK. They are known to be active in purifying the Christian church of false Christians. Some have been implicated in re-programming our young people."

"This is unbelievable! It's like you guys are jinxed," Silvia reacted.

"Pastor, how is the evangelism center doing?" Diana changed the subject

"Great! We're getting indications that our blogs and emails are getting around the world. Already two E-Centers are getting started in Europe and Asia. Silvia, please don't worry. Diana's ordeal shows us in a very real and tangible way that God is protecting her for a purpose."

XXXXX

Detective Hardine returned to his only lead, the vehicles used in the abduction. This time, he went to viewing videos of nearby intersections going and coming from the Johnsons' house at the time of the murders.

He cataloged all of them and compared their license numbers to residences in the area and narrowed the list further, excluding service visits. Pared down, the list became more manageable, but now he had to do the footwork to eliminate innocents. Unfortunately, no unmarked police vehicles were on the list. He groaned at the prospect of sorting through the prospects. Entering his cruiser, he saw the evidence bag with the leaflet inside. It struck him that the leaflet was the one variable common to all incidents. He wanted a shortcut. He pulled out his notebook and looked up the number for Pastor Lange.

"Hello, this is Detective Hardine. We met before. Can we meet?"

"Sure, I remember you, Detective. When?"

"Now."

"Okay, I'm not at church or at home, I'll text you the address."

XXXXX

A late lunch cluttered the stove and the kitchen island. Silvia had put together a repast from items she found in the larder. They were about to clear the dishes when the routine weather forecast got interrupted by a red screen.

ZZZZZ

We interrupt your regular programming to bring you this breaking news. Our president is about to make an announcement.

My countrymen and ladies, I have received good and bad news. Your networks will be reporting that cholera has broken out in epidemic proportions in the Southeast and the Caribbean. The CDC and IFRC are rushing assets to contain the spread of this infection. FEMA is already on the scene. Clean food and, very importantly, clean water, at this moment, are being rushed to the affected areas. This continuing aftermath of the earthquake and tidal wave disaster is an ongoing nightmare. I want it to end. And that leads me to tell you about the good news.

I have already told you about how we are solving these problems. If we want this to end, we need to speed up our loyalty posture with God. He wants us dedicated to Him. This is the way we must go. We must be united in our faith and the practice of the same.

The apparatus is now completely in place. WCF is organizing the world into one solid expression of faith. The Knights of Malta are handling the world's commerce and banking. And, this is the great news; the WCF has appointed the pope to head the WCF. This is a smart move that will give the WCF the leadership it needs to operate in virtually every country in the world. All the puzzle pieces are in place. I count this as the signature accomplishment in my presidency. We can mobilize the world into one mighty coalition to affect all of the changes we need to convince our Father in heaven to remake the world into the Eden He originally designed.

Starting this Sunday, anyone donating to their place of worship will be counted as loyal. The credit card used will be recorded, and the IRS will be notified to double the deduction off of their personal taxes, no matter if the donation is large or small. It becomes a benefit to both their church and to our world.

See you in church Sunday.

ZZZZZ

Chad and Diana were alarmed, and Silvia didn't know what to make of it because she saw their eye language. As a couple, they were in the initial phase of developing nonverbal communication, their look at each other communicated they shared knowledge that this news item confirmed what the Adventists had been saying. A religious alliance had formed, world governments endorse the coalition, and world commerce is controlled by a spiritual-based institution. The events predicted in the Bible were coming together. It was time to throw their efforts into helping everyone to get ready. Now, they were wondering when Jesus' words in Matthew 24 were fulfilled or about to be fulfilled, "When you see the desolating sacrilege … standing in the holy place … flee."[17]

Silvia watched. They appeared determined. She had many more years' experience in detecting eye language. "What's going on?"

"What's happening is Bible prophecy for the end is coming true," Diana told her mom.

"How so?"

"The WCF is a fulfillment of Revelation 13. Our country is in concert with other countries to support the WCF, also mentioned in Revelation 13. And then, in Revelation 18, we see merchants involved in world commerce through the instrumentality of the WCF. The time of the end is upon us," Chad answered.

---

[17](vs. 15, NRSV)

"This is the material you promised to read, Mom," Diana added. "Chad, I think we should go to the E-Center."

"But, you're supposed to rest. You can't ignore the inner trauma of having endured what you endured. Right?" Silvia reminded her daughter.

XXXXX

Detective Hardine walked through the front door and found Pastor Lange leaning over Brian's shoulder, gazing at a monitor. He pointed at a line and then patted Brian on the shoulder. Upon turning, he saw the detective.

"What can I do for you?"

"Remember this?" Hardine said without preamble. He held up the evidence envelope with the brochure inside.

"Yes. Have you made any connections with that?"

"There have. I talked to you about the one at the Johnsons' house. Then there was one at the scene of Miss Cross's abduction and at several other abductions of ladies connected with the SDA church. It is a common link. I came here to see what it is all about. Could you give me a tutorial on what the SDAs believe? Do you have time?"

Pastor Lange could not refuse the smile that came across his face. "Sure thing. I'll take all the time you require. Let's go into the lounge. We have some nice sofas and some Bibles to help. That's the first thing you need to know about us is we find all our beliefs in the Bible."

"Thank you for taking the time. Let's get started," Hardine instructed.

The young workers at the computer terminals could not refuse the smile that spread across their faces.

CHAPTER 11

S audi Arabia's fossil water hidden in underground aquifers had all but disappeared in twenty short years. It took only a generation to become accustomed to the benefits of crop production and then for them to feel the loss when the wells ran dry. Fields of rock and sand became green overnight, flourished, then stood stark and dry twenty years later. The last aquifer produced zero water, having pumped out all of its contents with rainfall as the only method for refilling the underground caverns. The annual, next-to-zero rainfall in Saudi Arabia cannot replenish any of the many fossil water sources that have been drained by large mechanical straws poked into the sand over the years.

Isa stood on the edge of one of those dusty fields above the Al-Ahsa aquifer in an eastern province of Saudi Arabia. He raised his arms into the air and called for water to gush forth. The wells had been left open to extract every drop. The electricity was turned off, but the pipes were open. A gaggle of Bedouins shifted their gaze from Isa to the nearest outlet. Nothing happened. They shifted eyes back at Isa, and then a sound gurgled from the pipe. Sandstorm dust the consistency of talcum powder had blown into the pipe, and a thick mud belched out of the orifice. The slop dribbled to the ground. Then, thick soup ran out, and finally, pure, clear water spewed forth, gushing as if under pressure, the water hurled itself fifty feet away from the opening, landing in an old dusty canal. The empty catacomb reservoir, beyond the point of being replenished, jetted forth without the aid of electric pumps acting like an artesian spring.

A few voices shouted in victory. The remainder ran for the water. It took five minutes before they acknowledged their benefactor. Contrary to expectation, in a virtually uninhabited desert with nothing in the way of infra-structure, news travels fast. In two days, Isa became an un-urban urban hero. Wherever he went, crowds followed, asking for help, demanding to see a miracle. What he wanted was a bigger audience. He healed a woman suffering from spina bifida. Within a minute, she stood and walked an unsteady walk to her benefactor, who passed her on to one of his new disciples. He headed in a vector toward Riyadh.

> *Finally, pure, clear water spewed forth, gushing as if under pressure, the water hurled itself fifty feet away from the opening, landing in an old dusty canal.*

At first, this nomadic medicine man attracted little attention from the upper class. His crowds came from street vendors, beggars, and poor children. They were not very interested in his oratory, just what he could do for them on the material level. Gossip about him consisted of the story of his ability to heal and bring water to a thirsty desert. Interest waned. Then a deaf child clutched him around the legs, and Isa put his hands on both of her ears. Her instantaneous reaction could be seen and heard. She delightedly twirled while listening to her own voice call for her mother. More clamored after him, and then a white Mercedes honked its way through the crowd to the market wall upon which he sat. He knew this to be his moment. Shushing the crowd with his arms up in supplication, giving the impression something was about to happen from heaven, he slipped off the wall and strode confidently to the expensive sedan. When a young, mangled boy came out in the arms of his father clad in the accoutrements of royalty, Isa took the child's hand and asked that he be placed on his twisted feet. Nothing else needed to be done. Isa returned to the wall as the crowd gazed in awe at the healthy boy dancing in perfect symmetry. Instead of sitting on the wall, Isa stood atop the wall in full view of everyone in the marketplace.

"I have come to bring prosperity to my children. You are my children. Follow me to a better life."

XXXXX

The Seventh-day Adventist church was declared an extremist group and an enemy of the state by the justice wing of the People's Republic of China. SDA missionaries with foreign citizenship were deported after being held for two weeks and released upon pressure from the US Embassy. Other church leadership was tried, convicted, and sent to reform camps. Adherents of the faith were given an option to renounce their association, and their social credit score would improve, otherwise, they would willingly submit to reform camp. The only reason that didn't happen immediately is because the reform camps were overloaded with radical Muslims.

XXXXX

They were a little nervous when they knocked on the door. This would be the very first time in their lives that they had set out to teach someone about Bible truths. They weren't really prepared because they didn't know ahead of time what the questions would be. They did know that the Holy Spirit would help them with the correct words. Chad intended to speak when the Perkins opened the door; he didn't have to because the littlest girl jumped out beside Diana and invited her physically by pulling her into the entryway.

"You'll have to excuse Emilee. She has been excited ever since you called. She can't stop talking about being a healer just like you," explained Mrs. Perkins.

"Emilee, you are a sweetheart. You want to help people. God will help you to be what He wants you to be. Who knows, that might even mean healing people," Diana said while picking her up and giving her a big hug. Mrs. Perkins was very pleased. With a smile, she directed them to sit down. Diana went to the same comfortable spot she was in before.

"Let's have a word of prayer," Chad suggested. It was the beginning of a rewarding Bible study that added to a faith the Perkins family had already acquired.

XXXXX

The last field of grain in upper Leer County, South Sudan, flourished in a secluded glen cut off from the local population by a swamp on two sides and a rugged hill of rock boulders reaching up a steep incline. The only ones knowing of the small field were the refugees hiding in the swamp. Rebel soldiers usually didn't bother hiding in the mucky lowlands, nor did they venture more than ten yards into the rocks to set up an ambush. They waited there. The local people guarded the knowledge of the field because it meant life to starving children. Fish and amphibians from the swamp provided some protein, but they needed grain. Hunger existed as the norm because warring factions used food as a weapon to fight the opposition by starving the support base. This was nothing new. In past iterations, in this on-again, off-again conflict that seemed to last forever, they always abused and starved the populace.

Today, the government troops were there to burn their field. The Sudan People's Liberation Movement (SPLM), once again active, was lying in ambush in the rocks. The entire village knew. Children and the elderly were visibly absent, especially the young boys who were often conscripted into government forces. A crippled beggar, acting as a look-out, rattled a rusty tin can at the only intersection in the little town. He would signal the people when it was safe to return. Loitering next to the trucks, the government soldiers waited for orders to move out. Hidden in the rocks, SPLMs eyed the enemy, wiping sweat from their worried brows.

Naziya walked confidently down the middle of the dusty road. Thirteen years old, but mature by double that figure. She stopped directly in line between the soldiers and the hidden rebels. Raising her arms, she held one out toward the rebels with her palms against the rebels, like telling them to stop. It exposed the hidden to the ones in the open. The soldiers sprang into action only to be commanded by Naziya to halt where they were. They would have ignored her, but their weapons would not work. Pulling the triggers as much as they could would not unleash the death they were designed to deal out. Every rifle, pistol, and grenade launcher became inert. Befuddled, they shook their weapons as if they could wake them up. Naziya spoke in a commanding tone, "Put down your weapons! We have more important missions to perform!" The Rebels and the troops were still shaking imaginary sand out of the mechanisms. She repeated her order. In frustration, both entities ran at each other with knives drawn. Naziya again called for them to stop. They didn't. A shock-wave of considerable force flattened both sets of antagonists, leaving their leaders standing. The commanders began to realize this was some serious mojo. They started to pay attention to this oddity in a dirty dress that stood before them.

XXXXX

President Hertzog decided to slow the injunctions against the university. He knew the inevitable was going to happen, but he also knew that the end could be delayed because the world needed to be fully informed about the good news, according to Matthew 24:14. If the word failed to reach everyone, God, in His infinite love, would delay until that happened. The president contacted the legal department of the General Conference, asking for an appeal to a federal judge to put a stop to the requirements on housing and Sunday attendance record-taking. The appeal went big and included all of the SDA universities and hospitals, as it turned out. If predicted events continued to move forward as indicated in the Bible, they could close down and head for the hills, literally. Prophecy comes true, in its own time, like Nineveh. Nineveh did fall as predicted by Jonah. Jonah didn't take into account the everlasting patience of a loving God.

Students continued to attend classes. Professors taught sessions and handed out grades. Overshadowing all activities abided specific studies in the transpiring issues of evil. Hertzog believed there shouldn't be a break-off in training young minds to be ready for the end. One bonus to the new status was the establishment of an E-Center like the ones sprouting up around the world. Hertzog sensed in his inmost heart this had to be the end.

XXXXX

Chad and Diana were surprised to find Silvia coming with them to the church she considered strange. They made neither request nor innuendo. She sat at the breakfast table with her Sunday dress complete with massive earrings and a bright, eye-catching red necklace that matched her lipstick. Diana couldn't resist her curiosity at her interest.

"Mother, I'm surprised you wanted to come to our church today. Why?"

"Perhaps because I want to know firsthand what goes on in your church, as you said, 'our' church."

The night before, Diana suggested to Chad that they bring something for the potluck. This morning, they brought a pasta casserole Diana put together. She hoped it would pass muster in this vegetarian environment. They were mobbed at the front door. Many had heard through the media of Diana's ordeal and rescue. They came to her, praising God for her rescue; others, telling how they prayed night and day, still others, weeping for happiness. When they had to wait to tell her of their joy, they spoke to Chad and Silvia. The outpouring of sentiment elevated their feelings of friendship and comradeship. Their solidarity centered on Diana. She was their emblem of God's protection in the midst of evil. She gave them courage. She was also a token of the Holy Spirit's outpouring in the latter rain. Interestingly enough, they knew of her healing gift, but none asked for any demonstration because an evil generation seeks a sign.

Pastor Lange waited patiently until he could greet Diana and then turned to greet Chad and Silvia, "It's so very good to have Chad and Diana invite you."

"Actually, I invited myself before they had a chance to ask. You're probably wondering why."

"Ah, well, yes. Why did you want to come today?" Pastor Lange thought of several possibilities, but her reply surprised him.

"I came because of you."

"Me?"

"Yes, you. The way you answered my questions. You weren't argumentative or trying to be smarter than me. Anyone could tell I was doubtful, and you didn't put me down in any way. I was impressed. And, another thing, I have always avoided the book of Revelation, and you made it sound so clear. I read it for myself afterward and could see that even though it has symbols, it can still be understood. It was beautiful when it talked of God Himself wiping away our tears. I wanted to learn more."

"Thank you! What a wonderful thing to say. I think you'll appreciate my sermon topic today. It will be in the book of Revelation. I hope it will help you even more."

Sabbath School music began, and people started to find their seats for the adult class. Children's divisions could also be heard singing downstairs. After a prayer, the teachers stood in various parts of the sanctuary and taught from mini-pulpits that slipped over the pew backs. Lesson quarterlies were provided to everyone, and the topic came from the book of Hebrews. This Sabbath, the study focused on chapter eleven. The participants couldn't help but steer the discussion to current events. The teachers tied the current events to the faith of the individuals listed in the chapter. The unmistaken need to be faithful in times of controversy permeated the room. Silent and public prayers appealed to God for strength to live through the turmoil ahead.

After a short break, the worship service began. An opening hymn and invocation started the service in the usual way; then, Pastor Lange changed the service. He called up to the platform several of the workers at the E-Center that were in attendance. He started an interview, asking them about their work and successes. The congregants responded positively. Then Pastor Lange called for a season of prayer inviting anyone and everyone to join in when the Spirit urged them.

Silvia didn't know that this order of service deviated from the norm. It was drastically different from what she had known all her life. She watched and then prayed aloud with interest and fervency. Once again, the Spirit attended their entreaties. The supplicants began asking for help and forgiveness to be clean of all sin. Then they evolved into a necessity for unity. Church members endeavored to drop dividing issues between them. They asked each other for forgiveness. Like the disciples at Pentecost, they became of one accord. The permeating sense that the Spirit abode within their thoughts could not be dismissed. Each felt several dispositions simultaneously. Comfort radiated outward to consume the fears they had for the future. A sense of community flowed between them. A sense of quiet urgency lent them a feeling of mutual purpose. As the prayers slowed, the community of believers refocused on their need to worship their Creator.

Pastor Lange indicated at the outset that it is always difficult to do anything after experiencing the Holy Spirit as they just had encountered. He then introduced his sermon, saying that it was always important to focus on our Redeemer, the One who gave us the confidence to approach the throne of grace in a state of purity. Introducing his subject, he explained that the book of Revelation was a misunderstood book, sometimes ignored by Christians. Silvia had to agree.

He then went on to say that John, the writer, receives more credit than he should. He is called, "John the Revelator" when it is Jesus who provides the message. The first words of the book are, "The revelation of Jesus Christ." Throughout the book Jesus is in the middle of everything. The last two verses in the book mention Jesus by name. From the beginning to the end, Jesus is the subject and the messenger. He is described with seven attributes in chapter one, verses five and six. Then, He is physically described with seven characteristics as He appears in heaven in verses fifteen to sixteen. Then these characteristics are used to introduce each of the seven churches in chapters two and three. Chapters four and five depict Jesus before the throne of God as the only one qualified to open the scroll with the seven seals. The prophecy of the seven seals in chapter six and the first part of chapter eight is introduced by Jesus, the Lamb, by His opening of each seal.

At this point Pastor Lange said, "We have to acknowledge a trend of sevens. Jesus is the perfect Savior. I showed you in the first chapter that Jesus is described with sevens. In chapter five, verse twelve, He is praised with seven blessings by those who are before the throne. The number seven is significant to the ancients, like the Babylonians. It meant to them perfection and deity. Whenever the number seven showed up in architecture or literature, it spoke immediately to them that this was a god. Translated into the Christian environment, it meant The God, and in the book of Revelation, seven refers to Jesus, God's son." He then recapped the descriptions in chapters one, four, and five. He pointed out that the seven churches where a description of the Christian church down through the ages to the present day. The church is the body of Christ, and interestingly, marked out in seven sections. From there, Pastor Lange went on to detail all the combinations of sevens throughout the book; seven churches, seals, trumpets, thunders, portents, plagues, not to mention the descriptions of Jesus in series of seven. One reading of the book will yield an understanding that seven is a theme, and seven equals Jesus.

Pastor continued explaining that later on in Revelation, Jesus' incarnation is described briefly in chapter twelve. He is the male child born to the chaste woman and is caught up to God in heaven. Jesus is the commander in chapter nineteen who returns on a white horse with the name, Word of God, King of Kings, and Lord of Lords. He takes the saints to heaven to the marriage supper of the Lamb, and there, Christ sets up a one-thousand-year reign. After the thousand years, He returns with the saints and the Holy City to this earth where God and the Lamb (Jesus) are in their temple in the midst of the city, New Jerusalem. He explained that Jesus is the sum and subject of the entire book. Putting aside the book of Revelation because of its plethora of symbols is ignoring a multi-dynamic picture of Jesus.

> *Putting aside the book of Revelation because of its plethora of symbols is ignoring a multi-dynamic picture of Jesus.*

The pastor also pointed out another repeating phrase in Revelation. The phrase, "Those who keep the commandments of God and the testimony of Jesus," is repeated in chapters 1, 12, 14, and alluded to in chapter 19:10. In the last reference, the phrase "testimony of Jesus is the spirit of prophecy" means that the book of Revelation is the spirit of Jesus' prophecy, and also His gift of prophecy is a talent for humankind. The repeating phrase also testifies to the people of God who are loyal to God by keeping the Ten Commandments.

Another point was brought out about the structure of the book of Revelation. He told of how Jesus is more than named by name or symbolized by the number seven. Another symbol was used to depict Jesus. In early Christianity, when Christians were persecuted, they used a sign to identify each other, the Greek letter, *Chi*, a large curved X. It looked like a shape of a fish, and Christians liked that because the letters in the word fish, "ichthus," were the first letters in words that described Jesus in this order: Jesus, Christ, God, Son, Savior. Christians marked locations of secret meetings and would use the letter to identify each other by a scratch in the dirt or drawing one upon the hand. It was popular by the time the apostle John wrote down Jesus' message of Revelation. Structural linguists analyzed the structure and found chiastic forms throughout. Chiastic meaning the shape of a Chi or X in content. For instance, the seven churches are described in a way that illustrates that topical form. Studying Jesus' message to the seven churches shows parallels with the first and the seventh, the second and the sixth, the third and the fifth, leaving the fourth as the center hub. Looking at a chiastic form is like looking at an hourglass. The "Chi" is Jesus in literary form. With the 'X,' Jesus is indicated within and throughout the book of Revelation.

"Every time I read the book of Revelation, I learn something new," he explained. He then went on to urge readers to look at the content of the book and read the cross-references listed in the margins of many Bibles. The majority of the texts in Revelation have connections to and/or illusions to the Old Testament. That spells out, according to Pastor Lange, that the book of Revelation is a conclusion for the entire Bible, which also is a before and after treatise on the work of our Savior; prediction and fulfillment. And also, Revelation puts the focus on the termination of evil and the triumph of Jesus' true church.

"This book should be studied in detail. It is Jesus talking to his followers before the canon of Scripture was complete. It is the ribbon that ties up the Bible beginning to end. We cannot ignore this book," Pastor Lange concluded.

XXXXX

Isa's popularity soared as he healed more children. He traveled from province to province, preaching Allah's deliverance. Some whispered, asking if this might be the expected Imam Mahdi. Imams invited him to their mosques to speak to their people. Healing sessions followed each service. The phenomenon of Isa spread, and he was invited to be interviewed on Saudi National television. The question-and-answer session was picked up by affiliates in international networks, and the salient points of the conversation were translated into other languages.

The key moment came when Isa answered the question about the call to unite with Christians by worshipping on their Lord's Day of Sunday. "Allah and Jehovah are pleased that we pray to Him. If we pray every day at the appointed time, it is important. If we pray on Sunday with our brothers, that is good, too. Muslims and Christians all have a common mother that means they are one human family. All need to unite, praying together to end this world's disasters and famines. Different names, same god. He would be honored and appeased by our solidarity in prayer," he answered. His answer confirmed for many Muslims the need to bring an end to the animosity between the two large faith groups. His miracles, both for suffering humans and a thirsty landscape, supplemented his authority. Scientists were already analyzing his bringing water to an empty aquifer when no source for the massive amounts could be found. His words could not be denied by a hungry citizenry. Living under extreme privation, people search for any help no matter how scant. When presented with a solution beyond common expectation, they are ready to grasp at the possibility. They wanted what Allah's hand could provide. Radical extremists were losing what popular support remained. Extremist cell groups were being reported to the authorities, and their activities were curtailed to a large degree.

XXXXX

Naziya's power over their weaponry gave them more than pause. They were flattened by an unseen power, a force from an unknown source, a source that had to be recognized. The more superstitious of the soldiers and rebels ran for the horizon, dropping useless weapons in their wake. Others stood their ground, waiting for commanders to tell them what to do. Naziya spoke with authority. "Sudan must catch up to the rest of the world. If we don't unite here and now, we will perish!" The listening commanders waited for more. "There is a plan to bring this world into prosperity once again. If we continue to fight amongst ourselves, we will be left behind. I want to be brought to the president, now, without weapons." She then turned to the rebel side and said, "I want your leader to come with me without weapons. Do I have both of your support?"

"No!" roared the rebel leader. To his response, the rebels yelled in support, holding their rifles high, pumping them up and down. Their yelling suddenly stopped when the leader fell flat, paralyzed.

She turned to look at the commander of the government troops. Under her gaze he hastened to say, "I'll take you there." She then turned to the rebels to find at least a dozen subordinates gathered around their commander, asking him if he was in pain. They straightened up as if they were doing something wrong when they felt her gaze upon them.

"Do you have a second in command?" The men around the commander stood, slowly shuffled, and then furtive looks went to a tall man dressed in military pants and a dirty, blue, half-tucked shirt. He cleared his throat and then answered, "I can bring our party leader here."

"Okay, then we'll wait."

XXXXX

No judge wanted to accept or back the SDA appeal. They were caught between Scylla and Charybdis, between a rock and a hard place, beneath a president backed by international opinion no longer in favor of minority religious practices. They didn't want to grapple against the popular beast. They didn't want to be seen as unwilling to change the horrendous events wreaking havoc on the world. This resistance on the part of judges meant that Adventist institutions had to go forward in voluntary civil disobedience. The legal department of the General Conference of Seventh-day Adventists advised the presidents of their universities and hospitals that they may be arrested if they continued disobeying the presidential order. Every single president decided to stay the course. All but one hospital president agreed to operate in defiance of the order. Under the constitution they knew that they would be exonerated from any culpability based on the now passé doctrine of religious freedom. Today, however, the end of the great controversy between Christ and Satan drew near. These dedicated leaders were ready to greet Jesus after flying through the broken walls of their various prisons.

XXXXX

Chad's attention during the service and during the sermon never wavered away from the front of the sanctuary. But when it came time for dismissal, he looked around a bit while waiting for his row to stand up. He caught sight of a short little figure in a familiar tweed sports jacket slipping out the back. It occurred to him that he wanted to talk with the detective after he saw him, but it was too late.

"You were right, Pastor. I did like your sermon. I have never heard a sermon from Revelation, let alone one that put Jesus in the center of it like you did today. What I can't understand is why other Christians dislike the book," Silvia remarked.

"It's so sad. There is so much that can be learned from the prophecies. More than a couple of thousand, almost three thousand prophecies are in the Bible. Eighty percent are fulfilled as predicted. Twenty percent are yet to be fulfilled in the future. We can watch those being fulfilled in our lifetime," Pastor responded.

"That makes it kind of exciting to be living in this time," Silvia responded.

"And scary," Diana reminded her mother. They shook their heads in agreement. Vonnie touched her arm in sympathy.

"I'm sorry, sweetheart, I didn't mean to—"

"Don't worry, Mother, I know you didn't mean it," Diana came to soothe her mother's embarrassment. "I was thinking of what I read in Matthew 24. 'There will be great tribulation, such has not been from the beginning of the world until now, no, and never will be. And if those days had not been shortened, no one would be saved.'[18] We are in for a difficult time. I'm not sure I'm ready for this. It's kinda scary," Diana added.

"I agree; the hope we have in the Holy Spirit is what will carry us through. The Spirit will comfort and protect us, as He promised. We all know that for a fact because we saw how He protected you," Chad looked at Diana.

"The Lord is a stronghold for the oppressed, a fortress in times of trouble," Vonnie paraphrased.

Pastor hastened to validate that excerpt from Psalm 9:9, "That is so true. In the last week, we've had countless fire bombings of Adventist churches, here in the States and abroad, and not one person was hurt, even when meetings were scheduled. Somehow, our Lord made people late or not able to attend."

---

[18]Matt. 24:21–22, NRSV

"I have a question about your E-Center. Is it guarded?" Silvia asked.

"No," both Cynthia and Brian answered at the same time.

"Why?"

'Cause we know we are doing the Lord's work. He has given us every-thing we need to do this work, validated us with the presence of the Holy Spirit, and demonstrated we are within His will by the successes we are seeing on a daily basis. If God allows this to be destroyed, then that means we're supposed to move on," Brian answered.

"Okay, I guess I should try to get used to this faith-trust thing," Silvia said.

XXXXX

"I don't get it. They're not bad people," Hardine told his boss.

"How in the world do you know that? Can you read minds?" his cap-tain answered in return.

"I studied them with the intent of finding a motive and maybe a pos-sible perp or perps. I went to their church today. At this point everything indicates a group involved in hate crimes against these good people. It would be advantageous to get the perps behind bars."

"Or maybe these Seven Day Evangelists belong behind bars. It's not the first time these people have been the subject of questionable behavior. I don't know if you remember the David Koresh mass suicide in Texas a while back. That was them."

Hardine shook his head. "So far, I haven't found anything like that in my research. I'll keep digging."

"They seem on the surface to be straightforward Christians, but they're known to hide their true intentions. Let me know if you are in over your head and need backup. I want to know every clue you discover. Maybe I can help, you know, two heads are better than one." The captain left him sitting in his office. His inward thought was, *Well now, I at least have his support. If only he would give me a partner, that would be great.*

XXXXX

Years ago, the Minjur aquifer represented a massive source of water. Like all the others, it, too, was sucked dry without regard for the future. Isa stood again near an outlet. This time, a huge crowd gathered about the outlet waiting to see, with their own eyes, a miracle beyond the capacity of an ordinary magician. Technicians were in attendance, this time differing over the mechanisms of the first event. The crowds were amassed around a number of high-end luxury cars from the upper echelon of Saudi society. With simplicity, he raised his arms and spoke, "Allah brings water to his loyal people."

Similar to the first, the pipe belched sludge and muck and then fountained into the desert. The technicians were amazed because the old pumping equipment came to life, and this time, siphoned water from the deep caverns below. The children in attendance frolicked in the ad hoc water park. Isa pronounced, "The wilderness and the dry land shall be glad; and the desert will rejoice and blossom as the rose ... rejoice with joy and singing!"[19] Reporters swarmed around Isa like locusts on green crops. Round, sponge-covered microphones in the shape of black Q-tips assaulted Isa from all directions. The one all-encompassing question coming from every direction, "What's next?"

"I go where I am needed."

XXXXX

Two convoys approached from different directions. The beggar's tin can started to rattle, indicating incoming. Naziya rose from her seat under a tree and strolled out into the middle of the road. The rebel leader came upon the scene a couple of minutes before the five-star general of his imperial majesty's government. He stood in the road, glaring at the under commander. What he really cared to scrutinize stood nearby, eying him with alert thirteen-year-old eyes. This held his attention, and he couldn't fathom her strength over weapons. His manhood would not allow him to stare at her in fear. He chose instead to ignore her the best he could.

The beggar's tin can started to rattle, indicating incoming. Naziya rose from her seat under a tree and strolled out into the middle of the road.

The general came in an armored personnel carrier. Dust swirled around, and he strolled out to one side, giving the fifty-caliber machine gun a clear vector to eliminate his counterpart. If he could kill the rebel leader, it would be a very fine day

[19](Isa. 35:1, HCSB)

indeed. This was true even if one of his sub-commanders got hit in the fusillade. Without a cue from him, the gunner pulled the trigger. A fifty-caliber would put a hole in his enemy the size of a man's fist. It didn't happen; neither did the unmistakable concussive explosion. The general made a slight turn to his left to take a glance at his appointed executioner. He didn't like what he saw. His man was performing a weapons check, trying to clear it of its malfunction. The general then turned back toward the rebel and found him laughing in derision. He let his anger show. A subordinate aide de camp ran at the rebel leader trying to perform for his commander what he desired. He slammed into an unseen wall. He became a believer, lying flat on his back.

"Finally," Naziya emphasized. "it's time to go to the president."

XXXXX

It was early evening when the threesome got back to Chad's home. They were abuzz about the day's experience. After the potluck, church members stayed by, talking of events and God's purpose in all this chaos. Fulfilled prophetic events spiced the conversation and spurred them to prayer and self-commitment. All the way home, Silvia couldn't stop talking. She even asked about the marital status of Pastor Lange.

"Gosh, Mom, I don't know. It never occurred to me to ask."

"He doesn't wear a wedding ring. So, I'm assuming he isn't married."

"I could ask Vonnie the next time we see each other." Diana had a wry smile directed at her mother.

Silvia also indicated her inclination to join in with this group of dedicated believers. She acknowledged that the end must be near. She even thanked Chad for getting her and Diana connected with God's remnant people.

Before closing the garage door, Chad went to the mailbox to get the mail. He came into the kitchen a bit mystified. "Diana, did you give this address as your new address?"

"No, why?"

"Because you and your mom have a letter addressed to the both of you, to this address of all things."

"Whaaat?" Diana took the letter, and Silvia looked over her shoulder. "Open it," Silvia said. After ripping it open, they found one letter addressed to Silvia. Diana's name appeared in parentheses. Silvia took it and began to read. Soon her hand went to her mouth in surprise.

ZZZZZ

Dear Silvia (Diana),
I am a clairvoyant. Yesterday I was in session and contacted a gentleman named Roger Cross. He asked me to send you a letter. I took notes and have been as faithful as possible in writing his message to you.

MME LaFonte

Dear Honey,
I am grateful for this opportunity to send you this warning. Before I get to the warning, you need to be sure this is really me. Remember when we were dating? We took a walk along a river trail and talked of our future. The only two people in the world who know what I am going to say are you and me. Remember the first proposal? You told me that I had to make it romantic before you would accept. I guess it was because I used a pop can ring to make the proposal. I'm glad you made me purchase a real ring because I enjoyed every minute of our time together.

This is my warning. I have been watching you. I am worried. Please don't go to the Seventh-day Adventists. They are liars. Their theology seems logical at first, but below the surface, they steal money from the members and casual attendees. They are against the world faith coalition. They are a cult trying to ruin the noble goals of the world church. Promise me you will stay away from them.

Diana needs to read this letter. Show it to her. Ask her to promise you that she won't pursue this cult or stay with Mr. Johnson if he continues to worship their false god. I love you both and await the time when we can be together again.

Love,
Roger

ZZZZZ

Silvia wept profusely. The letter came in such an unexpected manner. It collided with her emotions in abundant manners. Receiving a message from her deceased husband shocked her to her core. Having him watch her hurt even more, and then telling her to avoid SDAs confused and enraged her about being duped all at the same time. She felt faint and had to sit down. She looked with teary eyes at her daughter for something; she didn't even know for what reason.

Diana couldn't help. Her mind raced in divergent directions trying to think of what this meant. Never before did she have any connection with a psychic. This was unexpected, unknown, and unbelievable. And, it was a message from her father contained in a grief context.

Chad had a different angle on the problem. Vonnie's comment about the dead remaining in the grave, unknowing until the resurrection meant that his folks couldn't be reached by a clairvoyant, and neither could Roger be reached. He looked at this letter as a cleverly devised plan to pull Diana and her mother away from the right direction. He remembered reading in his father's book, *The Great Controversy*, the statement about the doctrine of "the immortality of the soul" being used by Satan to bring people under his deception. He did, however, feel that his hands were tied in saying anything because of the emotional reaction of the two women. He spent his energy comforting Diana and Silvia in their renewed grief.

XXXXX

There wasn't a white flag to precede them, so the general led the way. When the rebel leader appeared, many guards leaped into action, ready to strike him down. The general commanded them to stand down. It worked in most cases; however, there were two instances where loyal soldiers tried to take down the well-known enemy. One weapon failed to discharge; the other had to be blown back with an unseen force in a spectacular way, which resulted in his tumbling over a balustrade to the marble floor below. He received a concussion and a dislocated shoulder. Once in the president's inner chamber, Naziya took over, demanding that the civil war must end.

Striding forward as the rooster over the henhouse, he sought to intimidate what looked like a frail, undernourished waif. With bluster, the president ignored her and spoke to his general, "What's the meaning of this charade? You bring me a child beggar and my flea-infested enemy. Guards! Take these vermin to be executed, including this stupid general who dares to confront me by dialog with treasonous scum."

Once again, Naziya had to demonstrate her leverage. The president became a statue. If his feet hadn't been spread in a defiant manner, he would have fallen over. Instead, he froze in place, unable to move or talk. Naziya began to explain how life in South Sudan would be from this day forward. Everyone in the room waited for the president to assert his dominance, but he didn't move. Aides began to sense something was wrong. They approached hesitantly. Moving their hands in front of his eyes indicated that he could blink but nothing more. Horrified, his aides started to lay him down. Naziya commanded them to stop. She then snapped her fingers to let him go. He came out of his imposed stupor to start a demanding rant against her witchcraft. Holding up her hand, he halted involuntarily. She warned him that if he were unwilling to cease the war, he would be punished. Again, he was released, and he raged at her. Moving violently, he unholstered his luger. Instead of freezing him once again, she used her force to propel him through the air, out the window, and over the banister of the balcony to the concrete porch below. A broken neck killed him instantly. Naziya asked, "Is there anyone else unwilling to bring this war to an end?" Everyone in the room answered they were not.

Pointing to the general and the rebel leader, she told them to form a new coalition government with one the president and the other to be the vice president. They were to flip a coin to decide. If there were any more unrest, she would be back. She left the building and a coterie of stunned individuals.

XXXXX

Chad and Diana had some time to talk alone. Diana calmed considerably with Chad's arms around her. They sat and quietly spoke in the living room. Silvia had retreated to her guest room.

"It is a little over the top to think that my father is watching everything we do. It must hurt him to see all the stuff my mother and I have endured. And then my kidnapping; it wouldn't have been heaven for him to see my jaw broken. It just seems to be too much," she said.

"It kind of doesn't make sense to resurrect the righteous at Jesus' second coming if they are already there in heaven. Why bring them back?"

"I know. My studies of late have been very revealing. I can't believe that people who are rescued by angels are two-faced liars. And besides, I have never had a hint that they are hiding something." Diana's head turned because she sensed her mother at the edge of the living room.

"Roger would never lead me astray!" she said emphatically.

"Mother, I didn't know you were listening. I didn't mean to hurt you."

"I know you didn't, Sweetheart. I didn't mean to eavesdrop. I was coming back for something to drink and heard you talking. I thought of that, too. You and every one of those girls were saved. It was miraculous. It's hard to dismiss the facts. Yet, Roger loves me and …"

Then Chad made a suggestion, "Perhaps we should check what the Bible says about life after death."

CHAPTER 12

"We just wanted to see if we could help," Chad explained after the three walked to the door of the E-center. Silvia was somewhat mollified after they talked it out before. Bible study on the subject of death taught them, among other things, that there are no thoughts or the praising of God in death.[20] Those texts helped them to see that a letter from the other side could not be authentic. Nonetheless, the letter was still tucked in Silvia's purse.

"Thank you for coming. I'll show you around, and you can see what you feel the most comfortable doing. I just set up two more terminals to cover the extra volunteers," Brian answered.

They saw a dozen people studiously working their keyboards. Pastor Lange was one of them, along with Cynthia, Vonnie, and Raphael. The computer systems and social media intimidated Silvia, who had no idea of how she could help. She whispered to Diana her reticence. When her mother went to the restroom, she tapped on Pastor Lange's shoulder to tell him of the problem. He suggested that Silvia help someone by looking up Bible texts. That was the plan. Diana wanted to get her mother to help the pastor. She waited to make her suggestion.

Chad asked Brian how the message was getting out, and Brian explained about buying specialized bots. "These bots are APPs that

---

[20]Psalm 146:4 and Psalm 115:17

187

multiply messages by accessing posts and showing activity on the message. It costs a little to buy the bots, but it is worth it to gain the attention that the truth needs. Businesses use the bots and get the costs back in purchases. We consider it the cost of advertising."

Diana suggested to her mother that she help the pastor in his scripture search. The response was immediate. "Not if there is a chance that Roger might be watching," she responded. Diana could see that the biblical study about death hadn't been completely put to death, so to speak. Vonnie came to the rescue by suggesting that Silvia could help her. She had heard the interchange between mother and daughter and knew she might be able to help because one of the dialogues she was working on had questions on the subject of the immortality of the soul.

Within Silvia, there arose a feeling of relief. This would be the first Sunday worship service she had missed in thirty years with the exception of childbirth and one case of pneumonia. Working in Bible search represented a religious act. She did, however, miss her friends at church. At first, she helped Vonnie by locating on the companion laptop a passage in the Bible that spoke of hurrying the second coming of Jesus. Her search brought up 2 Peter 3:12, "Hastening the coming of the day of God." It turned out to be the passage the online person wanted. Silvia felt she had accomplished something.

Another seeker wanted an answer about whether she should even try to become a Christian. She had heard that God picks some and rejects others. Silvia was launched into a search of Scriptures that mention predestination. This wasn't easy because Vonnie didn't believe that some were eliminated, whether they believed or not. Silvia had been taught all her life that God chose, and only His elect would eventually make the right move. Vonnie had to be diplomatic with Silvia and try to encourage her chatmate online at the same time.

Meanwhile, Silvia found a text juxtaposing those who go to heaven and those to everlasting contempt. Silvia had a moment of cognitive dissonance when she read Daniel 12:2 where it said, "And many of those who sleep in the dust of the earth shall awake, some to everlasting life, and some to shame and everlasting contempt." She was conflicted because the text taught sleep in death and then confirmed for her that some go to heaven, and some do not, i.e. predetermined. Vonnie texted the passage on the sleep of the dead, and, at the same time, dialogued with Silvia on the text's slight reference to some saved, and others are not. Vonnie tried and failed to make the point that the passage was talking about the final result of people making a choice pro or con. She added that God allows free will. Predestination eliminates free will and faith ceases to be a factor in salvation. She suggested that Pastor Lange could probably help explain better, but Silvia seemed uninterested and excused herself to use the restroom again.

XXXXX

Mt. Pinatubo, Philippines, sputtered and spewed. Lava cascaded down the flanks of the mountain, rolling toward the far-off sea, encompassing small communities on its way. Lake Pinatubo, occupying the old caldera no longer existed. The eruption had completely decimated the rim that held back the lake. Magma flowed over the villages, burning buildings in a matter of seconds and then smothering them. Families initially fled the released lake water with only the clothes on their backs. The tourist village of Capas, infamously known as the endpoint of the Bataan Death March, was on the watershed, but now in the lava path from the mountain. The poor villagers were first deluged, then slowly encompassed with hot liquid rock. Infrastructure was destroyed; roads to safety blocked, electricity, clean water, and food were cut off. Nothing was getting through on the ground. Helicopters were lifting survivors to safety one or two at a time.

Isa stood on the road at the point where the lava flow closed off access. Camera crews were making their video reports from the closest point to the disaster. Without preamble, he began to walk straight at the searing hot torrent. Officers detailed to keep the citizenry at a safe distance jumped to prevent him from serious injury. They were prevented by what they saw. Isa halted the flow. Magma banked on the uphill side like the one side of the parting of the Red Sea. On the downhill side, the lava oozed away, leaving dry, cool ground. Once the way became clear, Isa waved the rescue crews to drive through. True to their nature, the news vans charged through first, and then the EMTs walked out to test the ground, and then went to their ambulances to race through. Several slowed to wave thanks to Isa. A miracle takes second billing to rescuing people in need. They were the noble ones on the scene.

XXXXX

Diana sat alone in the break room with her feet up on the easy chair, knees to her chest, and her arms hugging both legs. The catalyst propelling her to this posture came from a dialogue Cynthia had in a chat room. One individual used harsh language to threaten Adventists with certain death and dismembering. The typed words reminded Diana of some of the cuss words used by her abductors. She asked Cynthia if they could be the same people. And the answer was that it would be impossible to tell for sure. It looked like the sender had entered the conversation from a terminal in Dubai. The gutter English and the usage of street words made it more logical the writer sat somewhere in an obscure American ghetto. No matter, it ignited a PTSD flashback reaction within Diana.

Cynthia read the body language as Diana slipped away. She immediately went to Chad to tell him what had happened. Chad went to the room and sat next to his love. Diana slumped over on his shoulder, and he shifted around to encircle her with the patented Chad Johnson protective hold. A familiar posture they had assumed many times before.

Vonnie and Cynthia came into the room to see if Diana was alright. They came and kneeled down near to her and extended their hands to hers. They said nothing, their touch more important than words. Diana patted their hands in response. Silvia entered and saw the foursome surrounding her daughter. Slightly jealous, she wanted to get into the middle of it because, after all, Diana was her daughter. Diana shifted, and Vonnie moved closer to Cynthia to make room for Silvia to sit next to her daughter. After a moment of reflection, Cynthia began to pray. They all prayed, focusing only on Diana. Diana prayed and thanked the Lord for her mother, Chad, and her good friends. Then they had a sympathetic conversation.

"I know God is with me. He has honored my faith by allowing me to be His conduit for healing. Amazing to me is that He used me to heal myself, very surprising. What is interesting is that I can't heal my flashbacks. They seem to be there when I hear a sound or close my eyes," Diana explained.

"Sweetie, I need to take you home and take good care of you," Silvia instructed.

"I know, Mother. You and Chad are doing a wonderful job. I guess it will take some time."

"I mean *our* home. I can't help as much as I like while at Chad's place. It's just not the same." Chad sat a little straighter. Diana reacted with concern, "But, Mother, it's just the two of us. I don't feel safe with just two females. Remember that voyeur who didn't seem to quit. Always peeking into our windows; we had to constantly keep our blinds closed and everything locked? We called the police, and they got tired of trying to catch him. I don't want that feeling again."

"But I want you near me."

"Why can't we … Chad doesn't mind if … Why? I mean, what has changed?"

Silvia looked around and then stood up. "I don't want to be near these people, and I don't want you near them either." After delivering her ultimatum, she stomped out, leaving a room in shock. In addition to shock, Diana was split in two. She hugged her knees and looked down. Once again, positive, silent support surrounded her.

"What happened? I thought she was one of us," Cynthia asked.

"I don't want to be indelicate, but she seemed to be conflicted about the state of the dead and predestination," Vonnie responded.

"I don't know what to do. I should go home with her, but I need Chad to keep me safe, help me feel safe. And that presents a problem in that if I stay with Chad alone, it will look bad."

"Which would you rather do?" Cynthia asked.

Heaving a sigh, she answered, "I guess in a perfect world, I would stay with Chad when it's dark and spend quality time with my mom when I'm not at work. It's awfully difficult to sleep when I'm worried. Then, on the other hand, my mom has always needed me since my father's death. I should at least spend some time with her. I thought she was getting over it when she started asking after unattached males, like Pastor Lange, for example. Now she seems to be reverting back. Oh, I wish she would change her mind."

"I might be able to help. I am temporarily staying with my folks. I could stay with you guys to play chaperone if that would help, at least until your mother changes her mind," Vonnie offered.

Diana reached for Vonnie's hand and squeezed it. "You are real friends, why can't Mother see it?"

"I think that letter from *MME LaFonte* plays into her change of attitude in a large way," Chad observed. Cynthia and Vonnie looked inquisitively. Chad and Diana explained the letter and how it arrived at the house. The two listeners were stupefied by the tangible act of Satan's deception. Spiritualism, playing on people's grief, propels them in any direction he chooses. This reality came uncomfortably close in affecting a person they knew. They were quiet, reflecting on the problem. They decided to pray for Silvia, bowing their heads.

"Hey! Are you expecting me to walk home? Are you coming, or should I call a taxi?" Silvia stood half in the breakroom door with one hand on her hip. Chad and Diana stood, moved toward the door with nary a look at their friends, trying not to irritate Silvia. Chad pulled his phone out of his pocket and waved it at his friends as he escorted Diana out the door. It was an unmistaken message that he would call.

Driving out to the parking lot exit, he stopped to check the traffic. The sounds of racing cars caused Chad to pause even longer. Angry road rage participants were screaming out their fury at each other as they careened and feinted toward each other down the road, trying to force each other off the road without wanting to scratch the paint on their shiny new sports cars.

"What's the holdup," Silvia demanded. Her words were drowned out with the high pitched sound of crumpling metal and screeching brakes. One of the cars shot into the air, twisting over to a topless top landing, abruptly coming to a stop against a family minivan folding it in two halves. The other racer bucked like a wild bronco across a verge decorated with shrubs, trees, and flowers. Sod flew in multiple directions until the front end suddenly acquired an accordion-shaped hood when it collided with a concrete barrier protecting a veteran's memorial. Debris from the fragmenting car took out a Vietnam vet as he stood astride his bike. In total, the victims were six.

Aghast, Chad, Diana, and Silvia watched the unfolding cataclysm. They pulled out of the parking lot and went to the scene of carnage, where they stopped. Exiting the car in a rush, they left the car doors open. Out of the E-Center concerned e-witnessing bloggers raced to provide first aid. Diana went to the family van, Chad raced to the veteran, and bloggers spread out to the two vehicles. The upside-down convertible driver was unreachable, already encased in a leather-lined metal casket. The other driver was out cold in his vehicle that had long ago deployed and deflated its airbags before it ran into the barrier. Brian and Cynthia helped him to the lush grass nearby. Diana, Vonnie, and a host of E-Center associates surrounded the minivan. Silvia kept her distance from the van, watching and calling 911, her way of helping without mixing in with these Adventists.

The mother in the van lay unconscious with a concussion from her head slamming into the side door as it suddenly crumpled inward in her direction. Her teenage daughter had been driving and received lacerations from flying glass and a snapped neck from side impact. She was paralyzed from the neck down. The ten-year-old caromed around the backseat interior because she had unbuckled her seatbelt in anticipation of a frolic in the park. Her injuries were around her body; a broken leg, a dislocated shoulder, a sprained wrist, and a deeply-cut forehead at one temple.

Diana immediately thought of God's gift of healing. She asked Him in a silent prayer, *Is this the time for me to ask You for these people?* She helped extract the ten-year-old from the back seat, not knowing what to do. She was still a novice as to how and when to call upon God to appeal for a healing. When used before, she had never asked. She was about to ask for healing for Karen's bruised legs when God healed anyway while she was praying and without her touching. Now, she desired guidance from above. The quickly-formed team lowered the girl to the ground. One pressed a handkerchief to the bloody wound. It wasn't enough to stanch the pulsating flow. Diana deliberated, looking at the extent of her injuries. Her thoughts were interrupted by a plea from the front seat, "I can't move my arms!"

The revelation stopped Pastor Lange and Raphael Wilson from unbuckling and pulling her out of the front seat. They needed to get both the teen and the mother out through the driver's side door. They were afraid of moving a paralyzed patient. They were stymied. Urgency entered the equation when the engine compartment belched smoke with fire creeping around the buckled hood. Diana heard the deliberations and moved to look. It was then she felt the distinct requirement from above to heal the teen to open the way for the comatose mother.

The teen got even more hysterical as it dawned on her that her head could not move, and her legs seemed detached. "Mom! Help me! I can't move!" Helplessly, she appealed to the only person she could see. Diana leaned in and spoke quietly, "Please relax. Our Lord will make you whole." Diana gently touched her shoulder, instantly, filling her body with radiating heat. The first reaction for the teen was to turn her head to see her benefactor. She found a radiant smile approximating that of an angel.

"Thank you," she whispered as if in a cathedral. She didn't even realize that she had reached to touch her healer's hand. Full realization came with tears of joy. She reached for her unresponsive mother, bringing a fragment of reality back to the moment.

Diana asked, "Can you unbuckle your seat belt for us?" The distraction helped the girl have something to do. They helped her out more to clear the way to help her mother than to assist a girl in peak condition. The two men were euphoric and somber simultaneously. They needed to get to the mother in a hurry but couldn't dismiss from their minds the miracle brushing past in front of them. The increasing conflagration motivated them to surge into the van and unbuckle the mother's belt. As carefully as possible, they manipulated the woman over the center console to the grass next to her teenage daughter. Fire spread around the edge of the hood out from the wheel-wells. Oily black smoke spread along the ground, distributed by a small breeze. An acrid smell accompanied a foul taste as rescue workers breathed in the fumes.

Waiting for the men to get the mother out and to safety, Diana heard a request, "Does anyone have a handkerchief or a Kleenex?" Diana immediately remembered the small pack of tissues in her hip pocket, insurance for her bouts of trembling and worry.

"Here, try these." Diana started to remove a couple but decided to unwrap the entire wad when she saw the wound and the amount of blood. She handed the wad to the attendee and turned to the pastor, who had called for her help. The concerned EMT wanna-be made a quick switch of a completely soaked, makeshift compress for a pristine white wad of tissues. The instant the tissues touched the wound, the bleeding stopped, and the other injuries disappeared. Eyes moved over the child's limbs, watching the transformation. It only took a second for the helper to check the substitute Kleenex bandage. Not a dot of red dwelt on the bandage. No gash. No effulgence of precious fluid. The hyperactive kid wanted to be up and moving; to experience the excitement of a three-car accident. Diana knelt near the mother as the pastor checked the pupils for concussion. Diana touched the woman's cheek, and the pastor watched as the pupils returned to normal functioning. Her memory of the accident would return much later, all one fraction of one second later.

Diana had witnessed two miracles—one she was summoned to, and the other by mere touching. Behind her another grew in happy celebration. She turned to see what was happening, and realization dawned on her that another person had the ability to heal. The only indication of injury was the bloody sop that lay on the ground completely ignored. As expected, the Spirit of God was flowing in great proportions in the midst of last day events. She moved to acknowledge the gift in another when the person said, "That was amazing! It was just like Paul in the book of Acts sending a cloth to a person who needed to be healed!" Now she couldn't be sure of what had happened. Her role in God's plan needed some focus.

Brian and Cynthia called Diana over the rising tumult of yelling bystanders and sirens in the distance. She looked around twice at the family of three, and then to her mother, and then to Chad, and finally back to Brian and Cynthia. They were signaling Diana's need to go to Chad with the veteran. The couple had their hands full with their casualty who had come to and was exhibiting drunken behavior, probably the initial cause of the road rage.

Chad kneeled back down next to the veteran. He had been hit with a chunk of the front grill as it flew off of the car. It sliced open the man's right side, exposing ribs and organs, ending at a hip pointer glistening bright white. Chad had his shirt off, using it to hold the ragged skin and innards in place and trying to keep the patient from bleeding to death. He wasn't winning the battle. The veteran was awake and in agony. The gentleman had a stark memory of when he was wounded during Operation Iraqi Freedom. He wanted to call out for a medic but knew this was a different time, a different place.

Diana hustled toward Chad; Vonnie started to go with her and then stopped. She saw Silvia watching. Her mind raced to the importance of helping Silvia see that Adventists were honest and trustworthy. She went to her and stood next to her. Silvia finished her call to 911 by saying that the EMTs were on the scene. The first ambulance pulled in at the same time as a fire truck, which went straight to the burning van. As Silvia began to walk away, Vonnie said, "Did you see Diana? It was wonderful, beyond wonderful!" Silvia stopped.

"What was wonderful? I saw Diana help the victims out of the van."

"She healed them. Well, I mean, God healed them using the spiritual gift He gave Diana."

"She healed them?"

"Yes."

Their attention became distracted momentarily when the veteran hooted with fists extended into the air. He jumped up and down, his tattered and bloody shirt flapping. The medical personnel arrived, asking him to sit down. They needed to get him calm. They saw the blood and wanted to determine what was needed. Silvia was proud. "It was a good thing for them that Diana was here."

"I agree."

"Those SDA women that were abducted with Diana were lucky she was there, too. Without Diana and God's Spirit, who knows what condition they would be in now," Silvia stated. Vonnie didn't know what else to say that would convince Silvia that the Lord was indeed with the Adventist believers.

XXXXX

In Memphis, Tennessee, a large clinic on the end of a strip of stores sported a sign that said, "Collierville Family Planning." Three ladies were delayed moving in the front door because of a mother holding a teenage daughter exiting. Two other women were passing by on their way to a nail salon about fifty yards down the line of stores. All seven were blasted in, among, and on top of parked cars as the clinic disintegrated outward in debris, smoke, and brilliant light. The sign split in two pieces, landing on cars at the far end of the parking lot.

Because that there Seven-dayer church has been agin' this clinic from the get-go. They're anti-abortionists. I knew it! I knew it. They did this, 'n who knows what else! They're agin' good healthy pork an' the Christian Lord's day, almost ev'r' thin' I can think of.

Fire rescue, fire engines, and police cars swarmed to the scene as good Samaritans sought to apply first aid to survivors. News vans staked out their territory to scoop the story and ask questions as to what and why of witnesses who had no clue.

One interviewee stood on the sidewalk, and confidently said, "I knew this would happen someday!"

"How so?" a reporter asked.

Pointing down the street to a church on the opposite corner, he answered, "Because that there Seven-dayer church has been agin' this clinic from the get-go. They're anti-abortionists. I knew it! I knew it. They did this, 'n who knows what else! They're agin' good healthy pork an' the Christian Lord's day, almost ev'r' thin' I can think of."

XXXXX

Ever since the Arab Spring, Syria has been one of the bloodiest conflicts of the modern age. Yet another fresh uprising started. Naziya planned to end this civil war as well. This was just another cog in the greater machine working toward a resolution. Walking into the presidential palace, she looked like a lost youth separated from a tour of the grounds. Guards sought to redirect her back outdoors. Every one of them became realistic statuary, just like all the real still-life sentinels spaced at strategic locations at the gardens and palace entrance outside.

She marched into the parlor, where the president reclined with a cigar. Seeing her made him jump from his couch like a cat surprised by a snake.

He wanted a more positive image than a lounging grandpa with nothing to do. "Where are my guards?" he spoke to his detail with a voice that could carry to the top of Mount Qassion.

"You have an opportunity to keep your position as president."

"Guards!"

"If you don't act, you will lose it all."

"Get out of my home!" The president went to her and attempted to grab her arm and escort her out of the chamber. It didn't happen. His hand could not penetrate an invisible barrier. Mystified, he walked to the door, searching for his missing guards. Naziya, with superior strength, pushed him out the door. There he saw his guards, permanently rooted to their positions. He went to the nearest and saw blinking eyes. He tried to shake him into activity and succeeded in knocking him over. The guard fell awkwardly like a plastic GI Joe doll.

"You need to tell me if you are willing to end this civil war now," Naziya demanded.

"What will happen if I don't?"

"You'll die."

"All right. What do you want me to do?"

"Remain here. Don't go anywhere. I'll be back with the opposition. Be prepared to compromise." To the president's total astonishment, Naziya flew out the window, heading northeast.

XXXXX

Diana took her mother home. It was only a matter of repacking her overnight bag, and she was gone. Diana, fresh with the feeling of closeness to the Spirit of God, thought she could stay with her mom. God must be protecting her if He needed her for special interventions. Vonnie had volunteered after her interchange with Silvia. Diana thanked her but said she would try to help her mom to get a better perspective. That letter was the culprit and had to be defeated.

At their apartment Rose waited in the parking lot. It didn't take an advanced degree in sociology to see that Rose and Silvia were in cahoots in an endeavor to get Diana out of this cult of Adventists. It all began cordially. Rose asked after their health, and then Silvia told Rose about the accident and Diana's part. That discussion carried them all the way through a quick supper. Reverent awe emanated from Rose. "This is wonderful. Those Adventists don't have healers like we do," Rose reacted.

Diana shook her head in dismay. She wasn't seen because Rose and Silvia were in total agreement, facing each other. Diana felt her mother would never make a studied decision. Her connections with friends from the old church and their prejudicial opinions were a wall of stubborn ignorance. When she thought it couldn't get worse, Silvia showed Rose the letter from Roger. After reading the letter, Rose once again responded that the true church always has the advantage over these satanic offshoots. They turned on Diana and emphasized the unmistakable evidence.

"See? The world is getting on the right side, and these Adventizers are completely missing it. Diana, you've got to see these are not the people to be associated with. You need to have an open mind. Chad is getting lost just like his folks. You're going to have to break the relationship," Silvia gave her an ultimatum.

Rose was quick to back her up. "Your mother is right. Reverend Tucker told me as much a month ago at church when we were talking about the Johnsons' murder."

"I need to think this over. I need some rest. I'm exhausted," Diana made an excuse.

XXXXX

A conclave of Roman Catholic and Eastern Orthodox prelates and more than nine hundred Protestant denominational leaders from around the globe met in the lush surroundings of Maison de la Radio, a concert venue with a colossal pipe organ. It was the perfect place for an accord of epic proportions with the ability to celebrate with the hymns of the ancient church.

The master of ceremonies opened the session with the words, "The protest is over! There is now only one worldwide Christian church and more. This is historic. We are one church of all God's elect." His words were met with universal applause. "The rift between the multiple religious groups and the former partitions of Christianity are now healed; all animosity finished." The emcee introduced, with a dynamic flourish, the keynote speaker, the new leader of the WCF, Pope Sextus VI. The Emcee detailed the pope's rise through the clerical ranks until recently being elected by the conclave of cardinals to the pinnacle of clerical leadership. Not to mention his nomination to the headship of the WCF.

The pope had difficulty beginning his speech because of the standing ovation. Everyone in attendance was thrilled. He wanted to celebrate the moment, but he also wanted to capitalize on the momentum of the church. When he did begin to speak, he used the words "Unified Alliance" to mean the brand new coalition of the newly formed world church. This Unified Alliance was proud of the fact that they were one faith, one God, one grand plan, and one world. Knowing this, the audience erupted in applause every time he said the words. They owned this Unified Alliance. They were proud of their baby. The pope's speech gathered momentum, riding on the wave of enthusiasm. He felt confident to make appeals and reveal plans. The grand design was moving forward faster than hoped.

"This coalition has come together from many perspectives. For example, within the Christian perspective, all the different faith varieties came together because of the John Seventeen Movement. This movement focuses on the words of Jesus before His death. He prayed for unity for all faith groups. Another example is how our Muslim brothers and sisters were drawn into our circle of love. They were drawn to our dear mother of God. Every one of us follows a different path to world unity. Let us welcome each other. Please let us stand and welcome each other, our wonderful friends. Welcome family, welcome, welcome."

The WCF chairman moved onward to his other objectives achieving the strategic purpose of this newly-formed Unified Alliance.

"I call upon all of you and your followers to appeal to the secular leaders in your parishes and precincts where you live and work. We must begin to clean this world in preparation for the returning Savior. Ask your mayors, governors, congressmen, ministers of parliament, assemblymen, representatives, yes, even presidents and prime ministers, to enact legislation to enforce the keeping of the Lord's Day. I know we don't have a consensus of opinion on the unfolding future. Some of us believe the Golden Age begins before the Promised One comes back. And then, some of us believe that He will come and begin the Golden Age on earth. This difference should not divide us. If we begin achieving the Golden Age now, it will be a noble enterprise, whether or not our Beloved returns before or after we achieve success. He will be pleased in either event. Let us roll up our sleeves, start the work this world has needed for centuries, and once and for all appease our Creator. We have everything we need. Now we can act. It is the Unified Alliance's destiny." The gathered listeners erupted in praise once again. If one were to analyze the subject for the applause, one would have to agree that it was self-praise.

Days later, the first indication of the spreading influence coming from the conference would be felt when leaders told subordinates and so on. Then, those individuals reached upward through their secular leaders, indicating the will of the people and the will of the WCF, the new world church.

XXXXX

Diana could not sleep. Even in her familiar bed, the visions of a dimly lit room with a smudged window slightly illuminating a sticky, gooey floor commanded her memories. The memory of the sickly smell was real and took charge of the moment. She could not shake the experience from her head. Getting up in the middle of the night, she crept out of the apartment. She could tell by the breathing that Rose was in the bedroom with her mother. It was two in the morning. She had lain in bed for hours unable to sleep, and then, when she did sleep, she was awakened by the flashback dream. Her mission was to get out to her car and phone Chad. At least she could talk to him and feel somewhat secure.

Chad didn't mind being awakened at that hour. He couldn't sleep either, worrying about whether Diana could sleep. He talked to Diana while getting dressed and then going to his car. By the time she had briefly explained she couldn't sleep, he was on his way. After one block, the Bluetooth in the car had synchronized, and he could talk hands-free. His actions were exactly what she needed. They mutually agreed that they couldn't return to his place because the ever-talkative Rose would have the news of their sexual faux pas all over the church by noon. They stayed in the parking lot in full view of her mother's bedroom. In the morning, when her mother called, she told her to look out the window.

The plan they made was to call Vonnie and take up her offer to stay with them. Diana didn't want to be ganged up on with Rose and her mother telling her what she must do. Her convictions were firmly on the side of what she had recently learned. Then, the blatant prejudice confirmed her conviction. She and Chad went in for breakfast, where Chad fell asleep in his chair halfway through his second toaster waffle.

XXXXX

Naziya had the heads of the Free Syrian Army and the Kurdish Rebel leader at the gates of the palace within the day. Both leaders were visibly cowed. The president had time to deliberate on his response to the other belligerent leaders. He was going to exert his position and historical claim to remain in power. To say the least, the negotiations did not go well. Naziya had to demonstrate power, the only factor understood by all parties. The shouting match ended abruptly when Naziya paralyzed their vocal cords. They stood for a moment and then began using insulting hand gestures. She expected that and brought into the equation candidates with the popular support without being tainted by the warring factions. Treason was the word no one could say, not because they didn't want to, but because they were unable. The little diplomat, really dictator, gave her ultimatum—cease this war or lose everything. They couldn't. She handed the reins over to the replacement team and went to assess the lower echelons of each faction, leaving the bodies of the uncooperative on the floor of the palace. It was as simple as that. People are either led or controlled by hope or fear, respectively. In this case, fear.

BBC reporters and other international media correspondences broke with protocols and conferred with one another about what they knew. They sensed that something had changed, which meant they were beginning to catch on to the fact that quick, quiet coups were happening in war-torn countries. They couldn't find the major players, presidents, generals, etc. Suddenly, they were gone, and new leaders were on the scene. To have unknown big news lurking beyond scrutiny caused a feeding frenzy. Reporters plied every source and went after any tidbit available, like piranhas hungry for raw meat.

XXXXX

Isa suddenly appeared in West Africa. Once again, ebola had raised its ugly head. A containment hospital sat in a lonely field, where no buildings or human activity was evident. The double-sealed tent stood in the quadrangle of a neoprene fence draped over a chain-link fence on land with no visible drainage, preventing oozing fluids from carrying the virus into the water supply and thereby to populated areas. Only one access allowed authorized entry. A large double-lined tent was used to scrub and sanitize any worker entering or exiting. Isa walked deliberately toward the zippered opening.

Assistants who checked credentials and helped with suiting up were all taking a break. They were locked into looking at the floor. They neither heard nor saw Isa walk past them to the hospital. Strolling across the open space, he entered the precincts of pain. His presence caused nurses to react. If he had just walked around a corner, they would have thought of a patient on the rebound, but he came through the opening from the out-side. Wearing no protective gear telegraphed that he was one very stupid dude walking into a deathtrap. They moved to save him.

Isa gazed at the pathetic patients, emesis basins nestled next to pillows at the ready, some of which had fresh bloody vomit. Their eyes were ooz-ing bloody pus. The foul smell emanated from unseen diapers. Two nurses took hold of Isa, intending to guide him away.

"I'm here to help."

"Are you a patient wanting help?"

"No. I'm going to heal these people." The nurses surmised they had a wacko on their hands. They were about to remove him when he stretched forward his hand and touched the closed, blood-rimmed eyelid of a sleep-ing teenage boy. The pale death-pallor vanished, replaced by healthy, glowing chocolate skin. The boy's eyes flashed open in reaction to instant health. He looked around in wonderment. A smile with whiter-than-white teeth blazed across his face.

Isa moved to the next bed. This time, the nurses stood in amazement. Isa asked the man to stand up. He was greeted with a disbelieving grunt as the helpers coaxed him to sit on the edge of the cot. The new-found strength propelled him to jump to his feet. Now the nurses were more than willing participants. Isa progressed down the row of cots designated as terminal. Blood emanated from day eleven victims, from their eyes, nose, and ears. These symptoms were disappearing rapidly. Sufferers now vaulted, leaped, and jumped in celebration. This was a reprieve of magical mega-proportions. Medical projections had given them one more day of life. Now they had a new contract on life. They could choose what and where they wanted to go.

A small crew of reporters was in the support area, making reports on the hopelessness of the new outbreak when the miracles occurred. They now had a giant scoop of the century. They could see visions of a Pulitzer dancing before their eyes. They rushed the entrance tent with cameras rolling and microphones poking into the folds and links of the barrier fence. That evening, their report would be on all the wires for worldwide consumption. Isa would be an idol.

CHAPTER 13

Checking on the new players in South Sudan brought Naziya back to the spoiled farmlands. The people needed food, and the new hierarchy had their hands full, creating a new government without war. Instead of working in semisecret, Naziya tipped off the press, indicating that the famine would be turned around. Curious, a few correspondents showed, wishing and hoping for a good story. They found Naziya standing in a field of melons all ripe and ready to eat. The village beggar rattled his tin can, signaling the people that an event of note

The village beggar rattled his tin can, signaling the people that an event of note had suddenly appeared.

had suddenly appeared. There was a rush toward the melons. Reporters approached Naziya with questions. She ignored them. Instead, she walked to the edge of another field and pointed to the burnt crop spreading into the distance. Beginning from where she stood, the rubble transformed into a ripe, amber sea of wheat. The videographers juddered cameras in surprise. Like a wave spreading away from an oceangoing liner hitting the sea for the first time, the grain rippled outward to the horizon. Bushels upon bushels of wheat were ready to be milled into flour and baked into bread. The media went wild for the astonishing serendipity. They wanted an interview and ran after her. It took some doing to corral her at another field, suddenly ripe with potatoes.

"Who are you?" one correspondent blurted.

"Naziya."

"How do you do this? Is it some kind of magic? This is amazing!"

"The one who created can recreate," she simply said.

"What does that mean? Are you saying you are a creator? You, a child in a dirty dress?"

"Don't downgrade a gift by criticizing the wrapping. Excuse me, I need to move on and feed hungry people and solve world conflicts." Naziya moved onward, the reporter stood in her place, thinking, putting far-flung tidbits of information together. Wild eyes marked the fact that she now knew the secret to the curious goings-on of quiet coups. The next wonder that confronted their senses was a massive horde of Bunyoro rabbits. Village men hustled to capture them in cloaks and makeshift nets.

XXXXX

Friday night sundown services are not universally held in SDA churches. However, recently, many more began in light of the fact that the world events foretold to the membership that the time was near. Prayer occupied the major portions of the services. A core of thoroughly dedicated constituents was huddling together. Prayers were offered on behalf of unbelieving family and friends. The major concerns were for eleventh-hour conversions.

Power failures struck hundreds of SDA churches. Individually, people thought it was only their church. By the next morning, it was more than apparent this was a planned attack upon their denomination and other groups that kept Saturday services. Phone calls to electric companies yielded, in most cases, a courteous answer that they would check into it and restore services immediately. No service was restored until Sunday morning. One unconfirmed report came in that the Sabbathkeepers didn't need electricity.

XXXXX

Hardine attended church once again, seeking information and also inquiring about why electrical service went off at the time of Sabbath observance. This morsel of information was attached to the other items.

He could see a broader comprehensive design. Having worked all his adult life on making the criminal elements pay for their felonies caused him to see this as out of place. Frequently, crimes are committed against fellow offenders. These good people invited him to eat with them and were concerned for his wellbeing. These individuals were not deserving of retribution in any way. The perpetrators were on a mission, a mission he could not figure out. He wanted more time to discern the underlying purpose behind this focus. If he could get to that, he might be able to find names to match the hatred.

Without electricity, worship went forward with piano and voice. To show preference to the hearing-impaired, the congregation clustered close together for prayer and the sermon. Moveable seating was brought forward to bring hearing-challenged worshipers in a ragged circle at the front.

The Perkins family sat with Chad and Diana, their presence adding celebration to the achievements of many witnessing members. Spontaneous songs rang out, and children sang with understanding because many of the songs were at their level. Pastor Lange's sermon aimed at the assurances of God's protection in the final tribulation. Without realizing it, the worship service went longer than normal. They were nourished, revived, and stimulated. The happiness enveloped them as they went downstairs for dinner. Some of the food was slightly warm, not having completely cooled after the electricity ended. Chad accompanied Detective Hardine and got him linked up with the pastor for another session on the unique beliefs of Adventists.

One round table comfortably sat six people; the Perkins were with Chad and Diana. Emilee, at first, ate and then turned in her seat to look at one elderly lady with a walker by her side. Diana watched her. Then she got up and knelt next to Emilee's chair.

"The Lord has told you something, hasn't He?" Diana asked.

"I think so," she answered. Everyone at the table stopped talking to listen to the interchange.

"I know He has because He told me, too. Why don't you and I go over to the nice lady."

"Okay." She slipped off her seat and took Diana's hand. They walked to about a yard's length from the lady, and Diana bade her to go ahead. The fellowship room hushed, sensing something serious was happening. Emilee touched the wrinkled elbow. The woman looked at her with a smile. "I want to make you feel better. Can I pray for you?"

"Of course you may, my dear."

"Close your eyes tight and don't peek, okay?"

"Okay."

"Dear Jesus, make this lady better. She needs help to be better. I know You can do it. Amen."

Mrs. Perkins was about to move to her daughter to console her because nothing seemed to happen. Then, there was a wonderful moment when Emilee was swept up in suddenly sturdy arms. The two swung around in a whirl on formerly feeble legs. Frieda kissed Emilee on the cheek, thanking her for giving her the health to go through the trouble ahead. There couldn't have been a happier moment at a common fellowship meal. Emilee squealed in delight, her benefactor shouted with tears on her cheeks. She placed the young girl on the floor, who ran to her mother. The Perkins were animated in wonder and surprise. Emilee jumped up and down. Nobody could eat; all were into the fun of newfound health. Many congratulated Emilee. She was overwhelmed with the praise and personal attention. Her mother found time to talk with Diana.

"Did Emilee actually heal the lady, or did you do it for her?"

"No, it was Emilee. I am learning to hear God's voice telling me when I should go ahead and work one of His miracles. I heard His voice telling me that He was telling Emilee to heal Frieda. I saw her looking at Frieda and knew she was questioning what she was hearing. I had the same problem figuring out how God works through us. So, I helped her to do what God wanted her to do. It was Emilee and God working together."

Mrs. Perkins began to cry. "We have a wonderful God," she sobbed. "He even lets little hearts do His will."

Later, when some of the jubilation calmed down, Diana took Emilee aside and told that she should not tell anyone how God talks to her. Diana explained that the connection she has with God is very precious and private. No one else should know how it works because Satan might try to pretend he is God. Very solemnly, Emilee shook her head in agreement. Diana told Mr. and Mrs. Perkins the same with a little more detail as to why.

XXXXX

Tiny Adventist day schools in Mumbai have existed for years. Small groups of nearby residents have relied on the schools to educate their children. Nutritious meals accompanied the curriculum. For their ministry, the neighborhoods praised them and begged for them to start more schools in areas where relatives lived.

A graduate from one of those little schools went on in his education to become a celebrated brain surgeon. His most recent success came when he removed a brain tumor in the son of the vice president. The many media outlets carried the vice president's gracious, tearful thank-you, awarding the surgeon a medal of distinguished humanitarian service. The highly-esteemed diplomat heaped praise for his healing powers. The doctor demurred. He explained that he was "the hands of God who does the healing."

To cover the story, networks mobbed the mini-school. It was only a matter of time before the school, its associated church, and its doctrinal stance became the discussion on all media outlets, print and video. Specifically, they zeroed in on the medical ministry of the Adventist church. Monetary gifts for SDA schools poured into the coffers of the church. The news blitz about the surgeon would have died a natural death like all news stories, except for the miracle of a physical healing in New Delhi by a Seventh-day Adventist woman. Again, the country was showered with articles, written and audio, to highlight the compassionate work of the church. The recently-established E-Center could barely answer the multitude of queries. Spicer Adventist University sent two busloads of students and faculty to answer the call. Soon tens of thousands were asking for the locations of SDA churches.

XXXXX

Maracanã Stadium seats almost seventy-five thousand. Today, it was filled to capacity and overflowing with seating on the floor of the venue. It was a convocation of world peace and unity. Media covered the event from every angle. Pope Sextus was the keynote speaker, and delegates came from almost every district in Brazil.

In the rural area of the Amazon basin, where medical missions and ADRA relief provided sustainment ministry to millions, a large coterie of believers existed. They believed in keeping God's commandments and the testimony of Jesus. For decades, SDA student missionaries and medical missionaries had established schools and churches to aid the poor communities and teach them the Word of God. Not a single delegate from these provinces went to the convocation in Rio. Representatives from the majority church met with village leaders and were mystified by their refusal. At first, they thought it might be uneducated naiveté, but when explaining the importance of world spiritual unity and how important it was to please God to bring in a stable climate and righteousness, the local leaders replied that they believed that God does not need to be appeased. He loves us and wants to save us. He wants to rescue His people from world-dominating systems that require His people to disregard His commandments, especially the day of worship.

WCF representatives were taken aback by the perspicacious nature of their boycott. These citizens were not ignorant or uninformed. They felt they needed to be reeducated. Returning to their headquarters, they made plans to help these poor people who needed to be guided by strong, authentic teachers.

XXXXX

Reporters caught up to Naziya at a warehouse that the World Food Programme had filled months ago, and then the government forces had carried it away. It stood empty, not just empty of food, but the shelves, tables, forklifts, and trucks were also gone. The media had a suspicion that Naziya had something to do with at least one of the coups from rumors and secondhand comments. They wanted, yea, longed to ask her if she had a play in the changes. It was too far beyond comprehension for this slight girl to have had an impact on politics, let alone politics of countries in longtime civil wars. They stood there, watching this waif with her hands on her hips.

It was a dramatic silence as she lifted her arms high and then swept them downward. Pallets upon pallets of wheat, rice, beans, and lentils appeared as if a curtain had been pulled aside. A bright, shiny, new forklift stood nearby. New desks with swivel chairs were near one wall. Normally talkative hardcore correspondents were unable to speak. WFP workers were stunned, and then tears began to flow, their prayers answered, answered in a staggering manner.

Naziya moved to slide out unseen. She was unsuccessful. The reporters blocked her exit. Two dozen foam-covered microphones shot forward, aimed at her like Nerf lawn darts. One intrepid journalist inveigled herself into her face, towering over her by at least two feet.

"Why did you restore this food? Government troops will just steal it again."

"No, they won't."

"What makes you so sure?"

"Because I changed the leadership to be a more compatible group. They know they will have to answer to me."

"You changed them? How could you? You're, you're … a child," a second reporter blurted.

"I spoke their language."

"Language! What language?"

"The only language they understand, the 'or else' language."

"Where did the former leaders go?" another asked.

"To their graves. World peace is on its way," she said, and then slipped through their cordon by gliding on air, yet another jaw-dropping occurrence.

"But wait! Wait, please. I need to ask you a question," the first reporter pleaded. Naziya stopped and paused, appearing to think about whether she should talk or not.

XXXXX

Isa stood in the Vatican plaza. The pope was about to appear for his daily address. Crowds waited. Many were there to receive the pope's blessing, which usually happened afterward when the pope mixed with the faithful. As always, there were people, some with children, who needed the blessing in hopes of a cure. Isa saw one wheelchair-bound boy supported with oxygen tubes and a headrest. Isa went to him, knelt, and unbuckled the restraining belt holding him in the chair. Startled parents quickly responded, but not swiftly enough. Isa had the boy standing on his footrests and then helped him to step out onto the cobblestone plaza. The child looked so mystified with eyes of wide-open wonder. The parents swept up their son and whipped around in swirling circles. Isa made to walk off when the family enveloped him in their arms, profusely praising God and thanking him for the miracle.

Another couple watched in deep thought. The wife wore a knit cap, hiding a bald pate. Her husband supported her frail form. No psychologist was needed to interpret the inner thoughts of the couple. Isa extricated himself from the family and approached the couple. They straightened up. Eyes lit up in anticipation. Isa held out his hand, and the woman took it. Immediately, strength surged into her bones. Her face manifested a smile broader than her cheeks. The flesh returned to her gaunt frame. Even more astonishing, her hair started to grow in long, lustrous waves. It was as if she had been in a salon moments before. She clapped her hands like a happy child.

At that moment, an announcement introduced the pope. Isa stood with arms on shoulders between the healed woman and the father of the healed child. They tried and failed to concentrate on the pontiff's words. Joy overwhelmed their concentration. The homily seemed shorter than usual because of personal elation. Before they knew it, the pope began moving through the crowd. What formerly had been first on their agenda, now didn't matter; other families with more critical needs would have a better chance to surge forward. The pope stood up from bending over to kiss a young lad. As he straightened, three Uzi's opened fire, tattooing dark spots on the pontiff's chest. A moment later, crimson stains spread outward as his body hit the ground. Swiss guards sprang into action, pulling weapons on the aggressors, while one fell upon the prelate to protect him from further harm. It was too late. Guards fell, and the little boy cried out in pain. More shots were fired with a different echo signature. Handguns brought down felons, while their automatic weapons spasmodically emptied into the air. The crowd of priests and bystanders screamed in unison as they raced away to every angle of the compass. Seconds later, the plaza had bodies strewn about like a sleep-in demonstration.

> *The pope stood up from bending over to kiss a young lad. As he straightened, three Uzi's opened fire, tattooing dark spots on the pontiff's chest. A moment later, crimson stains spread outward as his body hit the ground.*

Isa stood alone; the crowd around him had fled. Policemen and Swiss guards gave him a glance to see if he presented a threat. They quickly moved on to check the perpetrators as Isa moved slowly toward the prone pontiff. A crowd of aides ministered to him, knowing instantly that no hope lingered in the lifeless body. Some moved to shield the body from cameras from the media or from smartphones. Isa was invisible to the cordon around the prostrate form. He knelt and extended his hand toward the chest. That was when the guards reacted. They moved to stop Isa from desecrating the body. A moment of pause came when they saw his hand hovering above the pope's chest. He wasn't touching, just praying. Isa then offered his hand for the pope to grasp. To everyone watching, astonishment became the norm. The pontiff lifted his hand. Isa helped him stand.

A hush spread across the plaza despite the chaos. It must have been because people were taking in large amounts of air. The pontiff patted his chest in surprise and then bowed in respect to his healer. They exchanged a few words and then, arm-in-arm, moved to the nearest victim where Isa raised up a guard, then a priest, and next, another priest. Surprised police officers froze in place, watching the incredible drama. The only sound that could be heard was the many sirens screaming their way from multiple directions. Escaping crowds slowly came back into the plaza. Individuals who had sought safety behind the columns encircling the plaza peeked around the ionic pillars, wonder replacing worry. More of the victims were raised up. Wounded sufferers were cured. The healed boy became wounded and then was healed again.

The story began to roll out from everyone trying to bring understanding out of the unnatural.

"I was dead, I think!"

"What happened?"

"I don't believe it!"

"I was shot right here. Where's the hole?"

One survivor pointed to his stomach, "I'm okay?" Reporters started to snake their way to the pope and his benefactor. Oddly, guards began to perform their responsibility of protection in the shadow of divine providence.

A teen held her bloody arm where she had been hit with one of the many errant Uzi rounds. She approached Isa. Isa spoke to the pope, asking him to touch the girl. After a moment's hesitation, the pontiff obeyed by touching the arm and healing the trauma. The pope became Isa's disciple.

XXXXX

The presidential executive order landed in everyone's consciousness. For many, it meant that the government was serious about changing the world forever. Others, such as the baser elements, considered it license for mischief. The concept of a republic governed by the will of the people would never exist again. From now on, the world would be an oligarchy, a government by the privileged few. This rule of the few would eventually sit over a mountain of anarchy with local posses enforcing the will of the elite by any means they enjoyed performing, also grabbing anything of value wherever they found it. Those who have are never willing to give up what they possess. They will fight to keep it. If they can't fight for what they want, they work the political system to share the pot. They will go along with any fad or fancy to feather the nest of their future.

On the spiritual side of the coin, the presidential executive order sobered the students of Bible prophecy. It evinced the culmination of the forming of the image of the beast. This meant that the final movements of evil would be swift and furious.

ZZZZZ

Presidential Executive Order Observing the Lord's Day
EXECUTIVE ORDER
OBSERVING THE LORD'S DAY

By the authority vested in me as President by the Constitution and the laws of the United States of America, and to ensure the faithful execution of the laws, it is hereby ordered as follows:

Section 1. Definitions. As used in this order:

(a) " The Lord's day" means Sunday, the first day of the week.

Section 2. Policy. It shall be the policy of the executive branch to promote, enforce, and observe the Lord's Day Law.

(a) Observe the Lord's Day Law. In order to promote economic and national security and to eliminate natural disasters by pleasing our Creator.
(b) Observe the Lord's Day Law. In order to create the Golden Age, bring in world peace with less crime and warfare, higher self-esteem, and prosperity, it shall be the policy of the executive branch to rigorously enforce and administer the laws governing this law.

Section 3. Immediate Enforcement and Assessment of Domestic Prosecution According to Observe the Lord's Day Law.

(a) Every agency shall scrupulously monitor, enforce, and comply with the Observance of the Lord's Day Law, to the extent they apply, and minimize the use of waivers, consistent with applicable law.
(b) Within five (5) days of the date of this order, the heads of all agencies shall:
   (i)   assess the monitoring of, enforcement of, implementation of, and compliance with the Observe the Lord's Day Law within their agencies;

(ii) assess the use of waivers within their agencies by type and impact on the Observe the Lord's Day Law, and,

(iii) develop and propose policies for their agencies to ensure that, to the extent permitted by law, federal financial assistance awards and federal procurements maximize adherence to this law in the United States, and,

(iv) synchronize with WCF agents to ensure compliance with the spirit and letter of the WCF directive.

(c) Within three (3) days of the date of this order, the Attorney General shall issue guidance to agencies about how to make the assessments and to develop the policies required by subsection (b) of this section.

(d) Within five (5) days of the date of this order, the heads of all agencies shall submit findings made pursuant to the assessments required by subsection (b) of this section to the Attorney General.

(e) The Attorney General, in consultation with the Secretary of State, the FBI, and CIA, shall submit to the President a report on Observance of the Lord's Day Law that includes findings from subsections (b), and (d), of this section. This report shall be submitted within five (5) days of the date of this order and shall include specific recommendations to strengthen implementation of Observe the Lord's Day Law, beginning as of today.

Section 4. Judicious Use of Waivers.

(a) To the extent permitted by law, public interest waivers from Observe the Lord's Day Law should be construed to ensure the maximum observance in the United States.

(b) To the extent permitted by law, determination of public interest waivers shall be made by the head of the agency with the authority.

(c) This order is not intended to, and does not, create any right or benefit, substantive, enforceable at law, or in leverage by any party against the United States, its departments, agencies, or entities, its officers, employees, or agents, or any other person.

DANIEL B. CRENSHAW
THE WHITE HOUSE,
September 18.

ZZZZZ

There were many in the United States and abroad that nervously inhaled a giant lungful of air.

XXXXX

Piazza San Pietro couldn't have been more beautiful with rejoicing believers being blessed, healed, and kissed. It was greater than a multitude of holiday papal rituals. This was a menagerie of miracles. The only negative to the scene was the three dead bodies of radical assassins. The Italian police, on loan to the Vatican for murder investigations, were super slow in setting up crime tape in deference to the ongoing reverie. They wanted to watch.

Hours later, the crowd needed to eat. None wanted to leave. The pope felt thirty years younger and could sustain hours more excitement. He invited Isa into his apartment, but secretly wished he could continue. Isa suggested they invite the crowd into the Vatican Gardens. He asked the Secretary of the Congregation (CICLSAL), also wounded and healed, to have tables set up in preparation. Then he told the papal party to leave the refreshments to him.

Leading the crowd through the Vatican museum entrance, the pope and the celebrity of the moment chatted like two buddies in the pope's native language. Ahead, servants raced to set up tables as commanded. Every one of the legates, aids, and recipients of ad hoc cures were thrilled to be a part of this magical event. Many had smartphones out recording the views from every angle. Several had selfie sticks. The media followed the crowd without being restricted. None worried about security because healers were fixing and could fix everything in their wake. Entering the gardens, a double door opened to a set of steps with curving balustrades leading in two directions. To wondering eyes, the tables were laden with food. Loaves of bread, piles of fruit, petit fours, assorted cheeses, steam-ship rounds, La Pan, Fra Gras, and a multitude of cakes, pies, and pastries overloaded on folding tables not designed for such weight.

Nobody plowed into the food. They waited for the blessing. Normally, the pope would bless the food. This time, Isa was asked to do the honors. Cameras small and large, focused on the center of attention. He stepped behind the table of bread, took a large loaf, looked straight into heaven, and broke the loaf in two. The transformation, straight out of a fantasy movie set, flabbergasted everyone. Isa looked like Jesus.

XXXXX

Early Monday morning, Vonnie shuffled out of her bedroom to find Diana curled up in Chad's arms on the living room couch, "Oh, you two are up early."

"Diana couldn't sleep because of her memories," he whispered because he didn't want to wake her, but the voices caused her to rouse anyway. Her sleep was light at best.

"Morning." She yawned.

"You couldn't sleep?"

"No, every time I close my eyes, I see that creepy warehouse and … other things. I know I'm safe, but …"

Vonnie sat next to Diana and patted her legs. "I understand. No one should ever have to experience what happened to you." She then looked at Chad.

"I heard her moving around and got up to see why. That was about one-thirty. So we sat in here and prayed."

"I think I fell asleep while praying. I didn't finish my prayer. I guess I left God waiting for the rest of my prayer."

"He doesn't mind. I finished for you and thanked Him for answering my prayer for you to sleep comfortably."

"Thank you," she cooed and stretched to kiss him on his cheek. "I think it would be good to have some Bible study and prayer right now." Mrs. Johnson's Bible was open on the coffee table to 2 Corinthians 7:1. Diana picked it up. "I read this yesterday at the E-Center about promises and our growth in spirituality. I liked it and started to read it again last night."

They read and prayed over the admonition to become holy, and for Diana, the promise she has the Comforter who will help her. Vonnie took the Bible and started turning pages. She came to another highlighted passage, 2 Corinthians 11:13–15. It spoke of Satan disguising himself as an angel of light. They read it together and discussed the importance of not getting fooled by a false angel.

"I know my angels that helped me were the real thing because there were no strings attached."

"How so?" Chad asked.

"Because they helped. They didn't hang around to receive credit or be in the media spotlight. And they weren't trying to push some theological agenda."

"That's a good point, Diana. We can use that when Satan pretends to be Christ," he replied. "Is either one of you hungry? I've been starving for hours!" he added. Diana cooed again, knowing that meant he stayed awake just for her. He rose, intending to invade the kitchen and glanced back to see if they would follow. Diana and Vonnie looked at each other.

"I guess we need to feed the growing boy," Vonnie joked.

"Man-sized boy," Diana corrected. "Dear, do you want quick or big?" she asked after Chad's disappearing form.

"Huge!" he answered as he went down the hallway to the kitchen. The two ladies followed in a hurry to help Chad in appreciation for his TLC in Diana's distress.

In the kitchen they inventoried the possibilities and decided on Swedish pancakes. Chad set the table and collected the necessary toppings, Diana cut fruit and readied the pan, and Vonnie mixed the batter. They were all too busy to turn on the news. The shocking news waited to be reviewed.

XXXXX

Naziya slowly glided back to the semicircle of correspondents, touching lightly to the ground. Photographers were thrilled with the eyewitness footage of a Superman-like flight with no propulsion or wings to explain.

> *I am the Lord Jesus Christ, your Savior." As she said this, a sphere of light enveloped her, and she was transformed into a tall figure in a white robe with long, wavy, dark hair.*

"Who are you?" Many heads nodded in agreement. They all wanted to know the answer.

"I have come to bring you peace. Ever since I left this world, you have had almost continuous wars. Now is the time for peace and prosperity. I stop the fighting, and I fill the warehouses. Once the hungry are satisfied, we can build the Eden this world was designed to be. Peace from horizon to horizon. War will be no more."

Another asked with a trembling voice, "Are you an alien?"

"I am the Lord Jesus Christ, your Savior." As she said this, a sphere of light enveloped her, and she was transformed into a tall figure in a white robe with long, wavy, dark hair. The light diminished into a cloudy light surrounding her, and the observers gaped as they looked upon a representation of Warner Sallman's famous painting of Jesus. The cameras rolled.

XXXXX

"Diana, Diana! Turn on the TV. Jesus is here! He has actually come! Quick, they're showing Him on TV." Diana signaled to Chad that he should turn on the TV. Then she thought of the need to put on the speakerphone so Chad and Vonnie could identify their presence.

"Mom, I've got you on speakerphone, and the TV is coming on."

"Hi, Mrs. Cross, this is Vonnie. Oh, oh, I see it now; they're showing him standing next to the pope." Vonnie looked at Chad and Diana, shaking her head.

"Mother, that isn't Jesus."

"How can you say that? It looks like Him, and if you listen to the story, you'll see he raised the pope from the dead!"

"Really!? The pope died? Still, the real Jesus is supposed to come from the heavens on a white horse with all His angels with Him. This must be the antichrist," Diana answered.

"Can't be! They were periodically showing the scene in St. Peter's square where people and the pope were killed, and then he raised them back up. You can't fake that."

"Diana, this is Rose. Another thing is they told us that his Arabic name is Isa, which means Son of God. He _is_ the Son of God! You can't dismiss the evidence. And, and, Jesus appeared just like He did with the two on the road to Emmaus when He gave thanks and broke bread."

"This is Chad speaking. In the book of Acts, when Jesus ascended, two angels told the disciples that Jesus would come back in the same manner. He went into the clouds and will come back among the clouds. So far, I don't see where this happened as the angels said."

"Stay out of this, Chad, Diana must know that Jesus is here, and you and those Adventists have it all wrong."

"Mother, he's right; this is not how Jesus is supposed to come back. 'Every eye shall see Him.'"

"Oh, for Pete's sake, just watch and see." She hung up.

Diana wanted to cry for her mother at the same time as being irritated with her. Vonnie rubbed her back, sensing the conflict in her mind. They watched the news. Various reporters had different aspects of the story inside the garden and outside in the plaza. Violence and healing transfixed viewers on the plaza scenes. Pictures of the long-awaited and expected Jesus compelled viewers to worship or pray. Commercial breaks seemed to disappear. Every channel was the same. Disbelievers were held spellbound, like the three finishing breakfast. After a stunned silence, Chad suggested the family room where the television was larger. Without comment, all three went for their Bibles before sitting down in front of the large plasma screen.

Breaking news broke into breaking news. In some cases there were arguments behind the scenes about what could possibly be more important than the news about a returning Savior, or at least, a two-thousand-year-old historical figure. When the networks did break for the competing news, viewers were also in consternation about what could possibly be of higher import. Then, the story began with pictures of a hovering Jesus in front of a stocked warehouse. Correspondents explained where and what they were seeing. Then, separate perspectives told how Naziya produced ripe fields of wheat, fruit, and fresh meat. Then, others told what they knew of her intervention with warring factions.

Their expression of wide-open eyes in shock once again became a duplicated reality. Two false christs appearing at the same time and in manners of mystical dimensions boggled minds around the world. Diana could not pass up the opportunity to call her mother.

"Mom, what do you think about this development? There can't be two Jesuses, right?"

"No, Diana, I'm not stupid."

"Mother, the only reason I called is because we have to study which one is the right one. The Bible is our only hope of sorting this out."

"Well, if you take Chad's comment, this little girl who became Jesus is in a cloud. Maybe she's the right Jesus."

"No, Mom, neither of these fit the right criteria."

"Rose and I are going to call Reverend Tucker. I'll talk to you later. Bye."

Then there came another breaking news event following the abrupt exodus of both Jesuses. A tactical (low-yield) nuclear bomb blew up in the South Korean port of Pusan.

XXXXX

The initial shock wave emanated from an oil tanker parked two miles out in the harbor from the port activity. The tanker was unscheduled and had to wait until dock space allowed them into the inner harbor. The wave of destruction leveled every building involved in shipping and port support. It did considerable damage to structures within three miles of the epicenter. Because the bomb was in the hold of the tanker, it also blasted the water out of the bay and threw it in all directions. Ships were crushed and hurled onto land. No siren blared a warning. The electromagnetic shock killed every electrical circuit in the area. Phones and computers were unresponsive. Cleanup and emergency care were the only priorities. Getting away from the effects was futile unless you were upwind and five miles away. This was a W54 device used tactically (not strategically) in a land battle—a nuclear explosion from what is called a "backpack" nuclear weapon. The damage would have been much greater if it had been a typical device.

Jesus and Jesus flew in from aloft. As twins, indistinguishable from each other, they came down in front of distant cameras unaffected by the electromagnetic pulse. They were video-logging the mushroom cloud. There was a short, sharp negative interchange between the two that could not be heard. Isa told Naziya to go to the left, pointing in that direction. Naziya told Isa to go to the harbor and then flew right. Instead of going where Naziya pointed, Isa went to the edge of the destruction and started uprighting cars, fixing buildings, and what looked like resurrecting the dead. It was difficult to tell for sure because of the distance.

Naziya saw the effects of Isa's work and turned to the mushroom cloud and shooed it away like a stray dog. The cloud vaporized into the stratosphere. She went to the boats and raised them up, placing them back in the harbor in proper shape and afloat. Ambulances followed her/him, stopping to help the casualties that were supposedly brought to life and needed no care.

Isa would not be out-performed. He blew out all the fires in the blast area and cleaned the streets of debris. Correspondents felt little fear and raced forward to see the miracles performed by either Jesus. Isa was the closest. They watched as charred bodies struggled out of newly restored buildings, barely able to walk. Isa pointed at them and waited a dramatic moment before allowing their bloody skinless forms to suddenly possess healthy skin complete with clothes, shoes, and, in some cases, suits and ties.

When Naziya was done, she flew by the cluster of local media and headed west. Isa looked at her, hesitated, then flew after her/him, whatever.

CHAPTER 14

President Hertzog drummed his fingers on his desk blotter. The appearance of the two false christs was strong evidence to close school and send students home. He debated with himself. The Bible said false christs would arise. If that were the only event happening, he would stay the course just a little longer. However, their flying around like Superguy and Supergirl made a convincing argument on its own. Then the president's executive order to enforce Sunday observance tipped the scales. He had to execute his directive to dismiss. However, he wanted to equip them with the advice to stay true to God and His righteousness. He felt like a father with a very large host of nestlings. He picked up his phone and called the Ministry Department, the Department of Religion, and the seminary dean. He was going to set up a seminar on survival. It would be difficult to rip the students and faculty away from the news on the TV sets.

XXXXX

An irritating boil did not rank large on the news of the day. If it got worse, a trip to the pharmacist might be the easiest solution or to a doctor, if even more mucous appeared. What wasn't known was the widespread infection that was slowly and quietly disseminating around the country. Most people chose to deal with the minor skin irritant on their own.

XXXXX

Many were wondering how the president's executive order would impact them. They heard from local news networks that churches, mosques, and temples needed to report to their nearest post office to collect national card readers that would record their attendance. They explained that the cards needed were a regular use credit or debit card. When the card registered a gift to the religious organization, it was automatically reported to the IRS, the Attorney General's office, and the State Department. The gift had to be the minimum requirement of five dollars. Amused officials thought it a stroke of genius to help religious establishments with this requirement. After all, churches helped the indigent.

Waivers were announced for the elderly, feeble, and hospitalized unable to attend on Sunday. Those waivers needed validation from doctors, social workers, and hospital/nursing home administrators.

XXXXX

"Mrs. Cross, you can be sure that the Jesus that brought the pope back to life is the real Jesus," Reverend Tucker assured her over the phone.

"Why do you say that?"

"Because that healing preserved the WCF. That is our only hope of recreating our world. You see, the false Jesus wouldn't work against himself. 'A house divided against itself cannot stand.' That's what Jesus said."

"I see. But how can we be sure which is which? They look the same, and they both do miracles," Silvia asked.

"The Bible says that Satan will be able to appear as an angel of light. Time will tell. Their behaviors will eventually show who they are. They are the definition of an antipode; direct or exact opposite."

"I guess we have to wait and see."

"Exactly!"

XXXXX

Jesuit teachers, prevalent in Brazil, and priests, also prevalent, met with the village people in their small towns and hamlets scattered far and wide through the Amazon basin. Reporters came via boats and launches to record the meetings and send their reports to their news outlets and AP and UPI connections. The Jesuits wanted to have the country see their beneficent, indulgent ministrations for these poor people who had been wrongly persuaded to a false viewpoint.

After introductions in one meeting, following the practice of respect to elders, a frail, elderly man was picked by the visitors to speak on behalf of the local people. Surprising the officials, the elderly gentleman spoke with authority, turning the visitors' mission back on them, "We have a purpose to teach *you* the truth that will save your lives. You must come out of your church and join the truth. God does not need to be appeased like you teach your people. That is a false belief. God provides for us a way to be saved because He loves us," he affirmed with a commanding voice.

"You're not yet aware of how important it is to have the elements of Jesus' body and blood in the Holy Eucharist. You can't be saved without it. You should know this."

"I do know that the Eucharist is a false rite. If you recreate Jesus' sacrifice every day in the mass, you are taking away from Jesus' sacrifice on the cross. His act on the cross was for everyone if they ask, not because they take a tiny wafer. Jesus saves, not by ritual but by faith in Him. You're making His redemptive work worthless by your repetition and your belief that you are actually recreating the body of Jesus. You must come away from that kind of worship. Worship the Creator and the Redeemer, not a piece of bread." This elder spoke with power even though his wrinkled face and bent body visually spoke of weakness. Maybe that is why they picked him first. The lead priest signaled to the cameraman to cut. Reluctantly, he complied with a smile on his face because of the old man.

The meeting in the next stopover up the river brought another debate. This time, they were ready. They planned on selecting someone with less chutzpah. The villagers were already sitting in triple semicircles like attentive children. The delegation chatted among themselves, looking for the one they could dominate. They settled on an unsuspecting dupe. When beginning the meeting, a youth stood to their surprise and asked, "Why do you come to teach us? We don't need your teaching."

"You can't mean that. We've come to help you see the better way."

"We don't need your help. We are ready."

"Ready for what may I ask?"

"Jesus is coming, and we are ready."

"Haven't you heard Jesus has already arrived? It's all over the news," the priest informed her.

"No, He hasn't. We'd be on our way to heaven right now if He had."

"Here, let me show you on my smartphone." The priest brought out his phone, and the whole village moved in to see it. It was like flies moving on honey. The video was about the healing of the pope. "See Isa brought His Holiness back to life. The name Isa means Son of God. And look at this. Here, he changes into Jesus. Watch." The entire group crushed forward heads ear to ear. Then to the priest's surprise, they began to chuckle. "What's so funny?"

"That's not Jesus!"

"How can you be so sure?"

"Because, Jesus will come in the clouds of glory and 'every eye will see Him,' and all His angels with Him. We would've seen Him, up there," The youth pointed upward through the leafy canopy to a single star shining through. "Up there, Padre. Not down here."

> *The entire group crushed forward heads ear to ear. Then to the priest's surprise, they began to chuckle. "What's so funny?" "That's not Jesus!*

"But Jesus healed Our Dear Father."

"That was nice, but that ain't Jesus. Jesus would heal all of us in the wink of His eye. I'll wait for Him." The young girl lifted her leg, revealing a missing foot. While this fact worked its way into the consciousness of the listening priest, the young girl appealed, "Please, sir, you have to come away from that church. Wait with me for the real Jesus."

The teams really didn't find very many people that wanted to accept their teaching. Some did, but not the majority. Their excursion into the jungle did not reap the benefit they sought. They returned to the big city, working in their collective minds what their next move would have to be.

The contracted photographers were thrilled with a story of active revolt. How could anyone deny the facts when presenting them in such a clear manner? They edited the videos and presented it to their outlets. The video was snapped up and fielded worldwide. Soon, the story was presented as a counterpoint to the huge story of the ages, generating large-scale reactions pro and con.

XXXXX

Streets around the globe began to be battlefields. Angry drivers acted as if they should be the only ones on the road. Accidents quadrupled. E-Center operators had difficulty getting to work through the hubbub of stalled and diverted traffic. They delayed the morning devotional to accommodate the tardy ones. Everyone had the same excuse. No one faulted them. None really wanted to move to their homes. The night crew loitered around to get in on the prayer session. Prayer is attractive, but with the Holy Spirit in attendance, prayer is addictive.

Chad and Diana wanted very much to be in on the reaction that the E-Center would receive in the wake of the two Jesuses appearing. Vonnie had asked them to give her a full story when she got off of work. Pastor Lange read from the Bible and from a devotional book. "'Because lawlessness is increased, most people's love will grow cold.'[21] Also, in 2 Thess. 2:9–13, it tells us, 'The coming of the lawless one is by the activity of Satan with all power and false signs and wonders, and with all wicked deception for those who are perishing, because they refused to love the truth and so be saved. Therefore God sends them a strong delusion, so that they may believe what is false, in order that all may be condemned who did not believe the truth but had pleasure in unrighteousness' (ESV).

"This is what we are in the middle of right now. Lawlessness is multiplying. We can see it in how people are driving and acting. Similar to the news in competitive sports, there's more fighting rather than playing. This is also like what happened before Noah's flood. In Genesis 6, 'Everything man did was with an evil purpose and all became corrupted … Then God said unto Noah, The end of all flesh is come before me; for the earth is filled with violence through them; and, behold, I will destroy them with the earth.'[22] As God's ways were abandoned back in Noah's day, it gave way to a spreading growth of iniquity and violence. There was no government in the antediluvian world to control this widespread lawlessness, yet, God's Spirit was there to restrain evil and uphold morality in those who were open to His promptings. We are open to Him. We pray, and He responds. Let us have a season of prayer."

The team prayed fervently. Knowing what was happening in the world, with false messiahs flying around convincing the world they were the Savior, caused the team to long for the real Savior. When they opened their eyes, they were refreshed as if they had never worked the night shift or fought through maddening traffic. They began to talk.

'I'm starting to see people with boils. My neighbor has one on her arm, and I was grocery shopping yesterday, and a man had one on his neck.

[21]Matt. 24:12, NASB
[22]Gen. 6:13, RSV

Is this the beginning of the first plague? It's not a lot, but we're close now. What do you think?" Cynthia asked.

"The easy answer is, I don't know for sure. But, you're right; we are close, and we could expect to see that anytime now ..."

"Pastor, that brings up the question of should we stop our work here in the E-Center?" Brian asked.

"That's a difficult question. I have always believed, but I could be wrong, that Jesus' intercessory ministry ends when He steps out of the heavenly sanctuary and prepares for His return to earth *before* the plagues begin. I asked myself, why would He pour out the seven last plagues on people who may still turn to Him? It doesn't seem logical, knowing our loving Lord. If the Holy Spirit is withdrawn from this earth in preparation for His coming and the end of sin, then there is no way for sinners to repent because the urge to come to Him comes from the Spirit. Now, to return to your question, Cynthia, the first plague is boils, and when that comes upon the earth in abundance, we should take notice that it has begun. Will it begin slowly or quickly? Do the plagues build up gradually? I have to shrug my shoulders in ignorance. Back to you, Brian, if the first plague starts in earnest, perhaps we should head for the hills and leave this center behind. I hate to think of all the great effort and expenditure you have put into this work being left behind. Then I also hate to think of ending our ministry too early. Do you guys know what I mean? I would urge that we put out the last loud cry for people to get out." The team members nodded in agreement.

"I was wondering if we could do something for Diana," Chad asked as the participants looked eager to help.

"Sure, anything. Diana, what do you need from us?" Cynthia responded. Diana didn't answer. She looked expectantly to Chad.

"Can we all pray for Diana. She can't sleep because she's reliving the abduction every time she closes her eyes," he explained.

"Sweetie, I told you it will eventually go away. It's just a matter of time. You can't erase history. I know you're concerned for me, but I'll be alright."

"You don't mind if we pray for you, right?" Cynthia asked.

"No, I don't mind. It's just that I don't need anything for myself, really."

Pastor Lange decided to cut in, "You know what I see, Diana? I see you are very other-person centered. You want the best for others around you, and you put yourself behind that. I see you as a very caring person.

That is wonderful, and maybe that is why God bestowed on you His special gift of healing. It won't hurt to ask God to act on your behalf. Let Him decide. Would that be okay for you?"

"No, it would not hurt. It's a little uncomfortable, though, to be the center of attention."

"Just for a little bit," Chad smiled. The group clasped hands and bowed their heads. As they prayed, hands began to search for Diana's hands. Soon they were holding her hands in the shape of a wheel with arms like spokes meeting at the hub. The prayer was open, with prayer coming from random directions. They ended smiling at their good friend, only to find her sleeping comfortably sitting next to Chad. Without a word, they rose and left the breakroom. Chad gently lowered her to the cushions and put her feet up. He placed a pillow under her head and spread a couch throw over her form. Like the others, he went to work in the E-Center.

XXXXX

Ever vigilant, the media found the two messiahs at two different locations known for the hideouts of militants attempting to destroy the world's blossoming unity. Isa, landing in a mountain sanctuary in Pakistan's Hindu Kush Mountains, brought two vigilant sentinels to action who were spying for the media. They didn't fully expect an individual flying in from above, but the news stories had reached them in their lofty perch. They grabbed their long-range cameras and moved in to record the excitement.

Suddenly they saw and felt a massive explosion that sank a large portion of the mountain complex. The cameras documented dust as it rose over the mass grave. It took hours before they could see the missing formations of rock and ridge. Isa moved to another complex within the rugged range bordering Afghanistan and Pakistan.

XXXXX

Naziya wasted the desert places where hovels hid radical Islamists in Oman, Iraq, and Syria. She flew over the terrain, spreading fiery destruction in her wake. Her attack was perfect in its precision, weeding out cells of fanatical extremists who perpetrated attacks on the general public. Obviously, she believed these terrorists were beyond diplomacy.

The whole world wanted their nonsensical violence to stop. It was meaningless to all but a very few. If anyone could bring this violence to an end, they would be lauded from Sunday to Sunday. That was Naziya's intention—to bring it to a quick end. And their cameras caught her actions.

XXXXX

Across the world media discussions were basically the same as the one taking place in New York City at a local television talk show.

ZZZZZ

"It's illogical to have two Jesuses running around claiming to be the real thing!"

"Yeah, which one are we to believe is real?"

"Neither!"

"The first one, the one who healed the pope."

"How can you tell which one is that one? They both look identical. We can't believe in both."

"This is asinine! It's a mockery of true faith!" a male panelist responded.

"How can you say that? They have been healing people, bringing back crops, filling empty warehouses, reversing the effects of an atomic blast, not to mention stopping conflicts that have been going on for years, even decades. This is a huge benefit for the world. How can their work be asinine? They seem to be working together. We are on the cusp of peace, peace, I tell you, world peace!"

"Don't forget they fly! They have to be aliens from another solar system."

"I know it is politically incorrect to quote the Bible, but the Bible says, 'There will be false christs.' Jesus predicted there would be more than one. He used the word in its plural form," a female panelist explained.

"So you're saying that both of these are false christs,"

"No, yes, I don't know. When I was young, my folks made us go to church. It's been a long time, and I'd have to research this to see what that quote is really saying. I'll get back to you on that."

"Then why bring it up if you're not prepared for this discussion?"

"Hey! How can anyone prepare for this? Identical twins on a mission to fix the world claiming to be the saviors of humankind," she retorted.

"I have a suggestion," another offered.

"Go on."

"Take the meaning of their names. That might tell us something." No one asked him what he meant, so he told them. "Isa means 'son of god.' And Naziya means 'high aspiring,' in Sudanese if you will. If they are both from the same place, or whatever, then Isa must be the leader because he is the son of god, and the other is aspiring to be like him."

"That's nuts. I don't believe either one is the son of God or a god, for that matter, just aliens trying to take over this planet. They're using mankind's mystical beliefs to their own benefit."

"If we look at their work and their abilities, they are like the mythical Greek gods, only real."

"Well, there you have it, folks. The full spectrum is before us; gods, aliens, and false christs, signs of this crazy world we live in."

ZZZZZ

The sound went off, but you could still see the panelists arguing with each other on the studio set.

XXXXX

God's commandment-keeping people were streaming away from SDA universities and academies. Parents, teachers, and fellow students were aiding each other in getting home and planning the flight to sanctuaries away from the public all-seeing eye. A number of the E-Centers closed operations because of their link with students from Adventist institutions.

Diana stretched and yawned. She looked around for her praying companions and found the room empty. Without looking at her phone, she opened the door into the work area. They were buzzing in animated conversations as keyboards clicked in a flurry of activity. Paper cups and plates were everywhere. They had obviously been eating on the fly. Then, it dawned on her that time had passed for lunch to be finished. She checked her phone readout and found that it was four in the afternoon. It was an answer to prayer. No intruding flashbacks had ruined her rest. She had to ask herself why she thought God would not be interested in her individual plight. Right there, she thanked her Lord.

"Hey, look who's up? Good afternoon, sleepyhead," spoke Cynthia in jest. A number of workers broke off and came to Diana to celebrate her undisturbed sleep. Chad was there in a flash, happy with her hours of rest. Diana had a big smile.

"Normally, I might be offended being called a sleepyhead at four in the afternoon. But today, I am delighted." Diana touched Cynthia's shoulder and smiled at her friend.

"So, tell me. How's the dialogue on these two false christs?"

"Oh, you wouldn't believe it; we're enjoying a tremendous response. Remarks are all over the spectrum, from strange to completely weird. I think we've helped people with a better perspective. Also, we've started to call them out of the world coalition by advising caution," Cynthia responded. Before Chad and others could give their responses, the main door crashed open. Two police officers burst into the room. Everyone looked up in alarm.

XXXXX

Vonnie saw movement out of the corner of her eye while she scanned the documents laid out on her desk. She looked up. Mrs. Greene was coming in her door. She started to stand.

"Please, don't stand for me. Keep your seat."

"Okay." Vonnie watched as her boss closed the door and took a chair next to her desk. She said to herself, *This looks serious.* "How can I help you, Mrs. Greene?"

"I'm debating with myself whether I should have you call me Mrs. Greene or Leticia. Let's keep it at Mrs. Greene for now."

"All right."

"The company is making sweeping changes immediately. The word came down an hour ago. And, I've been in deep thought ever since. Anyway, here's the situation. I have been asked to supervise the evening shift. That means all activities, personnel, and productivity ..." she paused.

"That means you've been promoted. Congratulations! I think. You don't seem to be celebratory. What's wrong?"

"Nothing's wrong. You're right, I am being promoted, and a lot of people are being moved up or out. I feel complimented by the selection. It's an honor. But, and it's a big but, I have to be a part of the selection process. I'm supposed to handpick my second and reform the entire swing shift to conform to the new protocols."

"That is big. How can I help?"

"Well, I want you as my second."

"Me? Why me?"

"'Cause you're trustworthy and reliable. Your salary would triple, and you would have stock options. It would mean that this company would have finally broken the glass ceiling on the swing shift with two of us at the top. And women would be in the majority when combining all three shifts and the head shed.

"I am wondering, what days, er, hours would I be working?"

"Weekends." Thoughtful quietude lingered as Vonnie realized she would have to turn down her boss and the confidence she was placing upon her. She almost began her denial when Mrs. Greene continued. "I know what you are thinking. Normally, I would find a way to accommodate your beliefs, because I think that makes people like you loyal workers. However, this time, the head shed wants to take advantage of the times. Saturday Sabbath-keepers are to be eliminated. I want to appeal to you. I need your reliability. I don't want anybody else, just you. Please take this job. I can actually boost your salary to the next level of seniority. Will you please accept the job for me?"

> *Saturday Sabbath-keepers are to be eliminated. I want to appeal to you. I need your reliability. I don't want anybody else, just you.*

Vonnie didn't want to disappoint her mentor. This was a giant leap up the career ladder based on her connection with one person. "Mrs. Greene, I must decline. I'm sorry. I have to stay true to my conviction."

"Maybe God would forgive you if you broke His law occasionally. Don't you agree?"

"God always forgives us, but breaking His law purposely to have a better job working for a wonderful boss is not right. I owe my allegiance to God, and I don't want to disappoint Him. Also, we are near the very end. I want to greet my Savior without a guilty conscience."

"Are you sure? This is a great opportunity. You may never have a chance like this again."

"I'm sure."

"I'm sorry to tell you this, but tomorrow is your last day. The brass wants to rid itself of all Sabbath-keepers before they become an embarrassment. You'll get all remaining pay and will be paid for your accrued vacation time. You might want to bring some boxes with you tomorrow to clean out your office, or, if you don't have enough, I have a few upstairs you can use. Again, I'm sorry."

"Please don't be sorry for me. I expected this, sometime. It has been predicted. I count myself fortunate to be on earth at the time of Jesus' return. Thank you for thinking of me, Mrs. Greene."

"Call me Leticia."

"Why the change, may I ask?"

"Because I'm quitting, too. I want you to teach me about your faith." She smiled.

"Oh, I see, that's why you have boxes."

"You're right."

"So, this was a test!"

"I knew you'd pass."

XXXXX

"You must cease and desist now!" The one officer commanded.

"Ah, sir, do you have the right place? We aren't doing anything illegal here," Chad answered while sweeping his arm around, indicating the bank of computers.

"This center has been reported being active in fomenting dissent against the federal government. Move away from those computers."

"We are loyal citizens. We wouldn't do that. We are not law-breakers," Brian explained.

"The complaint is that you are teaching people to observe a day other than what is required by the president's executive order."

"Officer, we don't mean to be troublesome, but we are protected under the constitution for free speech and the free exercise of religion," Diana answered.

"Not when your speech is treasonous. We are not going to debate this anymore. Get out before I lose my cool. Are you going to leave peacefully?"

"Yes, sir, we'll leave now. If you could give us a chance to collect our personal belongings, we won't give you any trouble," Brian answered for the group even though Pastor Lange was the spiritual leader. They all recognized his and Cynthia's investment in the E-Center. They would be losing all the money they put into the endeavor. However, they all knew things like this would happen. It caused them a degree of happiness.

The officers watched carefully as they packed, not allowing them to get near the terminals to finish conversations or alter evidence. Diana noticed several boils on the less verbal of the two men. She approached carefully.

"Sir, I see you have a painful irritation on your cheek. Can I help?"

"What can you do?" he said dubiously. A knowing pause permeated the room. People stopped to watch the coming miracle. The other officer was alerted by the behavior and the gaze of the people in the room. When she stretched out her hand, he moved his face away. "It may be infectious."

"In a second it won't be," she answered.

Her statement caused him to stop, giving her the opportunity to gently touch his bubbly skin. The transformation was instantaneous. A soft 'ah' filled the room. It interrupted the harsh side of the watching policeman. He changed his mind about these people. He still had to evict them, but he didn't have to take them into custody. He could just tell the waiting team that arrests were unnecessary.

The exodus was smooth and uneventful. Brian left with Cynthia touching a kill switch at the edge of the door as they went. All electricity snapped off. Computers would have to reboot, and then complicated, extra-long passwords would prevent access until a very capable black hat could hack into the system. Brian correctly anticipated that evangelism in any form would be curtailed by any means possible. After losing thousands of dollars in sophisticated equipment here and all over the world, Brian had a smile on his face as he left, especially when he saw the replacement workers waiting to enter his building to reverse the work of his team. They would be delayed getting to work, and he knew the close of salvation's probation was at hand. It meant the work of counter-witness would be ineffectual.

Two police officers looked upon the departure of the team with mixed feelings. This experience didn't add up in many ways.

XXXXX

Vonnie and Leticia indulged in a very long supper at a salad buffet. Their conversation was comfortable and informative. Leticia had sensed that stressors in the world were extreme, and then when two fake Jesuses had entered the scene, she had to revert to her childhood training in a Pentecostal church. For her, the Holy Spirit was always near, even when she had turned down her connection with God and aggressively sought a career in industry management. The rapture was her escape route if she returned to Jesus in time. Then, she got online in a chat room where some bloggers explained that the second coming was a visible, loud, culminating event where the unbelievers were slain with the brightness of His coming. Then, she watched Vonnie's commitment to her admirable friends, her church, and to God in the middle of prejudicial harassment. She wanted to know more and began a study on her own. Now she faced a friend possessing the knowledge she needed.

They had their Bibles open in front of them and searched together. Their discussion was interrupted by a nasty waitress, "Are you finished? 'Cause we've got customers to seat. Order more or leave!" Leticia looked at Vonnie and said, "I've got this—my treat." Leticia ran her card with a zero tip, then changed her mind and left a nice tip. After all, money no longer counts for anything in the new world.

In the parking lot, Vonnie invited her to Chad's place after calling him to see if that was okay. It was more than okay. It was great.

XXXXX

Pastor Lange had two surprises, one after another. The E-Center's closure, not unexpected, yet stunning in that it happened in front of his eyes. Then, he pulled into the driveway of the church to find a crew of hard hats working around the large brick sign identifying the SDA church. As he got out of the car, every one of the men backed away from the sign. The crew boss came straight at Peter, telling him to remove his car immediately. His first reaction was to ask what was going on. The boss said, "It's your car. What'da I care." He then walked off. Pastor Lange watched him stride to the truck, quizzing the meaning of his hand signal as he went out of sight behind the vehicle.

Bam! The blast blew apart the sign, driving broken bricks in every direction, several hitting the side of Pastor Lange's car. His reflex was to duck, but he wasn't fast enough to avoid shards of masonry zipping past his head and the blast knocking him backward. He ended up flat on his back, looking straight into the sky. Ringing in his ears drowned out the laughter from the lawn by the front entrance. He looked like he had been killed. Nobody bothered.

Out from behind the truck came two men carrying a temporary sign announcing the new location for a Sunday-keeping church. The small group of people, by the entrance, were clapping. The applause was for their new acquisition, a fully complete church building younger than their older building with the crumbling foundation.

Peter groaned as he rolled over and pushed himself to his knees first and then to his feet. He staggered a few steps before he could walk normally toward the pastor's office door. He could see this as his last trip to his sanctum sanctorum. The small group moved toward him.

"What do you think you are doing?" one man asked. Peter's eyes cleared enough to see that the voice belonged to Reverend Tucker.

"I ah, I ah, was going to get some of my things out of my office."

"It's not your office anymore."

Peter thought about it for a brief moment and then thrust his hand into his pocket, pulling a keychain out. He took a ring of church keys off of another ring containing his car and residence keys. "You'll be needing these. You won't have to hire a locksmith."

CHAPTER 15

The narrow streets leading to the Temple Mount, where the Dome of The Rock was located, were crowded. They weren't crowded because of commerce; they were crowded because of a rumor. Jesus was there. Surging forward, the feeble and the young were beset and fearful of the press of frenzied bodies. They sought safety against walls and in doorways. All eleven gates to the site were open, and the Islamic guards could not contain the push. Ten gates were for Muslims and one for non-Muslims. Besides, the guards were also in awe as Naziya hovered above one of the four minarets near the Al-Aqsa Mosque. Everyone wanted to catch a glimpse of the flying Jesus.

In a brilliant flash, the gilded Dome of the Rock disintegrated. No one was seriously hurt, a miracle in itself. One second it was there; the next it was a pile of rubble.

"This structure has stood in the way of unity between Judaism and Islam for centuries. Now it is gone, and peace can begin." The Naziya Jesus spoke, her voice echoing off of every wall and alleyway.

Before the gathered witnesses could return to natural breathing, Isa Jesus appeared low in the eastern sky with thousands of angels with him. The murmur from the crowds was a cacophony of clamor. Isa moved downward and forward toward the eastern wall, which contained the sealed Golden Gate. It was from that direction that Jews expected their Messiah to come from. It appeared as though he would slam into the Golden Gate in a spectacular collision. Crumbling blocks of rock fell away from the gate as if by magic. Then, a slanted slope allowed Isa to glide through the gate and up the newly-made promenade to confront Naziya Jesus. A dramatic pause built into the climax of the day.

"Naziya, you are a pretender. As your name represents, 'High Aspiring,' you have been aspiring to raise your throne above the Father's throne from the beginning. You are Lucifer, and it is time to tie you up and send you to the abyss." An angel with a heavy chain appeared over Naziya Jesus and took hold of his arms. He did not struggle. Then Isa Jesus instructed the angel to take him away. "Take him to the Krubera Cave in Abkhazia and seal him in for a thousand years." She/he was flown away unceremoniously, and Isa turned to address the crowds and the assembled media.

"The antichrist is gone. I am here to bring in the planned millennium." In the midst of his words, the Dome of the Rock assembled back into its former glory. "Destroying this shrine won't bring us together. Our unity comes from our determination to achieve one world organization that will allow us to become what I originally designed. All of our paths have taken us to this point. It is time to enjoy solidarity. Come, let us walk together." Isa Jesus landed on the ground and blended in with the adoring fans.

> *The antichrist is gone. I am here to bring in the planned millennium.*

XXXXX

"Well, that settles that. Jesus got rid of the antichrist. I've got to call Diana. She can't dismiss *this* willy-nilly."

"She has to leave that cult. Don't forget to tell her that the facts prove she has to get away from those false teachers," Rose directed. "We have the facts this time," she added.

They looked meaningfully at each other as they waited for Diana to answer. Spread out before them, they had notes garnered from watching TV and from phone calls to Reverend Tucker.

"Hello, Mom. How are you doing?"

"I've been studying like you said."

"Great, Mom, that's what we need to do. The Bible is very important."

"You saw the news about Jesus, right?"

"I did."

"Well, he came in a cloud of angels and put the antichrist into a pit, a bottomless pit. Just like it says in the last book, Revelation."

"I heard about that and turned on the news to see it. We studied together the texts relat—"

"This is so great. That pit is the Krubera Cave on the eastern shore of the Black Sea. In the western Caucasus mountains. It is the deepest point on earth at 7,208 ft." Rose was holding the notes for Silvia to read.

"We must have been watching the same channel." Diana was waiting for the other shoe to drop. Her mother was working up to something.

"We don't have to worry about Satan anymore. He's gone. We can focus on putting this world back together. Like Jesus said we should."

"Mother, that's not the real Jesus. When Jesus comes, He won't touch the earth. We will meet Him in the air. That's what the Bible says."

"He conquered Satan and had two of his angels seal him in the abyss. Our millennium is starting now. He is bringing Christianity, Islam, and Judaism together. I found out that this Isa is considered the returned Imam Mahdi by Islam. He is another Buddha by Buddhists. He is the Krishna by Hindus, and because he came through the Golden Gate, he is the long-awaited Messiah. Billions can't be wrong. It's working for every-one except people like the Adventists. Diana, listen to me. You've got to get away. Come home. Stop spending time with them. Chad can come, too. But if he won't, you have to save yourself. Those people are going to jail." Rose nodded her head in approval.

There it was; the other shoe. "Mother, this is just the beginning. It—"

"Yes, that's right; it is just the beginning. We are going to have heaven on earth."

"Mother, please listen to me—"

"No! Come home! For ——————! Escape from those idiots!"

"I've never, ever heard you swear. What's going on?"

"You have to be stopped. It's good you aren't going to that E-Center anymore. Stop having sex with Chad. Now, get home this minute!"

"Wait, whoa, mother, Chad and I aren't … we … How did you know the E-Center closed?"

"I called the state's attorney general and told them what's happening in that … place."

"Mother!"

"Come home when you wake up. That is if you can get to sleep." The phone call ended. Diana wept. Her mother had never been so mean. After all the years she had stayed with her when she grieved inconsolably over Roger. She wanted to yell. She wanted to shout at her mother. She wanted to fall into a hole. Her own mother had turned on her, misjudging her, belittling her PTSD, calling the authorities to stop her witnessing. This came after all the years struggling through grief aftereffects.

On the other end, Rose congratulated her compatriot. "She needed that! You did the right thing! Actually, she needed to hear this months ago, before she got wrapped up with these numbskulls."

"I shouldn't have said that about her getting to sleep."

"No, you should've. It's her own fault. She deserved it."

"She didn't deserve it. Nobody deserves that."

"Yes, she—"

"No! Absolutely not!"

"Yes!"

"Get out! Now! Get away from me!"

XXXXX

Isa Jesus toured the Dome of the Rock and Al-Aqsa Mosque with the obsequious Islamic leaders, who felt compelled to explain everything as if he never heard a word of history surrounding the third most important site in all of Islam. He accepted their reverence towards him, allowing many to kiss his ring. Then he strolled through the prostrate worshippers surrounding both locations. Outside, it was chaotic with crowds pushing and shoving to glimpse him through crowds of angels and clusters of fans.

A small delegation of his angels had gone ahead to the Knesset, setting up a visit for when Isa Jesus could extract himself from the adoring masses jammed hip to thigh in every approach to the Temple Mount. It was a good thing Isa could fly because the avenues were a torture with tempers raging and open battles in the clogged streets. When he did take his leave, individuals took out their frustration on those they supposed prevented them from seeing the Imam Mahdi.

In the Israeli parliament (Knesset), every seat was occupied. When he walked in, every knee hit the floor in respect.

"I know you expected me in a certain manner. I took care of that today, along with the false messiah. We are ready to move forward. I have brought you and your enemies together. Those unwilling to cooperate are almost gone. This world is ready for one leader with equal opportunity, equal riches, and equal access to basic necessities for everyone who remains. Are you with me?" The response was unanimous.

XXXXX

It was a shock to learn the fragment of information he acquired earlier. It put him in a tailspin. An overheard remark at the Perkins house came back to him, and it launched him on a new tangent. Someone had said, *I wonder if the NEO-KKK did this.* He wanted to see if there was an active group in the area. Additionally, if so, he wanted to know if any police officers were members. Tracking down informants wasn't easy. Days went by until he found a member willing to talk. He had to pretend he was willing to join. It made him want to take a long, soapy shower afterward. The informant was more than eager to get credit for a new inductee and bent over backward to appeal to him. He asked, "Would I be the only policeman in the local Klavern?"

"Oh, no. We have police chiefs, captains, lieutenants, and patrolmen alike."

"So, I won't feel out of place?"

"Right, we'll welcome you with open arms. We're like a family."

The conversation went on for another half of a racially-prejudiced hour before he received a phone call that made it easy to break off the interchange. He went straight back to the precinct.

Now he sat, pondering. He couldn't be upfront with his captain because the captain could be a suspect if the NEO-KKK were involved. If he went forward with the investigation, he would be tackling the department all on his own. The voice brought him out of his contemplations.

"How many cases are you working on?" the captain asked.

"I've had four cold cases going nowhere. Then yesterday, they caught the guy I identified in the Stephensville murder. It seems he was hiding in Georgia. That one is now closed. Then, you know about those gang war murders. No one is talking, of course. And lastly, the Johnsons."

"Here's three new cases. Beat cops are putting up yellow tape as we speak." His boss dropped three almost empty folder jackets on his desk.

"Why three folders? Isn't this three dead in one scene?" Hardine noticed a blotchy left hand on his boss.

"No, three different places, three different murders. You better get a move on. You have a lot of ground to cover."

His eyes went down to the hands covered in festering boils. "What about the other detectives? Why can't they help?"

"'Cause they're busy with five more homicides. Get going! By the way, you're off the Johnson murder." He moved to leave.

"Who's taking over the Johnson case?"

"I am."

Detective Hardine looked down at the folder jackets with addresses clipped on the covers. He saw a milky, bloody drop of pus splashed on the top. He slipped his evidence-collecting gloves on. He was going to clean the folders on the way out. For the second time, he wanted to take a soapy shower.

XXXXX

The news about the church takeover flew around the members at warp speed. Again, members were surprised and not surprised. They hadn't thought that their church would be stolen, but given the predictions of the end times, it didn't seem logical that early Christians had to hide in caves and catacombs while last-day Christians would ride out the tribulation sitting on soft, padded pews.

Chad had an idea. He suggested that the church worship in the park next to his house. It had sections that were secluded. The number of cars would not be out of place, parking in a public area. If the weather turned bad, he said they could walk to his house a couple of hundred yards away. Diana suggested a potluck to follow at the house.

Chad and Diana, Vonnie and Leticia, and Peter Lange spent some time the day before around the dining table, planning the Sabbath in the park and filling in details for Leticia of prophecies being fulfilled. Detective Hardine stopped by to tell Chad he was off the case, and when he found everyone there, he really wanted to join in the discussion. After getting settled in his chair, they asked what he was interested in studying. He quickly answered, "What's next? That's what I want to know."

"The seven last plagues," Vonnie quickly answered.

"Okay, I'm a novice on all this stuff. I wouldn't know a thing if it wasn't for my interviewing you and Pastor Lange. You made me see how important it is to claim Jesus' sacrifice on the cross and to be loyal to Him and the commandments of God, as it says in Revelation. It has dominated my thoughts for the last several weeks, making it very difficult to go to sleep. Then, I remembered a comment about false Christ's coming.

All this information is synchronizing with the news events. I'm wondering, what's next? What kind of plagues?"

"The seven last plagues mentioned in the book of Revelation," Chad answered.

"I'm sorry. I've never read it."

"No need to say you're sorry. The plagues detail how God destroys Satan's system of oppression on God's commandment-keeping people. They come right at the very end of time. Jesus is coming very soon. The plagues are: boils or sores, then the seas become like the blood of a man, then—" Peter Lange was interrupted.

"Wait. You said boils?"

"Yes."

"My captain had a severe infection on his hands. Could that be ..." He stopped because everyone around the table was nodding in agreement. Hardine looked to the ceiling and then adjusted himself in the chair. "This is it, then?" More head nods. Several shared their observations, confirming the fact that the first plague had fallen in earnest. In some cases the description was rather gross. Faces were somber. Diana had to excuse herself because she received another text from her mother.

"Detective Hardine, I don't know your first name," Vonnie said.

"Lucas, call me Luke."

"Luke, if I could be so brave as to try and put the oncoming events together, I'll do my best. Pastor, correct me if I go wrong. Very simply: first boils, second bloody seas, third bloody fresh water, fourth scorching heat from the sun, fifth darkness, sixth is foul spirits that act like frogs gathering satanic forces against God, and lastly, there are the effects of Jesus coming. The last plague is His coming when Satan's forces are completely defeated. In the middle of all that is the mark of the beast, prohibition of buying and selling, and death decree. How did I do, Pastor?"

"Basically correct."

"Death decree?!" Leticia reacted. "Us? Against us?"

"Don't worry that decree comes right at the very end. When Jesus is on His way to rescue us. He won't let His people die at that time. The controversy is over. Satan is seen in all his hatefulness," Vonnie spoke to her friend.

"If the last plague is His coming, that sounds nice. A plague for them and a blessing for us."

"For us, yes. For everyone who has the mark of the beast, no. All of the plagues are designated for those who go along with Satan's kingdom.

For instance: fresh water is turned to blood, but God leads his people to 'springs of living water,' as it says ... here look in Revelation chapter seven. 'For the Lamb in the center of the throne will be their shepherd. He will lead them to fountains of living water, and God will wipe away every tear from their eyes'"[23] (vs. 17), she addressed her friend's concern.

"The promise has some other information in the verse right before the one about tears. Ah, look what it says in verse sixteen, 'Never again will they hunger, and never will they thirst; nor will the sun beat upon them, nor any scorching heat.'[24] This tells us that we won't be affected by the fourth plague," Chad added.

"All right, everything revolves around this mark of the beast and the seal of the living God. What is the mark?" Luke asked.

"We don't know for absolute sure. There are a lot of theories. Some suggest a physical mark in the forehead or hand; others say that it is a symbolic mark. I favor the latter, but I'm willing to be surprised. Those who don't have the mark will be unable to buy or sell. That hasn't happened. When it does happen, then we will have a good idea of what the mark is," Pastor Lange summarized.

"It isn't going to be easy, though. We will be safe, but Jesus tells us that time will need to be shortened to preserve the elect," Chad reminded.

"That's Matthew twenty-four," Vonnie said to Mrs. Greene, who, in turn, agreed. "We're in for a rocky ride, starting now," Vonnie tacked onto her first comment.

"Here's another negative we should watch out for. On the way over here, I had two near-misses with possible accidents. The Spirit of God's restraining power is being withdrawn like it says in Genesis six, verse three, 'My Spirit shall not strive with man forever.' And now people are driving like there are no laws. Everywhere selfishness is the norm. We have to be super careful not to get in an accident or cross people who will delay us or put us in jail for spurious reasons. In Nahum 2:4, there is a description of people going crazy with vehicles, 'The chariots shall rage in the streets, they shall jostle one against another in the broad ways: they shall seem like torches, they shall run like the lightnings'" (KJV).

"I can help us with these." Luke put his badge and revolver on the table.

"I like your team spirit. We are together in this problem. However, the weapon is not needed because God is a mighty fortress. We let Him fight

[23]RSV
[24]Rev. 7:16, NIV

our battles for us. We'll get through this together, together with Him. The badge might help a little. But, again, God will help us completely.

Diana came back to the table. She had made an attempt to dry her eyes to avoid detection of her inner turmoil. They knew. Diana grieved over her mother's behavior. Texts came on a regular pattern; they were nasty and pleading at the same time. It seemed like her mother couldn't clear her mind to stay on a single, purposeful objective. In this text she blamed her.

"That was another text from my mother. She thinks she got her boils from eating Adventist food. She says I have to come home now or else." The two women at the table were quick to show their compassion with their touch. The others, including Chad, verbalized their concern.

Mrs. Greene spoke of a concern she had that Diana's situation brought to mind. "My husband didn't know what I know now. I have learned a lot of things about God and His commandments and how important they are, but Stewart died never knowing about these truths. He was a born-again Christian. He died as a soldier in Iraq many years ago. Is he going to be saved?"

> *"That was another text from my mother. She thinks she got her boils from eating Adventist food. She says I have to come home now or else."*

This was a sensitive subject. There was a hesitancy to address this subject because of the grief factor and because of Diana's present grief over her mother. They were surprised when Diana answered. "My father died many years ago. He, like your Stewart, was a strong believer. He died of kidney failure after two transplants. My mother never really got over it. Anyway, he, like all of us, came to the knowledge of God's salvation in Jesus and began his faith walk. We all are on our own faith walk, which takes us on different paths to the kingdom, each with different testing points. If our walk is interrupted, we are saved no matter where we are in our faith as long as we remain true to Him. At this time, our faith walks are, I guess, accelerated due to the fact that Satan has manifested himself and defined the rules for his kingdom. We are coming together as God's people." Diana interlaced her fingers together to illustrate her point. "We have to be in agreement with God's kingdom and His precepts. Our faith walk is here and now. My father and your Stewart are safe. We are safe if we stay true to the Lord and stand strong at this testing time."

"Amen. I could have never answered that as well as you did just now," Pastor Lange pronounced.

"Yes, amen!" Chad smiled at his approval. Then Diana added a subscript.

"I wish my mother had passed this test. She got tricked by Satan!"

"Unfortunately, she did. Maybe I can add a postscript on what you said that puts it all together. The saving truth is Jesus' work on the cross. Here, at the end of time, the Sabbath is a testing truth that separates the loyal from the lukewarm Christians. The Sabbath is a testing point predicted in Jesus' revelation when He has John write the words, 'here is the patience of the saints, those who keep the commandments and have the testimony of Jesus.'[25] Satan can catch those who don't study the Bible thoroughly for themselves."

XXXXX

News broadcasts featured multiple upon multiple angles of the appearances and ministry of the messiah (lower case 'm'). In a negligible manner, other stories would slip into the dialogue. One was medical in nature. Concerns for the epidemic of skin carbuncles had network doctors explaining what to do and how to avoid the contagious nature of the outbreak. Explanations were all over the place, mostly centering upon the lack of preventive measures and medicines to treat these detestable boils. Normally, pictures of disgusting eruptions of the skin would not be telecast. However, the prevalence of the contagion necessitated people making every effort to avoid contact with infected persons. Pictures of ripe boils festering and erupting like volcanoes upon mounds of fevered flesh caused viewers to convulse and avoid tactile contact as designated by the networks. Identifying the problem supposedly would help curb the spread. Of interest was the fact that no broadcast spoke of the pandemic in terms of a plague.

Another small blurb slipped into the heavy emphasis on the messiah. This news article detailed the first problem of the reshuffling of food. Multiple shiploads of wheat, rice, and corn were shipped away from the United States to famine areas. Those shipments would temporarily produce a shortage in warehouses and mills that would eventually reach retail outlets in a minor way. News of this possible problem in the future caused

---

[25]Rev. 12:14

people to stock up on flour and grain products. The artificial shortfall came sooner than expected. Local store owners had to call the police to quell riots breaking out in long lines. Television announcers blamed the Knights of Malta for enacting their redistribution of resources too hastily. Social justice needed to be mindful of the hordes of starving children in fat America. Demonstrations poured into the streets of major cities across the nation.

XXXXX

A large publicized convocation at Saint Peter's basilica included on the dais Pope Sextus and Isa. At the very beginning, Pope Sextus abdicated his position, offering the position of the papacy to Isa-Jesus. "I yield to his holiness, Jesus Christ the Righteous." He didn't bow; he prostrated himself full length upon the floor. All prelates in attendance did the same. Watching reporters spoke in hushed tones as if they were calling a golf match, saying this was expected and overdue. The ceremony was meticulously planned to look as though it were impromptu. A robe, a miter, a mozzetta, and a pallium, specially made for the messiah, were brought and placed on him. Applause broke out among the attendees. Pope Isa stepped to the podium and began his speech. He first announced that Pope Sextus would continue to be the head of the WFC. He then pronounced his papal name. "I have taken a new name. Holy Fathers have traditionally taken symbolic, meaningful names. I plan to do the same with five names that encompass all that I am and want to achieve. I am Pope Domenic Clement Leonardo Xavier Sextus. I take Sextus because I wish to honor my predecessor. Domenic because I am the Lord. Clement because I am merciful, Leonardo because I am the Lion of God, and Xavier because when I am done, this world and everything in it will be one new house."

Reporters reverently repeated the new pope's name, "Domenic Clement Leonardo Xavier Sextus." They made reference to how the name summarized the hopes and desires of the people. They said that the people are hungry for a strong leader who is like a lion and merciful. They pointed out to viewers that acknowledging Pope Sextus' work and keeping his leadership in the WCF signified his reign would utilize great men as when Jesus picked Peter to lead as the first pope in His infant church. If one could make a visual representation of what these correspondents were saying and doing, it would be a bunch of bobbing bobble-head dolls.

Meanwhile, in the Caucasus mountains, reporters in helicopters hovered over the Krubera Cave nestled in a snowy ridge about ten miles from the east shore of the Black Sea. As the choppers descended, two angels came into view. They were in front of the entrance, holding swords of brilliant yellow light. The light swords were crossed in an arch over the cave. Many videos caught the guards in an imposing posture keeping an unseen Naziya supposedly locked below.

XXXXX

"This is all moving so fast! I don't know if I'm ready," one believer stated while the outdoor church was being organized. Members were placing camp chairs and blankets in a semi-circle.

"How do you mean?" Pastor asked.

"Jesus says we should flee. I don't know where to go."

"Oh, I was worried you weren't ready spiritually."

"That bothers me a little bit, too. I have always claimed Jesus as my Savior. I've never turned from Him, and I ask Him to forgive me for what I might've accidentally done every day."

"You are an example the world should follow. About fleeing, what Jesus is telling us to do is avoid the people who want to round you up for their brand of final punishment. Our signal is the desolating sacrilege standing in the holy place. We are at that right now. Perhaps, we should start leaving now. We are sure that Jesus will rescue you and all of us, but I'm guessing it may not be pleasant before that. I'd rather avoid that if I can. So, perhaps, you will want to go where you can't be easily found. For myself, I'm going to the mountains with my backpack, tent, and sleeping bag. Does that help you?"

"A little. I can call some friends, I suppose. Maybe."

"Jamila? Come with us. We have room at our cabin, room enough for you and your kids. Will Kevin be back from his deployment soon? If so, we have room for him, too. Don't worry," a member added.

"That's wonderful! Thank you."

"Yes, it is very wonderful," Pastor commented. "It is a very good idea for us to pool our resources and make our plans."

"I have some suggestions," Detective Hardine stood up from his blanket seat. He got a go-ahead nod from the pastor. "My entire career as a detective has taught me techniques we can use, I mean, to avoid for this moment. Here is how they will track us down. They'll use our electronic devices against us. They can tell where we are and who we are talking to. Anything that can access the Internet can tell them where you are if you are using it. I suggest we dump our electronics when we flee. Then, if they're trying to find us, they will track our cars. All license plates are read on every major highway. All they have to do is enter in your registration number, and whenever you pass one of those readers, they'll know where you are going, at what time, and how fast. Video cameras are everywhere; stores, gas stations, traffic lights, parks, you name it. They will employ facial recognition software to read those videos, and again, they will know where you have been and when. Credit cards are your only means of purchase; as soon as you swipe your card, they will know what, when, where, for what, and how much. Aircraft and drones will be employed to follow or find you using infrared scanning. They can see where warm bodies are hiding amongst the trees. They will study and interview your friends, social networks, and relatives, asking them if they have seen you and where you might be hiding. They will offer them rewards if they tell them where you are. I know because I used these very things to find perps. What I am saying is that you have to go completely off the grid, completely away from people you know. Of course, that doesn't mean our fellow believers."

"Should we throw away our phones now?"

Luke Hardine looked to the pastor for that answer.

"I think we should begin leaving as the situation dictates; by that, I mean that some may not be able to move quickly like the elderly, et cetera. The desolating sacrilege has happened. He is there, claiming he is Jesus. We saw it on TV. He's standing in the place of the world's alliance of religions. That is done. The plagues have started, I think. When the seventh is complete, Jesus will have been here, and we will be with Him on our way home. We don't know exactly when. However, in Revelation 18:8 it says, 'her plagues come in a single day.' A day in prophecy is a year. So, we are at one year or less. We really don't know exactly when the first plague of sores started, yesterday, the day before, or last week. I'll throw this out to all of you. When do you think we should go off the grid?"

"I really thought you would tell us," said Cynthia.

"Looks like we've got a whole year before Jesus comes," a formerly nervous gentleman said in relief.

"Not necessarily. The Bible says, 'No man knows the day or the hour.' What I was implying about the plagues coming in a single year is that the prediction is indicating a year's time frame, perhaps within a year. We can't really start the clock ticking on this prophecy. What we are facing is no more than a year, and we don't know what portion may be cut off from that year to be 'shortened for the sake of the elect,' as Jesus says. If anyone wants to stay around for another Sabbath, I will be with you, so let me know. Ah, maybe we should start the clock on our church service. I suggest a prayer and then a song."

They quietly bowed their heads for prayer. Unseen by the worship company, a cluster of policemen were watching with binoculars. Chad and Diana sat together on a blanket. Near to them on one side was the Perkins family, minus Emilee, who chose to sit with the lady she had healed. Detective Hardine shared part of the blanket on the other side, because Chad was the most familiar to him, excepting the pastor, of course. Heads lifted when Pastor suggested they sing, "Lift up the trumpet and loud let it ring." They all knew the words and the sentiments which heralded the coming of Jesus. The reality of the nearness caused them to sing with gusto. They were interrupted by an invasion of blue.

A half-dozen officers circled the group, and another three went to Pastor Lange and arrested him, putting him in handcuffs. One officer announced, "This is an illegal gathering for the purpose of worship on the wrong day. If you don't wish to be arrested, then I suggest you disperse."

Detective Hardine began to stand. He stopped when he saw his friend, Peter Lange, lightly shake his head in the negative. When he sat back down, Peter smiled at his friend. The unspoken message was that now was not the time, and people needed to be spared the discomfiture of jail. Protest, at this time, would be futile. Nothing would change the conditions of oppression, which would go forward to the end.

Brian felt leadership had fallen to him. The head elder hadn't attended the last several Sabbaths. As an elder in attendance, he wanted the people to be safe. When he stood, Chad stood with him. Brian asked for the officer's attention. "Sir, we will leave. Let us collect our families." The parallel with exiting the E-Center did not escape him. He wondered if all he would do in these end times would be withdraw while pacifying imposing police officers. He longed with earnest inner yearning for that day, not too distant in the future, when he as a black man would never have to be obsequious again. Chad recognized Brian's leadership and whispered in his ear. Brian spoke to the company. "Folks, it has been pleasant, just like when we had potlucks with Chad and Diana. See you soon." Everyone caught the message underneath.

Diana noticed one of the officers at the edge of the gathering. He did his best not to look directly at Diana. Embarrassment kept his head down and away. He was the officer at the E-Center who was relieved of his itchy, suppurating boils.

Standing between two policemen, Pastor Peter Lange watched his flock disperse in different directions. He smiled broadly as he heard them hum the tune, "We Have This Hope."

XXXXX

Prayer for Pastor Lange predominated worship in the crowded family room/kitchen area. From different directions the entire company rejoined at Chad's place. Without delay, they put their beloved pastor before the throne of God. Sober thoughts occupied minds. To have their pastor arrested put starch in their resolve. It was difficult to focus on Brian's reading and remarks from Luke 21:12. "But before all this, they will seize you and persecute you. On account of My name, they will deliver you to the synagogues."[26] He explained to those gathered that Jesus was speaking of the early Christian church, "But that it can also be applied to the present situation. If Jesus tells us this, then I take courage, knowing because He knew this, He also will take care of our pastor, and He will take care of us." Amens could be heard in concert around the room. Then Brian went to Matthew 24:36–44 and made the point that we must be ready because we "do not know what day your Lord is coming."

Although Brian's comments were not delivered in a smooth, professional manner, they were received in good faith. He took the situation and put it in a positive light. All were confident that Jesus would rescue them in time, and Pastor Lange would burst forth from his prison cell and fly up to his waiting Savior.

All were confident that Jesus would rescue them in time, and Pastor Lange would burst forth from his prison cell and fly up to his waiting Savior.

Pastor Lange would burst forth from his prison cell and fly up to his waiting Savior. Toward the end of his sermon, he made the observation that this might be the last time they could meet together in a large group. They may have to split into smaller groups. Another sobering thought.

They ate their potluck meal together. The Perkins invited everyone to their home next Sabbath, unless, of course, circumstances dictated

[26]RSV

otherwise. They were still trying to figure out the best time to leave hearth and home. One suggested that when they were no longer able to buy or sell, they should leave; another said they should wait until the death decree is announced. Chad said that *The Great Controversy* indicates that people exit the cities when the death decree is issued, and governments abandon the people of God to those who desire their destruction and allow anyone to do what they want with them. It was an extrapolation of the passage, but not too far from the truth. The discussion turned to the position that living between now and the death decree might be very difficult, and "We might be put in prison like Pastor Lange!" Many agreed that avoiding that would be nice. Many decided not to wait another week.

Everyone agreed in the final analysis that God will protect them in whatever situation. They also covenanted with each other that they would pray every day for each other as each day passed. They spent the remainder of the Sabbath praying and studying with each other in various portions of the house and in the backyard.

XXXXX

Sunday, they went shopping for needs with an eye toward what they might need if they had to drop everything and run. They watched with interest to see if their credit/debit cards would process. They did. Everywhere they went, people were suffering. Signs at the entrances of grocery stores and restaurants asked people with open sores to stay away unless their sores were properly bandaged. In the middle of the bakery section, Diana received a text from her mother.

ZZZZZ

Guess where I am? I'm in our new church building, where the Seventh Day people used to worship. They're real losers!

ZZZZZ

Diana showed the text to Chad and Vonnie. They both commiserated. What they noticed was that Diana was coming to grips with her mother's awful behavior. It was like she had suddenly become a schizoid personality, an entirely different person.

"In my expectations of my future, I never envisioned this. I expected my mother to be my friend and cheerleader," Diana remarked.

"I think I was in your future, right?" Chad wanted to turn the conversation positive.

"And, soon, we'll be in heaven," Vonnie followed Chad's lead.

"Right. Both of you are the best. I know what you are doing."

"As far as our planning goes. I'm thinking bread would be nice, but look, nothing." Looking around, he could see bare shelves. The only thing available was crackers in boxes. "Crackers last better, we could buy some for later."

"Why do we need crackers if the Lord is going to provide bread later?" Diana asked.

"I am wondering how much later? If we leave too early before we're supposed to, will we need something to eat? It won't hurt to have extra."

"If we have extra, God won't have to provide," Diana said.

"I've always heard 'God helps those who help themselves,'" Vonnie added.

"O, great now you're taking his side," Diana reacted with a smile. "After crackers, what's next, goose liver paté?"

"We're vegetarians now, remember?" Chad reminded them. "What's next after dry blah crackers is we need some backpacks. I have one, but both of you need some nice comfortable ones. And we need some rugged clothes for the woods. That's what next. Well, maybe we can get some preserves for the crackers on the way out."

"This is strange. Normally I'd be shopping for a new purse."

Their conversation was interrupted with a loud shouting match in the dairy department. A quick look down the aisle showed empty refrigerators and two ladies on the floor punching and kicking each other.

XXXXX

Hardine was at his desk, sorting through collected information from the new cases. He had to be sure that he didn't confuse data on one case for another. Running in and through his mind was the question, *Why am I doing this?* The nearness of Jesus' coming changes everything. He didn't need to make more money. He didn't need to further his career. He couldn't bring closure to grieving survivors. Even if he did find the culprit or culprits, the legal system would take months, maybe a year, to get a conviction. The Lord would be here before then. Again, the question nagged at him, *Why am I doing this?* The only answer was that he needed to keep up appearances.

A clerk from the office pool plunked another four folders on his desk. "What's this?" he asked.

"More murders."

"If I may ask, why me? I have enough work already."

"The captain divided the cases evenly amongst all the detectives, even the first years."

"I see, thanks." Luke Hardine turned to his computer and started writing his resignation without an effective date. He could fill that in later at the right time.

Because he could, he planned on visiting his friend Pastor Lange in jail.

XXXXX

Pope Domenic Clement Leonardo Xavier Sextus made his tour de force in the nation's capital. He went to the White House and then to the capitol. From a joint session, he went to the upper balcony to address the crowds. It was a massive convocation. White robes covered every part of the pope's body except his face and hands. There was no mingling with the crowd, ostensibly to avoid contact with people who might be infected with the prevalent skin disease. For some reason, he might not be able to heal himself.

The content of the speech the Pope delivered primarily revolved around a strong call for unity. He made passing reference to the pestilence of sores being a lingering effect of the devil's legacy. Now that he had banished the devil, i.e., the antichrist, he could create a new age. He emphasized that time will tell how determined the world population is to convince his father that they are sincere about cleansing this world of those individuals who choose to impede progress. Of special note, he said if people don't willingly comply, then concerned citizens should be allowed to clean up the population themselves. It meant individuals outside law enforcement would be allowed to take the law in their own hands. Interestingly, none seemed to be bothered by the departure from proper civil decorum.

CHAPTER 16

S ome people believe that what is not on the news must not be important. When colossal events crowd the airwaves, minor but significant stories get bumped off the nightly news. A couple of matters were happening at an alarming rate. Emergency medical personnel were being called to traumas so frequently that sometimes they didn't have the time to return from one event before they were summoned for another. Suicide cases had increased to an alarming trend. Domestic arguments were reaching dizzy heights with many ending in vows to divorce or, worse, violence. Desperation without hope breeds despair. God's presence provides hope. Without the Spirit of God, people are on their own without the inclination to reconcile. Their anger consumes them, not allowing them to cool or modify their thinking. They strike out at others and at themselves.

One item of news seemed to remain in its own sphere of interest, i.e., astrological observation. The sun has been more than active in solar flares, which usually precludes a CME, a Coronal Mass Ejection. Nothing was for sure at this time, so news outlets did not carry the story.

Normally, news reports would make a big deal about a bear entering a residential area foraging for food. The preoccupation with a world on the brink of nirvana kept them from videotaping predators prowling neighborhoods for fresh, easy-to-get meat. The Spirit of God no longer held animals in check. Their fear of man left them when the Spirit left the earth.

Several incidents of mothers protecting infants from coyotes occurred daily. People were afraid to take walks in semi-rural areas. Handguns and clubs accompanied gardeners. One greens-keeper was attacked by a puma, who took him off of a mower and dragged him, kicking and screaming into the woods. The mower continued onward, crossing several fairways through a split-rail fence before getting wedged between two cars in a parking lot. Later, his half-eaten body was found with the typical leaves and twigs kicked over his carcass, awaiting a second serving.

Eerie and very strange was the phenomena of normally docile deer attacking humans. Some would espy a human at close range; see them as a threat and attack. They would ram them with horns or trample them under their hooves. Anger is not something associated with the cervine species. Those attacked thought maybe they were rabid.

Safety warnings should have been issued by way of the media. However, network personnel was locked in studio squabbles about who should tell what, and what should be told on air. The public was not being served.

Another story began to evolve slowly and imperceptibly; poisonous red plankton, pseudo-nitzschia, infested various parts of the ocean away from areas not usually traveled or fished. Large-scale mortality events occurred. Fish floated belly-up, bleeding, creating islands of rotting flesh. Flies somehow managed to show up, even though the putrid mess was hundreds of miles from land. Poisoned shellfish percolated to the surface, joining the red blooms and the silvery bodies, making it looked like a bouillabaisse strong on tomato sauce. These islands of floating dead fauna steadily grew until a few ships encountered them and left them scattered in their pink wake.

XXXXX

It was Tuesday when Chad and Diana found their debit cards blocked. No announcement told the world that those who did not agree with the new national worship requirements, i.e., worship the red dragon's beast on his day, would not be able to buy or sell. It just happened. Their shopping for the forthcoming turmoil still had some to go before being completed. Chad had an ace up his sleeve. He went to his father's bank.

There, he opened the security box and took out every gold coin. He figured gold would always be in vogue. Some of his father's associates greeted him, not knowing that his card was blocked. He didn't use it; his identity was well-known. All those coins weighed him down considerably. It felt funny to be carrying pure gold when it added nothing in the balance toward salvation.

On the floor of the living room, they stacked their necessities. Three backpacks, three air mattresses, three stuff-sack sleeping bags, and some cooking and eating utensils. He had some oddities which included six spray cans of clear IR blocking paint. Typical of Chad's planning behavior, he wanted everything ready and at hand. Non-perishables, rain gear, and rugged clothing needed to be added before they were ready. On top of the pile, were three pocket-size Bibles, the most important item in their estimation.

Diana's phone rang. It was the receptionist at her office.

"Diana Cross?"

"Yes."

"This is Gina. I was told to call you in case you came. Some imbecile clients brought that disease here. So, stay away. Got it?" The line went dead immediately.

Diana looked a little puzzled. "That was the receptionist at my work. She's usually the nicest person on the planet. The plague has infected the office, so I was warned to stay away. Not that I was going to go and finish my research anyway. I doubt that there will be many drug-affected families in heaven."

"Life sure has changed. We–" Chad stopped because of the racket in the backyard. A large dog was going nuts barking wildly, and a cat was hissing in return. They went to the sliding doors by the deck. A white cat was putting up a brave fight on top of the fence as a dog kept lunging from below on the other side. For his effort, he received a raking slash on his nose. The feline carefully moved along the fence toward a tree limb and to safety a bit higher off of the ground. Diana wanted to rescue what she termed a 'kitty.' Vonnie was right behind, stepping out on the deck, heading for the tree. Chad followed in typical male fashion, calculating what a cat in the house would mean. His attention was distracted by the ruckus on the other side of the fence. It wasn't one dog but at least three. They were racing back and forth, trying to find a way into the yard. His mind hurried forward, checking his memory banks for any holes under the fence. Then he thought of the gate. The ground under it was lower. That's when he saw eyes looking at him from over the top. Menacing snarls told the story of what must be a rabid dog. He decided to call the girls back when Diana reached up to take the cat down. She was attacked for her efforts. She quickly withdrew her hands.

"I think we need to get inside *now*!" Chad emphasized. He stood at the foot of the deck stairs, signaling with his arms for them to hurry up, watching the gate as the canines assaulted the wood and the ground beneath. The growling and snarling multiplied to the point where he had to recalculate the number of dogs on the other side of the gate and doubt that they were after one single cat. Once Diana and Vonnie made it by him, he backed up the steps and pushed the BBQ grill in front of the deck opening. It was providential, as the gate lost its integrity and broke inward at the latch. Instead of a pack of dogs, it was wolves streaming into the yard and surging as one organism toward the humans on the deck. Chad hustled the two women into the house as the wolves squirmed around the grill in a mad dash to get at the humans. They hit the glass, snarling and yapping at the three on the other side. Saliva dribbled down the glass.

Chad hustled the two women into the house as the wolves squirmed around the grill in a mad dash to get at the humans. They hit the glass, snarling and yapping at the three on the other side.

For the next several hours, the pack of wolves circled the house in an attempt to gain entrance. At one time, the three looked out the front window to see four men in a car parked across the street. The wolves attacked the car from all sides, and at times, stood on the hood and the roof. Finally, the men drove off.

XXXXX

Luke Hardine managed to solve one of the first three cases and two of the four that came the next day. Individuals were locked up or put on APBs for pickup when they used their cars or devices. Evidence came easily in these cases because rage was the basis for each, and rage causes perpetrators to forget anti-forensic measures. The high number of incidents reminded the experienced detective that the Holy Spirit had been withdrawn. It made him sick. One of the highlights in his day-to-day activities was his visits to Pastor Lange. If those ended, he would have only his connection with the strange church that he had been introduced to because of the Johnsons' murder. As a reminder of his good fortune, he kept the prophecy brochure in the pocket of his tweed jacket.

All his adult life, he never felt life was on his side. His accomplishments seemed to exact a toll on his happiness. He got married and lost children to miscarriage and stillbirth. He graduated from the police academy, and then the long hours and danger pushed his wife away. The divorce was nasty. He moved into detective work and got lost in the day-to-day grind. The only time he went to his studio apartment was to sleep. He was considered bad luck because he lost two partners in firefights with crime lord soldiers. No one wanted to be his partner, so he worked alone.

He wanted to quit, but quitting meant he would have no access to Peter, and Peter would have no one to visit him. Peter had messages for his members, and Luke would carry those messages to them for as long as he could. He had a higher purpose than he ever had before.

XXXXX

Leticia wanted to come over. It presented a problem with the roving band of wolves. They could leave by simply driving out of the garage. Once out, where could they go and be at ease? They preferred to work, plan, and study in private. Chad suggested that the girls draw the wolves to the back by enticing them. He also suggested that Leticia bring some red meat if she had it on hand. Vonnie called Leticia immediately, and Chad went to the garage and removed one car, parking it on the driveway. He went in through the garage while the animals were distracted around back. When he came into the kitchen, he saw that Diana had received another text from her mother. She pushed the phone over the counter to Chad because she and Vonnie had already read it.

ZZZZZ

You can't hide behind those animals forever. Sooner or later, we'll be there to take possession of that house. You don't deserve it. I've got 4 men who are waiting to kick you out. If you stop this Saturday crap then you can stay with me.

ZZZZZ

This told Chad several things at the same time. The carload of men were kept at bay by the wolves. God's providence was unique, to say the least. The next thing he thought of was their tenure at this location was limited. People were ignoring the law for their own benefit. Anarchy was upon them. It was not in the streets as yet, but it was beginning. Then, he saw Diana's mother consumed by materialism. One does not have to have money to be in love with money, the root of all evil. All those years, she lived cheaply in an apartment with no property to her name. Watching her church acquire a new building without sacrifice put her on the track for moving upward.

"I'm sorry, sweetheart, this is another stab in the heart for you," he empathized.

"I guess I'm expecting it. I'm seriously considering not reading her messages. She's not acting like the mother I know, I mean, I knew."

"We are going to have to leave sooner than we might think. I'm not too excited about spending a year in the woods," he opened the discussion. The barking and growling outside erupted over some unseen provocation.

"And I'm not interested in fighting off wild animals while I avoid the anarchy in the cities," Diana retorted.

"What do we do?" Vonnie asked.

"It'd be nice to go to a cabin if we had one."

"What about that cabin mentioned last Sabbath?"

"That would be nice, but we can't all end up in the same place. It would attract attention, and then where would we be? We need to let them have their hideaway without ruining it for them. And, they are offering their place to some who really need it," Chad answered. Leticia's phone call indicated she was close. Chad told her to drive into the garage when the door opened. Diana went to the garage, and Chad went to make provocative noises out back. While there, he saw yet another example of animal violence. The white cat attacked a squirrel. In the ruckus the cat and the squirrel fell to the ground, where a wolf pounced on both of them. Other members of the pack wanted in on the snack. Parts of rodent and feline were flying in all directions. Chad didn't have to make wolf-enticing noises. He stood at the glass door and watched. Three ladies joined him with different reactions of horror.

"Did you start this?" Diana asks with incredulity.

"No, it's just a symptom of this sick world. Cats and squirrels are natural prey for wolves. But this degree of violence is over the top. The wolves are more concerned with fighting each other than eating. Look, what's left of the cat is just lying there. None of them are trying to make off with the meal."

The foursome closed the curtains and wished that drapes could seal out the sound. On the floor in front of them was a large cooler. "What's this?" he asked.

"Meat. You asked for red meat."

"Wow! That much?"

"I emptied my freezer."

"That'll work. We will use it to get out of here and go shopping."

"Shopping?"

"Yes. I'm going to see if gold coins carry their weight in ... Never mind. Detective Hardine said they will use infrared to find us. I know the military uniforms have infrared blocking capabilities. We should get some. Let's go to the army surplus store. I know, I know they aren't very chic."

"Okay. We throw raw meat out the back, and we drive out the front. Do they have infrared blocking purses?" Diana asked. The other girls smiled. Chad had a puzzled look on his face.

XXXXX

Luke Hardine needed food. His cards didn't work. As a bachelor, he ate out almost every meal. He went home to have a meal of cereal and milk. When there, he found the milk had soured. He munched his way through dry bran flakes and called Chad. As a proud man used to standing alone, it didn't come naturally to ask for food. Chad didn't hesitate. He invited him to join them at Jaxson's Army Surplus.

A few minutes later, they cruised through the stacks of tactical gear and piles of Meals Ready to Eat. The girls were selecting their sizes and showing displeasure on the colors and absence of flattering design. The uniforms were crudely practical, not pretty.

"How are you paying for this?" Luke whispered.

"Remember those old westerns where the good guy flips a single coin on the bar, and it pays for room and board, stabling for his horse, and a round for a crowded bar?"

"Yes."

"That's what I'm going to do."

"Really?"

"Yep, partner." It took less than thirty seconds for Chad and Luke to look at the shelves for the uniforms, select the correct sizes, and plop them in the cart. They then went for Boonie hats with a circular rim all around and in the same camouflage material as the uniforms. Those also were infrared-scattering. Chad dropped a packet of ten space blankets into the cart. The men looked at the women expectantly. They took the hats, put them on, and, of all things, checked to see how they looked in the mirror. Diana decided to pin one side of her hat up with a hairpin to make it look like an outback Aussie hat. Combat suave.

They pushed two loaded carts to the checkout stand. The heavy stuff was the MREs. They found the vegetarian MREs were on sale because they were more difficult to move off the shelves.

The clerk totaled the cost while whistling a merry tune. He was the owner of the shop. At the end, Chad asked the owner, "Have you ever seen one of these?" He held up a gold coin and handed it to the man.

"Yes, I know what that is. I have several in my investment portfolio."

"Then you know that it's worth is equivalent to what we owe you. I'll give you the one you have there, plus another for good measure." For a moment, the owner was putting together the import of the situation.

"Give me two more, and you have a deal."

"Deal!"

As they left, the owner was whistling and drumming a beat on the countertop.

Chad offered Luke to come stay and eat with him, but he declined, taking his new clothes and two cases of MREs with him. Chad handed him a half-dozen coins, just in case.

XXXXX

The oceans were changing colors dramatically. More dead fish surfaced. Known fisheries which had provided sustenance for millions for centuries were empty. People were clamoring for food. Ships full of grain plied the waterways, and mercy flights flew in emergency supplies until the ships could arrive. The widespread influence of the Knights of Malta was pressed to the limits to shift food from the haves to the have-nots. The United States no longer had artificial shortages; there were real gaps in various food types. Items that did not perish quickly were moved overseas.

Fresh vegetables were in supply. Leaders encouraged people to start back-yard and rooftop "Unity Gardens."

In addition to the seas turning red, they were rising. A billion people lived within forty feet of sea level. A quarter of those were within forty inches. Masses of people were being pushed out of their homes because global warming added more ice cap water to the equation. The edges of the polar icecaps receded, exposing more ocean surface. Sunrays were being absorbed into the water instead of being reflected back. Water temperatures rose, creating more melt from below the visible ice. With tides creeping higher and higher, filthy red sludge reached further up beaches to be deposited closer to, and in some cases into, dwellings. The smell battered the senses of oceanside dwellers into submission. Many fled their homes, escaping inland.

Spreading ever outward, the red tides clawed at every beach and rocky point around the world. Ships churned wakes of pink "Vs" behind them as white oxygen bubbles mixed with blood-red water. At estuaries fresh water pushed at the red clouds for a few yards before merging into obscurity. Mariners complained in salty sea language. The air above didn't have the intoxicating smell of adventure. It reeked of death and decomposition. Fish farms were destroyed. Kelp farms died on their long tethers, leaving putrid tatters. Everything in the oceans died; flora, fauna, and coral creatures combining animal, mineral, and vegetable. The oceans would have shriveled into compost fertilizer if it wasn't for the fact they were primarily liquid.

XXXXX

"I think we should go tomorrow. I have been praying about this, and I just feel we should leave. This is not how I work. I added up the data, made up alternative options, and then decided. I don't usually feel my way through a decision. Do you understand what I mean," Chad shared his feelings.

"I do. I have the same conviction," Diana agreed.

"You two belong together," Vonnie observed.

"Are we all going to … wherever, together?" Leticia Greene asked.

"Yes, most definitely. Starting tonight, we are linked together until the end. I know we have to get out of here. I do know a place in the moun-tains—" A dog started yelping in pain from the neighbor's yard. It was clear that the wolves had made another kill. "—where the trees and the underbrush have grown over a small rock building. You can be ten feet away from it and not know it's there. I found it when I was on a campout with my Boy Scout troop. Anyway, it's an excellent place to hide, but not a place where we could hide for months and months. It would be good for maybe a little while."

"We could stay at my folks' house. They're low on food, but they're safe for now," Vonnie suggested.

"Or we could go to my place. We'd be crowded," Leticia offered. "Wait, did you say they were low on food?"

"Yeah, important. Why didn't you say anything about your folks needing food?"

"Because they said they didn't need anything for at least two more months. They think Jesus will be here before two more months are up. Somebody in their church convinced them that the fifth plague is on the throne of the beast, and that means that the only way darkness can fall upon the beast alone is if God's people are already gone."

"Pardon me for saying so, but it is clear that the seventh plague describes the second coming if one compares that and the sixth and seventh seals," Chad pointed out.

"I know. I don't agree with them. It is understandable that people will want Jesus to come sooner rather than later, and they'll grasp at any hope."

"By helping them, we can help ourselves. We can go there first, and when we leave, we'll leave enough food for them to last." Diana helped make the decision. They had purchased boxes and boxes of food, intending to last out a year.

They stacked some of their provisions in a pile in the garage, stuffed backpacks, boxes, and bags of food. Diana wanted to know why they weren't putting everything in the cars. Chad explained that he had a plan to acquire a vehicle that would be difficult to track. He was secretive about it and busy at the same time. This would be the last time he would be in his home. He wanted to take too much. He wanted to spend time in his father's study. He even lingered at the old clock on the mantel. It didn't take a PhD in sociology to figure out what Chad was going through. Diana came and rubbed his back. She followed him around without saying a word. She didn't even remark when he loaded his toy helicopter and toy drone.

Finally, they were ready, and they settled in the living room to talk. It was then that he noticed that all three had their hats on with a fashionable double fold on both sides with the chin ties tied in pretty bows at the top. They looked like movie stars on safari. He had to laugh.

"Whose idea was it to make those into designer bush hats?" They looked at each other and giggled. Diana slowly raised one timid finger with a coy look. It eased Chad's serious demeanor.

They talked idly about redemption and salvation. They shared their inward worries. Leticia worried about not knowing enough. All her Christian life, she had accepted the good-neighbor sermons from pulpits. She never got into the meat of the Word. The best that she got was a social gospel of doing well toward others. Nothing informed her of

he noticed that all three had their hats on with a fashionable double fold on both sides with the chin ties tied in pretty bows at the top. They looked like movie stars on safari. He had to laugh.

her dire need to have sins forgiven and her character ready for meeting the Creator. The good news had entered her consciousness recently. It revolutionized her thinking and challenged her to dig deeper. At every turn she discovered more about a personal Savior who had died for her sins and could be a close friend. She wanted to know more, feeling she didn't have enough time. She doubted if she was ready for the ordeal ahead, yet knew her Savior would assist.

Vonnie didn't feel righteous. Her life had always been in the world of the church. She grew up attending church as an infant in cradle roll. She always loved Jesus as a childhood friend, as a rabbit's foot for passing a difficult test in high school algebra, and as a sounding board for a stressed-out college student. She never knew a time when she didn't pray. She couldn't put her finger on a point in time when she had invited Jesus into her heart for the first time. As an adult, she realized she had used Jesus rather than putting Him first in her life. She revised her prayer life and began a morning devotional commitment. Becoming more knowledgeable enhanced her prayer life and her worship. She shared the fact that knowing one is saved and forgiven is different than feeling one is righteous. Was there something more to it? She didn't know and worried that it might be an impediment to her suitability at a time when absolutely everything was on the line.

Diana worried about her attitude toward her mother. When she went to a youth retreat a decade ago, the speaker did something she had never experienced before, an altar call to accept Jesus. She marked that as the time she brought Jesus into her life. Since then, it was explained to her that God had picked her out for salvation long before she was born. She was only acting out the will of God. When working on discovering the why of the Johnsons' murder, she found a belief that made more sense. Faith must be a choice, not an enactment of a preprogrammed path designed ahead of time. Faith was an act of loyalty to a God who provided a way to salvation, and it was up to an individual to accept. Learning that confirmed her choice of so many years before as valuable rather than cheap. The downside of that truth was that her mother was not automatically saved, and she had turned her back on God, losing the fruits of the Holy Spirit, love, kindness, gentleness, and patience. The ache within her heart over her mother's behavior dominated her goodwill. She hated the clairvoyant that had written the letter. It was because of that her mother had changed, deciding against the biblical evidence. Was her frustration, maybe her anger, with the spiritualist and her mother's hateful attitude, a sin? Could she ask for forgiveness for the sin of anger when she still held the emotion? This worried her, making her doubt.

Chad still held angst toward those who murdered his parents. He had unresolved grief with no closure. He had spiritually found a purpose at long last. The relevance of religion had escaped him before. The relevance of truth found him now. He had a desire to dwell in God's benevolence and tell others of his newfound knowledge. Love for God blossomed, and because of that, he was able to let love open to include a woman. Guiding people into truth at the E-Center helped him even more. Leading Diana, Vonnie, and for a while, Silvia, established in his heart the desire to work to His will. He regretted not having more time to perform within the Divine commission, "Go therefore and teach." He would do all to lead those around him to safety.

However, he debated in his heart the nature of his urge to get to the bottom of the crime performed upon his parents. Was this motivation wrong? Should he seek God for its removal? He shared his concern with his friends.

They didn't debate with each other; they comforted each other in that God understands where you are and how you feel. They spoke of the fact that they were His children, and their questionings were indications of their loyalties. If one is not concerned, then that would mean the Holy Spirit was unable to work with one's conscience.

Vonnie made a summarizing point that was important. "We are not talking about something we did. We are talking about thoughts, thoughts rather than actions. It has to be in the direction Jesus wants us to go. He wanted us to stop at the thought before sinning. We are sitting here worried about thoughts, feelings, or the lack of knowing, not committing. God looks at this conversation and smiles with happiness that we get it. We have grown in our Christian walk to the point where we are concerned about preliminaries way before volition. Volition is acting on a will. We are not acting on our will to sin; we don't even have the *will* to sin. Am I making any sense?"

"Yes, you are. When we are linked with Jesus and His will, we become like Him in heart and mind. That means our feelings and thoughts are approaching His design. That means we are wearing His robe of righteousness. Therefore, we are wanting every part of our character—thoughts, feelings, and concerns—to be consistent with Him. Thank you, Vonnie, for making me understand this a little better. By being concerned, I am really acting on His prompting toward His righteousness. My volition, as you say, is His will."

Late in the evening, Chad asked to lead them in prayer, "Father in Heaven, we are grateful for Your righteousness, Your perfection, Your goodness. We appreciate that You are so great because You give all that to us. We are righteous because You give it to us. We are perfect because You give that to us. Your robe of righteousness is our robe of righteousness. We are like wedding guests with rented tuxedos and gowns. We look like we are rich because it is Your apparel that we are wearing. People would mistake us for being of the upper class. We *are* of the upper class, the upper, upper class, the class of the redeemed. Thank You, Lord!"

They liked that thought. They smiled, thinking of how nice it will be to dress formally for the great wedding feast in heaven. Their odyssey would begin tomorrow. Tonight, they would dream of a celebration where they would wear garments of unknown material.

XXXXX

Leaning on the bars to Peter's cell, Luke told him what he knew about the various members. He told of conversations where Vonnie was checking on other members and what she had heard from Brian and Cynthia as they had been checking on an even wider circle of believers. It was a she said, he said, she told, he told all over the length and breadth of the member-ship. Any other time, it might be a symptom of a gossipy church. In this case it was a characteristic of a caring, loving church. Jamila and her chil-dren were safe with the Nashes at their cabin. Some of the members were clustering together because of house-jacking. Nobody had been hurt, just inconvenienced. Luke had overheard several conversations where people were sadly grieving over the loss of some members to the world. Of spe-cial note was the surprise and sorrow of the head elder's defection. When Peter heard that, he grieved as well. At the park he didn't want to believe it. He had spent so many hours with him working on the details of church-manship. One lady had seen him filling his car with very visible sores on the side of his face. It was difficult to believe that someone who had spent so much of his adult life in the church would not see the signs of apostasy in oneself.

He told of Chad's ideas and the purchases at the surplus store. Peter realized that Luke didn't have a lot of food with just two cases of MREs. He told Luke where to find the hidden key to his house so he could use the larder he would never use. The purchase of IR blocking military uni-forms to wear to avoid IR detection interested Peter. It wasn't something he would know to do, but he thought, *look at me—I'm behind bars*. The two friends had prayer, and Luke left to work on appearances. He didn't realize that the whole conversation was recorded.

At Peter's house, he found several imposing men at the front and side door. One had a pry bar at the edge of the door jamb. It told him everything he needed to know. He jumped out of his unmarked police car and held his badge in front of him. He let it lead him to the crowbar man. The men hesitated until Detective Hardine pulled back the flap of his sport coat and rested the heel of his hand on the handle of his service revolver. He felt guilty as soon as he did it, guilty because it was a selfish use of power for his own benefit. He could argue for the fact that he was protecting the property of a citizen, but in the present context, this world's possessions were about to be destroyed, and the owner would probably never use this residence again. Then, he had to admit that the dynamics of these last days were between God's way and the world's way. However, it worked. He realized his old ways needed to be replaced with the new ways he was trying to learn. Here forward, he would let the Lord fight his battles for him. He watched the men grudgingly get in their vehicles and leave.

XXXXX

Brian and Cynthia were coming to the same conclusion that Chad and Diana had—they needed to leave. Their apartment building managers were telling them that because they had two bedrooms, and they only used one to sleep in, that meant a homeless person needed their spare bedroom. They talked about it. If this had happened outside of the current situation, they would have counted it as an opportunity thrust upon them by God's providence. A suffering soul thrust into their home ripe for the call to His kingdom. But in the present situation, it was courtship with the devil. They had also received a letter from their bank that the state government would take funds out of their account by way of garnishment for humanitarian purposes. No legislation covered this action. Watching prejudicial eyes had made a decision independently from normal protocol. They were forced to understand that the new world plan meant for them to share whether they agreed or not, and despite their record of charity.

They packed their car with everything they might need to survive the next several months or the remainder of a year. They didn't know where they would go. God would provide the way. They planned to visit all the members to encourage them to stay the course and not lose heart.

Tomorrow morning they would leave the apartment empty and unlocked with a note welcoming, whoever. Cynthia also baked a cake and spelled out with blue frosting on white. *'Welcome to Our Home.'*

XXXXX

The Hixons called their daughter about a TV presentation. Once again, a disaster was unfolding. Vonnie told everyone else that they needed to put on the news. They, of course, did not tune in to the beginning of a story, like Hollywood TV. They came in at the end. They had to switch several channels to get a more substantive account. They put it together from what they were watching and what Vonnie was hearing from her folks.

The recent volcanic activity had vents under the polar sea. Superheated water jetted upward toward the ice-covered surface. Almost instantly, the warmth carved out a dome, which acted like an oven spreading along the surface of the water, creating a massive cavern that had to collapse. When it did, hunks of ice the size of mansions looked like ice-cubes bobbing in hot coffee. They disappeared in minutes. With the way clear, boiling water ejected steam into the air, which formed precipitation in the form of acidic rain. The hot air created its own weather, and the result was a warmer local climate to soften the icecap from above. Seas were rising.

Farther south, the rise in the sea had registered in coastal communities except in the way of what people would consider an extraordinarily high tide that did not recede. Shoreline beach businesses closed shops because no one could endure the smell of rotting fish and rancid seaweed. Birds were eating the abundant carrion and then dropping out of the sky dead. Finally, news outlets were recording the destruction of the vacation/recreational economy. None wanted to take a day at the beach; beaches were all but gone. What was not detailed on the news was that people were loathing leaving their homes unguarded and having house-jackers move in. It was a simple thing to do legally. If they could manufacture a letter or e-mail purported to be from the property owner saying they were invited into their home, the resultant litigation to get them out could last for months on end.

Mrs. Hixon was pleased to have her daughter coming back home and her friends with her. She said so at the end of their phone call.

Leticia Greene repeated the question she had asked before. She knew the answer in general, but not specifically. "What's next now?"

"The rivers and fountains of water … become blood.'" Chad answered.

"Do we need to start collecting water?" she asked.

"If it comes to us running out of water, I know God will provide. But maybe we should collect, ah, well … Why listen to me? I've never done this before," Chad waffled. Mrs. Greene had a very downcast look on her face.

"I know I'm saying something we all have been avoiding, but I'm scared." They looked at Leticia, agreeing, yet not knowing what to say to ease her worry. Diana answered, "I'm not scared, I'm petrified. Tomorrow, we leave this place not to return. Our lives are changing every new minute, and the Bible tells us that if this time isn't shortened, no human would be saved."

"Even worse, it was Jesus' words that you just quoted. This time we can't be lightly ignored," Vonnie added.

"I hope you don't think I'm okay with all this. My way of dealing with fear is to be as ready as possible. I realize that may look like confidence, but it really, really isn't." Diana reached out to her love tangibly by clasping his hand in hers. It comforted her greatly, maybe more than comforting him. They quietly worried together, each with their own thoughts. They were leaning into the wind, more like a strong gale. After acknowledging their plight, they prayed. They prayed for strength, endurance, and most of all, they prayed to keep the connection with their Creator unbreakable.

XXXXX

Luke made himself a nice warm dinner. He could have returned to his apartment but felt an unnecessary need to protect his friend's property. It didn't feel right to sleep in his friend's bed, so he stretched out on the couch.

CHAPTER 17

He made a fantastic breakfast. His morning started like it had the last several weeks—with prayer and study. He had to make up for years of not knowing Bible truths. He wanted to read and remember God's promises, especially the ones relating to the end times. His studies with Pastor Lange had emphasized God's love. Because of Hardine's search, Pastor Lange had also focused on the unique beliefs of the SDA church, which are now the beliefs that it seemed that the whole world was interested in eliminating. Ending his study with a prayer of commitment, he felt like devouring an entire cafeteria steam-table of food. Fortified, he went to work to keep up appearances.

> *His morning started like it had the last several weeks—with prayer and study. He had to make up for years of not knowing Bible truths.*

At the door to the precinct, they relieved him of his revolver and his badge. They took him to the interrogation room, where he sat on the other side of the table. They didn't handcuff him to the table, but they did let him "cook" for several hours as if he had information they needed. When the captain did come into the room, he feigned compassion.

270

"You really do need to take time for yourself. You work too much. You forgot to go to church and use your card to validate your loyalty. If you had been paying attention, you would know that you can go downstairs and reactivate your cards. It's so simple, and yet you didn't do it. Why?"

It didn't take a detective to discern that the captain knew the answer to his own question.

"I do not ascribe to this world and its denial of Bible truth. People are being forced to deny their conscience and—"

"Spare me the crap! Can I assume that you didn't neglect to validate your cards on purpose and that you are in protest?"

"Yes."

"Then I must consider you a belligerent and outside the law. You will be booked and held for trial along with your preacher buddy."

"Have you solved the Johnson murder?" Detective Hardine asked.

"I filed that under, 'who cares?'" Luke Hardine felt handcuffs on his wrists for the first time when they put them on and led him down to holding. He had wondered in the past what it felt like to be arrested and shamed in the eyes of peers. Walking past associates, he didn't feel shame, he felt proud.

According to procedure, he received one phone call. Instead of calling a lawyer, he called Chad. He wanted to tell him about the captain's remark and apologize to him for not solving his parents' murder. He also relayed a message from Pastor Peter.

XXXXX

Chad answered his phone, hopeful of some news about his parents' case before he started going off-grid. Caller ID indicated it was from the police station. As he expected, it was the detective, but the tale was not expected. He listened and then encouraged Luke as a friend, praying for strength. Literally, the dragnet was being drawn closer and closer. Two arrests of people he knew.

They were ready to exit the house, waiting for him. He explained the phone call and then took a folder and said, "I'll be back in a moment." He went across the street to a neighbor.

"What do you want?" the man spat out the words. The exchange didn't look promising.

"I want to make a trade."

"Trade for what?"

"I have here the deeds for my house and the two cars. I will sign them all over to you for your truck. Three for one, deal?"

"You want to give your house for my truck? Are you crazy?"

"No, I need a truck 'cause I'm going off the grid."

"Oh, I see. You're one of those. Just like your stupid ol' folks. You deserve what they got. I'll take your house if it will get you outta here. I'll get the keys."

"And the deed."

"Yea, yea."

Chad signed the documents on the front step. He handed over the folder when he saw the deed to the truck signed. The keys for all the cars were exchanged, and he drove the truck to the driveway of his former residence. He piled the remaining supplies in the back and drove away, following the other cars. He saw in his rearview mirror his neighbor walking across the street with a shotgun. He thought that was logical because of the wolves and then realized he hadn't heard a sound from them since last night and hadn't seen even a nose or a tail; another mystery.

The girls drove to Vonnie's folks, and he drove to a filling station to fill up with gasoline. He checked with the manager first, and he was willing to sell gas for over three thousand bucks in coin. He got a full tank with extra cans of oil and filled some portable five-gallon containers. He was still conflicted about how much he should plan and how much he needed to survive.

When he got to the Hixons' home, they greeted him by saying, "We are really getting close now!"

XXXXX

The Kings were going from one member's house to another. Many were not home. Where they were home, they prayed and encouraged. Their spiritual leadership as it came to the members helped to a great extent. A familiar face, a word of hope, and a handshake or hug made the dire news palatable. Ministry vs. melancholy in moments before worrisome events has the capacity to bring people to their knees before their Savior. The members were pliable, open, grateful, dedicated. If only past ministry could have been performed with believers with this degree of personal commitment and urgency.

Cynthia called ahead to alert Chad, Diana, and Vonnie of their desire to visit. They expected to meet them at Chad's place. They changed course and went to the Hixons'. It turned into a Friday evening vespers service after they compared notes on the newest events and shared a supper together.

XXXXX

When Isa brought water forth from the Al-Ahsa aquifer in Saudi Arabia, the local media set up a camera to show the ongoing miracle that he had created. People talked with awe of the Great Imam Madhi. Posters of the Madhi with the water spewing from the pipe seemed to be on every building, wall, and mosque in every city in greater Arabia. The pictures and the video of the pipe became a symbol of the new Islam. Then, in full view, it happened—a belch stopped the flow for a couple of seconds, and then clumpy blood came out of the end. Other locations found rivers changing to blood from their sources downward to their deltas in the oceans. Long rivers didn't change overnight, but populations were signaled ahead of time that bloody water was on the way. In third world countries where people relied on flowing water, the reaction was a rush to fill their water barrels, buckets, and bottles. Wells located near unconfiscated Adventist churches in Africa remained pure for the time being. Room at the edge of rivers and lakes came at a premium. Riots broke out, fights turned into brawls, and then all-out wars.

This phenomenon could not be ignored. The worldwide media covered every detail. Reporters stood by springs and wells, showing the blood coming out in slow ooze rather than a splashing, gurgling stream. This time, the media could not dismiss the parallel with the biblical account of the final plagues. The preceding phenomena added to the story. International news plied Isa Jesus with the problem of the plagues being poured out upon the world. He replied, "This is what was predicted. 'True and just are Thy judgments.' With these plagues the wrath of God is ended. God the Father is pouring out His wrath upon this world because we are not in unity as yet. We must purge the earth of those who will not agree with the principles of His government. Sunday, The Lord's day, needs to be universally observed so the world can focus on the Father. The plagues will end when we all comply."

His words fell like a death knell upon the world. Something had to be done. The world could not go on like this. The government signaled that it didn't have the resources to find all of those who would not submit. Citizens were called upon to turn in their neighbors and associates. The entire world became, in one fell swoop, a toxic environment.

XXXXX

Diana didn't want to enter into a dialog with her mother, even if it was one single text. The question that stood before her was, "Is the water reddish where you are?" She knew her mom was asking if there was blood coming out of the faucets in Chad's house. Her mother did not know she was at another location. It presented a dilemma between answering or not answering. She could say "no" because last she knew, it was true, but now, maybe not. If she said "no" it would tell her the plague was not affecting God's people. She wanted to communicate the truth that her mother had missed. She decided against a reply, and then another text came in. "Answer me. Blood; yes or no?" So she texted a simple, "no."

The Hixons' had a nice dinner. With six guests the dining table was full with all leaves inserted into the table. They also used their very best china. Why not? Their next formal dinner may well be in the kingdom, and the guests of honor would be all eight of those sitting at this table. Not just guests, they would be the church as the bride of Christ. It would be the marriage supper of the Lamb. Diana asked, "I wonder what kind of china we will eat off of up there?"

"Nicer than this china for sure," Mrs. Hixon answered.

"Oh, I didn't mean it in that way. This is beautiful china!" Diana responded.

"I know you didn't mean it in that way, honey. I just think that whatever we eat off of up there will be way beyond our expectations. I can't imagine it. But I do feel that it will be outdoors, don't you?"

The house party enjoyed talking about heaven and guessed at what it will be like. The conversation was fun. It was not like the first moment of dread that hit Chad when he walked in the front door. That's when he heard that the third plague started and the quote from the fake Jesus. Marching forward, one plague at a time sobers the soul. A lot of "maybes" were in the thoughts. Maybe they should be out of the way in the woods. Maybe they should be purer. Maybe their theology isn't correct. Maybe they should be having a more difficult time. Then there were all the "oughts." They ought to be witnessing. They ought to be better prepared. They ought to trust the Lord more and not make so much preparation.

With Isa Jesus calling for mankind to stop the plagues with unity, boggled the mind. For that to be true, it would mean that Bible prophecy would have to be false. That meant Jesus' message in the last book of the Bible would be incorrect. If Isa Jesus was really Jesus, he would have to own up to the fact that he didn't tell the truth in His message given in the book of Revelation. Yet, the world accepted his incredible stupidity and marshaled resources to end the natural disasters caused by the plagues.

That evening, they welcomed the Sabbath, feeling the sanctuary of peace it provides. In its arms they nestled into the love of the Lord. Their prayers were accompanied by the Spirit, and they rejoiced in its assurance. Fortified, they reveled in fellowship with the divine. Whatever happened in the days ahead counted as nothing compared to the time they spent with the Holy Spirit this evening. The hours of spiritual pleasure were lengthened when they found out that Brian and Cynthia didn't know where they were going to stay that night. The Hixons' invited them to stay there, and the final resolution of the sleeping arrangements put everyone in sleeping bags in the living room on the couch, floor, and easy chairs. They talked deep into the night.

XXXXX

The Perkins' house was full of worshipping "illegals." Not all of the church members were there. Some, unfortunately, had fallen away, and some had fled to who knows where. The house was not large, but it was warm with fellowship. Emilee had a friend from down the street. A child with cerebral-palsy had been a playmate for years. She didn't get the call from the Lord to heal her until just before the time when everything had to be finished. Her friend and her friend's parents were brands plucked from the fire at the last possible moment. They were alive with questions, and they were fresh, brand-new believers in the testing current issues of the time. New believers excite a congregation. Having these people come in before the curtain fell felt like a victory before the last seconds of overtime. Upbeat attitudes about God's work within human lives trumped any minor exhilaration about doing something illegal. They were outside the law and inside the law at the same time. The law of the land vs. the law of God. Again, one trumps the other.

Brian stood to begin worship. Before he even opened his mouth, some others asked for the attention of the group. He thought they were just trying to help. They weren't, they had an agenda. One spoke and gave a personal account of an experience. He spoke of the ministry of Brian and Cynthia on the phone and in person. Another validated that sentiment. Yet another wanted to praise them, and specifically Brian, as a great elder for the church. She wanted to recognize Brian as head elder for their church and elect Cynthia as a second elder. "Amen's," seconded the call for him to be their leader.

Chad stood up and raised one hand for attention. They gave him their respect. Starting with his relationship with Detective Hardine, he explained the phone call and that the detective had given him a message from Pastor Lange as his one call after being arrested. He said, "Pastor Lange wanted to tell the church that he had the utmost confidence in Brian King as a spiritual leader. The result was more "amens." Brian was officially the leader of this little church of stalwart believers and Cynthia, his right-hand man, er, woman. Deep inside Brian this validation with all the smiles and verbal confirmation gave him the reverse of those horrible stops by racist police officers. Inside he thanked his Lord and Savior for knowing what he wanted without asking. He looked at his loving wife to see an understanding smile.

"My brothers and sisters, reading from our Bibles is the most sensible thing we can do at a time like this. Let me illustrate. In Psalm ninety-one we read, 'He who dwells in the secret place of the Most High shall abide under the shadow of the Almighty. I will say of the Lord, *He is my refuge and my fortress; My God, in Him I will trust.*'[27] So much of this psalm speaks to me today. We start by dwelling with Him and then find the following benefits. Look in verse three. 'Surely He shall deliver you from the snare of the fowler *And* from the perilous pestilence.' Have you seen any perilous pestilence lately?" They nodded their heads. It was a "Duh" moment.

> *So many were choosing to go with the world of the now rather than the world of the future. Friends and relatives were throwing away eternity, thinking that life would be better in the immediate days ahead if they went along with a spurious charlatan.*

Brian pointed out that practically every verse spoke to the now. He reminded them the truth mentioned in verse four was the reason that they were going into hiding, and the truth was their shield. When he got to verse seven, the mood became somber because it really was true that thousands and ten thousand were falling on every side of them. So many were choosing to go with the world of the now rather

---

[27]*vss. 1–2, NKJV*

than the world of the future. Friends and relatives were throwing away eternity, thinking that life would be better in the immediate days ahead if they went along with a spurious charlatan.

Brian had chosen the perfect text to encourage the little flock of refugees. It talked of things they were seeing, and it gave them hope. He ended by saying, "Look at where you are right now! There's absolutely no plague. No sores. No blood coming out of the tap. We are blessed by the presence of God. Wait—we are blessed because we are in the fortress of God. We have gone to Him. We have fled to His stronghold. I love this psalm. Do you love this psalm? Let me hear you, do you love this psalm?" He was greeted with hearty amens. Yes, they loved the message of the psalm. They also loved their new leader.

Leadership is a fickle thing, but not this time. In volunteer settings leaders usually lead by permission of the followers. Brian was their leader before Pastor Lange's message of validation. Brian had voluntarily selected Jesus as his leader, and his leader had validated him in a personal way, as He always does with anyone who is willing.

They sang songs of hope and victory. They recounted close calls and miracles. They praised God and asked for protection. They told each other where they planned to hide and prayed about each plan and its success. They prayed for the pastor and the detective.

Diana received a text from her mother that told another story.

ZZZZZ

You take the cake! You call yourself Christians! You're worse than criminals! You, I mean Chad, shot at us. You could've killed us! What did you do with those dogs? Kill them?

ZZZZZ

She leaned over to show Chad. It confirmed for them that the wolves were there for a purpose. For Diana, it demonstrated once again, her mother was bent on acquiring a nice house for nothing. She had never noticed her mother's capricious desire for wealth. This had to be a selfish spirit entering her life. Her mother was a different person, one she did not know. It disappointed her and confirmed to her that one never knows what is in a person's heart. God knows the secret intents of the individual's core.

Chad related to the group about the wolves, and how they had kept men away from them while they prepared. Mr. Perkins asked if maybe they should have stayed there if the wolves were their protectors. It was a good question and one in which he had an interest because of his responsibility to protect his family. Chad's answer was that he had a sense that he should leave, which was confirmed by a similar feeling by Diana. "It still is the big city, and we are encouraged to get out of the cities, but I must admit my decision is based primarily on that feeling." Mr. Perkins thanked him for his answer and went quiet, thinking.

"Has anyone heard from Raphael?" Vonnie asked.

"No, nothing recently. Cynthia and I tried to visit him yesterday. His place was open and empty," Brian explained.

"Did he move?" Vonnie came back.

"I don't think so. The door was open, most of the furniture was gone, and the place was wrecked. I think someone trashed the place after taking what they could," Cynthia answered.

"I know his folks live in California, and he would want to help them. They were close as a family. Being the only son would mean he would feel obligated to help. He's a good son," Brian added.

"So, we pray for him, his folks, and plan on asking him what happened when we get to heaven. We should have enough time, don't you think?" Diana smiled as she commented.

The aroma from the kitchen overwhelmed them as they talked and prayed. Mrs. Perkins had this desire to provide a huge lunch for members who were struggling to eat in the shadow of austerity. Some went to the kitchen to help chop, cut, and slice the vegetables. The items that worked magic on the senses were apple pies, pots of chili beans, and several pans of flavored vegeburger for haystacks. One of those helping wanted to know the reason for choosing this type of food. Mrs. Perkins explained that one of the church members had told her that the former president of the Arizona Conference, Tony Anobile, had always said haystacks would be eaten in heaven. She giggled when she said, "I thought this would make us all homesick."

XXXXX

Peter and Luke were two cells apart. The holding center in the basement of the five-story justice building contained twenty, two-bed cells, which were all full. The county jails were also full. In Luke's cell there was an almost comatose drunk, who had destroyed his car by running it through the showroom window of a car dealer. As incoherent as he was, he still managed to splatter his and Luke's bunk with foul-smelling emesis. The odor wafted through the cell block, driving the guards away and allowing the two friends the chance to worship and pray together without interruption. Other internees had their heads, and more specifically, noses buried in their pillows and blankets. The Lord blesses His people and gives them opportunity to worship Him.

Peter asked Luke if he knew "Amazing Grace." He said, "a little." So Peter began to sing. He sang quietly but soon heard a third voice. He stopped. "Luke, did you hear an angel join us?"

"Hardly an angel. I heard you guys praying and quoting Scripture. It was just what I needed. My name is Richard. What are yours?"

"Peter."

"Luke."

"It's good to meet you. I won't say it's nice. What's that smell?"

"That would be my cellmate. Arrested for drunk driving, and his stomach is rebelling."

"That's awful!"

"Maybe, but it's keeping the guards from stopping our illegal worship service."

"On the Sabbath," Richard added.

"Are you a believer?" Peter asked.

"Yes."

"Tell us about how you got here."

"I, ah, knew that Saturday was the true Sabbath of the Bible in both Old and New Testaments, ever since about ten years ago. But I was the music director at my church, and my check came from my work at Sunday worship services. I kept the Sabbath quietly on Saturday until these restrictions started on Christians to keep Sunday. It was a matter of conscience. It would have been so very easy to swipe my card and let it go at that. I just couldn't. Then I heard a small voice calling me out. I had to resign. So, I did. And that was that."

"How did you end up in jail?"

"The police came to my house looking for church property. For years, I've had a filing cabinet in my home office with church sheet music in it. They went right to the files and then arrested me for stealing from the church. Voila! Here I am."

"You don't seem worried?"

"God is protecting me. Us, He is protecting us. I read in 2 Thessalonians that the *Lord is faithful. He will guard me against the evil one. What gives me hope is that the promise of protection follows a statement about the Lawless One who* takes his seat in the temple of God proclaiming to be god. I'm watching the Lawless One fulfill one prediction, and I'm relying on the promise of the other. Enough about me, let's continue morning worship."

"You're the music director, what do you suggest?"

"I'll start singing, and you join in." Richard began to sing, *Jesus Paid It All*. Tender tenor tones reverberated through the concrete walls of the basement. Luke and Peter didn't want to join. They wanted to listen. This was serendipity, an unexpected blessing.

"Sing another one, please." He did sing another and another. He gave them a Sabbath concert. He paused for Pastor Lange to give a sermon on the twenty-third psalm, "Yea, though I walk through the valley of the shadow of death." The last song for the impromptu service was, "It Is Well."

As if by magic, the cell block erupted in noise in complaint immediately after the final prayer. It seemed that the sense of outrage over the smell automatically kicked in, and everyone demanded ammonium hydroxide as if it were hyacinth in full bloom. Over the rancor Pastor Lange called to Richard, "Did you know you are mentioned in Revelation eighteen?"

"What haven't I seen?" he yelled in return.

"Verse four says, 'Come out of her, my people,' you came out. You're one of the Called-out Ones."

"No, I didn't pass out once?"

The noise prohibited any conversation. Peter answered the best he could, "I'll talk to you later."

"You're right; it doesn't matter."

XXXXX

Vonnie received a call from her folks while she was eating lunch on the Perkins' deck overlooking the backyard. She had her feet up on a cushioned stool. As soon as she heard her mother's voice, her feet came off the stool and hit the deck. "What's wrong? Oh, no. What are you going to do?" Conversations on the back deck came to a halt. They listened to Vonnie breathe as she listened to her mother. "You're sure? That's what you want? Don't worry, Mom; it won't be long now. We have a plan, so don't worry about us. We'll meet in heaven. Yeah, soon. Tell Dad I love him and … yes, I love you, too."

Cocked heads told Vonnie everyone was waiting for an explanation. "Armed men are sitting on the front porch of my folks' house. They can't go home; neither can we, for that matter."

"Oh, phew, I thought something terrible had happened," Diana deadpanned. "What are they going to do?"

"It *is* odd that we are kinda expecting things like this. My folks are staying with some friends from their church, and they are going to the mountains if anyone tries to take their friends' house. Making an observation: so far, it looks like people are going after property, not trying to kill our people. I'm guessing the death decree hasn't been issued yet," Vonnie observed.

"It's only a matter of time. I know, theoretically, that it won't come to death, but it's still scary to think someone might want to come after us and try. Looking down the business end of a shotgun is not on my bucket list," Diana said.

"What is on your bucket list?" Chad asked.

"Nothing. Bucket lists are for people who want to do things before they die. I'm not going to die," she responded.

"That's the spirit!"

"So, what are we going to do?" Leticia asked.

"Move up our schedule. Go to my hiding place," Chad answered.

"Tell us about this place."

"It's very secluded. It is covered in trees and brush so thick you can't see it even if you are standing ten feet from it."

"How did you find it?" Diana asked.

"I was hiking with some friends, and I needed to, you know, take a moment. So I tried to go behind some bushes, and I saw a stone wall through the leaves. I decided to investigate. It turns out that it is an old dairy shed for a nearby ranch house that is nothing but rubble."

"What's a dairy shed, Chad?" Vonnie asked.

"Back before refrigeration, pioneers would build a rock shed close to a stream. It was cooler next to the water, and the rock would keep the heat out."

"How big is it? Will we be able to sleep in it?" Diana asked.

"It'll be tight with four of us, but maybe we can keep out of the way. The big plus is that if they're looking for us, they could walk right by us and not know we are there."

"Unless, of course, if they have to go to the bathroom," Diana quipped.

The conversation had been with the four up to that point. Mr. Perkins spoke, "You can stay with us."

"Thank you. That is nice. But you extended the same invitation to Brian and Cynthia. If too many of us stay in one place, it will attract attention. We have to spread out a little. Besides, we are not like some of the other believers; we have a place to go."

"How much time would it take to get there?"

"About a two-hour drive and then another little hike."

"You'll have to stay with us at least tonight because if you left right now, you only have maybe forty minutes of daylight left. It'd be dark when you got there. How would you find this place in the dark?"

"You're right; that wouldn't work."

"So, stay with us tonight, and leave in the morning."

"That's a good plan. Thank you."

XXXXX

Commandment-keeping people were finding different places to avoid the coming trouble. Technically, they were already in trouble. The plagues were falling. The mark of the beast had made it difficult to buy and sell. The general populous was capitalizing on bargains at the expense of commandment-keepers. Animals were unrestricted by the controlling Spirit of God. And people were acting without the internal locus of control. God's people were in the middle of chaos, and yet, they knew it could get worse. They wanted sanctuaries insulated from the anarchy to come.

President Hertzog, at first, took in Andrews' students who did not have a home to go to that supported their belief. Every corner of his campus home was filled. Then inhuman elements started taking over the campus buildings and dormitories. They had to find a more secure location that didn't have immediate appeal to the greedy masses. That was true even for the small community of Berrien Springs, Michigan. The president and his wife had to make a decision to move. One of the campus buildings was not of immediate appeal to the public. The kids' club Pathfinder building was down a steep hill and up next to some trees. A chain crossed the road at the top of the hill blocking curious traffic from going down the hill. Since the closure of the university, the chain had remained in place. At night, the president led his charges down the hill, bringing as many non-perishables with them in suitcases, backpacks, and tote bags, a strange cavalcade in the wee hours. They used flashlights instead of the electricity, so as not to attract attention. Two hefty youths dragged two dead trees across the road near the chain to discourage anyone from driving through the chain and down the hill.

XXXXX

Raphael drove through the night to California. His folks were delighted to see him. Both parents had arthritis and limited movement. They had saved up foodstuff for the end, but staying in the inner city slowly became untenable. Teen gangs were preying on the elderly, stealing anything of value they could lay their hands upon, any object for resale or trade. It was only a matter of time before some would attempt to break in. That was the fear Raphael's folks worried about daily. Their prayers for protection contained belief in God's ability to intervene, yet every noise at night caused them to jump in fright.

Teen gangs were preying on the elderly, stealing anything of value they could lay their hands upon, any object for resale or trade.

Having their son there helped them to believe in God's wonderful protection. Raphael felt leaving the home was the better part of wisdom. He loaded up the family pop-up camper trailer, hooked it to his car with a bumper hitch, put all of the provisions and warm clothes in the car, and took off toward the uninhabited parts of the Sierra Nevadas.

Climbing the hills fronting on the edge of the Sierra Nevada Mountains provided an intermittent view of the valley they left behind. As the road curved to gain altitude, sometimes the view of the populace areas was on the right, then later, on the left. Raphael thought looking back was not for nostalgic reasons, but more of relief as he put mile upon mile from the danger that lay behind. He could estimate approximately where his parents' home was by spotting the tall downtown buildings. Turning his attention forward, he suddenly jerked back because he thought he saw a streak of lightning. It wasn't lightning. It was a large fireball screaming down from the heavens. He had seen shooting stars, but this was massive. He could not estimate the size because of the distance. He pulled to the side of the road to watch. In two seconds, he wished he had not stopped. The flaming ball smashed into the city, and that's when Raphael could judge its size. It was at least 500 feet in diameter, not counting the surrounding and trailing ball of flames. The fireball engulfed the city, dwarfing the tall buildings, crushing them like sandcastles under an M-1 tank. A massive crown-shaped crater formed instantly with fiery debris flying out in fountains of rock in every direction. The valley rippled like waves on a pond when a rock hits water.

Raphael stomped on the accelerator pedal as he saw the shock wave of fire and dirt heading his way. He needed to flee. His mother and father were inhaling air in huge gulps. The camper trailer was fishtailing behind the car as they sped up the road. Raphael's head kept juddering back and forth as he watched the road ahead, and the concussive shock wave ranged outward toward him at Mach 1. His only hope was to get around a shoulder of a hill out of direct impact with the wave. He calculated the distance and knew he didn't have enough speed. He prayed aloud for help as the distance to safety suddenly collapsed. The corner and the edge of the hill seemed to race toward him, and the wheels below did not touch the ground. Like a bobsled on a curve, his vehicle slid behind the protective hill as the rubble flew by and above them. They were in the shadow of security in the material world and in the shadow of the Almighty in the spiritual world. The storm of fire and rock blew over them, darkening the sky into night and covering them in heavy dust, gravel, and fragments of a destroyed city.

CHAPTER 18

Pope Jesus supervised the huge port support operation of moving massive amounts of food into truck caravans to the interior of Africa. Tons of wheat, rice, beans, and potatoes bundled on pallets were craned out of ships onto flatbed trucks. The operation did not need another supervisor. The pope was there for the media and for what he expected to be a photo op. As he spoke to the cameras of the wonderful redistribution of food to famine-stricken areas, the docks were flooding. Seaside docks usually float up and down with the tide. This time the piers were at maximum height for what would be the highest tide. The water was overflowing the planks. Trucks could not get close enough to receive the pallets; the first truck on the dock had to pull off the dock to avoid being submerged.

The entire operation was crawling to a stop as water rose by natural tide and unnatural melt. The pope could do nothing about the flood stage and suggested nothing about the rotting red color. He, however, remained on the positive subject of love for hungry humanity and provided a miracle by pushing the waters back as in the parting of the Red Sea. In a semi-circle around the port, a watery wall waited to rush back in to swallow the harbor. He kept the extra tide away until all the lowboy trucks could clear the port and proceed inland. Behind the miracle people wanted to know why there was so much water.

Unseen and unknown, under the polar ice cap, volcanoes were bubbling pillow lava over the seafloor. Lava at two thousand degrees Fahrenheit cools down quickly in Arctic water, but not fast enough below yards upon yards of pack ice. Seawater responded by heating up. Huge chunks of ice melted like cubes in excessively hot coffee. Ocean levels were raising because of these North Pole volcanoes spreading coastal woes around the world.

There were now many more individuals struggling with livelihood issues beyond that of famines because a quarter of a billion people lived within one meter altitude of the old sea level. That meant almost three hundred million people were displaced, having to move inland. The largest refugee migration ever! Some island countries were completely decimated, almost like sunken Bermuda. Fishing boats floated above the problem but, the facilities that processed the catch and the stores and restaurants could not purchase and use the catch. This is in addition to the fact that so few of the fish populations could survive the nasty red aquatic environment. If oceans got any deeper, some coastlines would have submerged cities.

XXXXX

It looked like Chad was in a stupor. He suddenly stood up and called for attention to the group assembling in the living room. They were ready for vespers, and he was concerned about their safety. It took a few false starts before he realized he needed to wait until after the close of the Sabbath. He apologized for his lack of consideration but asked for their attention afterward.

Both Cynthia and Brian led out in a song service followed by prayer that moved naturally into asking God for intercession in helping fellow believers, relatives, and those incarcerated for their faith. When they were done, Brian drew a parallel with the prayers they just uttered, and the imagined prayers early Christian church believers said for their loved ones being persecuted. He emphasized that this was different in that we know that there is no more need for martyrs for the cause of God. In a few short weeks, maybe months, everything will be finished. One voice said, "I prefer weeks over months! Actually, days over weeks! I don't think I can take much more of this worry!"

"I have to second her feelings," Leticia added. "I feel like I'm sort of two-faced. On the surface I'm singing and praying, and deep down inside,

I'm agonizing over what will be next. I say I have faith, and yet I doubt—doubt His protection. For two millenia, Christians have been tortured and murdered. How is this different today? The Richards … well, you know about that. Is what we are facing now different or just the same as before?"

"It *is* different. Let me assure you, prophecy in Daniel chapter twelve predicts that in the time of trouble, Michael, the great Prince, will arise and deliver His people, those whose names are written in the book of life. According to the book of Revelation, your name is written, and you are in charge of blotting it out. So, if you haven't turned your back on God, you will be protected by Michael, the great Prince," Cynthia confirmed and gave Leticia a hug. "We're going to be okay, you'll see."

"I wish I had your faith."

"Nonsense. God gives you everything you need. He never puts you in a place where you cannot prevail because He gives you what you need. I get that from the text, 'He never tempts you above what you are able to withstand.'"

"And, everything you need is a gift from God," Brian added. "Chad, what did you want to say?"

"It's not spiritual. It's more practical."

"Okay." Brain answered, but many were interested.

"Remember when Detective Hardine told us about how we might be tracked? Well, I've been thinking. He said they would track our cell phones. That made me think. When they start tracking us, they will know where we are and where we have been. Like a breadcrumb trail. If they were to start tomorrow, they would know all of us were here today. They would see all these phone tracks here in one place."

"What should we do, turn them off?"

"If we turned them all off, then the last signal they have is here. They will come here looking for us. I suggest we take our phones away from here. Leave the phones on so the trail leads them away from the Perkins. Then turn the ringers off, but leave the phones on, and put the phones in logical places that will confuse them."

"How so?"

"Put your phones in a mall or an apartment. Here's one idea I got—leave it at a church. They might think that you are there, trying to turn your credit cards back on. Maybe they might leave you alone for a little while, at least. I was thinking I might go home and toss the phone up on the roof. They just might turn the house upside down, trying to find me."

"After having a shootout with the new owner," Diana quipped.

"I hadn't thought of that. I was thinking that it would be logical since my last name is still on the utility paperwork. There's another thing—if we get a chance to worship here again, we should park a distance away and walk in. All the cars could be a giveaway."

"We won't be able to phone ahead to see if it is safe to come here again next Sabbath because we will be turning off our phones, so, I suggest we plan on meeting here, unless there is a brush-off signal," Brian suggested.

"There might not be very many of us, but being careful is the better part of wisdom. What kind of signal do you suggest?" Cynthia asked.

"I suggest I put a small green felt pen circle on the stop sign on the corner. If it is there, keep driving. If it is not there, then it means it's safe," Mr. Perkins instructed.

"So, it's a plan. Now I suggest we protect this place and get our phones out of here," Chad said.

XXXXX

Domoic acid collects in crustaceans, i.e., shellfish, and poisons those animals who eat them, including humans. With the crisis in oceanic food production, there was increased competition for what remained. Domoic acid is acquired from algae and spreads upward through the food chain, sometimes as a factor in the Red Tide. If eaten in large enough quantities, it can be fatal; otherwise, it causes vomiting, nausea, diarrhea, and abdominal cramps within twenty-four hours of ingestion. Desperately hungry people will eat almost anything that resembles food, even rotting shellfish. Medical emergencies were soaring in shoreline communities in third-world countries. Rushing food to these locations couldn't be done fast enough.

Pope Domenic Clement Leonardo Xavier Sextus, aka 'Isa-Jesus,' aka 'son of god,' felt pressed to the maximum extent, trying to cure so many cases of amnesic shellfish poisoning (ASP). He swept into the seaside hospitals and raced through the wards, healing as he went. No sooner had he left than ambulances refilled the wards. It was the same in the Pacific and the Atlantic. All day long, he was on a mission to prove that the returned savior of mankind could save the world from disease, famine, and strife. He turned to the media to help him accomplish changing the world. The nirvana of the here and now could not be achieved until "his father" was pleased with the people of this world. Fault needed to be placed at the feet of the rebels. If they couldn't be induced into complying with the norm, they had to be eliminated. He called an emergency council of world leaders, both civic and religious.

XXXXX

The foursome drove to Vonnie's home, where they had left their cars to avoid having so many cars parked at the Perkins' house. It would be dicey collecting their cars if there were armed thugs nearby. When they got to the corner down the street, they stopped to see who might be lurking nearby. One tall individual stood by the curbside mailbox with a sawed-off shotgun in his hand cradled in the elbow of the opposite arm. If he wanted to, he could interfere with any one of the cars they desired to drive away. They debated whether it was worth it to fetch their cars. They all agreed that it wasn't, but Chad said they should at least try and then use the cars to lay false trails later. He proposed a distraction. He drove around the block, leaving the three ladies off on a blind approach to the house. It was blind because the trees and bushes blocked the view from one angle. He went to the other side of the house, stopped, got out of his truck, and yelled over the cab at the man, asking for directions. His body was shielded by the cab. It worked. He got the fellow's attention with very little in the way of directions in return. Chad got the gist of his comments by watching the shotgun waving around, trying to encourage him to move on. At one point he pressed the horn on his steering wheel for no apparent reason. The sound blocked the sound of engines starting. By the time the guard knew what was happening, the three cars were moving down the street. Chad yelled heartfelt thanks, and then drove off. They finished their simple plan by linking up at a nearby shopping center.

They laid plans for meeting up after depositing their smartphones. Diana told them she would be taking extra time because she wanted to talk with her mother. Her reasoning was, "I can't just let her go." They understood. Chad volunteered to go with her, but she declined, knowing her mother's negative attitude toward him. He drove along behind her and watched as she walked into her mother's lair. From his supplies in the back of the pickup, he extracted some binoculars and went to a small hill opposite the apartment. He watched from a distance through the balcony sliding glass door.

Diana knocked on the door and totally surprised Sylvia, who peered through the peephole. "You came to your senses. It's about time!"

"No, Mom, I've come to help you."

"You've already helped me by leaving that idiot, Chad. Now, tell me, why's he shooting at us?"

"He's not. He sold the house to his neighbor. It's the neighbor who is shooting at you. Mom, you were trying to steal a house. That's not right. It's against the Ten Commandments."

"Stop telling me what you think is wrong. Those commandments were for the Jews. Sit down!" Diana sat at a kitchen chair. In her mind she tried to think of the words that might hit a responsive chord with her mother. She silently prayed for the right words. From behind, Rose approached with a man from church. They grabbed her arms, and a belt went around her waist, trapping her arms to her sides. They cinched it so tight it bit into her flesh.

"You have to tie me up? I came to you willingly because I love you. I wanted to show you the truth. Please, let us talk without this, this, this restraint."

"We don't think you are in your right mind. There's some kind of spell over you. You're not thinking straight. We need to keep you here until we can get a psychologist to put you in your right mind."

"Who's in their right mind? You're trying to steal a house. You are swearing. You believe in clairvoyants. You know enough to realize that the seven last plagues are falling. Blood is running out of your faucets. And you can't see that this is the end? Mother, you have to come out of this stupor and recognize Jesus is coming soon."

"Jesus has come! He banished the devil to the bottomless abyss. You have to stop this make-believe drama and see the real drama that is playing out in the world. Jesus is fixing this, and we are going to please our heavenly father, and everything is going to be all right. You aren't going back, even if we have to keep you tied up."

"Tying me up is not how God works. God gives us freedom of choice. Faith and love are voluntary, not coerced. If we are forced to love God, then it is not love, it is oppression. Mother, what you are doing is not coming from heaven's environment. It's coming from—"

"Shut up!" Sylvia moved threateningly toward her daughter.

XXXXX

Outside Chad watched. He saw her enter and converse with her mother. It appeared to be a neutral conversation, neither positive nor negative. He had hoped against his better judgment it would have started with an embrace. That would have been a positive omen. He watched her sit down. He could see Rose standing nearby and a man on the other side. He didn't know what it meant to have so many so close. He was disturbed by it. Then he saw Sylvia slap her daughter.

XXXXX

"Mother, you have never hit me before. You never swear. You have always been a model citizen. You taught me as a child to love Jesus and act like Him. Never, never would you have been like you are now; you have to shake the devil off. Go back to what you were; my loving, kind, caring mother. You loved Jesus; act like Him. Please, you're my mommy!"

"Why, you insolent, disrespect-ful child! I shall ..." Her hand was raised, ready to backhand Diana. Diana ducked, knocking herself over onto the floor, chair and all. Sylvia was prepared to pursue her to the floor tiles when her attention diverted to the opening door. Chad came through with an ad homi-nem defense. Holding out gold coins, he proffered them in trade for his Diana. The gold glinted in their eyes. Just when they were about to lurch forward, he tossed them in their general direc-tion and dove for the belt buckle that held Diana to the chair. They were scurrying out the door before the coins were corralled.

With the art of a quarterback, he threw a spiral all the way to the roof. The phone hit the slanted roof, bounced twice, and slid down to the gutter. He went back to Diana, and they slowly disappeared from the life they used to have.

They ran to his truck, leaving her car behind. In the truck Diana explained that the keys to her car and her phone lay on the kitchen table. It was as good a place as any to end her electronic breadcrumb trail. Diana cried as Chad drove to his old home. Up the block he got out and walked to the edge of the lawn. With the art of a quarterback, he threw a spiral all the way to the roof. The phone hit the slanted roof, bounced twice, and slid down to the gutter. He would have preferred it had landed in the center of the structure, but he wasn't going to make a correction. He went back to Diana, and they slowly disappeared from the life they used to have.

XXXXX

There was another ignored event of colossal proportions. Astronomy is a discipline of science overlooked by the majority of the population unless there is an eclipse or a visible comet in a cloudless sky. Other astral phenomena are avidly watched by select amateurs or professional astronomers. What was happening was not reported in scholarly journals. A CME (Corona Mass Ejection) churned within the sun, ready to blow any second away from the sun, ranking almost on the level of an undersized supernova. No records could lend enough information to predict all the effects this would have on the earth if it was aimed directly at our planet, or how fast it would travel. It would expand outward from a large sunspot on a direct collision course with earth, colossal in speed. Light takes 8.3 minutes to fly to earth. A CME would take anywhere from half a day to eighty-three days to reach earth, depending on its mass. Coming from any other galaxy, it would mean nothing. In the Milky Way, and in this solar system, it was significant, and the media should have paid attention. Other distractions kept most everyone focused on the immediate concerns of organizing the world to fix humanitarian concerns.

CHAPTER 19

Not a cloud in the sky blocked the rays of the sun warming the truck as it drove away from Leticia's car, their last diversion. They talked seriously about their morning, especially about the friends they left behind. Many had left the night before, but Brian, Cynthia, and the Perkinses were staying for as long as circumstances would allow. Emilee tried to be an exception; she wanted to go with Diana. Emilee was mollified when she was told she needed to be a guide to her friend down the block. They were left planning an extended sleepover. Remaining at the house had its advantages. The home was away from built-up areas. Eight homes clustered in a loop leading off a state highway, winding through a small forest. Two of the other residences belonged to fixed-income retirees away in southern climes. As they drove into the mountains, they wondered about the next time they would see them.

Diana tried to be upbeat and participate in the in-cab conversation about how close they were to the second coming and the reunion of friends and fellow believers. There was also the great feeling of little things, such as never locking a door or better yet no locks at all. Like running and not getting weary, or like traveling to any beautiful spot in a universe full of possibilities. They drove higher into the mountains with vistas for miles around. Snow clung to higher elevations, cleansing the landscape with swaths of purity. Yet, her feelings were not elevated because she could not dismiss the stranger who inhabited her mother's body. The ugliness exhibited last night blocked out the natural wonder still seen around them, and the security and beauty of perfection ahead. The lethal infection of sin attacked her mother, putting her in the terminal ward of her mind. She could do nothing to save her. There's no beauty in sin.

Chad laid out the plan. They would hide the truck and then portage the equipment and supplies to the stone hut and remain out of the public eye. He explained that it would be cooler than what they were accustomed to down in the city. He reminisced about his scout troop days. It was this road they drove up when he went to camp. When he was young, the tents were set up ahead of time. When he was older, they had to pack in their own pup tents and set them up themselves. He never could wait to get done setting up and start exploring. He roamed the hills and knew every cave and creek. He looked upon the dairy hut as his personal secret hideaway. He never dreamed that his discovery would be a sanctuary from evil. He mused over the fact that experiences from more than a decade ago could come to his aid now. Did God plan ahead for this eventuality? Did He see Chad with this future need? Chad felt in awe of God's foreknowledge.

Soon, they broke out into an alpine park that stretched outward to cover dozens of square acres. Chad turned onto a gravel road that led toward a high ridge. The hillside was heavily wooded, perfect for hiding. A narrow gorge led upward to a sub-timberline reservoir used to irrigate hay fields for cattle down on the edge of the open grassland park. Chad pointed to the left side of the gorge. "The ranch house used to sit up there, and the dairy shed is up the ravine in all that brush and timber. I used to camp in the shed and fish out of the dam farther up. I'm pretty sure there aren't any fish alive in that bloody soup." The red scourge cascaded over boulders, spreading out into a meandering wash. In the truck they were calculating what their new home would be like and how long they would have to exist there.

The road led upward to a circle in front of a path leading to the ruined ranch house. Chad drove off the road and into a pile of brush near the red stream. A few yards farther, and he had the benefit of a copse of aspens to hide the truck. Apart from the ugly stream, it was a spectacular day. The sun was shining brightly, splashing rocks and trees with lumens of light. He took the binoculars out, stepped back out into the open, and trained the binos up the ravine. Of course, he couldn't see the hut, but he was always inspired by the vista of perennial snow clinging to the rocky ridge hanging above him. He was surprised by what he saw. People were scooping snow for drinking water. The colorful shirts were standing out against the white and rock-gray background. With fresh water at a premium, scraping snow off the mountain was a plausible substitute.

They had plenty of time to set up housekeeping, yet there was a sense of urgency on his part to show them how wise he was in bringing them here. He wrestled his backpack on and grabbed a couple of boxes of MREs, then put them down because the girls had not organized their burdens. He shucked the backpack and helped them with theirs. In a few minutes, they were walking up a game trail through the steep-sided gorge. Just as they were thinking this might turn into an ordeal, Chad stopped. "We're here."

"Where?" The women swiveled their heads around, trying to find a rock building. About them there was nothing but shrubbery. Chad smiled. A bloody brook burbled by the stone hut, which was encased in fallen trees, massive pines, serviceberry bushes, and long, overhanging branches.

XXXXX

As elders and spiritual guides, Brian and Cynthia went about encouraging members to stay the course. Most of the time, they met with empty houses and ruffians patrolling purloined property. Out of curiosity Cynthia opened her phone to check their bank account. She wanted to know if the money-hungry extremists had hacked into their account. They had. A zero balance greeted her eyes. For her, it was not a loss but a confirmation, confirmation that politico-religio forces had their eyes and hands everywhere. She immediately turned her phone off and tossed it in the back seat, being careful not to leave an electronic trail. In being careful to press the off button, she held it too long, and it cycled off, then back on. When authorities began to track them, they would have this trail to follow.

XXXXX

"What was that?" Raphael's father blurted out a question that was more of an exclamation. His mother in the back seat was speechless, trying frantically to breathe.

"It was an asteroid, Dad. An asteroid clobbered our home," he answered.

"I know that, son. I meant what was it that picked us up and put us here?" They knew that it was divine intervention, but exactly what was a mystery. They knew somehow their Lord or an angel had picked up and carried their car plus trailer around the corner into the shadow of safety. They looked out their dusty windows and only saw the providence of a gracious Savoir. It took fifteen minutes for the small rocks, gravel, and dust to stop raining down upon the car. They didn't even think about the noise. Gratitude overtook their senses. Prayer and praise, thanksgiving and tenderness were all aimed heavenward. A benevolent God was the only thing they could focus on as they sat in their sanctuary of dirt and dust.

XXXXX

The inside of the dairy hut exuded a dank, musty smell that soon dissipated when the decrepit door was opened wide, and they moved in and out, preparing their hideout. Chad's plans included, it seemed, everything. Limited space and a rocky floor made it impossible to sleep four people on the floor. Chad anticipated that fact, bringing hammocks and equipment to hang the hammocks from the walls. He nailed pitons into the rock walls. Soon the hut took on the appearance of a sleeper rail car, comfortable, yet crowded. Chad made several trips down to the truck to bring up the remainder of the supplies. Bundles of water bottles were the most arduous. They were heavy. The ladies helped by carrying supplies and divided bottles of water into backpacks between them. At the end of the day, they had a well-provisioned refuge. They relaxed on the edge of a small talus and watched the activity and listened to the sounds of the small valley that stretched out briefly between the sharp cliffs on either side of the gorge. Day was dying, and the shadows were long. They ate some of their food. Leticia offered some snack-sized chocolate bars as dessert from a bag she had in her backpack. It sponsored a discussion on whether there would be chocolate in heaven.

They felt relatively safe, as no humans were in the area below the reservoir. Of course, they didn't know for sure if the authorities were looking for them. They were off the grid, as survivalists liked to say. If anyone was after them, they would probably hear the noise in the still silence of the mountain. Usually, the creek would make gurgling, splashing sounds, but in this case, the bloody sludge oozed around rocks and logs. A localized rain cloud blew moisture over them and chased them into their refuge. It caused Chad to complete his preparations by installing a camouflaged poncho on top of the shed with a space blanket inside that would block any infra-red scanning that would betray their location to authorities.

The ladies were impressed with his cunning preparation and told him so. Diana felt proud.

XXXXX

Several meteors had struck the earth. Professionals were mystified by the lack of warning and debated as to whether it was a full meteor shower or an asteroid that had broken into many pieces. It was the only news on all media outlets. Having a celestial object the size of a small-town softball stadium hitting the earth was news on any day. Having a half-dozen hit the earth at supersonic speeds, causing massive destruction to two metropolitan cities, was beyond belief. Huge burning craters were all that was left of thriving communities. Accusative fingers were pointing in every direction.

"How could this happen without advance warning?"

"Why didn't the politicians act?"

"Who knew?"

"Who is responsible for this? Somebody had to know! Why were the astrophysicists asleep?"

"Did NASA know about this?

Then others got to blaming God and then more began to shift blame toward the messiah. Reporters were mobbing the last known location of Isa Jesus, Pope Domenic Clement Leonardo Xavier Sextus VI. A news conference was set up by his aides and publicized in hopes that Isa would hear and come in from wherever he was at the moment.

XXXXX

A constantly blaring television was permanently set to a mainline media channel in prison as a means of occupying inmates like an inattentive mother uses a TV to babysit her children. Pastor Lange and Detective Hardine watched in awe. In fact, everyone watched the wall-mounted set silently. The images were too gruesome to be true. If one knew what Hiroshima looked like one day later, then they would have something to compare to the scenes flashing before them. Tree fragments, twisted metal beams, and heaps of bricks smoldered in a circular basin all black and charred by the hotly burning meteoroid. If there were bodies in the video, they would not be recognizable because of the instantaneous cremation they had experienced. No commentator could form words to describe the carnage. They simply moaned as the camera panned over the wreckage.

The three imprisoned friends were appalled. They also moaned, but added to their empathy was a touch of confirmation. Here was yet another reminder of the end of all things. Pastor Lange quoted 1 Peter 4:7, "'The end of all things is near, Therefore be clear-minded and self-controlled so you can pray.'[28] We need to pray with all our hearts for what's coming," he advised. He received two "amen's" in response.

Quietly, so as not to bring upon themselves the wrath of the other inmates, they prayed for the believers they knew would be enduring extreme stress. They thought that was the ministry they could perform. Little did they know their own trial was around the corner?

XXXXX

The car and the top of the camper trailer looked as though it had been through a hail storm. Every square inch of the surfaces, hood and trunk, had dent dimples. Using small pine branches, they brushed off the dirt and gravel. The branches were everywhere because the debris from the meteor fallout had stripped pine boughs and leafy twigs from the flora near the road. It was if autumn had arrived before the trees could oblige with the necessary color change.

"I hope our friends are okay," Raphael's mother whispered in awe.

"Everyone I know left," his father answered. "They took Jesus' warning to flee when the antichrist was taking the place of the head of the false Christian church."

"I should have gotten here earlier, and we could have left sooner. That way, we wouldn't be cleaning all this gravel off our car," Raphael opined.

"Don't bother yourself over this. We have clear evidence of God's protection," she counseled her son.

"Amen. I agree."

XXXXX

The media of every ilk and every persuasion were gathered en masse. A forest of microphones dwarfed the speaker's podium. It was only a few minutes, and the new pope came to the platform, crossed himself, and strode to the dais. A hushed silence permeated the scene, including all points of the world, as they watched with hope.

---

[28]Author's paraphrase

"The latest calamity of meteors that we have witnessed has hurt our Eternal Father and me deeply. You cannot imagine how we watch this world stumble on and on without heeding our counsel. These are natural events that can be turned aside if this world changes direction. We only wish that our commands for unity had not been ignored. We hate to see pain and suffering.

"I have been in deep communication with my father and our God. He informs me we are not united as yet, and we must come together to stop the end of this world's calamities. These events have been set in motion by man's mismanagement of our creation. Our father will stop this destruction in a moment only if we come to understand his divine will. He refuses to have a disjointed humanity who does not care to act and perform the needed measures to bring about 100 percent agreement with his plan of restoring Eden once again. Mankind's original purpose was to tend this garden world. Over and over, we have sent you messages through a multitude of prophets and a plethora of faiths to come together. Now is the last call. Time is at an end. Come together under our leadership, or we will have to start all over again with a new creation out of the remnants of this polluted world. Humans are starving, people are dying,

You must be one voice, one body, one church, worshipping on one day. Explain, urge, and coerce them to join the world to save this experiment of life. Do what is necessary to bring the obstinate spoilers to heel.

children are suffering; you have the answer to solve these issues. You can stop the evils of this world. I will assist you with energy and stamina. Are you with me?

"I appeal to you; unity must come now. All worship together or all will be destroyed. I am standing between you and destruction. I pleaded with the father that you can get the work done. I told him I believe in you. Therefore, I beg you to bring everyone together. You must be one voice, one body, one church, worshipping on one day. Explain, urge, and coerce them to join the world to save this experiment of life. Do what is necessary to bring the obstinate spoilers to heel. If they won't comply, persuade them with force, and if they still won't join us, they must not continue in their selfish rebellion. This comes to an end now! You know what you have to do. Get it done!"

Pope Isa Jesus exited the stage to cheers. Those yells echoed around the world.

XXXXX

The inmates were concerned for their friends. They couldn't stop themselves from sinking to their knees next to their bunks and praying for those out in a very hostile environment developing exponentially into bedlam. Detective Hardine knew immediately that the result of the pope's admonishments would mean the loss of the rule of law. It would mean that millions of vigilantes would be out forcibly persuading individuals with higher principles than they to change to the majority opinion. It would create a cacophony of chaos; an anarchy in league with a false hierarchy. He knew this would be bad, very bad. He prayed for others, not himself. "Dear Father in heaven, I deserve no favors from You. I am a sinner saved only by Your amazing grace. I have come to you late in life and on the edge of the end of time, but I ask of You to protect Your precious children who are out in this awful world of hate. Soon, unprincipled people will take advantage of the clear mandate to compel commandment-keepers to keep Sunday as the day of worship. Please hide or rescue those in harm's way. I only wish I could be out there helping them avoid trouble; however, I know You can save to the uttermost. Your will be done. Give them strength, and me, too. In Jesus' name, ..."

Loud noises, slamming metal doors, and yelling of epithets crashed into the consciousness of the inmates. Something was up.

XXXXX

The four mountain denizens lounged on the hillside above the obscure hut in the valley below. They were sharing small, fun-sized chocolate bars Leticia had brought along for something a little special. Each had just one, even though they were small. She asked the second time just for fun, "Will there be chocolate in heaven?"

"I hope so," answered Diana.

"Why not? Chocolate is vegetable-based," Vonnie added.

The three ladies looked at Chad, who was nibbling on his little bar. "Don't look at me. I'm not into speculation on absolute unknowns," he responded. "You're not a chocoaholic like the rest of us," Diana smiled.

"Is this the calm before the storm?" Diana changed the subject, pointing to the valley, ridges, and the mountain in the background.

Late-day sun bathed the scene in long, lazy shadows. It didn't look as if the world were ending. And the four fugitives from the law of the land did not know of the papal mandates that now doomed the keepers of God's Commandments and the testifiers of Jesus' love. They were totally unaware of the faux messiah's inflammatory comments and how they inflamed the baser elements of society. Every ad hoc civilian vigilante jumped to the opportunity to inflict vengeance on those they hated. The CPF (Community Police Force), various Posse Comitatus,' MS-13, the 101 Posse, the Patriot Posse, the Klan, and many others were springing up like grass on golf courses. They headed in different directions, some toward the high Sierras to look for non-compliants hiding into the mountains.

Vonnie answered Diana's observation. "It certainly is tranquil. It's not what I expected for an intense time of trouble."

"However, we don't know what they may be going through down in civilization. Without phones, we have no idea what's going on," Chad added while toggling his controls on the toy drone.

"Thanks to you, we are sitting up here on the side of a mountain not being hassled," Diana smiled again at Chad as she spoke.

"Preparation is key. I have to add my applause for your planning, Chad," Leticia agreed with Diana.

"Hey, look at that! Are those deer playing? No, that isn't playing. Whoa, that's weird. What are they doing?" The group looked in the direction of Vonnie's gesturing hand. What they saw was normally docile deer trampling each other or something with their hooves. Then they were horrified when Chad's binoculars were shared by the ladies, and they saw a poor rabbit being trampled to death as the rest of the herd fought amongst themselves to do the same. After more observation, they discovered that several rabbits had attacked the deer, biting them in the legs. It was completely absurd, yet in a world without the controlling influence of the Holy Spirit, it wasn't outside of the possible. The group could only shake their heads in disbelief.

The sound of a 4×4 truck echoed around the valley's walls as the lower gear growled, climbing up the hill toward their hidden pickup. The 4×4 was obviously loaded, judging by the sound it made. They could not see it; only hear its ominous tone.

XXXXX

There was a long line of traffic moving slowly. Usually, the cars moved at around fifty to sixty miles per hour. Today, they were stacked up due to numerous jaywalking incidents. People felt they had the right to cross any road at any location for any trivial reason. Interestingly, a patrol car sat at the side of the road, doing nothing about the blockers of traffic. They were pleased with the slower traffic because they were on the watch for non-compliant defiant breakers of the civil regulations to support the world effort of stopping chaos.

Brian and Cynthia rolled by the black and white cruiser. Cynthia's phone had been sitting in the back seat for days. She thought it was off. It wasn't. As they drove by the cruiser, the officers were deep into their tech systems. Like an electric shock, the policemen both jerked heads up to spot the car containing the wanted offenders. It was so sudden and unexpected that they were befuddled in trying to leap into action. In their confusion they focused on the wrong car and started attempting to get to it in the heavy traffic. Brian saw the patrol car struggle to move into the line of cars after avoiding several oncoming cars go by in the other direction. Even with the lights and siren on, the drivers were unwilling to yield to the police. Brian watched this in his review mirror, all the while wondering if the police were after them legitimately, so to speak, for non-compliance or for reasons he had faced in multiples before, illegitimately because of his race. No matter, he was not willing to go through any harassment, especially at this time when all notice could be painful.

The light changed to red, cutting the traffic in two halves. They were able to drive on, while the patrol car screamed its anger behind uncaring, unmoving motorists. Finally, the official vehicle jerked out past the waiting cars and drove straight at the oncoming cars that careened out of the way. Soon, the police were three cars back. A red SUV pulled over, and the police advanced to the second car. They were getting closer. The officer in the passenger seat was monitoring the satellite feed on the computer. A quick pass around the next vehicle and a squeeze into a tiny gap between caused the car immediately behind Brian and Cynthia to pull over. The patrol car aligned itself behind the car at the curb, and the line of traffic went around. That is when the tech officer wildly indicated that it was the wrong car. For a few moments, Brian and Cynthia were free. They took the opportunity to take the road less traveled, turning up a side street.

At the top of a long hill, their car sputtered to an abrupt halt at the same time as they experienced a change in the type and intensity of light around them. Yellow-white light replaced the normal ambiance. Everywhere, light shattered the atmosphere, bathing everything in white spectral intensity. A moment later, they could feel the intense heat from a blazing sun. Power poles with transformers erupted in sparks, power lines sagged and snapped in a reaction to the dramatic change in the magnetic fields accompanying electricity. Transforming power stations were rendered inert when flashes and smoke obscured fenced-in areas. Brian and Cynthia knew that the fourth plague had begun. A glance behind them showed cars stalled everywhere, with the police cruiser with no lights or siren operational and trapped behind a vehicular flotsam. Up in the sky, a jetliner plunged, flipping over on its top, arrowing toward the earth.

XXXXX

Detective Hardine faced his boss across the table. It was nothing like when the captain visited in his office in the past. This was the interrogation room, and he was handcuffed.

"Luke, why in all that is sane and logical would you throw your life away for these people? You, I mean they, are destroying our chance at a better world. Join the majority who know what's right. All you have to do is agree to a small donation to the church, and everything will be forgotten. You'll get your job back, and all records will be expunged. Think about it. I can even get you a promotion. We need you. Come on, Luke, whaddya say? Please, I don't want to have to do this," the captain pled. He had never called Detective Hardine by his first name before.

"What do you mean, you don't want to do this? Do what?"

"Are you going to give up on this stupidity of yours? Decide!"

"Over the years, I have observed the worst that society can produce. That kind of day-to-day experience can turn one negative about life and people. Thinkers, psychologists, doctors, politicians, and yes, church leaders have said humanity can get better if given a chance and the right environment. I doubted it. If anything, mankind is getting worse. We are not, as they say, evolving upward to better and better. I can't believe that. I see humanity getting worse—"

"Get to the point!"

"I didn't see any improvement, so I decided to put the bad ones in jail. That was my motivation. Then I did a deep dive into yet another population group to find a murderer. I found a solution to my negative attitude. I had a solution to my mental dilemma. I found people that knew what was happening and where everything was going. They honestly knew Jesus as their Savior. I wanted to join them beca—"

"Shut up! You're done. Sign up, or you will lose."

"I won't. I am on the Lord's si—" His words were cut off by a punch to the middle of his face. The shock rattled his brain and disturbed him on several levels. This was legally wrong, it physically hurt, and it told him that the spiritual dynamic was Satan fighting the commitment of one of Jesus' own. That last thought comforted him, knowing he was on the right track in company with the people who "keep the commandments of God and the testimony of Jesus." Stars sparkled in his vision as he realized he was lying on the floor after being knocked out of his chair. Without a good head target, the captain kicked Luke repeatedly in his side, breaking several ribs. The beating continued until he was crumpled in the corner of the interrogation room. The captain grabbed him by his belt, dragging him to the door, then propped him up against the door and drew his arm back to deliver another punch to the head. White light bathed every corner of the building, changing windows into supernova-like intensity. Then, all electrical circuits failed, lending a fearful ambiance of dark evil to the room. All activity stopped in wonder of what happened. The captain felt responsibility to lead and discover the source of the problem. He yelled for a guard to return Luke to his cell, but not before delivering a right cross to his temple, which knocked him out. Every door had to be manually locked and unlocked because electronic locking systems were offline. Two guards had to drag the detective all the way to his cell. They had to use flashlights in the cellblock, as there were no windows with solid concrete walls.

XXXXX

Another sound added to the sound of the 4×4 as it growled up the grade. A high-pitched whir came overhead. A drone heavy with cameras, some fish eye, some infrared, patrolled the mountains.

"Get down! We should be in the hut where the infrared can't find us," Chad spoke as he toggled the levers to raise the toy helicopter high into the air. He wanted the upper hand if the drone came their way. The ladies squeezed themselves into little cracks and folds in the rock formation they were formerly sitting upon.

"I hope they didn't see us," Vonnie breathed out quietly.

"They already have. The drone has changed direction toward us," he answered. "Oh, nos" were sighed by all of them. Chad brought his helicopter over the drone and tried to match speed as he descended toward the evil eye in the sky. It was more and more apparent that they had been made. The bumblebee sound grew closer and more ominous. Then it stopped, hovering in a position that indicated it had eyes on the quartet. Chad landed the toy in the middle of the drone. Blade shards flew in every direction as the two meshed their props together and plummeted out of the sky.

The wreckage lay about fifty yards away, mangled with dirt and brush. Chad's victory lay in fragmented pieces. They stared at the scene for a brief moment before they heard the 4×4 and yet another drone coming their way. They had to get down to the hut to hide before the new threat could locate them and vector in the occupants of the truck. In single file they had taken a game path downward for about ten yards when the drone popped over the ridge and hovered above them. They were in confusion as to what they should do. Their hideout was a perfect place to be where electronics could not find them. However, with the all-seeing eye above them, they didn't want the device to watch them expose their sanctuary. They were helpless to know what to do. Diana made a suggestion. "Maybe we should split up."

"Ah, I agree. I will stay here and keep the drone occupied until you all can get away, and then we'll meet up at the hut."

"You're sacrificing yourself for us. I won't leave you. Vonnie and Leticia, run! We'll distract the drone," Diana commanded.

Chad climbed atop a rock outcropping and started throwing stones at the drone. He also called for the women to run. Every time he threw a rock, the drone jerked out of the way. His efforts only raised the buzzing of the drone to the point of sounding mechanically angry, if that were possible.

The sky turned from a gentle pastel blue to yellow-white, and it encompassed the entire heavens from horizon to horizon. The increase in light momentarily blinded the four, making it impossible to see their surroundings. Shading their eyes, they strained to make out surrounding features to give them orientation to move, which they didn't know if they should. The drone ceased its sound and dropped like lead. The silence overwhelmed them. Nothing made noise, no drone, no 4×4 truck. The massive CME wiped out every electrical grid, every electric transformer or coil, disabling anything that used electrons to move a mechanical system. The changed light turned into hot heat brighter than normal sunshine, and so bright that their eyes had to readjust to the new light, similar to turning on the lights in the room at night. Airborne surveillance had come to an abrupt end when the drone plummeted to the ground.

CHAPTER 20

Ａll media was affected by the Coronal Mass Ejection (CME). No television, radio, or printing presses were operational. There was no way for the leaders to communicate to the masses. Communication and geo-positioning satellites went inert because electrons were stripped from their metal components ionizing them. Reporters found that their small devices worked, but they could not use the power grid or access the Internet. The media, with contracted scientists, would normally attempt to explain the phenomena the world was experiencing in terms of natural events, but could not. And they wanted to but could not tell them that the protective layers of ozone or the magnetosphere could not protect them from harmful radiation, x-rays, a, b, or c UVLs, and gamma rays. They also wanted to assure the people that restoration of electricity would come sometime soon, but they could not. They were flummoxed with no outlet to ply their trade.

However, in the meantime, anarchy became the rule of life. Police, National Guard, and military active duty and reserves were powerless to communicate and to react to lawlessness. Commerce could not move. Human needs could not be supplied. Shipping by land, sea, and air stood still. Business tycoons could not ply their trade, and they turned their anger at the political-religious leaders who had promised to make this world a better place. They railed at the one global political-religious organization that had said it could stop the world's problems. These magistrates of trade were in tears at the ruin of their commerce and the loss of billions of dollars per day.[29]

Grocery stores knew their frozen goods would spoil, so instead of giving to the poor, they hoarded the goods amongst themselves and nearby relatives. Seeing what was happening, people began to loot the stores, brawls broke out, and bloodied and almost-dead victims crawled to hospitals that had no electronic equipment to diagnose or treat them, let alone lights to see them. Life had returned to primitive survival. Animals scavenged upon dead bodies, and the fowl of the air picked at the carrion.

XXXXX

Raphael huddled with his parents in a camper under tall pines to avail them of the shade from the scorching sun. The pine trees and the higher altitude helped to bring down the temperature a bit. In an effort to assuage them from the heat, they soaked handkerchiefs and tied them around their necks to cool their bodies. The discomfort was offset by the knowledge that the seven last plagues were limited in their duration. They read their Bibles ending at Revelation 18:8. They knew that because the whole book of Revelation is filled with symbolic references, this text meant the plagues would be a year or less, knowing a day equals a year in biblical prophecy. Their Savior was to come soon, and this was the fourth of the seven. They had flashlights and extra batteries for the next plague. What they did not know, was nothing electrical was working; they were off the grid and hiding in an unpopulated area. Off in the distance, they could see San Gorgonio Mountain. Yesterday, there were patches of snow hiding in the ridges leading to the peak. Today, the snow was completely gone.

XXXXX

Brian and Cynthia had to hike home. The sun beat down upon them with what seemed like white-hot intensity. They walked on the shadiest side of the street, nearest to rows of trees and some buildings. A blessing came in the form of a long warehouse that provided a city block worth of cooler shade. They had several miles to go before they reached the safety of the

---

[29]See Rev. 18:11, RSV

Perkins' home. Their first indication of God's providence in their behalf was a spring of fresh water that erupted at the base of the warehouse wall. They splashed refreshing water on their arms and faces, took deep drafts of drink into their bellies (natural canteens), and soaked their shirts in the water to cool them as they continued their walk. Leaving the shade of the warehouse, they looked back to see that the spring had disappeared, including the runoff that had moved into a nearby gutter. Then a miracle occurred; a small dense cloud interceded between them and the sun. Cynthia looked at Brian, and then they nodded and said almost in unison, "a pillar of cloud by day."

XXXXX

Luke lay oblivious to the calls of his two friends. It took a while for him to awake from his semi-coma. As consciousness returned, he didn't welcome it as one would think. He had a massive headache, his ribs throbbed, and his jaw could not clench like normal. The teeth did not align because the bones were out of place. What disturbed him the most was that he could not see anything. For a scary moment, he thought he was blind. He called out to God, his newest Best Friend. Then he realized he was wrapped in his own bloody blazer, which had been rudely pulled over his head as they dragged him to his cell. Being able to see in the dim light coming from under a door in an adjacent room didn't help. He had a concussion with blurred vision.

"Is that you, Luke? Did you call out?" Pastor asked. Luke could only manage a groan. "What did they do to you?"

"Thried ... trieb, Oow, They, uh ... ooo ... make mre," Luke attempted to communicate. His hand went to his aching head and came back warm with blood. He was in no shape to talk.

"Shut up! I'm trying to sleep," the cellmate complained.

"Luke, don't try to talk. I think I know what happened to you," Pastor Peter Lange consoled. "Richard and I will pray for you. Just relax."

Through the fog Luke could understand his friends were trying to help. The composite of his various pains was starting to register in their total enormity. It hurt to breathe, to talk, to move; if he did absolutely nothing, he throbbed, ached, and had points of stinging discomfort. Asking him to relax would be cruel mockery if Luke didn't understand what Peter meant. He knew he was supposed to relax in the Lord and dwell in His love with hope.

"Dear Father in Heaven. We are calling upon You, O Lord, in a terrible time. Our friend and Your child is in terrible pain because he did not deny You," Peter began. "Yes, Lord, he has been true to You," Richard added. "We humbly ask You to ease Luke's pain at the least, and, if possible, take away his injuries. All of us need to be strong at times like these. I …" Pastor was interrupted by a clear ungarbled, "Thank you." "Luke, Luke, is that you? Your words don't sound slurred."

Getting to his feet, Luke answered, "I'm, I can't believe it, I'm okay!"

"Okay?" "Okay?" Both Peter and Richard answered in the same manner.

"Yes! I'm really alright. Oh, thank You, God! Thank You! Guys, God healed me. No more pain. My jaw isn't broken. I can talk. Oh, praise God!" Detective Hardine was not a demonstrative person, but in this case, he was out of his shell and transfixed with joy. Peter and Richard were contemplating an awesome God who answered their simple prayer.

XXXXX

It was hot. The quartet sat under a ledge in the shade that they expected to be cool. It was only less hot. It might have been better in the stone hut; however, in their attempt to find a more temperate place, they left the hut again and hiked up to the ridge once more to the higher location, only to discover it was about the same. The sun beat down upon the earth like a sledgehammer on red-hot iron. Nothing moved. Birds didn't fly, and no rodents scrounged for food. Up on the mountain where a snowpack had been lurking on the north side, nothing remained. It appeared naked. The silence was eerie.

The 4×4 had stopped cold, and no amount of manipulation could get the engine to spark back to life. The overloaded engine coil fried many circuits, the battery, and some of the wires were compromised. The vigilantes that stood around the truck had to make a decision either to hike back down into town or try to find the banned individuals. One comment carried the day, "Let's have some fun before we have a very long walk."

"Yeah, we know where they are. Let's go get 'em." The remote wouldn't lock the 4×4, so they had to lock it manually. With their shotguns, they started to amble up the road to the valley where their quarry was last seen with the drone cameras. Below the stone hut, they fanned out to cover the valley. The four up on the ridge watched the progression as the posse searched. True to Chad's preparation, the men went right on by the hidden hut.

Heat prevented the aggressors from moving any faster than a slow amble. Then, as if by planned choreograph, they stopped. The rumble up the valley near the dam increased from a small cataract sound of water over rocks to a rushing deluge that was collapsing huge amounts of soil, including trees. What looked like a tidal wave spread out to fill the basin and swept everything in front of it. Full-sized trees tumbled top over roots. Boulders were pushed ahead of the flush that made them look like ping pong balls in a street gutter. The men saw the destruction unfold before them. They had no plan, no escape, but that didn't prevent them from scrambling toward the sides of the mountain gorge. One moment they were running, the next, they were gone in a swish of sloppy red water, logs, and muddy debris. The reason for this deluge was the almost instantaneous melt of the high mountain snowpack that overwhelmed the weir designed to slow down winter melt. In a moment, everything recognizable was gone.

The observing quartet was horrified by the swift justice upon the posse. Life was simply swept away. It was difficult to watch. They searched to see if anyone might have survived. The conviction of the loss came as they saw the destruction of the ground. All the trees were ripped up; the ground looked as if it had been scraped clean of foliage. What was left was sloppy, wet mud, trickling from every angle. Their horror for the loss of life was painful. It took a while before they were able to see the destruction of other objects in the valley. The location of their hidden pickup was empty; the truck was miles downstream and still tumbling away out of sight. Then, they looked at the formerly densely-covered hideout, where the hut was located. "Was" was the right tense. It was gone. Slowly, it dawned on them; everything they had brought with them was swept away—food, clothes, camping gear, and extras. All they had to wait out the time of trouble was what they had on them. Leticia gasped, "What are we going to do?"

XXXXX

Being in the dark, during the plague of scorching sun was strange. The inmates were in a concrete building with few windows, and with an adjoining room possessing the only natural light seeping under a closed door. Enduring the fourth plague seemed upside down, or more accurately, out of order. Very faint outlines of beds and bars were all they had for visual references. What they lacked in light, they gained in noise. The inmates screamed, swore, and slammed objects at bars, complaining of no lights. It was also odd because, beforehand, the lights were usually on constantly day and night. Food normally served at noon was delayed. No electricity to the kitchen meant it was only time before the internees would raise an unholy din, bringing even more unnecessary attention from the guards. It was not a good situation, boding ominous for those under the magnifying glass of public outrage.

Several battery-powered lamps were brought into the cellblock and left in areas for the best illumination. It only served to appease the inhabitants slightly. When the guards left, they took with them Richard and Peter for what looked like interrogation. It wasn't.

Luke prayed for his two friends because he knew firsthand what they might be going through. He knelt by his bunk and ignored the insults from his cellmate. Two guards returned from taking Peter and took Luke roughly to the same room as his friends. All three were handcuffed to a bar atop a central table and sitting on metal folding chairs. A few minutes later, they found out what the purpose was for this meeting. Five officers and the captain stood with their legs spread, and their hands clasped in front. They were waiting for the word to begin.

"This is your last chance. Get with the program. We don't have electrical card readers, but if you say you will join us, then we'll let you go until the electricity comes on. Got it!? Otherwise ..."

"I understand, 'otherwise' means you'll beat us into submission."

"Are you going to comply?"

"No, I will not turn my back on my Savior," Luke confidently replied.

"Let's see your savior keep you from this." The captain slapped Luke across the face. Luke was surprised to feel a faint brush of the hand while he heard a loud smack, and his head involuntary jerked to the side. Then a kick came to his side that knocked him out of the chair, leaving him hanging by the cuffs that were attached to a bar on the table. Again, nothing was felt. It was like he was swathed in bubble wrap. The captain's behavior released the other officers to act upon primal urges. They swarmed on the three in a melee of malevolence, punching, kicking, and gouging, pouring out their hate based on manipulated opinions of superiority over these men. The three were linked to the table that juddered back and forth. To the abusers, they thought they were inflicting pain, but the abusees felt next to nothing.

The supposed torture lasted until gunshots were heard in the building. It was miraculous how the officers exited the room in unison, rushing to the emergency. The faithful men used their feet to realign the chairs, sit down, and then, with their hands still linked in the center of the table, they prayed thanksgiving and praise to a protective Savior.

XXXXX

The center of rebellion against the throne of God was scorching hot. The fourth plague was poured out upon all those who were in on the plot against God's true believers. Since all unshielded electronics and the power grid were not functioning, air-conditioning did not work. There wasn't a sanctuary of comfort for those wanting an easy way out of the world's problems. Many curses were issued against those they thought God was punishing. They cursed the ones responsible for the power shortages, the non-compliants standing in the way of evolutionary per-fection. Even prayers were earnestly uttered, asking God to eliminate the ones who would not jump on the bandwagon of political-religious agreement. If only these malcontents were gone, then God's blessing could be poured out upon a united world, and the perfect millennium could begin.

XXXXX

"Don't worry; God will take care of us," Vonnie almost sang the last phrase.

"I know to survive in the woods, finding shelter is the first step, and then fire is next," Chad said.

"The psalm says, 'He who dwells in the shelter of the Most High ...' That takes care of that need," Diana said. "What about food and fire," she added.

"As far as food goes, I still have some chocolate," Leticia tried to help.

"That could help us with the fire need," Chad said.

"What! Chocolate isn't flammable."

"Hold on. Give me a moment. What I need is one of those chocolate bars and an aluminum can. I think I saw one in a cave I explored years ago. Let's go. Come on. The cave might be cooler than this open ledge we are under now." Chad was on the move. He moved into the hot sunlight and wove his way along a game trail along the ridge. The ladies followed, and to their surprise, saw a following cloud giving them respite from the direct sunlight.

Entering the cave, they found it had been a popular site for some beer bashes since Chad had last been in the cave. There was an abundance of beer cans from parties carelessly tossed in an angle behind some rocks. Chad sorted through the pile until he found what he wanted, and then he asked Leticia for one of her chocolate bars. The ladies were in a state of curiosity, watching him collect tinder to start a fire.

"Why do we need a fire? It's hot. We're not going to need warmth, will we?" Vonnie asked.

"Not now, but when the plague of darkness comes, we're going to need it, and we'll want to get some firewood ahead of time because collecting it won't be easy in the dark," Chad instructed, while he assembled small shreds of dried leaves, pine needles, and twigs. The women began to help collect wood and then watched as Chad rubbed chocolate on the concave bottom of the aluminum can. Then he started to rub, then buff the can with a corner of his shirt. With the fat from the chocolate and his buffing, the can bottom became bright as glass. Then he reflected the harsh light onto the pile of tinder. A few moments later, a wisp of smoke curled upward. Then a small flame licked at the small pile of fuel. Minutes later, they had a fire crackling around small broken branches. They planned to keep it burning until the plague of darkness plunged them into night.

XXXXX

Cars could not be driven. Cameras could not record or project important public service announcements. Electric trains and buses could not move the public. If people were within walking distance of work, they still could not perform their duties on dead computers, or electric tools, or use indoor lighting. Commerce ground to a halt. Few products could be made and brought to markets or shops. Leaders were powerless to communicate. Police could not coordinate their efforts to quell riots, stop looting, and curb any and all criminal behavior.

Attempts to equalize commodities to all levels of society smashed into an un-electronic barricade. The socialistic impulse for all elements and castes to be equally provided for found that transportation and refrigeration could not be utilized for the foods being redistributed. All seemed to be lost in the great endeavor to right the world of all its ills. The great global initiative had fallen on hard times. People were pointing fingers trying to find fault. However, the dialogue was not based on scientific evidence, and neither was it able to talk with people in the know. Hope and fear are motivators. The hope for a better world had started the global grand plan. Now, fear of roving bands of vigilantes and starvation caused people to fend for themselves. One solar phenomenon foils the best plans of Satan's minions. It was Satan's turn to ratchet up his game plan.

XXXXX

Brian and Cynthia made it to the Perkins home. The sun had set hours ago, but it was not dark. The brilliance of the scorching sun lit the sky from behind the mass of the earth. The full moon was four times brighter than normal; it actually radiated heat. The CME was over, and the sun was on maximum overload. Work crews were attempting to repair the damaged components on high priority circuits, such as those for governments, military, and police.

The Perkins and the extra church members were on the back deck, taking advantage of the relative cooler temperature. They compared notes on the day that had transpired. Everyone was surprised by the almost-complete failure of electronics. It served to protect many defenseless Ten Commandment=keeping lawless ones. It was an irony to be considered lawless when they held dear the commandments of God and the testimony of Jesus.

In the somewhat-diminished light, the sky started to sway and move like currents in the ocean. Then the currents became green and blue with small slivers of yellow and red mixed in. The northern lights had come south. It was the aurora borealis in all its glory. The reason they were normally seen in the north is because the magnetosphere that protects the earth from solar radiation is closer to the earth at the poles. Now, after the magnetic shock wave of the CME blasted the earth, solar radiation was closer on other parts of our globe.

"Are those angels, Daddy?" Emilee breathed out in wonder, hoping it was the beginning of the second coming.

"I wish it was. It is so beautiful it makes me think of heavenly beings. No, sweetheart, it is the northern lights. One of the beauties God has created," Mr. Perkins answered.

"Oh," Emilee said sadly.

"Well put," Brian added. "It won't be long now before we really do see angels in the sky.

The TV in the house blinked on, even though it had been turned off days ago. No lights were on. No electricity coursed through the wires of their home, yet color and sound came out of the set. Everyone was mystified and moved to see this phenomenon. Pope Isa Jesus was talking to the world.

ZZZZZ

All earth is in chaos because of rebellion against honoring my father. He and I are punishing the earth with fire until things change. I am calling fiery asteroids down upon workers of evil, especially cities known for their sins. Those who are loyal in their hearts, I will protect. I know all loyalists are not perfect as yet. Mankind is getting better and better as it evolves to a higher standard. However, on the road to glory, you will need to be forgiven along the way. All those who make efforts to turn the world into an Eden made new will have all sins forgiven if you are willing to purge the earth of disloyal persons. All of them must be taken care of as the antediluvian world. This is a noble cause. We are close to the end. We will soon achieve the objective together. When this is done, I will resurrect our kind to live in happy peace together with the mystical 144,000 who make it through.

The earth's communication network has fallen victim to an astrological event of epic proportions. The results have electrical grids and communications inoperable, making security entities unable to communicate and to act upon illegal persons boycotting the global initiative. I have repaired the communication system for those who are on our side. Soon electricity and other problems will be solved. Be patient. We will prevail.

Many of you recognize the pouring out of the seven last plagues mentioned in the Bible's last book. It is true. These are being aimed at the unrighteous, just like the plagues of Egypt centuries before the first time I walked on earth. Don't worry. These are only temporary.

I will have more information for everyone soon.

ZZZZZ

The television clicked off, and the house went dark.

"So, the pope serves himself to further his own ends," Cynthia remarks.

"What else did you expect?" Brian answered. "He's now using his powers to bring as many as possible to join his evil movement. He's got control of the media and can turn it on and off at his will."

"It's not really a time of convincing anymore. Probation is closed. Decisions are made," Cynthia reminded her husband.

"You're right! I guess I'm still thinking that people need to be convinced."

"Honey, you're still a little right. The antichrist wants more people to get involved in eliminating God's true believers. You know this is tantamount to a death decree."

XXXXX

The cellblock mates watched, rather listened, to the pope's message, as the television was turned to face the guards at the locked gate. When he was done, the guards and many of the inmates cheered. Normally, this would not bode well for the three. Now, they were buoyed up by the experience they had in the interrogation room. They had no pain with gain ahead. The noise died down, and they whispered their impressions of the pope's message.

"It sounds as if we are close to the death decree. He didn't actually tell us the decree has been enacted, but it was implied in his words," Peter whispered.

"Exactly, he didn't actually say it, but he was inciting a riot. Pastor, you said something about the people at the end of time not being killed. Something about not needing any more martyrs," Luke added.

"Yes, that's how I have always believed. When Jesus is done with His ministry in the heavenly sanctuary, called the investigative judgment, the seven last plagues are poured out on the earth, and the seventh is His second coming. In Revelation 13 Satan makes up his false church called Babylon and creates an image of the beast that must be worshipped in his way and on his counterfeit day. With all the people of the world either in one camp or another, there's no need to persuade them to one side or the other. They will be marked in one way or another with the seal of God on the forehead or the mark of the beast on their forehead or right hand. So, there is no more need for the people of God to testify with their lives. God rescues His people from Satan's wrath in the nick of time. It will seem as if there is no hope for our rescue, and then we will be saved."

"I understand what you are saying. If God or His angels are protecting us from pain now, it is reasonable to assume He will keep us safe from murder, right?"

"Right. I agree. I didn't expect to be helped with this pain relief. That was a surprise to me. What I can't understand is why you had to suffer in the first place."

"Perhaps it was a test. After all, I have only just begun to believe. I was a skeptic before all this."

XXXXX

"Chad, I was thinking."

"Yes, sweetheart."

Diana and Chad were sitting in the shade of the entrance to the cave. "We don't know what's going on because we are cut off from the news. Also, with Detective Hardine in prison, we don't know who is covering your parents' murder case. And, they could not call you and tell you if they have found the murderers. Does that bother you at all?" Diana asked.

"Months and months ago, I really wanted to know. I was upset, and I wanted justice, but now, I, ah, well, it doesn't matter anymore. I know they're saved. In the bigger picture, earthly justice is of less importance than the heavenly judgment. I know my parents' killers will be judged," Chad averred, then added, "How about you? Are you comfortable with God's judgment?"

Those who didn't study the Bible and then passed themselves off as authorities were duped by the spirit of Satan.

"I guess I have to be. My mother chose for herself, yet, perhaps, I'm more focused on the judgment of the people who led her to believe in a lie. Those who didn't study the Bible and then passed themselves off as authorities were duped by the spirit of Satan. I'm sure my mother would have stopped believing with them when they started stealing property, but she was under their spell of hate for what others believed. I know God is fair, and according to Philippians, 'Every knee will bow, and every tongue will confess that Jesus is Lord.' That means to me that everyone will acknowledge God's fairness. Am I right?"

"I think so too, sweetheart."

"I'm glad you're calling me sweetheart," Diana leaned on Chad's shoulder.

CHAPTER 21

The scorching sun desiccated every succulent plant into shriveled paper. Evergreen trees lost their needles after turning brown. The moisture in the ground evaporated into thin air. Dust swirled everywhere. A squirrel walking across a dead brown lawn could be seen a quarter of a mile away because of the trail of dust that rose behind his little singed paws. Lack of fresh water had to be replaced by moisture in food, and now that was disappearing. Many animals had to hibernate, or more accurately, aestivate, as the case was, to survive the unbearable heat. The fugitives of faith were doing essentially the same. They were in the shadows of cliffs, trees, and basements all in an attempt to avoid, like the animals, the fourth plague. For city dwellers, the plague would have been almost bearable with air conditioning, but with the power net down and slowly coming back in places, cursing became the norm, odd that the cursing came from those wishing to appease God the Father.

Then, everything changed. When the sun should have risen over the capital of Italy, it only went darker. No orb could be found. It just disappeared. No cloud obscured it; no smoke from a massive forest fire covered the sun. At first, that is what the professionals guessed as to the reason. Then, they had to admit that there was little in the way of explanation. Astrophysicists consulted a multitude of instrumental readouts to measure the light spectrum, visible and invisible, that came from the sun before the CME and during its radical burst of heat. No explanation came to them. They had to admit there was no theory that could encompass the phenomena now staring them in the face. If the sun had collapsed, then the earth and the nearby planets would be thrown out of their orbits because of the change in its gravity well, and that did not seem to be happening. No planets could be seen and measured as to their trajectories. The brilliant minds of science have theories for almost everything in an attempt to explain the universe we live in without a Creator but could not come to a final assumption or a guess for why the sun would blink out but not implode or explode. They asked why there were no telltale signs of what it was going to do. If the CME drained the sun of its elements of combustion, why didn't it fade out immediately afterward or give a clue to its sudden demise. One amateur astronomer suggested that a mass of dark interstellar matter may have intervened between our sun and our planet, but that required an explanation of how dark matter, which is supposed to be transparent (according to astrophysicists), could slide past our Oort cloud and heliosphere, and then suddenly become able to obscure the sun, and why dark matter did or did not exist within our solar system in the first place. This flash in the pan theory illuminated the desperation people were resorting to, to explain the unexplainable. None of their theories, instruments, or constructs of physics could put a spin on the darkness that enshrouded them on this day. The sun and stars just went out. Christians, on the other hand, read Romans 1:18–21and saw how scientists did not have any excuse for understanding the power of God over His own creation.

Later, as people became horrified by the impenetrable night, another inexplicable sight appeared. The full moon came up blood red, eerie in its portent. A natural full moon would be reflecting bright sunlight; this moon had nothing to reflect. Everyone, including the scientists, was saying, "How is that possible?"

XXXXX

Raphael had difficulty finding the flashlights they stored in storage bins in anticipation of the fifth plague. Everything was pitch-black. No ambient light helped. It felt like he was in a cave a mile underground. As he felt his way into the corner of the tent, a thought came to him from his physics class in college. "CME's destroy unshielded electronics; why am I searching for flashlights that won't work?" He had tried to start the car after he observed the effects of the CME. It confirmed in his mind that everything electronic might be compromised. Now, he didn't know what to do except continue with what he was doing, as he had no alternative plan.

"Son, have you found them yet?"

"Almost, Mom, I think I have the right box. Ah, here it is. I'm not sure if this will work. The CME I told you about would have …" In the absolute gloom, a beam of light shattered the dark like a sledgehammer. The light shocked his retina, blinding him for a couple of moments. What he thought of immediately was that his Lord must have protected their ability to see while camping in the mountains. Looking at the beam of light on the ground in front of him, a wry smile of understanding confirmed his inner conviction that God takes care of His covenant people and provides a lamp unto their feet. He looked at his mother, who said, "And the people of Israel had light where they dwelt." She spoke of the Israelites in Egypt. They had not started a campfire because they didn't need it for warmth. Now they would need flashlights instead of groveling around the forest floor for wood and tinder to start a fire. They were a few moments away from discovering a challenging dilemma.

XXXXX

Chad was glad that they had a fire going when the searing sunlight winked out. Without light, artificial or natural, how would they find the manna that was briefly located in shady places around the cavern entrance? Every early morning, they were rejoicing in the providence of God. It was a thrill to experience a taste from the Old Testament about three thousand five hundred years ago. The manna had appeared the very next day after they lost everything. It was a sobering detail that taught them their faith was not complete. They had planned and supplied themselves with everything they thought they would need. Then, in a moment, it was swept away. Their needs spoke most eloquently on their behalf. The next morning, they rose early because of the cooler temperature, and to their amazement, flat, irregular wafers of bread lay upon the ledges of rock and upon the boughs of dried fir and spruce. It looked like children had broken pieces off from a larger sheet without perforations.

"Wow! It does taste a little like honey, just like it says in the Bible!" Vonnie exclaimed.

"Perhaps you can get the recipe," Leticia quipped.

They were using their hats as collection containers. From the Bible, they knew they must not keep the manna overnight, but this was Friday, and they knew they must gather and keep enough for the Sabbath. "You know, the Israelites gathered manna before the Ten Commandments were given at Sinai. That means the Sabbath was expected as an act of loyalty and was taught by the miracle of manna before it was framed in the covenant. When my mother's friends and her pastor told her that the Sabbath was no longer necessary because the Commandments have been abolished at the cross, they overlook the fact that the Sabbath was kept before Sinai and in the Garden of Eden. Why can't they see it?" Diana stated strongly.

"I think it is called confirmation theology. That's where they only accept concepts or ideas that confirm what they already believe," Chad answered. "I'm sorry that my answer doesn't ease the pain. Your mother got taken in by false applications of scripture."

"Don't forget Satan also got to her with that stupid letter. That was a really deceptively evil tactic that could have gotten to anyone," Vonnie added.

XXXXX

The transition from the basement rec room to the outside backyard deck was almost instantaneous. When the sun turned dark, the ambient light disappeared. Even though the electrical grid was being repaired in many places, it was not out to this remote suburb as yet. They sat on deck chairs with scented candles gently flickering from atop deck rails. It was more pleasant in temperature and quiet.

"When should we say Sabbath begins?" Mrs. Perkins asked.

"That's a good question," Brian answered. "I suppose we could estimate based on last week, but today there is no sun to mark the exact time. It is simply an act of loyalty on our part. We want to worship Him on His day."

"And, there is the fact that we can't commercialize any day with the prohibitions that have been put on us commandment-keepers, I might add. We are removed from the day-to-day cares, and now we are totally focused on God for our very survival," Cynthia observed.

"And our total dependence, thankfully. The heat destroyed our fresh food, and we ate up what was left. And then, suddenly, manna started to appear. The Lord knew when we would need the miracle, not before, and not days from now. Right on time." Brian popped a small wafer into his mouth.

Emilee listened to the adult conversation as if she was one of them. "I've been thinking; other people worship on Sunday, which, ya know, is named after the sun—right? So with no sun, how do they worship? They don't know where it is."

"True, but they really don't mark the start and end of their day like God asked us to do for His Sabbath. Many of them work and buy and sell anyway," Brian answered.

"In one small way, Sunday has no meaning without the sun. The Bible says darkness was poured out on the throne of the beast, which is the false controlling power; the beast can't fix the problem of the sun. It is beyond their capability, and it is a moment where thinking people need to recognize that God controls all creation, including our solar system's star," Mr. Perkins added, even though he was usually a quiet listener.

"Did you hear that? That was a car. It has been so quiet because of the electricity being down that now a car on the highway a mile away can be heard," Mrs. Perkins spoke. "It means things are getting repaired, and the world moves on, I guess. What happens next?"

"The sixth plague is the gathering of the forces to stand against God. Three foul spirits like frogs go out to deceive with miracles the leaders of the world to gather at Armageddon," Brian spoke.

"Armageddon? Is that real or symbolic?" she asked.

"Symbolic. In Revelation almost everything is symbolic. The issues we face are too big and too spiritual to be brought down to a single place, a minor valley in some far-off country. The name means mountain ('ar, mountain) of assembly (mageddon, gathering from the Hebrew). It comes from Ezekiel 38, where the forces of evil come to fight the people of the covenant. The covenant people are mentioned at the end of chapter 37, and then the evil is destroyed in the next chapter at Mageddon, which is mentioned as the mountains of Israel in verse 8. So, the sixth plague is preparation for the Day of the Lord, which is the seventh plague. Jesus will come to save those who have His testimony and keep His commandments. All others, especially the lawless one, will be destroyed by the brightness of His coming (2 Thess. 2)." Cynthia explained.

"So, it won't be long now!"

"No, it won't."

XXXXX

"Uck! Look at this food!" Raphael's mom held a ruptured can in her hand. "The heat cooked this, and then it burst. It's spoiled. The ants are all over it. What are we going to eat?" Raphael and his dad looked over her shoulder. They had to agree that the food in that can was ruined. Immediately, they began to search the remainder of the supplies. Seeing the rest of their stores, they didn't complain. They stopped, looked at each other, and then began to pray. "Oh, Lord, we are now completely in Your hands. We prepared because we felt we should not presume on Your benevolence. Now, we totally put ourselves into Your care and keeping and await for either Your sustenance or Your soon coming. In Jesus' name, amen." Raphael's last word was reinforced by both parents.

XXXXX

More electronics were repaired. The powers of the global coalition communicated on newly-made networks. The civil, ecclesiastical, and commercial powers united to form a tri-fold image of leadership, which they called WFC and which they required all humankind to follow. They were at a terminal point. Fickle humans will follow any leader in chaos unless one can communicate strength. By instilling fear, they project strength. If that doesn't work, they will use physical force. The antichrist's cabal needed to project a solution to explain the unexplainable and fight against those who opposed the fundamentals of their right to lead. The triumvirate of leaders under Isa Jesus agreed that they would take the results of this teleconference and announce the decision when the whole world could hear the edict at one moment and act in concert at one agreed time. They had the electronic connection to plan but not to fully communicate, so they agreed to spread out the message by leap-frogging the message on the back of all the existing systems that were operational. Wrapping around the world, they could unite all forces into one resolve.

XXXXX

Brian watched them, using the lights from their motorcycles as the only way to see them. The Patriotic Posse circled their bikes like covered wagons on the Oregon Trail. No other light illuminated the area. The rally point was a field of dried corn stubble at the bottom of a hill near where the angel rescued the young ladies from the sex traffickers. As Brian watched, Mr. Perkins brought two pair of binoculars to help see the activity. They watched the gang as they drank and roughhoused, laughing as they pointed the weapons out into the forest. It did not look good for the secreted faithful. They wondered if their decision to stay in the quiet neighborhood was the right thing to do. Brian felt their tiny group of believers should leave. They slid back from the window and went to the dimly-lit basement to give a situation report. The adults weighed options and tried to figure out a place to flee to, where they would not be captured. Their options were limited because they would have to walk, and the posse might hear them leave. They debated the issues pro and con. One problem was their sustenance. Remaining meant gathering manna when listening ears were near; leaving, they knew God would provide, but walking in almost virtual darkness would be hazardous. Using flashlights would attract attention. They decided to watch the menacing gang to see if they would leave or approach the house. If they approached, Brian and Cynthia planned on distracting the bikers by fleeing out the front door, and the remainder of the group would slide out the back door and hike up the forested hill behind the house. Until then, they watched.

XXXXX

In the morning, they lit their flashlights to explore the woods for berries and perhaps some piñón nuts. Dad groaned from his arthritis, and Mom felt her back was tight, but neither wanted to miss the opportunity to see God's providence. They expected something natural growing in the forest, maybe something unharmed from the sun's onslaught. What they found gave them pause, literally. They stopped and prayed over the evidence of the formerly unseen proof of their faith. Also, they thanked God for His attention to their needs. They marveled at why the God of the universe would pay attention to the insignificant needs of just three people. "God loves us, doesn't He!" Mrs. Wilson observed. Collecting the manna was more delightful than eating it. But they couldn't resist tasting it. They saved the rest for a feast of thanksgiving.

That night, the campfire reminded them of family times years ago. They stared into the flames and talked of trial by fire that the three Hebrews faced in Babylon. They didn't think their trial had been as onerous as the one on the plain of Dura. Spiritual parallels did not escape them. There were three then, three now. The temptation to false worship was the same. The images involved, Old Testament and New Testament, were set up by governments. Fire was in a furnace, and they saw fire come down from heaven; both were scary. Then there was the majority opinion then that went along with the powers in control, and then the powers of the now that received the majority of adherents. The minority of true believers were dedicated to the commandments of God when everyone else obeyed Nebuchadnezzar, and then a scattered few were not obeying the WFC.

"What was that?" asked Mrs. Wilson.

XXXXX

By way of providing more room in the cellblock and punishing the three believers for their lack of compliance, they were located in one cell. It was a two-bed bunk for three individuals. It meant only two could sleep at one time. They did not think it as an encumbrance but as a blessing to be together. Now, they could communicate quietly without repercussions from angry cellmates.

The TV snapped on in the cellblock. It added a little more ambient light than what was available from small portable lanterns. Regular lights were not turned on, as they didn't want to overtax the system. The TV dominated the cellblocks with their light distracting cellmates from harassing the three worthies. After knowing nothing about anything on the outside, the twenty-four-hour news channel was perfect for keeping the peace. It also gave the three a picture of where they were in the countdown. It did not take long for them to see that the fifth plague was in full swing as the media was reporting the restoration of electricity and how long it would take for various neighborhoods. Major media discussions ranged around the disappearance of the sun. No adequate explanation could put all the facts together into a coherent whole. If the sun imploded, why then were the stars gone? And, why are they not freezing without the warmth of the sun? They argued that the moon keeps the earth rotating, and the earth revolves around the sun that produces seasons. If the sun was gone, then all orbits should be affected; seasons and times would also be affected. Pastor Lange quoted the words, "He changes times and seasons: He deposes kings and raises up others." Some of the cellmates asked aloud, "What does Pope Jesus say about all this?"

XXXXX

At first, it sounded like a boulder crashing through trees and brush. Then grunts and growls accompanied the thrashing noises as the bear drew near. It roared out his hunger as if his anger could fill his belly. The extreme heat had kept prey and prowler in privacy. Now, the night brought on the primitive need to eat and an intense need to eat as soon as possible. Glowing eyes behind the leafy foliage were the first visible indication that the bear was almost upon them. The campfire was illuminating the swaying bushes where the creature would emerge. Raphael grabbed his flashlight as did his folks. Their hopes were to blind the beast in hopes of stopping him. It raged out of the woods at top speed. Once released from the tangles, he was ready to taste blood.

The trio was frightened beyond comparison. The roar shook the ground, and the bodies of the small family. The flashlights jiggled, and the one held by his mother fell as her hands went to her face. In haste, Raphael grabbed a burning stick from the fire and threw it at the bear. It was just enough to get the black beast to slide to a stop, kicking up sod and dirt. Father and son threw some more flaming sticks to push the reluctant brute away. He only took up a circling patrol, scanning for a way to snatch a tasty treat near the intimidating fire. As one, they stoked the campfire with every piece of wood to extend its effect farther out, hoping to enlarge their safety zone. They had only one animal to watch, and they moved to keep the fire between them and him like children avoiding a playful parent seeking to catch them from around a coffee table. Then the situation became more complicated—another almost identical black bear appeared.

XXXXX

Strong evidence to the contrary doesn't seem to stop prejudice. Those who believe in a universe made from a big bang rather than a loving God want to hang on to their scientific data to confirm their foundational belief. They look askance at individuals who believe in a Creator God who created this world in six days. They treat them as ignorant. Even with an unexplainable event such as a sun and all the stars going blank at the same time, they consult their textbooks, huddle in convocations, and dialogue in think tanks of wisdom to posit an answer to what they are seeing, or not seeing. They have always thought that the sun's demise would be the end of life on earth. One conservative scientist who was a Christian quipped, "If the sun goes nova, don't return home for your cloak." Other mainstream scientists preferred to ignore the Creator, who is in charge of the universe. They don't completely agree with the religious global regime. They go along with the requirements to buy and sell, eat and drink, and ponder and speculate. Uppermost in their minds is the question, "How long does this world have before it becomes frozen and inhabitable?" And they wonder if there is enough time to construct a space vehicle to ferry them to a place of sanctuary to save humankind.

XXXXX

Three cruisers pulled up to the gang of bikers. The emergency lights whirled around the area, bedecking trees with blue and red flashing lights. After a brief conversation between the two groups, the cruisers turned off their pulsating lights. A huddle ensued with pointing, animated gestures, and nodding heads. The officers were not delivering instructions for the bikers to move off; they were coordinating a search. The two parties moved into about ten teams and headed in different directions on the various modes of transportation they had. Obviously, they were now in search parties, and the Perkins' house was the closest structure. Some with weapons at the ready headed for their humble hideout. They kept peeking through the drapes to see what would happen. Then for some mysterious reason, the cruisers stopped and put on their sirens as a signal for the others to regroup for more information.

XXXXX

Just when the news became repetitive, a special bulletin preempted the ongoing breaking news. Typical sounds and red notices indicated a change from the ongoing program. Reporters said, "We bring a live message from the WCF."

ZZZZZ

Isa Jesus stood at the podium in all his papal finery. Behind him stood all his cabal of aides, advisors, and assistants. Also in attendance were some representatives of the nations, heads of state, and, where distance and travel was a problem, presidents, prime ministers, and monarchs were seen on electronic panels in Skype-time. It was virtual reality in reality. It was an impressive moment in history for the modern technology involved, but as a world conference, it was momentous for the subject presented. The leader of the world confederation paused for effect. His words would be understood in every language, a miracle in itself.

Believing citizens of our new world order, I bid you blessings and good will. We are in solemn times. Assembled around me, you see an illustrious gathering of the brightest and best of our world. Is not this a great empire that we have built? We are in agreement that a brave new existence is just around the corner: A glorious halcyon day of the future. We are only a few steps away from nirvana. We need to maintain our resolve. [Isa looked around at his colleagues, who all nodded in agreement.]

There are those who think they can defy our directives. They think they know better than the son of god. We have been tolerant, even more than tolerant. These malefactors are keeping all of us from achieving heaven on earth. Radical bad behavior requires radical correction. This world must take the next big step to perfection. We gave the malcontents a nudge with the requirement not to buy or sell. They should have figured it out after a couple of weeks, but then it has been much longer. Now, we have to finish this, but with compassion. In love we need to bring this to an end. The sinners who disobey the laws of this administration need to be eliminated, purged to cleanse this evil world, and set it right with the universe.

I propose we execute this move with tolerance and love. The ones to be purged need to have a chance to repent. At the time of execution, ask them to repent. If they do change their opinion, provide them a quick and merciful death. They will be witnesses of our resolve. If they don't change, then give them a slow and painful death. This may seem cruel, but in reality, it will give them a moment to rethink their stance and repent. In the end, it might save them for eternity.

My dear children, the next days will be difficult yet rewarding. The goal is within our grasp. All that humankind was meant to achieve is just beyond this arduous stage. I appeal to every concerned citizen to act now. Finish the job. Let me set the example first. I have interviewed some of these malcontents, and they will not change; they won't recant. I have told them of the consequences and given them time. Behind me on this monitor is a video of these sinners. They are standing in a courtyard on a hillside north of here. [Isa raised his hands and arms to the sky and gestured for an imaginary object to move downward. Cameras gave a panoramic on-screen view of the landscape. Ten individuals stood in a group. At a distance they looked edgy, turning in every direction, looking for someone or something. Out of the sky, from a distance in the background, a streaming ball of fire streaked into the yard, blasting the epicenter with fiery plasma mixed with burning shards of iron. No humans could be seen, nothing familiar from the original view remained. Embers and flaming debris lay about.] *I brought the fire from heaven as an example of my authority and what needs to be done and of my hatred for those who go against the will of God. The time is set. Midnight tomorrow starts this noble purge. I lead, you will follow. Amen.*

ZZZZZ

The faithful cellmates were stunned. The others were cheering. Some exclaimed with whoops and whistles; others were awed by Isa's power. Calling fire from the sky is not an easy stunt to pull off.

"I don't believe those people who died were really believers who were against the system," Pastor remarked.

"How can you say that?" Luke asked.

"Because there's no longer a need for martyrs."

"That's right; you explained that before. So who were these people he executed?" Please explain."

"Well, when the seven last plagues started, it marked the end of witnessing, because, 'He who is unjust, let him be unjust still; he who is filthy, let him be filthy still; he who is righteous, let him be righteous still; he who is holy, let him be holy still.'[30] That pronouncement recorded in Revelation indicates that the end has come, and the two camps of righteous and the unrighteous are finally made up. That is why I believe there is no longer a need for martyrs. That demonstration of power was *contrived* to intimidate the masses. Satan rules by fear and God rules by hope."

"I see. His demonstration would also galvanize sinister elements into action," Luke surmised.

"God will remember His own," Pastor consoled.

"Yes, yes, but it is difficult to believe the Lord will accept me as one of His own this late in the game."

"I can. Don't worry, my friend."

---

[30]Rev. 22:11, NKJV

XXXXX

The light from the cave cast a soft orange glow out over the valley. Any movement near the entrance projected moving shadows outward. The foursome was careful to move in and out to collect manna because they didn't want to attract attention to anyone who might come looking for them. They were more concerned about human notice and less of animals lurking nearby. Diana was about ten yards from the cave opening, bending over to pick up a morsel of tasty bread when a roar shattered the silence and caused her to fall backward. She was so frightened she pushed herself backward with her heels in absolute panic. Chad came to the rescue with a firebrand in his hand in the nick of time, as the mountain lion was crouching ready to spring. He stood

Diana was about ten yards from the cave opening, bending over to pick up a morsel of tasty bread when a roar shattered the silence and caused her to fall backward.

between his love and the threat, flicking the flaming flagon before the desperate animal. The puma half-pounced half-leaped from side to side, trying to get around the blazing stick. Leticia and Vonnie came to Diana's aid to help her get closer to the fire. They all backed into the cave with Chad bringing up the rear while making light circles with an ember at the end of his wand. The lion was confused and roared his anger. As an extra added safety feature, they all stood behind the campfire.

"I thought when a predator wanted to attack prey they didn't give away their intent first. This one roared. Why, I wonder?" Vonnie asked.

"Desperate, I guess, or maybe he roared to fend off competition from his feline brothers and sisters," Chad answered.

"I'll second that!" Diana sighed with relief. "I mean the desperation part."

"We need to keep this fire going to avoid creatures coming in," Chad instructed. The party looked around to calculate their stash of firewood.

XXXXX

Two hungry bears were anxious to eat meat. All vegetation was no longer succulent. They wanted easy, quick food. As they circled the fire, they occasionally roared at their competitor, even stood on hind legs to threaten each other by their size. This puzzling circumstance kept the Wilsons standing and on the move constantly. It was wearing down Mrs. Wilson's stamina. It was only a matter of time before she would collapse. They needed more wood and a safe place to rest. Raphael pushed a burning log out of the fire to about six feet away and then started another fire with their last pieces of wood. Just when they started to settle in between the two daunting fires, another animal came to the scene, a grizzly. The hulk intimidated the other two into smaller circles on one side of the fire. He came in closer and tried to snap at Raphael as he shielded his folks. The grizzly took a few strides outward and sat down, roaring at the other two. He was claiming his prizes with his superior position.

"What's he doing?"

"I think he's waiting for the fire to die down, and he's not willing to share," Raphael answered his mother.

"Great, so I might come to a grizzly end."

XXXXX

Knowing what the pope had said communicated to the prisoners that the end was near. It meant that if their theology were right, God would save them. If they had gotten it wrong, they would die for their faith, and the end-time scenario would end in a different manner. Pastor Lange could not be persuaded that it would be dissimilar from what was described in the book of Revelation. Yet, their in-cell dialogue centered on the video of fire coming down out of heaven and killing the supposed anti-WCF believers. To believe, as Pastor Lange believed, meant that the whole development of the Isa Jesus build-up, including the struggle with Naziya, was a contrived hoax. His encouragement to his two brothers included a statement that a God of love, as Isa Jesus claimed for himself, would not be killing off opponents. It also meant that all the wonderful miracles, like raising the dead after the atom bomb explosion was faked. Additionally, the battle between Naziya and Isa was also faked. It would have been nice to see inside that deep hole to see if Naziya was still there. As they chatted, sitting on their bunks, officers came to open their cell. They had their weapons drawn and took one at a time out of the cell, handcuffing them as they went. Three police officers escorted each inmate in a separate direction than what they had experienced before. They took a dank, musty concrete stairway downward. The lower they went, the more ominous it became if that could be possible, after having been beaten in the interview room repeatedly.

A steel door stood open into a room where a sump pump was in one corner, and pallets covered in moldy boxes were in another. The smell was overwhelming. They closed the door with a clang, and the three were lined up against a wall.

"Hey, this is too soon for you to be killing us. The pope said tonight at midnight," Detective Hardine reminded the officers.

"Shut up! You have no authority here," an officer replied.

"John, you and I are friends; we used to be partners. What gives? You can't wait a few hours?"

"Not anymore, so shut up!" The officer cocked his revolver in emphasis. The other eight men charged weapons and aimed them at the three. Involuntarily, three courageous men drew in deep breaths, expecting the worst, hoping for the best.

XXXXX

The ruckus arose in crescendos as more and more motorcycles growled into life. Bikers spun donuts in the cornfield. The police cars moved in separate directions. Soon the bikers also headed outward like a pinwheel. It wasn't more than two minutes before bikers were spinning wheels on the front lawns of the small collection of houses where the Perkins lived. Brian and Mr. Perkins watched nervously from the living room window, peering from the edges of the curtains. Normally, the police would have been called. But staying out of sight was important now.

As if a bell rang, the bikers suddenly assaulted the house from all sides, looking into windows to see if there was anyone home. There wasn't enough time to get into hiding when window glass broke in the back kitchen door, and the front door jamb was shattered when kicked in. The insurgents must have known this was a house that had not complied with the law. The two men were caught trying to move toward the basement stairs. Flashlights swirling in many directions converged on the two men. They were caught.

"Hah! We've got some live ones!" One vigilante yelled, and the rest answered by shooting various weapons into the air, or ceiling as the case was. It was a signal to others in the area that they had found someone. The sudden and very loud gunshots evoked an involuntary response from the ladies. They yelped and screamed because, at first, the noise scared them, and then they thought the men had been shot. It alerted the self-appointed posse to their presence downstairs. A few moments later, the occupants of the basement were unceremoniously dragged upstairs. It was not comfortable, and it indicated the hate the posse had for these people. Rough handling disturbed the men, who were held between burly men ready to land punches. As soon as all were upstairs, the posse members escorted them brutally outdoors, off the deck, and onto the lawn.

Emilee was carried under one arm of a six-foot-ten monster. They must have thought she was a brat and expected her to resist. Instead, she was calm and compliant. When they got out onto the lawn, she was placed on the ground. She didn't try to run away, even though several men circled her with their arms extended. She began to address them as equals. Her face was serious, and her eyes moved from one to another of her guards.

"Ya know, Jesus is coming real soon, and you need to be ready. If you ask Him, Jesus will let you come along with us when we fly to heaven. You have to do that right now 'cause there's no more time. Okay? Please come with me, please."

"No, now get over there." He pushed her toward her mother, who extended her arms to receive her youngest. The family of five stood together with Brian and Cynthia, and a few other believers, awaiting the next move.

Flashing emergency lights came down the street, turning the dried leaves and dead pine trees into a psychedelic mixture of bluish-red, exploding upon an uneven tapestry. It looked like everything was vibrating off-sync. Standing calmly when bikers are getting ready to kill you is off-sync. When the officers came around the corner of the house, there was a moment of relief. It looked like they might be saved from the expected slaughter. Was this an intervention in the nick of time? The officers walked into the circle, and the bikers opened up enough to let them in. Smiles were exchanged, and then the officers in blue drew their weapons, and the entire mob lowered their barrels to draw a bead on the various targets. One senior officer said, "On the count of three. One ..."

XXXXX

Getting more firewood became a priority. They took firebrands out of the fire and edged out of the cave to hunt for wood and possibly manna. They found no manna; it was not morning, but they did find some small limbs and twigs to stoke up the campfire for warmth and primarily for protection from the puma pacing around, waiting for an opening. Diana, still a bit shaken from before, watched at the edge of the entrance. After a few moments, she thought she saw another shadow in the murk. It didn't move, it crouched, and no eyes gleamed in the night. She pointed a shaky finger and said, "What is that? Is that what I think it is?" All three stopped to extend arms and fagots in the general direction of the shadow. Without a word all four were backing inward when a third, smaller lion made a dash to grab Leticia. She screamed, and Chad stabbed his flaming stick like a sword at the new threat. But when he halted the one, another shadow darted in to make a snatch. More screams ensued. All four retreated into the cave behind the fire. They couldn't stop their heavy breathing.

The screams and the commotion alerted the wrong people. Out in the valley, a hunting party was homing in on the cave. They weren't hunting for game; they were looking for the people seen in the drone video before the dam break. The noise and the ruckus attracted their attention and made it easier to make the turn up the valley to zero in on the hideout. Then the light flickering from the cave told them where they needed to go. Climbing the hill to the cave was not easy, as it was steep, and flashlights didn't illuminate everything. They had their heads down, studying the terrain when a puma attacked one vigilante on the edge of the climbing group. The massive feline had the unfortunate posse member by the throat, ripping at his jugular. It prevented his screaming for help. Instead, he just gurgled. The wild thrashing attracted the others, and flashlights illuminated the ugly scene as the lion ripped at the poor fellow with hind claws tearing away at the lower body, shredding jeans into ribbons mixed with bloody skin. The posse was in consternation with the sudden attack. The nearest man had the presence of mind to pull his revolver, place the gun within a foot of the puma, and shoot the beast in the head. It did not help the man; he was already dead from a rapid loss of blood.

Lights started whirling around in every direction, scanning for other animals. A long tail was briefly seen disappearing behind a rock. Several weapons fired at the rock instantly. Automatic rifles peppered the rock, sending rock shards into the air and into the woods. In minutes, the posse realized the outlaws in the cave could be getting away. They turned their weapons at the entrance and started to fill the opening with a fusillade of bullets, intending to kill or keep them cornered.

Inside the four believers were crouched down next to the far side of the fire. They heard the first shot, and Chad stood. He couldn't see a thing; it was more of an alert response. The noise told him that there were armed people outside. He decided to herd the four into the very back niche in the cave and instructed them to lie down. He then pushed the fire apart to diminish the light in case people came into the cave. He wanted to make it difficult to be found. He didn't know what else to do. As it turned out, it was for the best. More shots were heard outside, and then a massive cloud of bullets flooded the grotto, pinging off of walls and rocks. Rock chips and dust showered down, while projectile fragments flew in every direction. Chad tried to protect Diana's body by covering it with his own.

CHAPTER 22

A hopeless situation begged for a response of desperation wrapped in a blanket of fear. Bullets, bears, and bikers were assaulting the redeemed. Pinging bullets, roaring animals, threatening officers, and vigilantes with menacing weapons could make anyone quake. The covenant-keepers faced their adversaries with as much confidence as they could muster. All their bravado came from the personal knowledge of a returning Savior on a white horse with myriads of angels behind Him. They didn't even look at their adversaries. They looked upward to their redeeming hope of a conquering King. The sky was still absent of any illumination. It was dark as black velvet. The eyes searched, and their thoughts asked, *Where is our Savior?* Some even said, "He promised."

Beneath their feet the ground trembled. It felt like heavy trucks were driving nearby. Or maybe they were losing their balance because of fear. They could not focus completely because they were divided between the physical present and the soon-to-be supernatural present. The trembling grew, and then huge thuds came from the soil around them. Then crashes were heard. Branches were breaking. Thuds, cracks, and smashes were coming from every direction. Personal safety changed from the threats they had been facing to confronting nature's rage. It was difficult to process all the information to know in this single moment what the events were telling them. They were hopelessly overwhelmed with negative stimuli to lock onto their eternal hope. One positive was the distraction the events had on the killers. They were now worried about their own safety. They started to run.

Running could not get them to a haven away from heavy objects falling from a mysterious sky. As the ground moved, their steps went awry, causing them to stumble like drunken sailors. Trembles became tremors, and then massive waves rolled the land in what seemed like every direction. It was now the killers' turn to be overwhelmed with negative stimuli. Weapons were dropped; fangs and claws were withdrawn. Consternation filled the minds of those who menaced the redeemed. They started to head for solid structures, buildings, and cliffs.

Standing in front of intimidating predators, the small Wilson family watched the animals flee to the sanctuaries they always sought when wanting to hide, the forests. They stared at the unmistakable signs of a massive earthquake. Ground swells rolled around about the solid piece of property shaped in an irregular triangle where Raphael stood with him out on point and his folks on his flanks slightly behind him. The miracle of solid ground reminded Raphael's mother of a familiar hymn where they stood on higher, solid ground. They marveled at God's protective providence as beasts scattered in fright, sometimes yelping from heavy hailstones that beat down upon them. A blast of a celestial trumpet stopped them, and the living beasts looked upward.

No number "Two" was uttered. Instead, several enormous ice balls slammed into the ground near the mixed posse of vigilantes and police. The would-be murderers jumped in fright and scrambled to get into the Perkins' house, leaving a clump of believers standing near a large blue spruce in the backyard. Some revolvers and shotguns lay on the ground. They made no attempt to pick them up. They watched. A huge, irregular hailstone buried deep into the lawn next to where they calmly remained motionless. At this point they thought nothing could surprise them. Then, an overly loud paean of a brass-like instrument vibrated through their bodies. The formerly unheard military sound directed their gaze upward to an army following a King.

Bullets still zinged around the granite-lined cavern like hornets on a mission. The reports of assault rifles were the only noises in the valley until ground rumbles and smashing massive ice chunks crashing through trees made a dreadful din. The four were convinced that the multitude of lethal ammunition bouncing around the cave was directed away from them. How could they have escaped so thick a cloud of projectiles? An unseen hand was deflecting slugs like a force field around a large magnetic object. In this case the force field was protecting four precious souls, half the number that was saved in a large boat long ago. Chad lifted Diana, and the four companions sprinted toward the ragged entrance, revealing only the blackness of a non-night. It wasn't that he was tempting God by presuming upon His goodness, it was because Chad knew it was the very end, and Jesus had to be coming sooner than soon. They stood there and watched with their ears. Thunderous bangs of rocks tumbling down the cliff eclipsed the thumps of hail upon the terrain. Then, from around all that cacophony voices could be heard cursing the hail and the moving earth. Then, as expected, the angelic trumpeter put all creation on universal alert. Jesus was on His way.

The concrete cellar nestled below a thick-walled, rock-solid jail was dimly lit and musty. It was not what anyone would choose to see just before their death. Yet, there they were, lining up against a wall while officers were chambering their weapons with deadly soft-point ammo. No one thought to struggle against the inevitable. God had demonstrated His protection so far; why not now. As the officers began to take aim with wide stances and both hands on revolvers, a sense of movement made their aim inaccurate. Then, a shuddering became quaking to the point of jarring. Huge chunks of wall tumbled inward. The predicted earthquake had arrived and in the nick of time. The detention center split in half from the sub-basement all the way up to the fifth floor. The dark sky lay bare above them, and the handcuffs fell off as they felt their feet lose touch with the floor below and began to feel the weightlessness of a slow ascension upward through the fragments of crumbling walls and floors. At the fourth floor, they heard the clarion call of the angelic brass section. Just around a jagged corner of concrete and protruding rebar, a bright light split the sky with wondrous brilliance. Without immediately seeing the source, they knew the center of attention. Richard began to sing the third stanza from a popular hymn with tears streaming down his face. "Long my imprisoned spirit lay, fast bound in sin and nature's night; Thine eye diffused a quickn'ing ray, I woke, the dungeon flamed with light; My chains fell off, my heart was free; I rose, went forth, and followed Thee. Amazing love! How can it be, that thou, my God, shouldst die for me?"[31] Luke and Peter wept as he sang.

---

[31]Charles Wesley

Fifteen miles to the north of the prison, in the Perkins' backyard, Emilee thrilled to the moment by shouting with glee. It sounded more like Weeeeeeeeeeeeeeee! She was flying. Her youthful exuberance was matched by similar feelings of supreme joy on the part of the surrounding adults and Emilee's sibling. No carnival ride could equal the thrill of gracefully lifting off the earth, gradually gaining speed as the compelling Lord of Creation drew them to His heart. Brian, Cynthia, and the Perkins family were in awe of the experience. Married couples held hands. Soon, others joined them as they ascended to the heavens. Emilee looked to her right and saw a handsome man with her. "Are you an angel?"

"Yes, Emilee, I am … your angel."

"You know me?"

"I've been with you before you were born."

"So, you protected me." The angel nodded his head in the affirmative with a big smile. Then Emilee got a little frown and asked, "Remember that time I skinned my knees really, really bad?"

"I do."

"How's come you didn't protected me that time?"

"I wanted to, but you needed to learn how to be more careful, to take care of yourself."

"Mommy told me I should'a wore my pads."

"I agreed with your mother."

"I know your voice. You whispered in my ears when I was supposed to pray for healing people. It was you!"

"Yes, it was I. When God instructed me to tell you, I was so happy. God is wonderful!"

"Yes, He is! I can't wait to see Him and say thank you. I'll draw Him a picture of what happened as a memory."

"He'll like that."

Brian and Cynthia changed from holding hands to embracing, flying in tandem, and one arm from each around each other's shoulders. They noticed an enveloping light that surrounded them. The radiance sparkled as if miniature diamonds were floating in the air with them. It was as if the luminance was attracted to them, clinging to their bodies. Two angelic beings came to them from above but flying in the same direction. They swooped down to almost lock arms on either side. Cynthia had heard the exchange between Emilee and her guardian. She then knew who this couple was. She extended her hand to grasp the hand of her protector. Brian saw that and copied her on the other side with his heavenly companion. Broad smiles were shared.

"Brian, I want you to know that I am very proud of your life and how you lived it," Brian's celestial companion spoke with a beautiful voice. After all the years of toil against prejudice, misunderstanding, and abuse, these words from his angel sentinel brought emotion to the surface. Cynthia squeezed his hand. Then Cynthia's angel looked at her and said, "You, too, are to be praised for your stalwart faith." These words brought both of them to the point of happy tears.

Raphael took his mother's hand, and his father took her other hand. They lifted off the earth as a trio of happy children. The campfire faded so quickly in luminance compared to the heavenly brilliance above. The Son of Righteousness shed His eternal light grander than the sun used to be. The light was not too bright for their eyes, even though they came from the darkest night. They could see with great clarity every detail of the angelic army's robes and mounts. The two parents who were formerly in their sixties were now in their youth. Joints felt alive, breathing was unhampered, and strength returned to their muscles. They had an odd feeling of wanting to run, jump, and leap with joy when they were flying without wings or propulsion. How does one skip with glee when there is no ground under your feet?

Coming up out of the inner city rubble, the trio of escapees ignored the chaos of screams and derision below. Instead, they focused on the purified scene above them. Trillions of angels were around and behind Jesus, who was sitting on a white horse singing in triumph along with the trumpets. As a commander, the Savior was at the head of His troops. Newly acquired eyesight enabled them to see the throne of God enveloped in a sea of glorious colors, which emanated outward, spilling over the flying formations. Their new ability to see great distances also gave them the skill to see a broader spectrum of colors beyond what man could detect before. Stars too small (too distant) to see before were now in crisp clarity, yet the light of the Father was beyond comprehension. They could make out the moving circles that propelled the throne forward. Spinning wheels were made of—they knew not whatmaybe nebulonic material like that which gives birth to stars. Because of their focus, they did not see the group they were joining. They heard the conversation Emilee was having with her angel. They listened. When she spoke of drawing a picture for God, they were reminded of how the God of the universe with billions of galaxies to manage would give her all the time she wanted.

Zinging projectiles stopped coming into the cave. The loud discharges diminished somewhat because many posse members were running for cover, dropping the weapons as they ran. Others held their guns and pointed them stupidly at the wonder of a coming King of Kings. Wasting ammunition into the air was purposeless. How could a common bullet reach to the height of the stratosphere? Chad and Diana stood at the lip of the cliff, taking in the grandeur. Flights of angels flew in every direction, linking up with ascending parties of resurrected believers who were ahead of most believers. The victorious trumpets rang out an announcement of change. It was an awesome wonder on multiple levels. Just when they thought of cheering for the winning team, they lifted up into the air. With hailstones crashing about them, they knew no fear. The providence of God kept boulders from dropping upon them. They glided upward in a rapture of ecstasy. Overhead groups of the resurrected flew toward the epicenter of the universe, the throne of God. Both thrilled to the sweep up to heaven and had difficulty looking at their two companions. They wanted to take it all in.

In front of them, several individuals raised steadily to the King. They had no idea there were others approaching from the rear. Diana was drawn to one in particular but wasn't sure. She didn't know how to speed up her flying. That's when an angel came alongside and took the hand that Chad wasn't holding. Without talking, he knew either she wanted to go faster, or he had someone he wanted her to see. As they approached the one she was looking at, he turned his head to see what lay behind. Their eyes met, and Diana squealed with glee, "Daddy!" It was as if she were a little girl again. She flew into Roger's arms and attempted to squeeze the eternal life out of him. For her father, it had only been a few moments since he had seen her last, and that was when he was sedated but in pain. All that was gone now, and he was happy to be united with his little girl. Emotion made talking difficult, but he did manage to blurt out, "Is your mother here?" Diana shook her head negatively. His head dropped. It took the edge off of all the grandeur around them if that were possible in light of all that was ahead of them. Before she could explain to him the bad news, the aura around them changed dramatically. Luminescence enveloped them, clothing them in light. Their heavenly robes of white light wrapped them in splendor.

Diana quickly introduced her father to Chad and then Vonnie and Leticia. She was distracted because she couldn't keep her eyes off of the robes. Their clothes had disappeared, and now they had these garments.

She couldn't resist touching the warm essence. It had substance without weight, texture without depth. She could lift what felt like a drape at her waist. The three women looked at each other in wonder. Diana, without thinking, blurted out, "Mother would love these!" Then she began to weep and clung to her father. "Dad, she got scammed by the devil. It was really mean. I'll explain later."

"I understand. We'll have plenty of time later for you to tell me what happened. Look, Jesus is calling us to come to Him."

Another reunion took place. As crowds of the saved merged, it became more difficult to spot friends and relatives unless they had lifted off of the earth relatively near to each other. Luke, Pastor, and Richard had united with Brian, Cynthia, and the Perkins family. Their flight joined together with Chad, Diana, Vonnie, and Leticia. It was magical in the spontaneous joy that overflowed. Everyone wanted to talk at once and speak to lost friends. Hands clasped in a web like skydivers linking up in a large interlocking network. Instead of diving, they were soaring, skyrocketing.

"Chad? Is that you?" The call came with an element of incredulity. The speaker was uncertain, not just because of the many changes in appearances. "Chad, you made it!?" This time, it was a female voice. All of the flyers looked up and to the right to see Daniel and Janine Johnson slowing down to link up with their son. Nobody knew how they managed to do that, but they would figure that out later. Janine wanted to see her son. Embracing while flying was another unknown, yet she managed it just fine. Talking in his ear, she asked, "When, er how, I don't know what to ask first. You didn't seem to care about church." She then saw Diana. "Diana and you, together? I have too many questions." She couldn't put it all together.

"Mom, Diana and I came to be close friends, and, thanks to Dad's sermon, we committed our lives to being close friends with Jesus. Diana and I came to keep the commands of God and have the testimony of Jesus." Chad helped his mother.

"Look who's quoting Revela ..." Janine started to say.

"Did you say my sermon? How did you hear my sermon?" Daniel was super interested. So many were excited and wanted to talk at the same time.

"It was recorded. Diana and I listened to it a bunch of times. It was key to my getting serious about God," Chad explained. It was wondrous news for a father to hear.

"Your robes are different; they have a red hem." Diana observed that both Janine and Daniel's flowing robes had an extra plus. Vonnie was ready with the answer. "The red fringe means they were martyrs, martyrs for the cause of God. You are to be honored for eternity. I am so proud of my friends. I wondered if it were so. Now I know for sure."

"Did you know who it was that killed you?" the detective inquired.

"You know, it doesn't really matter anymore," Daniel answered.

"I guess you're right. More importantly, I also want to say that because of your deaths, I was set on a path that eventually led me here. Praise God!" Luke responded.

"Absolutely, Dad. It doesn't matter anymore. We are here, and that is all that matters," Chad confirmed the feelings of the group, which echoed his words with hearty "amens" all around.

Clasping hands all around them, they ascended to heaven, singing songs with new voices and occasionally pointing at celestial objects.

"We had *this hope that burned within our breasts,*
Hope in the coming of our Lord."[32]

The curvature of the earth was dimly illuminated by volcanic eruptions. This gave the sinful world behind them a dark pall. The globe was streaked with ribbons of bloodlike lava and was in stark contrast to the majesty which was beside and above them. The glory of God, the rescuing Savior, the myriads of angels, the magnificence and multitude of stars, the gathering redeemed, the presence of friends, the appearance of lost loved ones, and the company of formerly unknown now known guardian angels, and their own changing bodies, represented way too many objects to center one's attention upon, not to mention the flying without wings. It was stimulus overload to the maximum. It was not like anything they had experienced before. They all felt honored to be among the redeemed. Chad was happy to be in company with his parents and his best friend. Just when he thought it couldn't be any nicer, an angel flew to his mother, holding a little girl in his arms. It was one-year-old Grace all clothed in pure light.

---

[32]Wayne Hooper

EPILOGUE

This novel is not *precisely* accurate. It is a guess. There is a very good chance that this novel is somewhat inaccurate in *non-theological* details against the real events that will unfold in the near future. However, the broad strokes of this story should be very close to accurate, but the minutia maybe not. It is hoped that it portrays a scenario that will cause the reader to want to understand the broad details of the coming prejudice against God's people; those who come through the great tribulation testifying of Jesus and remaining true to the precepts of God's will. Read, absorb, and study everything the Bible says about the last days so that you are not duped by the great red dragon's sophistries. As the Bible told us, "let the reader understand" (Matt. 24:15). The author's prayer is that you will be anxious to hear that clarion call of the angelic trumpet and not be surprised by it.

BIBLIOGRAPHY

White, Ellen G., *The Great Controversy*. Mountain View, CA: Pacific Press Publishing Association, 1911

White, Ellen G., *That I May Know Him*. Washington, D.C.: Review and Herald Publishing Association, 1964

TEACH Services, Inc.
P U B L I S H I N G

We invite you to view the complete
selection of titles we publish at:
www.TEACHServices.com

We encourage you to write us
with your thoughts about this,
or any other book we publish at:
info@TEACHServices.com

TEACH Services' titles may be purchased in
bulk quantities for educational, fund-raising,
business, or promotional use.
bulksales@TEACHServices.com

Finally, if you are interested in seeing
your own book in print, please contact us at:
publishing@TEACHServices.com

We are happy to review your manuscript at no charge.